THERE HE WAS

She'd waited so long to see James, and there he was at last. His light brown hair was shorter, his clothes finer, his build a bit leaner than the last time she had seen him. She noticed every difference even as she savored the sight of him.

She was a fool, she knew, but she was a willing one. It was just so *good* to see him, to have him around again. James wrapped Julia in a friendly hug, holding her so tight he actually lifted her feet off the floor.

"It's wonderful to see you," he said gruffly. "Happy Christmas."

My dear, she thought. *Call me "my dear."*

He didn't, of course. He never would. But held close to him, Julia's heart pounded all the same. She felt short of breath, and not because he was holding her so tightly. He was here, and he was holding her, and just for a second, she wiped from her mind that nagging awareness that he wasn't here for her.

Just for that precious second, she allowed herself to rest her head on his shoulder, allowed the feel of his arms to imprint her body with their heat and strength. . . .

SEASON *for* TEMPTATION

THERESA ROMAIN

ZEBRA BOOKS
KENSINGTON PUBLISHING CORP.
http://www.kensingtonbooks.com

ZEBRA BOOKS are published by

Kensington Publishing Corp.
119 West 40th Street
New York, NY 10018

All Kensington titles, imprints, and distributed lines are available at special quantity discounts for bulk purchases for sales promotion, premiums, fund-raising, educational, or institutional use.

Special book excerpts or customized printings can also be created to fit specific needs. For details, write or phone the office of the Kensington Special Sales Manager: Attn. Special Sales Department. Kensington Publishing Corp., 119 West 40th Street, New York, NY 10018. Phone: 1-800-221-2647.

Zebra and the Z logo Reg. U.S. Pat. & TM Off.

ISBN-13: 978-1-4201-1895-7
ISBN-10: 1-4201-1895-1

First Printing: October 2011

10 9 8 7 6 5 4 3 2 1

Printed in the United States of America

Acknowledgments

So many people helped this book exist. I owe my first, greatest debt to my husband, who put our then-baby to sleep every night while I worked on my new book—and then read pages and told me, "It's good. You should keep going." (And better yet, told me when it WASN'T good.)

I'm also grateful to my friend Amy, who read not-so-wonderful drafts and gave me wonderful comments; and to Ragan, who jokingly offered to design my cover when my book was inevitably published, then seriously offered to design my website instead. And to my other dear friends, who were surprised/amazed/thrilled/terrified that I had turned my hand to fiction. (Anna—I'll be sure to dog-ear your copy, just like old times.)

These typed pages wouldn't be a book without the tireless, limitless energy of my fantastic agent, Paige Wheeler; the faith and confidence of my editor, Alicia Condon; and the delightful serendipity of the 2009 Northwest Houston RWA Lone Star Contest.

Finally, thanks to my family, who is always proud of me, even when I don't deserve it. I hope I deserve it this time.

Chapter 1

In Which an Unbelievable Number of Biscuits Are Consumed

August 1817
Stonemeadows Hall, Kent

The clock on the drawing room mantel ticked away the seconds loudly, and James drummed his fingers on his knee in time with it.

Perhaps it was excitement that caused his every nerve to feel on edge. A man should feel excited to meet his fiancée's family, shouldn't he? Certainly not nervous, though. Not when that man was a viscount, accustomed to the sharp eyes and sharper tongues of the *ton*.

But ever since Lord Oliver had written to approve James's suit of the Honorable Louisa, James *had* felt nervous, as if something might go awry and upset his swiftly laid plans. Now that he was in the Olivers' drawing room, his feeling of anxiety grew even stronger.

He sighed and walked to the window, but his eyes could hardly take in the well-tended grounds outside.

Once again, he ran through his mental checklist of Reasons This Engagement Made Sense.

First, Louisa was intelligent and poised. Second, she came from an old and established family. Third, he liked and respected her. And fourth and perhaps most important of all, she'd agreed to marry him after a courtship that even he would have to describe as perfunctory.

Behind him, the drawing room door slammed open with a bang.

James whirled at the interruption, expecting to see the elderly butler who had shown him in a few minutes before.

Instead, a young woman burst into the room at a half-run. She was muttering loudly, her expression harried and the bodice of her frock askew.

"Curse and drat that girl, drat her. I *knew* she hadn't left her music in here, but where could it be? We'll never find it before the vi—"

As her eyes roved the room, she froze in mid-word upon seeing James. Her mouth dropped open. "Urr."

The clock on the drawing room mantel ticked off four endless seconds as James stared at her, still too surprised to speak, and she stared back with wide blue eyes.

The young woman spoke first. "Well, I'm embarrassed. I don't know what to say." She glanced at the doorway with an expression of longing. "Could I go back out and pretend this never happened?"

James stifled a laugh. "Please stay," he replied, bowing to his companion. "I'm delighted to meet you."

He was pleasantly surprised to find he meant those trite words. Since the door had banged open, his tension had begun to ebb, as if he'd simply needed a jolt to bring back his sense of self-possession.

"I'm sorry, you are . . . ?" The young lady seemed still to be struggling to comprehend James's presence in the drawing room.

"Lord Matheson. That is, I'm James, Louisa Oliver's fiancé."

She gasped and grew pink with embarrassment, so James prompted her in his gentlest voice. "May I assist you with anything?"

She met his eyes again, and he was pleased that the flush began to fade from her cheeks. She was rather pretty, small and fair, with a heart-shaped face and a wide mouth that was currently pursed in thought.

"I don't think so, but thank you. Unless you're willing to forget that this happened at all, which it seems you are, since you're being very polite to me. I hardly know why, unless that's just something that viscounts do. I promise, I did mean to have everything perfect for your arrival, but instead I've blistered your ears in the first minute we met."

"It's quite all right," James assured his companion again. He gestured her toward a pin-striped sofa. "Please, be seated if you wish. I've heard much worse language before."

"Really?" The young woman looked intrigued. "From ladies? What did they say?"

James coughed to hide another laugh.

Who on earth was this impulsive creature? She seemed to say whatever was on her mind, which he'd rarely encountered among females but found now that he enjoyed immensely. He'd never met anyone so unguarded in her behavior. His interest was piqued, and he tingled with an excitement quite different from his earlier anxiety.

Unable to keep a smile from his face, he replied, "It

would hardly be polite of me to repeat such words to you, especially since you've just complimented me on my manners."

"Nonsense," she replied at once. "I'll give you another compliment if you tell me. I'm sure I can think of something."

There was more than a small part of James that wanted to take her at her word, to say forbidden things to a young woman. He had a feeling this one wouldn't be scandalized; she'd laugh and ask for more.

And he was curious, too, about what she might offer him as a compliment.

Perhaps a little too curious?

"I'm sorry to have to disappoint a lady," he said. "But I really shouldn't."

His companion sucked on her lower lip, deliberating. "I suppose you're right. Anyway, I like your coat."

James stared down at the sleeves of the garment in question. It was well-tailored, but apart from that it looked ordinary to him. "Thank you?"

"That was your compliment. Or rather, my compliment for you," she explained. "You see, I followed through on my part of the bargain. Perhaps sometime soon you'll follow through with yours, since you'll be visiting our family for a while."

This was too ridiculous. James shook his head, protesting, "Absolutely not. There was no bargain. You're not going to manipulate me into teaching you how to talk like a guttersnipe just by telling me you like my coat."

"But I really do like it," insisted the young lady. "You look quite noble, if that's the right word for a viscount. I'm well aware that my own appearance is out of sorts, which is another thing I meant to remedy before your arrival."

She brushed an errant lock of blond hair from her forehead, looking rueful. "I intended to have my hair pinned up properly, but perhaps you know how it is when you are with young children. I'm always having to crawl after something or other, and it is just so much easier not to attempt misguided elegance when one is alone with family. Which I suppose you soon will be, but still, first impressions can be so lasting, and I didn't want to come across as a complete hoyden despite the possible truth of the matter."

The cheerful lilt returned to her voice by the end of this speech, and James was again transfixed by the play of her eager expression as she talked, the curve of her mouth, her animated hands.

Her hands. As if time slowed to a crawl, James watched as one of her hands reached for his.

He stared at her hand on his, feeling burned by her cool fingers. It was a whisper of a touch, but his skin prickled under it anyway.

But she was talking to him. What was she saying? He mentally shook himself to pay attention, trying to ignore the fingers holding his.

"Louisa seems to like you very much," the young woman added, still holding James's hand in her impulsive grasp. "Since I know she likes me too, I daresay I can tolerate me as well as she does, and we'll both get to like each other."

Her innocent words acted on James like a slap across the face.

Louisa.

His mind reeled. How quickly he had forgotten all his nervousness, and even his very surroundings, while talking to this girl. He drew his hand back slowly.

"We'll get to like each other," he repeated, avoiding his companion's avid gaze.

He feared that was too true.

He had to remember he was here to arrange a swift marriage with Louisa, not to banter with . . . who was this young woman, anyway? She was obviously a member of the family, but she looked nothing like his tall, elegant fiancée.

"I'm sure we will," he replied at last. His voice came out stiff and formal. The stuffy tone disgusted him, but he needed to place some distance between them.

"Forgive my ignorance," James began again in his best I-am-a-viscount manner, "but . . . who *are* you?" It was something a viscount probably ought never to have said, but really, sometimes it was so much easier just to cut to the essence of a subject.

"Who am I?" she repeated. "Why, have we really been sitting here these minutes and I never said? Oh, my lord, you must think I'm the rudest person you ever met."

"Not even close," he replied. "Remember all the words I know. I've been in some very rude company." Guilt twinged through him as the playful words fell from his lips. He really shouldn't talk with her like this.

"Rude company . . ." She gave a sigh of pure envy. "You're so lucky. Anyway, I'm Julia, Louisa's sister."

"Then you are lucky, too," he replied automatically. He was still confused, though. How had his dark-haired fiancée wound up with this tiny blond slip of a sister?

Julia seemed to read his confusion on his face, because she added, "I'm not really a blood relative, but I feel as close to Louisa as if we were. I mean, what I imagine I would feel like with a full-blood sister, though neither of us has one. Just half-blood. Though I feel as if they are full relations, too. Anyway, Louisa and I are stepsisters. Do you have any sisters?"

James restrained a smile as her cheerful words bubbled over him. "Yes, one elder sister," he answered when Julia finally wound down. "Gloria, the dowager Viscountess Roseborough."

Ah, Gloria. The smile dropped from his face, and he chose his next words carefully. Gloria's troubles had already been laid out before the entire *ton*, but they might not yet have made it to the Oliver household in the country.

"My sister is rather a . . . well, a serious-minded person, and very conscious of propriety. But then, her life has not been easy of late."

He berated himself for saying too much and averted the subject. "Still, I can vouch from my own family experience that being related to someone need not make you close, and I'm sure the reverse is true, too."

Julia beamed at this affirmation, and a jolt of delight shot through James. She'd accepted him; she'd perceived his reply as honest. Perhaps he could have told her more, after all.

Just as Julia opened her mouth to respond, a footman entered the room with a large tea tray. Immediately on his heels marched three girls and a boy of decreasing size.

Julia's attention was distracted by these new arrivals. "Ah, I thought someone would soon join us in here! We've all been wild with curiosity to meet you, you know. Hello, children. I suppose you want some biscuits?"

She motioned to the footman to set down the heavily laden tray on a table next to the sofa, which he did with an audible groan of relief.

Julia turned to James and introduced the lineup of eager young children with great formality and flourish.

"Lord Matheson, may I present Miss Elise, Miss Emilia, Miss Anne, and Master Tom." As Julia indicated each child, a well-grown and pretty girl of perhaps nine or ten years curtsied properly, a smaller and more saucy-looking version tipped him an equally fine gesture, a chubby five-year-old shyly flounced her dress and ducked her head, and a small boy bent into a giant bow, teetering as he hauled himself upright again.

James had long experience with small children, and dutifully matched the solemnity of young Tom's bow. "Misses Elise, Emilia, and Anne, and Master Tom, I am delighted to make your acquaintance. Would you care for some . . ." He trailed off, and peered at the tea tray. "What type of biscuits do we have?"

"Ginger and shortbread," Julia replied, parceling the treats out onto plates. "And they've given us watercress sandwiches, too. I can't imagine why. No one ever wants to eat them."

"Actually, I rather like them myself," James admitted. He pitched his voice casually, mindful of the eight small ears and eyes now regarding him, but disappointment nagged at him. He wanted to continue talking to Julia, to know what she would have said next had they been left alone. He had never felt such an immediate pull toward another person. Did she feel it, too? He wanted to grasp her hands again, to feel the gentle shock of her touch. Given a few more minutes, he might have unburdened himself completely.

Don't be a fool, James. His burden was his own, his and his family's, and not to be dumped onto young women he had only just met. He sighed again, but thankfully none of the family members noticed in the bustle over biscuits and cups.

With a great effort, he wrenched his mind away from the present, back to a silent library six weeks before, and a dark-haired young woman named Louisa Oliver who had hidden there to escape a crowded ballroom. The ballroom in which he'd been bidden to find a wife.

But Julia's voice interrupted his thoughts almost at once. "Children, why don't you sit on the sofa over there to eat your biscuits? You may fidget to your heart's content, and Lord Matheson and I will pretend not to notice a thing."

Amid a chorus of giggles, a bustle of cups, plates, and crumbs, the children scooted off across the room as Julia had indicated.

She laughed softly as she poured out two more cups of fragrant dark tea.

"Heavens, we *are* coming at you all wrong. I am so sorry, my lord. The only explanation I can think of is that we are out of practice in receiving Louisa's fiancés." She smiled at James. "Milk or lemon?"

James blinked. Surely she hadn't just said what he thought she'd said. "Er . . . have there been many?"

"Many what? Lemons? I suppose so. We all like them prodigiously."

"No, fiancés." He held his breath waiting for her answer.

Julia looked puzzled for a moment, regarding the tea tray as if looking for the fiancés in question. Then understanding broke over her face.

"No; you're the one and only, which I would have thought you'd have known. But it is so much easier to throw Louisa to the wolves than to blame the whole household for our topsy-turvy welcome."

She laughed, and James let a relieved breath whoosh out of his lungs. He settled against the sofa back again, considering her thought process.

No, it still didn't make any sense to him, but the distraction was delightful. After a moment, he gave up and just chuckled. "Miss Julia, your logic is impressive. Lemon, please, and one sugar."

Julia handed him a delicate cup, then prepared her own tea and piled up a plate of biscuits for herself.

Settling back on the sofa, she chose a piece of shortbread and let it crumble in her mouth. Their cook made the most wonderful shortbread, light and sweet. The only thing better in the world was her ginger biscuits. She chose one of those next.

Julia hadn't realized she was so hungry, but before she knew it, she was staring at an empty plate.

"Did I really eat all my biscuits?" The words slipped out of her mouth before she could stop them.

She looked up to see the viscount's green eyes crinkling at the corners with amusement.

"If you didn't, someone stole them from you very quietly indeed," he replied with a straight face, but his eyes brimmed with laughter.

Her treacherous face turned hot again with embarrassment. "I suppose that's possible," she replied, struggling for dignity.

She forced herself to set down her plate. She would have loved to refill it, but there was no way she was going to let this dashing young man watch her make even more of a fool of herself than she already had. More than once.

"Er . . . a watercress sandwich for you, my lord?"

He looked surprised, but accepted one of the foul treats. He actually began to *eat* it.

"Do you want some more biscuits, Miss Julia?" he asked between bites. "Not that it's my place to offer you food in your own home, but I'd feel better if I weren't the only one eating."

"The children are still eating, too," Julia replied, but she was too hungry to put up any more than a token resistance. She eyed the tray, considering how much food she ought to leave for her parents and Louisa.

They never ate much in the early afternoon. Perhaps two biscuits each would do? She took the rest.

"Admirable," the viscount spoke up, watching her pile biscuits onto her plate.

Julia could feel her face turning pink again. She never could hide her embarrassment, which itself was always embarrassing to her. "I'm certain everyone else will love to have the watercress sandwiches," she explained, knowing her words sounded lame. "No need to let these biscuits go to waste."

"Of course not," he replied, hoisting his teacup in front of his face and making a choking sound. "It's very resourceful of you."

Now Julia was suspicious. "I could have sworn your cup was empty."

He set it down, a poorly feigned expression of surprise on his face. "So it is. Well, my mistake." His face was serene, but his eyes were laughing again.

"I hope you choke on your horrid sandwich," Julia muttered under her breath, too quiet for him to hear.

Of course she didn't mean it, though. Every time the viscount smiled at her, she felt triumphant. Glowing, like she'd accomplished something wonderful.

She just wanted to keep looking at his eyes; she'd never seen anyone like him. It wasn't that he was the most handsome man she'd ever seen, though he was undeniably good-looking, tall and lean. It was more that . . . he seemed happy. As if he was exactly where he wanted to be.

If he'd only keep smiling at her like that, she'd keep eating biscuits to amuse him. Whatever it took to keep that smile on his face.

Actually, eating more biscuits was an excellent idea for her own sake as well. She wondered if it would be too rude to leave none for Louisa. Her sister had never actually *said* she hated watercress, after all. The mere fact that she'd never taken one of those sandwiches in her whole life meant nothing. It could just be a coincidence.

She reached for another ginger biscuit and looked at the viscount expectantly.

He picked up on her cue right away. "Must I take another sandwich to keep up with you?"

"I knew it. You don't like them either."

He shrugged. "That would hardly be polite for me to admit, Miss Julia. Perhaps I should just say that I preferred the shortbread."

She was seized by a sudden urge to break down the final barrier between them. After all, she'd already bullied, insulted, fed, and amused him. If she couldn't permit a future relative to call her by her Christian name after that, there was simply no good time to begin.

"Please call me Julia if you like," she offered. Then, wondering if she'd been too forward, she backed off, explaining, "Or if you insist on formality with one who is to be as a sister to you, then you must address me as Miss Herington. You see, I am the oldest of the Miss Heringtons. To be fair, the only one as well, as we are a family of remarriage."

Oh, dear, there she went talking her head off again. Louisa always said she never used a word where a sentence would do, and never a sentence when she could use a paragraph.

It didn't seem to bother the viscount, though.

"Very well," he agreed at once. "I'll be happy to call you Julia, and you must call me James. I am not the only Matheson, you see; I have a cousin with the same family name who's got his eye on my estate, so for his sake if nothing else, informality must be introduced so that we are distinguished from one another. Imagine the confusion if you were to shout for Matheson at a party and got the wrong one."

"It would be much more likely to raise eyebrows if I were to shout James and get the attention of a dozen young men, or more likely the whole room. Wouldn't everyone look at the ill-bred shouting girl? And then I'd have your attention regardless of how I had addressed you."

James looked at her with mock suspicion for a moment, and his green eyes kindled. But his face was sober as he replied, "Quite true, and most efficient it would be. Were you to take up the habit of shouting, you need never address me by anything at all. But perhaps we had better leave it at first names, to be spoken at a moderate volume."

First names. Spoken at any volume, Julia liked the sound of that.

James could hardly believe he was saying such ridiculous things to a young woman he barely knew, but he was

enjoying himself as he had never expected to when embarking on his journey to Stonemeadows Hall. An engagement of convenience ought not to be a matter of
concern for a man who'd spent his life under the
quizzing glass of the *ton*—and yet, he'd been as nervous
entering the manor house as a young man entering a
woman's bedchamber for the first time. He was shame-
fully afraid he wouldn't be able to perform up to the expectations of his audience.

All right, perhaps that was taking the simile a bit far.
But he'd been apprehensive. He was, after all, the head
of his family now, which was still a rather startling realization even after a year. And his family needed him, and so
he needed Louisa. It was as simple as that. But he hadn't
quite felt right about the situation until he started talking to Julia.

Why was it that his thoughts flew to the bedchamber?
To the heat of the physical? He swallowed.

Suddenly, the door swept open again. James was
grateful for the distraction.

Louisa's slim form appeared, attired for the outdoors
in sensible walking boots and spencer. She looked
proper and lovely, and as demure as a woman should be.

Her eyes at once found James's, and she strode to
greet him. "Oh, Lord Matheson—I mean, James—I'm so
sorry I wasn't here to meet you when you arrived. You
must have made good time on the road; I'm glad of it. I
have only just got back from a walk. I do apologize."

She looked worried, as if she expected him to be dis-
pleased. He gave her his sunniest smile of reassurance,
but the pucker remained between her delicate brows.

Something must be amiss with his face. Did he look
odd? Was Louisa bothered that he had been speaking
with Julia? Surely not; they were to be family, after all.

The thought made something twist deep inside him.

But he had made his choice, logically and irrevocably, and he knew how to act. He reached reflexively for Louisa's hands, hoping to soothe the troubled expression from her face.

"My dear Louisa, please don't give it another thought. It was a remarkably fine day for travel, and indeed I did make excellent time. I know I've arrived before I was expected. Since I've gotten here, I've been enjoying fine refreshments and some very, um, stimulating company."

Good Lord, had he just said the word "stimulating"? That came a bit too close to the truth. He could have bitten his tongue for that.

But Louisa seemed not to notice any unwitting double meaning in his words. Her gaze was instead drawn to the four small children swinging their heels in the air as they sat in a line on the long sofa at the back of the room, munching on biscuits and chattering among themselves.

Her dark eyes widened at the sight, but her voice, when she spoke, was calm. "How lovely that the children have introduced themselves already," she replied. "I suppose we are all to be family, and I hope you'll forgive us for being somewhat unconventional in greeting you."

We are all to be family. Yes, just as he'd reminded himself.

"Of course," he replied. He hoped Louisa wouldn't notice the catch in his voice.

He escorted her to a seat in a cushion-piled wing chair near the tea tray. As she sat, her brows again furrowed, and she shifted on the chair seat. "What on earth . . . ?"

Leaning to one side, she felt behind an embroidered cushion and pulled out a much-creased sheaf of sheet music. She held it, bemused, for a moment, then looked up at Julia.

"The music!" Julia exclaimed. "Emilia's pianoforte music. I'd forgotten all about it."

A vague memory stirred in James's mind. "Music? Is that what you were shouting about when you ran in here?"

"Shouting?" Louisa echoed, glancing from James to Julia and back again. The corners of her mouth began to curve upward. "I'm terribly sorry I missed that."

"Nonsense. No one was shouting," Julia said, eyeing James with a gimlet stare. "Honestly, the very suggestion is ridiculous. As our illustrious companion and I have already discussed in some detail."

Louisa nodded. "I'm sure his lordship is teasing you."

"I would never do such a thing," James demurred, wiping a poker-straight expression across his face.

Julia's hand rose to cover her grin, but not soon enough to suppress a snort of laughter.

"Watercress sandwich?" she finally choked out, extending a plate to Louisa.

"No, thank you," Louisa replied. "I know how much you enjoy them, Julia. You go right ahead and finish them all up."

Her dark eyes sparkled with mischief, and James was sure Louisa knew *exactly* how much her sister enjoyed watercress.

"I . . . I don't care for any more," Julia faltered. "I'm rather too full, and you know we'll be dining fairly soon."

"Full?" Louisa raised her eyebrows. "Have you already had several watercress sandwiches, then? I didn't realize they were such favorites of yours. Perhaps we should arrange to have them served to you more often."

James raised his teacup to his lips so the sisters wouldn't see him struggling not to laugh.

Over the rim of the teacup, he saw Louisa look back to the sheaf of music she still held. The impishness vanished from her eyes, and again that pucker of worry knit her brows.

James wondered what she was so worried about. Surely it wasn't anything to do with him?

Chapter 2

In Which the Viscount's Life Is Threatened, but Not Seriously

"Don't eat the fish, James," Julia told him in a low, urgent voice across the table as soon as they were seated at dinner.

Warily, he eyed the lemon-garnished trout arranged on a platter near his elbow. He wasn't fond of the head-left-on style of cooking a fish, but apart from that, they looked perfectly innocent.

"Er," was all he could manage before Lady Oliver shushed her daughter.

"Good heavens, Julia." The baroness laughed. "Lord Matheson will think we are trying to poison him." A cheerful woman with Julia's light hair and eyes, Lady Oliver had welcomed her guest with immediate warmth—and, it seemed, no murderous intentions.

"He shouldn't think that," Julia replied, "since if the fish were poisoned, and I wanted him to be poisoned, I would hardly have told him not to eat them. I would have told him *to* eat them. No, James, no one wants to poison you."

He blinked, unraveling this string of arguments. "I must say, I'm relieved to hear it."

"Well, we've only just met you," Julia answered. "Give us time; maybe we'll change our minds."

Louisa coughed. "Perhaps the viscount would prefer not to have his life threatened during his first family dinner with us."

"Why wait?" Julia asked breezily. "Good heavens, someone is always threatening someone else around here. It's all in good fun, though. It means you're part of the family now."

She turned that bright smile on him again, and James's insides clutched. Somewhere right between his heart and his groin—and truth be told, he wasn't sure which was more affected.

He would never have expected a family dinner with his fiancée to include forbidden foods and veiled death threats.

He was finding he liked the unexpected.

"Now, now," Lord Oliver broke in mildly. "It's hardly polite to tell our guest that we've denied him certain dishes, is it? My lord, that's an awfully fine trout there. I think you'll enjoy it very much, if you care to partake of it. I caught it myself in a lake not far from here."

James glanced around for guidance. Both Louisa and Julia shook their heads at him, Julia mouthing "no" as broadly as she could.

Mystified, James nevertheless took the unmistakable hint. "I thank you for the offer, but the rest of the course you've offered me looks so delicious that I believe I've already served myself more than enough."

Lord Oliver accepted this, and turned his attention to his wife. While James couldn't exactly follow the thread of their conversation, he very much feared it had to do with which type of excrement made the best fertilizer.

The baron shared Louisa's dark coloring, and he would have been a tall, gentlemanly-looking man had not his careless dress and distracted manner given him a shambling air. James could tell that his prospective father-in-law was as little aware of fashion as he was of subjects that ought to be avoided during dinner.

"Psst." Julia drew his attention away from his thoughts while her parents were still distracted by their talk of unpalatable organic matter. "The fish."

"Yes?" Puzzled, James began to hand her the platter, but she shook her head frantically.

"Don't eat it," Julia whispered loudly. "Papa never has the fish eviscerated. He thinks it gives it extra flavor to cook it with the guts in."

James shuddered at his near-encounter with a fish liver, and Julia gasped. "Oh, goodness, I shouldn't have said the word 'guts' in front of you."

Louisa's mouth lifted in amusement. "Now you've gone and said it twice. Whatever will his lordship think of us?"

"It's all right," James reassured his fiancée. "It's hardly the worst thing she's said to me today."

Just as he had hoped, Julia's mouth dropped open, and he could see her taking a huge breath for what was no doubt going to be a very impressive retort.

But just then Lord Oliver's voice rose to rejoin their conversation. "My lord, did we tell you about the new calf yet?"

"Please, do call me James," the viscount replied. "No, I have not yet had the honor of hearing about your latest born livestock. My felicitations to you."

"It's really most interesting," Lord Oliver continued

enthusiastically. "You see, we didn't have one of our own bulls cover the dairy cow. Instead, I was seeking to breed a—"

"Papa," Louisa broke in, glancing at James in worry. "I am not sure the viscount wants to hear about such a subject at this moment."

"Oh." Lord Oliver looked amazed. "Was I being indelicate? My lord—that is, James—have you never helped to deliver any of your own livestock?"

"Er . . ." James replied again. That was becoming a distressingly common reply in this house. He had to do better.

He cleared his throat and tried again. "No, Lord Oliver; no, I haven't had that experience, being only recently possessed of my title and a long-ignored country estate."

He did *not* add that his inexperience was a fault he hoped to remedy in time, since that would be the opposite of the truth. He believed he would rather wear a silk dress and attend a *ton* function in the guise of his elder sister Gloria than watch a calf being born.

He met eyes with Louisa, who gazed at him apologetically. He smiled back at her, delicious mischief filling him. Never in his life had he attended a dinner where the conversation had turned to any of the topics discussed at the Stonemeadows Hall table. It certainly took some getting used to, but he was adjusting quickly.

His smile grew as he considered his mother's reaction, were she to hear a conversation turn to excrement or fish guts. It would be amazing. Would the oh-so-correct viscountess have the vapors, or would she throw a tantrum? He wasn't sure, but either way, he'd love to see it.

"So," said Lord Oliver, serving himself with gusto from

the much-maligned dish of trout, "tell us about how you and James met, Louisa. Of course I was happy to agree to the match, but your letters didn't include much information."

Louisa looked down at her plate. "There's not much to tell, Papa," she said tonelessly. "We met at a ball near the end of the season. He courted me afterward, under Aunt Estella's chaperonage. You know how these things are."

Was that how it had gone? James could hardly recall now, it had happened so fast. When his sister's marriage had dissolved in scandal, his mother had summoned him to London in no uncertain terms to find a suitable wife, set up his own household, and help restore the family name. And there was no denying the dowager viscountess when she sent one of her summons. The woman could be positively frightening, even if she was his mother.

He'd chosen his future bride quickly, but he had chosen well. Logically. Appropriately. He knew that, as certainly as he knew that Louisa wanted to change the subject.

She'd been willing to make her choice hastily as well. He wondered why.

Julia was having difficulty following the dinner conversation. Which was unusual, since lively chatter was as much her meat and drink as the courses laid upon the table.

But tonight, she didn't want to listen to Louisa and James tell their story of love. She'd rather push her food around on her plate, unseeing. Or maybe throw it. At least a pea or two.

Something wasn't quite right about the conversation,

though. She could sense that much, even through whatever it was that was making her feel so odd. She narrowed her eyes, scrutinizing her sister's downturned face. Was Louisa blushing? She *was*.

As Louisa spoke, a knot in Julia's chest distracted her from her sister's words. She turned away from the table and tried, discreetly, to press it away with the flat of her hand. Where had that come from? She must be choking on her food without realizing it.

It didn't feel like choking, though. More like . . . smothering.

She took a deep breath to ease the tightness, and it went away. Until she looked up again, and saw James fixing his eyes on Louisa, and Louisa looking back at James at last, a whole host of unspoken words passing between them. And then the knot came back again.

Oh, dear.

She must be uncomfortable seeing them look at each other. Surely that was it. It seemed wrong to trespass on an engaged couple's conversation.

And yet, she didn't want to leave. No power on earth could have pulled her from that table, and those green eyes that she had lit—yes, *she* herself—with such warmth and humor earlier in the afternoon.

Those eyes were cooler now, shuttered, though his voice was perfectly polite and gentlemanly.

"Louisa was quite alone in the library," James explained, as Lord and Lady Oliver chuckled. "In my ignorance of Alleyneham House, I blundered in there thinking it was the card room.

"I collected that she wasn't interested in company, or in dancing, since she was in seclusion during the grandest ball of the season. There was also the fact that she gave me a piece of her mind as soon as I stepped into the room."

This, at last, drew Julia's attention. Such rudeness was unlike Louisa. But then again, her sister had been a remarkably poor correspondent during her stay in London, and none of them had known much about James until his formal letter arrived requesting Louisa's hand from Lord Oliver. Perhaps James had acted like a boor? No, that was impossible. Louisa would never have agreed to marry such a man.

"Louisa, what on earth did you say to him?" she blurted.

It made sense to ask, she justified to herself. She always loved a story that included a good emotional outburst. Purely for intellectual reasons, of course. She simply wanted to build her vocabulary. It had nothing to do with her sister's relationship with James.

Louisa turned even redder, and James laughed, a pleasant low ripple that Julia felt through to her very core.

"She said—and I do believe I remember every word exactly, because I was so surprised—'If you are inebriated, please go out to the balcony for some fresh air. Do not be ill around me, or around all these gorgeous books that no one ever reads.'"

"In my defense, you were hardly the first person to enter the library that night," Louisa explained. "But you were by far the most sober."

"I was completely sober," James insisted. "I just didn't know the house very well."

"Louisa can always find the library in a house," Julia broke in. "It's like an extra sense she has."

As several pairs of eyes turned to her in surprise at this interjection, self-consciousness heated Julia's face, and she knew her own cheeks must be as pink as Louisa's.

Drat. She hadn't meant to draw everyone's attention to herself.

Just perhaps one particular person's.

Since everyone was already staring at her, she tried to fix the situation. She'd never yet found a conversation that couldn't be diverted if you threw enough words into its flow. Since her sister still looked embarrassed, she began with compliments.

"Louisa's read more than anyone I can think of, and she's the smartest person I know. I know for a fact she's read every book in the library here. Even the dull old books of sermons our grandfather collected."

Perhaps this wasn't quite the right thing to say, since it might make James think Louisa prosy. Or worse yet, it might offend him if he happened to be the sort of person who liked reading books of sermons.

Somehow, though, Julia didn't think James made a habit of reading sermons. That twinkle she kept seeing in his eye was a bit too roguish and shrewd. In fact, it was so knowing that Julia wondered if he suspected she'd been trying to steer the conversation away from his proposal.

Louisa cast her eyes down again, but a smile lit her face at last. Louisa did like to have people appreciate her breadth of knowledge, especially since many of their Kentish neighbors regarded such a love of books in a female as eccentricity. And perhaps, too, she was relieved to have the topic shifted from her courtship, since the hot color of her cheeks at last began to fade.

Julia was so pleased at her success that the knot in her chest hardly came back at all when James replied.

"I can well believe what you say about her keen mind. She has always impressed me with her intelligence, and I was intrigued by her boldness, too."

"Boldness?" Lady Oliver looked surprised. "Louisa?"

James nodded. "It was certainly the first time I'd been put in my place like that by a young lady, especially since I inherited my title. I don't mean to sing my own praises by any means; it is just that matchmaking mamas and determined daughters are usually very effusive."

"Anyway, that's that," Louisa said, still looking down at her plate. "It all happened very quickly, and as you gave your permission to the engagement, Papa, here we are."

She must have been more agitated than her smooth speech indicated, because she took a serving of the undesirable trout and raised a forkful to her lips. It was only once she placed the bite in her mouth that she realized what she'd done.

Julia watched, fascinated, as her sister's expression changed from distant to horrified. In Louisa's place, she would simply have spat the bite into her napkin, but Louisa had always had better manners. She reached for her wineglass, only to find it almost empty.

"Take mine," Julia whispered.

And with Louisa's look of gratitude as she swallowed away the terrible taste, Julia felt the knot in her chest dissolve completely.

Chapter 3

In Which
Breakfast Is the Most
Important Meal of the Day

James awoke the next morning feeling much more at ease than he had the night before. A good night's sleep had refreshed him, and he looked forward with eager anticipation to whatever unusual greetings the Olivers might have in store for him today.

Would he be treated to a discussion of pig breeding? Or perhaps invited to consume a live chicken, personally captured by his lordship that morning?

Or perhaps . . . he let his thoughts wander. Perhaps, in such an unconventional household, the young ladies were regularly left unsupervised. Perhaps he'd be left alone with . . .

What was he thinking? With Louisa, of course. Certainly. Why shouldn't he be allowed to be alone with his fiancée?

He looked out his bedchamber window at the clear sky of a sunny morning, and his tangled thoughts straightened into a semblance of peacefulness at the pleasant sight of the bright day and the orderly grounds.

With a bit of help from his fastidious manservant, Delaney, he attired himself nattily—if not exactly with attention to his pastoral surroundings—in blue coat, pale yellow pantaloons, mirror-bright Hessians, and crisp white linens. He quickly messed his light brown hair into place, accompanied by the pained groans of the manservant, for whose tastes he tended not to be fashionable enough.

But James hardly noticed; he was looking forward with impatience to the first full day he had ever spent with his fiancée's family. The cloudless blue sky and his well-rested body lifted his spirits, and he practically hummed with satisfaction as he thundered down the main staircase and into the breakfast parlor, thinking of steak and eggs.

And found that there was no one there. And no food.

Bewildered, James blinked, stared into all corners of the parlor, and checked the room's dainty timepiece. It was only just now ten o'clock—what was going on here? He had heard of country hours, but this—well, this was ridiculous!

Now that he noticed, the whole house was like a tomb. Where were all the servants? Where were all those little children? Where was Louisa? And where was Julia?

He was just wondering.

He was less than surprised, then, when the door behind him slammed open, light footsteps hurried in and skittered to a stop, and a feminine voice muttered, "Hell's bells."

That could only be one person. Without turning around, he said, "Good morning, Julia."

She gasped. "Oh, no, not again."

He turned, unable to keep a teasing smile from his

lips. "What am I to make of that greeting? That's hardly hospitable, is it?"

She reddened and smoothed her hair back from where it threatened to tumble out of its pins. "That's not what I meant, and you know it."

She added primly, "It is just that it seems as though every time we meet I am running into a room and swearing. Which I really do *not* do very often, I promise. At least, not every time I run into a room. It's just the unusual excitement surrounding your arrival. We are all turned on our heads a bit."

Julia gasped again and added, "Oh, Lord, and I was rude again, wasn't I? I mean, good morning. I mean, I should have said that first before I explained myself. Or even before I came in and said 'he—'"

"Yes, thank you, I'll consider myself properly greeted." James cut her off before she could utter the improper phrase again. It seemed as if Julia wanted to retort, but she took a deep breath, snapped her mouth shut, and nodded.

"Well." James changed the subject. "We keep meeting over meals, don't we?" As if on cue, he felt his stomach growl. "Although there doesn't seem to be any food this time."

The redness of Julia's face had faded, but she still looked chagrined. "Right, I'm sorry about that. Believe it or not, we meant this as politeness. You see, we all eat breakfast around eight or so, but we knew a town gentleman would never want to keep those hours. So I had the servants clear the food and they were to make new when you got up."

"And the—ah, bells of the underworld that you mentioned?"

"I didn't think they would clear *everything*, so understand my surprise when I saw a bare and gleaming tabletop. And the upper housemaid had just told me you were almost ready and on your way down, and I thought—"

Puzzled, James cut her off again. "Upper housemaid? I didn't see anyone about."

She blew air out of the corner of her mouth and looked at him with pitying tolerance, her embarrassment finally gone. "You're not *supposed* to. They're servants. Good servants are unobtrusive, especially with guests. She did excellently to notice and come tell me—only apparently our other servants are good, too, or at least feeling energetic this morning, because I've never seen them clear so quickly. Perhaps they're trying to impress you?"

James gave a bark of laughter.

"But they are working on making your food, I swear it," Julia said in a soothing voice.

She then flung herself down into a chair, and James followed her lead in a more sedate manner. "Honestly," she added, "please don't take this the wrong way, but haven't you run a house before? Don't you know how servants act?"

"Honestly," he echoed her, "no, I haven't ever run a house. Nicholls, my own country estate, is a recent inheritance, but I've never lived there. All I've ever had since attaining my majority are my bachelor lodgings in town. And a single valet."

"Oh, I beg your pardon."

"No, that's quite all right. I ought to learn these things or my wife and servants will think I'm a fool. Which is much worse than merely having one's future sister think one a fool." As her mouth opened in protest, he raised a hand to quiet her. "It's only fair. I am, at least in this respect. Repeat that at a *ton* party, though, and I'll have your hide."

She covered her mouth quickly, but a giggle crept between her fingers.

The gnawing in his stomach lessened at the sound of her laugh. She distracted him, and he felt the urge to talk on, to prolong their conversation again.

He explained further. "You see, I never came to the country as a child, and I never visited my own estate until I inherited it. For both of my parents, there was simply nothing outside London. And since my father passed on, my mother has continued to live in Matheson House in town and run it to her own liking. So I now find myself in the position of having a title and no idea what to do with it."

"You have a secretary, don't you? And a steward?"

"Yes, and they're damned capable—if you'll excuse my language."

"Absolutely," she replied promptly. "Anytime. Say whatever you like."

"In fact, they're so good that they don't have a bit of need for me. But they live in London, and they focus on our holdings there. I intend to create a real home for myself in Nicholls."

A sudden worry struck him. "Does Louisa know how to manage a household?" Good Lord, he hoped so. An ignorant viscount was bad enough, but if his future wife was savvy, they would manage.

Julia looked doubtful, but she was nodding. "I expect most young ladies learn such things from their mamas or their housekeepers. We are well supplied with servants here, but we haven't had a housekeeper since the butler's wife died last year. It would just kill poor Manderly to see someone else in his wife's place—er, so to speak. And anyway, between Mama and me, and of course Louisa, too, we basically handle those duties."

James eyed her askance, this small, hopeful-looking blond person sitting so pertly in a chair across from him. The more he learned about this household, the more unusual it seemed. "How many jobs do you do? Governess *and* housekeeper?"

Julia looked surprised at his question. "I never thought about it like that. This is my home, and I do what needs to be done. Everyone's happier knowing they can trust the children to be cared for and the servants to be content, so why have someone else do it?"

"What will they all do when you get married?"

The question slipped out before he thought better of it. Julia looked even more startled, and James wished he could have called the words back. He knew—he *knew*—that was a very personal question to be asking a girl he had only met the day before. And it was doubly improper to think of her married, or in anything but the most familial of ways. An image of the marriage bed quickly flitted through his head, and he racked his brain to think of a way to change the subject gracefully.

Luckily, a welcome tray of food was brought into the breakfast parlor just then.

And then another.

And then the most perfect rack of toast he'd ever seen.

As Julia dismissed the footmen, James wondered aloud, "How many people are having breakfast with me?"

"It's all for you. We just wanted you to have a choice, since we didn't know what you usually breakfasted on."

He approached the laden sideboard and opened the first covered dish hopefully, and a heavenly smell of steak and kidneys wafted up. Under the second cover were ham and eggs. And that toast—his mouth positively watered at the sight.

"This all looks and smells wonderful," he said as he began to assemble a plate. "Thank you very much. I'm sorry to have put you and your servants to so much trouble for just one person."

"So . . . it's a lot of food? You might not want it all?"

Out of the corner of his eye, James saw Julia's taut pose. Her gaze was trained blankly on the wall and her fingers twisted in her lap. "You want something to eat again, don't you?" He carefully kept his face solemn as he turned to face her.

She looked up at him, an expression of guilt on her face. "I might have over-ordered just a bit. But if you're absolutely *certain* you won't want everything . . . well, the ham smells *so* good, and I can hardly believe it, but I'm hungry again already."

James laughed. "Serve away. Have as much as you like. Far be it from me to starve a lady in her own home."

The hungry pair ate in companionable silence for a few minutes. James crunched through the thin-sliced ham and crisp toast until his empty stomach began to feel pleasantly full, and his mind returned to the three objectives he'd had for the day.

First, find some breakfast. Done.

Second, find Louisa and set a wedding date. The sooner, the better.

Third, find Lord Oliver and get his approval for the wedding date and marriage settlements.

He felt a bit queasy all of a sudden. He wondered if he'd eaten too quickly.

Still in silence, he sipped at a cup of coffee until he felt more settled. He took a deep breath.

"Where is Louisa this morning?"

"Hmm?" Julia looked up from intently slathering an ungodly amount of butter on a piece of toast. "Oh, I expect she's in the library. Or maybe up with the children, if Mama's not up there. Or maybe they are all visiting the new calf. It's sure to be one of those." She dimpled at him. "You see, I do not do everything by any means. Or know everything about this house."

James nodded his acceptance, not quite able to respond to her smile. "Would you show me the way to Louisa, once you are done eating? I haven't quite gotten my bearings in the house yet."

Julia stood up so quickly that James heard the thump of her knees banging against the underside of the table. She winced, but replied, "Yes, sorry, let's go. I didn't mean to eat so much and keep you waiting."

"No need for injury," James assured her, the urge to laugh returning again. "Please finish your toast. In fact, try these preserves as well—they are delicious."

That was all the persuasion Julia required to sit back down and resume her meal. "Mmm," she agreed. "You're right, the cook's got a knack with blueberries."

James looked down at his own plate again, but the food didn't appeal to him anymore. It had been delicious, and he had been very hungry. But now, his insides roiled, and he wasn't sure why.

So, with no food to occupy him, he watched Julia.

She didn't notice his gaze, so single-mindedly was she eating. Her light hair was pulling out of its pins, and with curls around her face, she looked very young and untroubled. Now that he knew the breadth of her responsibility in the household, he could hardly believe that she appeared so carefree, or that she and Louisa were virtually the same age.

As he watched, he felt that warmth tickle through his

body as it had the day before. She really was lovely, despite her untidy hair—or maybe even, really, because of it. And she was so *unexpected.*

He suddenly wanted to touch her neck, or smell her hair, or drop a kiss onto those full lips. If he only could get that blasted toast away from her for a few seconds, to draw her attention. His hand even began to reach toward her as if of its own volition, and he forced it to pick up a fork and toy with that instead. But he wanted to grab her up and kiss her until she forgot all about her breakfast. He wanted to learn all about her. He wanted to . . .

He mentally drew himself up with a start as he realized what he was thinking. What on earth was he doing, getting heated up about a young woman who hadn't even made her debut yet? And, more importantly, with an intelligent, elegant, would-never-talk-with-her-mouth-full fiancée waiting for him somewhere in this rabbit warren of a house, too.

He quickly shuttered his face, annoyed with himself. Honestly, had he taken leave of his senses to let this friendly, chattery (*don't forget beautiful,* his treacherous brain added) girl get to him in that way?

He might well have, at that. But he wouldn't let it happen again. Couldn't he talk to her without thinking of her as a woman? He simply had to, while he was staying in her home. He couldn't make her—or Louisa, for that matter—feel uncomfortable.

But he couldn't stop looking at her, either.

Julia finally seemed to feel James's gaze on her and looked up. "I'm sorry, I'm done anytime. You're finished?"

At his silent nod, she stood up and stretched luxuriantly. The taut flex of her body did nothing to help banish the thoughts that James knew, *knew*, he needed to put a stop to.

"It is so wonderful to have extra meals in midmorning. I can't thank you enough for being a late riser and missing breakfast."

This broke James's feeling of internal tension; it was too ridiculous. At his sudden explosion of laughter, Julia hastily corrected herself.

"That is, not late for town, but early. Maybe late for the country, but not really, since you are a guest. And you can do whatever you like, and not worry about it a bit, since you *are* a guest."

"Family, I hope," James replied in his most soothing, normal, brotherly voice. "And not to be tiptoed around with special arrangements that cause you extra trouble, like second breakfasts."

As he said this, he thought with a pang of the hour at which he would have to rise for breakfast with the family. Eight o'clock. It simply boggled the mind. Well, if he was to run his own estate, he supposed it would be good to get used to these early country hours.

"Right, right," Julia was still talking on. "That's right, you are to be family. Anyway it's very kind of you to provide me with an excuse to eat as much as I want to."

With this, the pair left the breakfast room and proceeded down a corridor James remembered only vaguely from his initial trip through the house the night before.

"I still have quite a lot to familiarize myself with," he observed.

"Louisa will be happy to show you around the whole house," Julia replied with—was that a knowing smile? He arched a skeptical eyebrow back at her, but she seemed not to notice as she continued, "We'll check the library for her first. It's her favorite place in the house."

They came to a set of heavy double doors, and Julia

knocked before cautiously turning the handle of one. "She hates to be startled," she explained over her shoulder in a stage whisper.

James nodded his understanding. "Louisa?" he called hesitantly.

"Good heavens, come in," said an exasperated voice from inside.

As Julia opened the door, Louisa added, "Julia, you have got the loudest whisper anyone could possibly imagine. Good morning, James. How are you feeling today? Did you rest well?"

"Excuse me; I will leave you alone," Julia said in her loud whisper, and again with that knowing smile that twisted warmly through James's stomach like a fine brandy, she melted off.

Once outside the door of the library, Julia blew out a deep breath, her shoulders sagging. She looked up and down the silent corridor to make sure it was empty, then leaned back against the wall and slid down to the floor, folding her legs in front of her.

"Why am I so stupid all the time?" she muttered.

Why, she thought to herself, did she keep embarrassing herself in front of James? Good heavens, that was actually *Viscount* Matheson she kept insulting! It seemed as if she couldn't meet the man without some breach of propriety, whether chiding him for his town polish or, oh yes, giving him an earful of her most unladylike vocabulary words.

Well, they were not *the* most unladylike words she knew, but they were bad enough.

He had been kind about it so far, but she knew well that it was important that he like the family and want to go ahead with the marriage. Quite simply, Louisa's turn in London was over, and Julia was to go next if she was ever to have a prayer of marrying outside the limited social circle of the surrounding estates. Their parents had never made the smallest allusion to the fact, but she knew well that, though a London season was a heavy financial burden, an unmarried daughter—especially one of five—could be even more so.

Julia glumly dropped her chin onto her folded knees, curling her arms around her legs. Thus far, her family had behaved quite unconventionally toward their guest—that is, their newest family member, as he had referred to himself—but then again, he did seem to like it.

So, did he like them?

Did he like *her*?

From what Julia had seen of James so far, he was . . . well, wonderful. She couldn't seem to stop thinking about him. His clever face, his warm smile, his low laugh, his long body. She only wished she'd been able to see more of it. Of him.

She felt her face heat again. This time, the heat spread into her fingers, making them tingle, and into the pit of her stomach, tickling it with nervous excitement.

James was exactly the sort of man she wanted to meet in London. Exactly the sort of man she'd like for a husband.

She had to remember, though, that he was also the man who was going to marry her sister.

Suddenly, she felt like using *all* her most unladylike vocabulary words.

Chapter 4

In Which Louisa Is Offered a Bathtub Shaped Like the Sphinx

In the library, James and Louisa were completely oblivious to Julia's fit of confusion outside the door as they enjoyed their first private conversation in, it seemed to James, the weeks since his proposal. As soon as the door had closed behind him, he strode over to the red Grecian-style sofa on which Louisa was seated.

He wondered what type of greeting would be proper in this situation. A man should be affectionate with his future wife, of course, but he still felt the distance of unfamiliarity looming between them.

After the briefest of pauses, he caught up her hands in his and kissed first one, then the other.

"Good morning, my dear. You look more beautiful than ever."

This was no exaggeration; Louisa was a lovely woman. Her wide brown eyes were bright, and her thick dark hair was coiled up neatly and caught back from her face by a pale green band that matched her print morning dress.

The color brought out the rich tones of her hair and the delicate pink of her cheeks, which blushed in response to his words.

Louisa cast her gaze down and motioned for him to sit next to her. "Nonsense; that's just fine talk. But it's kind of you, so I'll let it pass even though I know it's ridiculous."

"It's the perfect truth, I swear. I'm very glad to see you alone this morning. It has been quite a while, and we have much to talk about."

"Oh?" she asked, lifting her eyes. "I am glad to see you, too, of course, but what subject has arisen so suddenly?"

"Nothing sudden; just talk about our marriage. Before I talk to your father—which is, of course, one of the reasons for my visit here—I wanted to consult your wishes as to the time and scale of the ceremony."

Again he reached for her hands as he moved closer to her on the sofa. Gazing at her intently, he added, "I would like to be married as soon as possible."

This had been his plan even before arriving at Stonemeadows Hall; a key motivation for his swift engagement had been an equally swift—though respectably so—marriage. Now that he had arrived, he was also disconcerted by his unexpected attraction to Julia, and he determined to squelch it at once by cementing his tie with his fiancée.

Except Louisa didn't react as he'd thought she would.

Based on his experience with women, he expected a warm, eager response, possibly even followed by an animated discussion of where to get the wedding gown. He wasn't sorry to be spared the discourse on fashion, but still—when Louisa only stared at him, startled, he felt his heart sink a bit.

"I see," was her only initial response. She hesitated a moment, then added, "There is no need for a rush, is there? Need we be hasty?"

Her lack of enthusiasm stung, and James drew back. "Hasty? I hadn't thought of it that way. No, there's no reason except my own wish to be settled."

It was mostly true. True enough. He *did* wish to be settled. At once.

Louisa bit her lip as she considered, then admitted, "If we marry soon, I shall have to sponsor Julia during her season next spring."

This was a total non sequitur to James, but he tried to respond as he thought Louisa would expect him to.

"I think that would be delightful. You could begin your life as a London hostess with one of your favorite family connections."

His groin tightened. Delightful. Julia, in his house, nearby always, saucy and willing.

Oh, yes. And under his wife's supervision. The vision popped as quickly as a soap bubble.

Unaware of his thoughts, fortunately, Louisa was struggling to explain herself. She raised one slim hand, as if to ward off James's suggestion.

"I would *not* find it delightful. In fact, I'd find it the opposite." She shook her head. "I can't think of it; I really can't. I do dislike drawing attention to my own faults, James, but it cannot have escaped your notice that I fit very poorly into the world of the *ton*. How would it serve Julia—or my own self—to try to take a place of prominence in that world and lead an unknown young lady into it?"

Her reluctance was startling, but after pondering her words for a few moments, James wasn't really surprised. He knew she hadn't enjoyed her London season;

good Lord, they had met because she was hiding from a ballroom.

But he had to persuade her to be married as soon as possible. How best could he do it?

Well, there were always his title and his money. They were worth a try.

"Is that all that's bothering you?" At her suddenly mulish expression, he added hastily, "Not, of course, that I mean to belittle your concerns. But you forget, my dear, that I bring connections to our marriage as well. As my wife, the new Viscountess Matheson, you will have the respect of all you meet." He grinned at her; his most charming grin, the one that had always caused young women to swoon and flutter. "If I do say so myself."

Louisa, of all young women, seemed immune to The Grin. "I know," she replied, her expression glum. "I know that you're very much a part of that world, and that it is important to you. But could I not be one of those wives who stays in the country all the time?" A hopeful smile peeped at the corners of her mouth. "You could tell everyone I misbehaved terribly and you had to rusticate me."

James responded appreciatively to her sly smile and the potential double meaning of her words. "A misbehaving wife? Surely not *my* wife."

He bent his head, intending to drop a kiss on her lips. Just a small one. Just to remind himself of what he had promised to be to her.

Louisa permitted him to draw within a breath of her face, but then seemed to think better of it and scooted away just out of his reach. "Apparently fictional misbehavior breeds genuine misbehavior," she teased, her voice trembling a bit.

James was startled by her movement, and caught literally off balance. He swayed, checked himself to keep from tipping over, and took a deep breath to collect himself. "Surely a kiss is not out of place from your future husband."

Louisa colored again, and he smiled inwardly. This was the blushing-est family he'd ever seen. He rather liked it; it made it easy to tell what they were feeling.

Although, judging from her appearance, Louisa now looked . . . a bit anxious? Her brows were knit over her flushed cheeks, and she bit her bottom lip in seeming agitation.

This wasn't working. Why wouldn't she agree to marry him quickly? He couldn't understand, but she seemed distressed by the idea.

Which, honestly, was a bit lowering for a man.

It seemed ungentlemanly to press her further right now, so James mentally shelved the topic for another time. Perhaps Louisa was always intractable in the morning, and she'd be more compliant under the charm of an evening sky. They could take a walk in the gardens, and in the presence of a romantic riot of flowers, he could broach the topic again.

For now, though, Louisa's thoughts were still in London. He knew this not because he was suddenly able to read her inscrutable expression. It was, rather, because she suggested, "If we are not married until after Julia's season, my aunt, Lady Irving, could sponsor her instead."

So now they were talking of Julia's season again. James wrenched his thoughts into the proper channel. But . . . Lady Irving?

"Good Lord, that woman is terrifying," he gasped. "She makes my mother look like the veriest lamb in comparison."

He realized at once that this was a rather rude thing

to say about a gently bred lady, an elder, and a countess—
and especially about a female who was all of these things
as well as aunt to his betrothed.

But Louisa nodded calmly, not seeming to mind at all.

"That is certainly an apt description," she agreed. "I
know sometimes I felt overwhelmed by the amount she
had planned for me during my season. But that would be
ideal for Julia's presentation, if Aunt Estella is willing."

An idea struck James. "Actually, your sister Julia's
rather like your aunt." At Louisa's look of surprise, he explained, "Not that she is terrifying in the slightest, but
she seems to say whatever comes into her head."

"Oh, well, that's true. I suppose it comes from growing up with . . . rather an unusual set of parents."

"I expect the *ton* will find her honesty refreshing,"
James added loyally, but he felt a pang of doubt. What if
they should not take to the young Miss Herington any
better than they did to the Honorable Miss Oliver? He
shook off the thought, remembering Louisa's own pain
at her invisibility during the season and determining to
do whatever he could to ensure Julia's success. For
Louisa's sake, naturally.

"I hope so," Louisa said, her expression uncertain. "I
don't know if she cares to go at all, but of course she
must marry. And probably she will enjoy London. Julia
genuinely likes people, so the crush of a party may seem
like a very fine thing to her."

They sat together in silence for a moment; James was
unsure of what to say. His own relations would sooner give
any amount of money, he knew, than admit that they
were ever ill at ease. The *ton* could be quite a minefield
for the socially awkward or timid.

A thought suddenly seemed to seize Louisa. "James,
what if I came to London, too, to keep Julia company,
and I could look for bride-clothes at the same time? I

could take part in events when I wanted, and it wouldn't matter if no one noticed me, because as an engaged lady, I am no longer in competition with the young misses."

Her spirits looked as if they were lifting as she spoke, and she continued in a rush, "Oh, James, it would be perfect. Please do agree. Aunt Estella will do a much better job as a sponsor than I, and Julia would not be lonely as I was, and you could show her around at any parties that I didn't wa—" She paused, her gaze dropping, and finished, "Um, that I was not able to attend. Due to, er, fittings with my *modiste* or some such thing."

The idea was unusual, but he considered it. Louisa was willing to come to London; this was more than he had expected her to grant after her initial reluctance, and he might yet be able to persuade her to come as his wife.

"It would be uncommon, but it seems like a reasonable solution," he granted. "Do you think your aunt would agree to have you both stay with her?"

At her eager nod, he added, "I myself would be delighted to have you in town for another season; otherwise there would be little reason for me to go. And you are right, I can ease your sister's path as I was not able to do for you." He smiled down at Louisa, whose dark eyes were now sparkling with excitement.

"Oh, James, it would be so much better with her there—and with you, of course." Her brow puckered. "But what would we tell people if anyone wondered why we had not yet married?"

That was a good question, and one for which he had no answer. He was marrying to subtract from the family's notoriety, not add to it.

He shrugged.

"We'd tell them to get their blasted noses out of our business," James replied straight-faced. Perhaps Julia was already influencing him; he'd never have dreamed of speaking so to a lady before yesterday.

Louisa gasped, then started laughing when his face broke into a smile. "Why not? Or perhaps we could tell them that my parents enrolled you in their livestock operations, and you were far too interested in developing new cattle strains to get around to planning a wedding," she suggested.

"Or that you refused to marry me until my entire home was decorated exactly as you like, with fashionable Egyptian furniture and a bathtub shaped like the Sphinx," he teased, pleased to see his fiancée shaking her head with laughter.

"Oh, no one would ever believe that one. That would be too repulsive," she said, catching her breath. "Unless—is this the truth of your renovations at Nicholls? Are we to be transported to the Pyramids when we enter your estate?"

"I'm afraid it's much more prosaic than that," he admitted. "I've got a sound roof over the place as a start, and the rest is repairing the damage of years of neglect. My father never kept more than a skeleton staff there, and many of the rooms have been closed off for years.

"Come to think of it, though," he continued, "it would be nice to have you put your own stamp on it as the work proceeds. You know, have things as you like—the wallpaper and draperies and whatnot."

Louisa nodded and offered him a small smile. "Your offer is generous, and your point's well taken. Maybe we could make a family party of it someday soon. I'd love to see Nicholls, and I'm sure you are keen to get back there as well for a time."

"It's settled, then," James said, and he stood to take his leave of her. "I'll go and speak to your father, and I'll acquaint him of your wishes for your aunt's sponsorship of your sister. And I will suggest an excursion to Nicholls sometime soon, whenever it is convenient for your parents."

"But what shall we tell people about our postponed wedding?" she asked again. She bit her lip.

He pondered the question for a moment. Nothing came at once to mind, which had become a disturbingly common phenomenon since he'd entered this house.

"Well, we'll figure that out if we need to," he said finally. "'For family reasons' is accurate enough." It wouldn't silence any gossiping tongues, but what else could he say under the circumstances? He tried to hide his perturbation with a small joke. "Or we can just say you're waiting for the Sphinx tub to arrive; whichever you prefer."

She shook her head, smiling, and began to reach again for the bound volume she had laid aside upon his entrance.

"I wouldn't tease Papa like that if I were you," she recommended. "He won't be able to tell that you're joking, and he'd think I had returned from London an extremely silly creature. Of course," she considered, "a Sphinx is part lion, is it not? He is so fond of animals, he may think it an excellent choice for interior décor."

James smiled and kissed her hand again, to remind himself again that he was a betrothed man. Louisa pinkened again, and as he left her, he was pleased—and perhaps a bit relieved—that he could affect her despite her worries.

Once outside the library, he leaned against the wall for a moment and shut his eyes. That conversation hadn't gone at all the way he'd expected.

True, his fiancée was going to visit his home, which he supposed was a good thing. But why the devil didn't she want to get married yet? Did she hate London so much? And if so, why was she willing to go back again to help her sister?

He opened his eyes, but shook his head in puzzlement. Louisa seemed to be offering him as much as she could, and it would be ungentlemanly of him to press her again right now. It would all work out eventually. They would be married, and with his wife at his side, he could help his sister and her young daughters.

As for that idea about Julia coming to London with Louisa—well, it would probably turn out very well for the two sisters. But he obviously needed to check his reactions better. His attraction to Julia was far beyond what he should allow himself to feel as an engaged man. He was going to find himself baying at the moon every night at the rate he was going.

Left behind in the library, Louisa was even more unsettled than the viscount. She laid aside her book, but in case James stepped back into the room, she kept her face carefully smooth.

It was an expression—or rather, a lack of expression— that she had developed during her time in London. There had been so many times her natural reserve had hindered her, it seemed small consolation that it also gave her the ability to keep her thoughts from her face.

She could show no fear when she entered a room full of hundreds of strangers, who looked her over and openly dismissed her. She could show no disappointment when she was overlooked for dance after dance; show no pain when her host, out of pity, took her onto the ballroom floor and trod all over her feet; show no chagrin when her aunt, who was gracious enough to sponsor her, lamented loudly to all her friends about how no one was coming along to snap Louisa up.

Truly, she was a talented young lady. The *ton* had had no idea just how talented.

Compared to the agonies of a single London supper party, her conversation with James had been a breeze. But she was left with an uneasy feeling all the same. She knew that the very reason for his visit was to discuss their marriage. She knew, of course, that he planned for them to be married fairly soon, at which point she would be his viscountess.

It was just that when he actually brought up the subject, she was terrified. Terrified of leaving her family again, of living in London, of always bearing the crushing loneliness she'd hardly even spoken of to Julia, her dear sister and closest friend.

She knew eventually she would need to get married, and while she didn't *love* James—after all, she had known him for such a short time—she certainly liked him very much. She knew, too, that a financially solvent viscount was really far beyond her touch. He could do much better than her, and she should be grateful. And she *was* grateful; there was no mistake about that. His proposal had offered her the chance to put a period to the loneliest, unhappiest time of her life.

But she couldn't help wanting to postpone the inevitable as long as possible. Fortunately, James was a kind man, and he'd been willing to accept her wishes even though they probably sounded lame to him. After all, how could she tell him—a man she hardly knew—that, despite everything he was offering her, she didn't feel ready for marriage at all?

She simply couldn't. She'd have to say nothing, show no sign of her doubts, and hope her feelings altered.

She sighed and straightened up. It was done; no more sense in thinking about it. James had come in, spoken with her, and left. He accepted what she asked. For at least a little while longer, she need not think about the changes in store for her.

She picked up the volume at her side again and opened it to the title page.

"Evelina," she read.

Evelina, who went to London and had a grand time, and made men love her, although she was a nobody. That old timeworn tale had seemed so entrancing once upon a time.

With all the force Louisa could muster in her arm, she threw the book across the room.

Chapter 5

In Which the Viscount Intentionally Walks through Manure

James's first full day at Stonemeadows Hall had already brought surprise after surprise, and it was still not yet noon. Thus the viscount was almost looking forward to having an extremely odd conversation with Lord Oliver about his eldest daughter's marriage plans, and in this he was not disappointed.

The older man welcomed James heartily into his study, but once the two were face-to-face across the baron's large, untidy desk, James felt unsure how to begin.

"Lord Oliver," he started, then paused as he met his future father-in-law's expectant gaze.

Should he say that the wedding was indefinitely postponed? Should he even try to discuss marriage terms at all? Was there any point until he and Louisa set a date?

He cleared his throat and tried again. "Lord Oliver, I've just been speaking with your daughter—"

"Emilia? Or Elise?" The older man's brow furrowed in confusion. "Not Anne. Or is it? Has Annie been bothering you to play bilbo catch with her again? I'll have Lady Oliver speak with her at once." He rose from behind his desk and began to head for the door.

James stood, too, but just stared after him for a second, trying to follow the older man's thought processes. "No, no. Certainly not. It was Louisa."

Lord Oliver stopped with his hand on the door handle. "Louisa?" He looked confused. "Why should Louisa want to play bilbo catch with you?"

James took a deep breath. All right, so this was going to be even more difficult than he had expected.

"No one was playing bilbo catch with anyone else, and no one wanted to," he explained with what he hoped was a respectful amount of patience in his voice. Good Lord, even as a child, he'd never enjoyed the cursed game of trying to catch a ball in a wooden cup. Why was the baron going on about it now?

"No," he continued, "I spoke with Louisa about our marriage."

"Ah." Enlightenment warmed Lord Oliver's expression into a beam of delight. "Now I understand. Very appropriate, that. But if you've come to ask my permission again, you really didn't need to. I've already consented to the match."

He clapped James on the shoulder and turned toward the door of his study again.

"I've been indoors for too long this morning. Would you care to walk with me? I'm just going to check on a few of the animals."

Unable to get another word in before his host left the study, James found himself trotting after Lord Oliver to the stables, trying valiantly to interject some comment— anything at all—about Louisa.

"We've decided to postpone the marriage until after

Julia begins her season," he gasped as he followed at a near run behind Lord Oliver's rapid pace.

"Hmm?" The baron was distracted now that they were almost to the stables. "Julia's getting married during her season? Yes, excellent idea."

This was the closest James was able to come to any of the calm discussion he had planned, in which he and his future father-in-law would sit across a desk from one another, set the date of the wedding, and perhaps even discuss the marriage settlement. The specific amount of Louisa's dowry wasn't really a concern for James, since the Matheson viscountcy wasn't at all short of funds; still, it felt like something he and his future father-in-law ought to work out.

Instead, he found himself trotting after Lord Oliver through a whirlwind tour of the stables. He was willing to profess admiration for the horses, but James split from his host when the latter professed a desire to check on a newborn calf and its mother. Saying he would meet Lord Oliver back at the house later, he trudged back across the muddy ground, looking dolefully at his mud-caked boots and remembering their mirror-bright gloss of the morning.

It wasn't as if he had never been in the country before, but getting into the stables of a manor house was an experience entirely new to him. He was used to grooms bringing horses out for him to ride, already saddled and bridled. Had he even been in a stable since he was an inquisitive young boy? Surely not since his father had tanned his backside and told him sons of the house didn't associate with servants.

He paused in his walk for a moment, regarding a clump of—yes, he was very much afraid that wasn't dirt on his boot, but something far more . . . organic. And suddenly, he felt his natural good humor returning. Cleaning his boots would be just the job for his valet, who tended to be supercilious at the best of times, and whose best personality traits were definitely not brought out by country life.

James's pace quickened as he imagined the man's face upon seeing his soiled boots, and he had to laugh to himself. He even veered toward a fresh-looking deposit and tramped through it with both feet.

He felt more cheerful at once. It would do Delaney some good to clean a bit of excrement off his master's boots every once in a while. And the Olivers were odd, true, but they were kind people—and at any rate, he was certainly gaining plenty of new experiences. He would hardly have wanted to marry into a dull family, would he?

The succeeding weeks of James's visit drifted by pleasantly, with few notable events to mar the placid country life he expected to constitute most of his days following his marriage.

But when, one day in mid-September, he received word over the dinner table of the impending arrival from London of the family's doughty relative, Lady Irving, he decided that this might well be a good opportunity to leave for a while. Only to oversee restorations, of course; not to avoid his future wife's relatives. Not even to escape from the aunt who could have taught lessons in sharp-tongued repartee to Attila the Hun. If Huns practiced repartee, rather than just whacking at their enemies with swords.

Actually, it wasn't all that difficult to imagine Lady Irving with a sword in her hand.

He waited until the next day, two days before Lady

Irving's expected visit, to broach to Louisa the topic of his return to his estate. He found her in the early afternoon; she was, as usual, in the library. As was now his routine, he knocked on the door before entering. When he did, Louisa was seated expectantly on her favorite red sofa, a book at her side, her hands clasped on her knee.

"Hello, my dear," he greeted her, kissing her on the forehead in their accustomed ritual.

"Good afternoon to you," she replied. "To what do I owe the pleasure?"

"Do I need a reason for coming to speak to my fiancée?" he answered gallantly.

She looked at him expectantly for a moment, and his bravado deflated. "Oh, very well, if you must know— I was thinking of returning to Nicholls for a time."

"To shoot partridge? Or to avoid shooting my aunt Estella?" she asked, quirking an intelligent eyebrow.

"Um," he replied. He hadn't expected to be caught out so quickly. "Well, perhaps a bit of both."

Louisa shook her head. "It won't do, James. You'll have to see her eventually, you know. She's going to stay here until we all go back to London for the season. She says she can't stand the London fog during winter."

"Probably she just can't stand for people to think that no one wants to invite her to visit," he muttered.

"Pardon?" Louisa's voice was innocent, her expression sweet, but he knew she'd heard him.

"Nothing, nothing," he said hurriedly, trying to end the topic of conversation. Honestly, he had dealt with enough difficult females in his life already just by growing up with his mother. He couldn't be expected to deal with them in the country as well; it was too much to ask of any man.

"Well," Louisa continued, looking mollified, "I think it would be lovely if you returned to Nicholls and made all ready for us to come for a visit. I am sure my aunt would love to come see your home. That is, our future home," she corrected. "Of course, I would love to see it as well. And I know you're mad with curiosity to see how things are shaping up in your absence."

A smile tugged at her lips, and James allowed his own face to relax into a mirror of her expression. "Yes, I have been wondering what the old place looks like now. I know I'll be surprised, but I don't know if it's because of how much or how little has been done in my absence."

"Perhaps it'll be best to keep your expectations low," Louisa suggested. "Just in case, would you like to set the date for our visit following your own arrival at Nicholls? If there's, say, a hole in the floor or some such nonsense, we'll definitely want that repaired before my aunt comes."

"Not necessarily," he murmured under his breath.

Louisa shot him a wry look and continued, "She's bringing her lady's maid with her as well, of course, and as the maid's French, she's very particular. In fact, she reminds me of someone." She paused in mock contemplation, tapping her chin. "Ah, I know; she rather reminds me of *your* servant."

James was relieved by her teasing mood, and, happy to play along, he put up his hands in surrender. "You win, you win. My manservant orders me around, and I think your aunt is quite the most terrifying person I have ever met, just slightly edging out my mother."

Louisa looked a little surprised by this chain of admissions, so James sought to placate her further. "But if it helps, I don't truly want to drop her through a floor. Nor any of your other family members, either."

If he hadn't known his fiancée to be such a lady, he would have had to describe her laugh as a snort.

"That's quite a relief, to be sure," she replied. "We will look forward to touring your home with the utmost peace of mind, knowing that a fatal accident is the furthest thing from your wishes."

A sharp rap sounded at the door, and Julia burst through it a moment later, panting with hurry, pale hair pulling out of its pins into untidy threads.

"Louisa, you'll never believe it!" she cried, and then noticed her sister's companion. "Oh, hello, James; sorry to interrupt you." She instantly turned red, and rushed on, "That is, not that I expected I would be interrupting anything. I mean, not that you would be doing anything you minded me interrupting. I—um . . ."

She wound down into a flustered silence, and James, inwardly laughing to himself, wiped a kind expression across his face. "Was there something you wanted to tell us? Or perhaps just your sister? I would be happy to leave you in private."

She looked gratefully at him for a moment, then blanched.

"Oh, Lord, no, it concerns us all," she blurted. "Aunt Estella is here *now.*"

Chapter 6

In Which They All Quake in Their Boots (or Slippers, as the Case May Be)

"Rot!" echoed a low but piercingly loud female voice as Julia careened into the entrance hall, followed quickly by Louisa and much more slowly by James.

A fabulous sight met Julia's eyes. A litter of trunks was scattered all across the polished marble floor, one dropped on its side and with its contents spilling out, which appeared to include . . . rocks? A slim, proud-faced, black-haired maid stood by in chic black clothing, her expression blank but her arms folded tightly in annoyance. Lady Irving, resplendent in magenta satin and bobbing yellow ostrich plumes, was pacing around and gesticulating wildly. A small green parrot sat on her shoulder, heedless of the fuss and nibbling at a ruby dangling from her ladyship's earbob.

It hurt Julia's eyes just to look at it. Her ears, too, actually. She made a mental note never to let that parrot anywhere near them.

Lady Irving continued in stentorian tones, arms flailing. "This is no way to treat a guest. No, better than a guest; your own flesh and blood! Just because a trunk is heavy doesn't mean your footmen have a right to drop it. In fact," she bellowed, "you ought to thank me for revealing their shortcomings."

Now Julia noticed her parents, plastered against the opposite wall of the entrance hall from where she stood. Her mother looked harassed; Lord Oliver merely looked vaguely at his elder sister.

"But why on earth did you bring rocks, Estella? You must know we've plenty out here in the country. Good heavens, they give the very estate its name."

He began to chuckle at his mild joke until he was recalled to the present by his wife's desperate tap on his arm. "Er, but very sorry about the mess, of course. We'll have your things packed back up and in order at once, I'm sure. While you're waiting, would you care to come see some of the animals?"

He at once headed toward the door, domestic difficulties forgotten.

Lady Irving replied witheringly, "I would *not* care to see your animals, and you know it. And I am perfectly aware of the name and location of your estate, as you also know. I brought this trunk"—here she waved at the offending article—"simply to test the management of your household. It was for the same reason that I came early. I wanted to know what type of treatment I was to expect now that you have no housekeeper. I can see that things have gone sadly to ruin."

Julia felt sympathy for Manderly, to be so reminded of the loss of his wife, although the butler was far too experienced and correct a servant to betray any unseemly emotion. But she also considered her aunt's statement to be more than a little unfair, considering the butler and the footmen struggling with the myriad trunks were in impeccable livery, and everyone was standing on the highly polished marble floor of a bright, high-ceilinged entrance hall without a speck of dust in sight. The only flaw Julia could see was the spilled trunk full of rocks her aunt had inflicted upon the poor footmen, whose balance must have been overset by the load as they carried in the inordinate amount of luggage Lady Irving had brought with her.

All right, it was time to say something, since the situation was degenerating and she could see no one else was going to stand up to her blasted aunt—and she meant that adjective with all affection. Lord Oliver was sidling toward the door again, his distant expression clearly showing that his mind had already traveled to the stables, well ahead of his body.

"My dear aunt," Julia began, stepping forward to make her curtsy. "It is an even greater pleasure to see you every year. And this year most of all, as you've so thoughtfully brought a trunk full of gifts from our great capital city. I am so sorry that it was spilled."

She straightened out of the curtsy and stood, hands folded behind her back, waiting for her aunt's reply.

Silence reigned for a few minutes. Then, blessedly, her ladyship snorted, and the corners of her mouth crooked into what almost appeared to be a smile.

"Good girl," she replied. "I like a young miss who can get her point across."

Emboldened, Julia continued, "It was kind of you to bring a pet for the children as well. Certainly such a parrot as that would do well up in the nursery."

Lady Irving at once turned a gimlet eye on her and said, "Not a bit of it. You should have known when to stop, my girl. This parrot leaves my shoulder only when my head leaves my shoulders as well. Or," she corrected herself, "when I change into a dress that doesn't match his plumage. At any rate, those children aren't going to pull Butternut's feathers out and plague the life out of him.

"There are too many dratted children about the place, anyway," she continued. "Tom," she rounded on her brother, "didn't I tell you not to marry a woman with a family? I told you not to marry a woman with a family. But you wouldn't listen to me, what was it, ten years ago? Twelve?" She tsked, shaking her head. "You should always listen to your elders."

Lady Oliver gaped at this impolite statement for a moment, then protested. "But, sister, all the small children are new. I mean, Lord Oliver's and mine. I only had Julia at the time I married your brother."

"Still," Lady Irving harrumphed. "You know what I mean. Although," she continued after a reflective pause, "I think you'll do very well in London, my Julia, after I'm through with you. You lack polish, but there's nothing wrong with that. It never hurt me."

"I can't imagine anyone ever telling you that you lack polish," Julia replied honestly. After all, who would dare to?

"No one ever has, but that's just because they're afraid of me," Lady Irving confirmed.

"Pieces of eight," contributed the parrot, and lunged for the rubies dangling at its side again.

Lady Irving removed the ruby earbob from the parrot's reach and continued, "Now, don't think you all can persuade me to give up my rocks. I want this trunk taken upstairs and unpacked, and when we go back to town, I will want them packed again and brought back with me."

"But *why*?" asked Lady Oliver, her pale, guileless face showing her confusion.

"To see if you'll do what I say," her unexpected guest replied triumphantly. "After all, you have a countess visiting you. Now, if it's not too much trouble, could I have my things conducted up to my chambers? Naturally, Simone will need an adjoining room of her own to care for me and my wardrobe."

"We could use those rocks for wall-mending," Lord Oliver chipped in, suddenly alive to the conversation, as if he hadn't heard a bit of what had passed before. "Estella, do let us have them. They'll be just the thing for the wall around the bull's pen."

Lady Irving stared at him in disbelief for a moment, then threw up her hands in surrender. "Fine, fine, Tom. Use them if you must." She shook her head, exasperated. "You people have no regard for rank."

"I'll show you to your room at once, Aunt." Louisa finally spoke up. Was she trying to put a quick end to the situation? Julia darted a sharp look at her sister, but Louisa's face was as expressionless and sweet as a painting.

James made a proper bow of greeting as Lady Irving finally took notice of him with the smallest of nods. "Ah, yes, Louisa's young rooster."

James straightened up, eyebrows raised so high Julia thought they might just shoot off of his forehead. "Beg pardon, ma'am?"

"Don't 'ma'am' me, you rascal. I dandled you on my knee when you were in nappies. Yes, yes, don't you pull that face at me, Matheson. Your mother and I led the *ton* together in our youth and married the same season. Naturally, I visited all the time when you were a babe.

"I think it is so much better to be a visitor than a parent," she reflected. "You and your sister were darling

creatures, of course. But children do so spoil the looks."
She patted her still-bright auburn hair.

"It is always a delight to hear your opinion, Lady
Irving," James replied, staring her straight in the eye. "I
am especially gratified to know you remember me during
my kindest and most innocent years. I do hope I never
spit up on you."

"Stuff," said her ladyship, the hint of a smile on her
face. "You are remarkably indelicate in the presence of
a lady."

"I do beg pardon, ma'am," James replied smoothly. "I
was under the impression, when you brought up nappies, that all topics of conversation were acceptable."

The sound that came out of Lady Irving could only be
described as a bark. With a nod of acknowledgment, she
cast an appraising eye up and down his form before
snapping to her maid to follow her up the stairs.

As Lady Irving passed by Julia on her way upstairs, the
younger woman heard her aunt mutter under her
breath, "At least he's got nice legs."

Well, that she could definitely agree with.

The household was back into a semblance of order by
the evening, though Lady Irving again upset everyone at
dinnertime by insisting on a strict order of precedence
being observed as they all went in to dine. James had
gotten rather used to meandering casually into the
dining room night after night, chatting across the table,
refusing every dish of fish—all behaviors that his mother
(whose forceful personality he now understood a bit
better, knowing she had been youthful friends with Lady
Irving) would at best have frowned on, and at worst have
had an apoplexy upon seeing. It was almost a novelty to

have his arm seized in Lady Irving's grip of iron and his less-than-eager steps led into the dining room.

He noticed that she was *not* carrying the parrot on her shoulder now. That, at least, was something to be thankful for.

Naturally, she most wanted to discuss the upcoming wedding and, once she got wind of it, the trip to Nicholls, both of which James was currently considering subjects non grata after Louisa's less-than-ecstatic responses. He informed the gathered family of his plans to return there for a few weeks, but was effectively able to stem a storm of protest—mostly from Lady Irving and Julia, neither of whom had known of his plans to leave—by inviting everyone to come for a visit as soon as he had ensured the soundness of the house.

"I suppose that'll do," Lady Irving granted. "It'll be sadly flat here without a good-looking young man to liven things up, though."

James could only gape at her in surprise, much to the detriment of his dignity.

Without further comment, her ladyship turned to Julia and added, "That expression right there. See it? *That* is why I say things like that. It's worth more than gold to me to get a viscount's jaw to drop."

"I want to make his jaw drop, too!" Julia cried. "James, can I?"

"If you ask me about it, you're not likely to surprise me," he explained. "And *no*. You shouldn't try to startle people. No offense is meant, Lady Irving, but she shouldn't come to London intending to shock the garters off the Prince Regent."

"That would be hilarious," Julia mused. "I wonder how I could get to meet him."

James thought of Prinny's good-humored debauchery,

his affairs and excesses. He didn't want Julia anywhere near the prince's garters. He shouldn't even have said it as a joke; the very thought was disgusting.

"You are *not* meeting the Prince Regent," he told her firmly.

"Rot," Lady Irving replied. That seemed to be a favorite word of hers.

Julia's face lit up with anticipation. "Aunt, I must have you teach me all the rude words you know before the season begins."

James met Louisa's eyes helplessly, and she just shrugged.

Yes . . . when faced with the combination of Julia Herington and Lady Estella Irving, what else was there to do?

Chapter 7

In Which No One Falls through Any Floors

The trip to Nicholls followed soon after Lady Irving's arrival in Kent, although it was not soon enough for Julia. She was, as she told Louisa, simply mad with curiosity to see the place where her sister was going to live.

Well, what other reason could there possibly be for her eagerness, after all?

Every time she mentioned Nicholls, Louisa's answering smile grew thinner. Probably, Julia realized, she was talking about it too much and making Louisa bored. But it was hard to keep quiet, especially as the set date grew closer.

The trip was planned for a week's length, and it was ultimately decided that Louisa would be accompanied only by Julia, who was wild to see how good the house looked; Lady Irving, who was just as eager to see what a terrible state the house was in; and Simone, on whose presence Lady Irving's every comfort was dependent. Lord and Lady Oliver were respectively preoccupied with the livestock and the children. Fortunately, in the opinion of all concerned except for Lady Irving, the parrot also failed to make one of the party, having become indispensable to young Tom, who was fascinated by the bird's swashbuckling vocabulary.

The day of the journey to Nicholls was sunny and warm for late September. The carriage ride and a brief pause for a luncheon at a respectable-looking inn transpired with only a few complaints by Lady Irving regarding the crowding on the Olivers' carriage seats, the stiffness of the "benighted" vehicle's springs, the shockingly bad condition of the roads outside of London, and the fact that Julia was sitting on her skirts and crushing their silk (which today was an eye-testing bright yellow).

As they arrived at Nicholls in late afternoon, each of the four occupants of the carriage had a unique reaction upon seeing the estate.

"The grounds are so *pretty*," said Julia.

"Good God, the drive is a positive cesspool," Lady Irving observed, looking pleased. "Matheson obviously hasn't done a thing to it."

"I hope we will be able to get some hot water at once," Simone commented in a low, lilting voice, looking at her hands with customary fastidiousness.

"The house is . . . larger than I expected," Louisa said, her eyes growing wider as they took in the immense breadth of the viscount's ancestral home.

"Large is good, my girl," Lady Irving replied. "More than you know, where men are concerned, large is good." She cackled at what was apparently, to her, an extremely witty remark, as Julia and Louisa stared at her blankly and Simone looked pointedly out of the window.

James came out of the house to meet them himself, drawing a derogatory sniff from Lady Irving. As he helped the women down from the carriage, her ladyship commented in a lofty tone, "Although I am a countess, my dear boy, you really need not prostrate yourself like a servant for all of us."

Julia saw Louisa's gaze fly, chagrined, to James's face, but the viscount only smiled benignly.

"Lady Irving, I would never deny you any attention that might make you the slightest bit more comfortable. After all, knowing you're the same age as my mother, I thought you might benefit from some assistance into the house, especially from the steady hand of an attentive friend."

Julia choked back a laugh, pleased to see her sister relax at James's easy but barbed rejoinder. Lady Irving, for her part, drew her hand away from James's arm and marched rapidly ahead of the party into the house without a backward glance. Simone stepped gingerly after her, placing her feet carefully to avoid the largest, muddiest ruts in the drive.

"I know it's in a bit of a state." James chatted with Julia and Louisa as he escorted them toward the house, one on each arm. "The workmen bring carts, the carts have big wheels and heavy loads—you see the result. I plan to cover it all over with crushed shell or some such thing. Unfortunately, that particular workman hasn't come with his cart yet." He smiled wryly. "It's all still very much a work in progress, but I'll do my best to make you comfortable."

When they stepped inside the house, Julia hardly noticed the high-ceilinged entry hall or the gracefully curved main staircase. She had eyes only for Louisa, who tilted her head back to take in every detail, turning slowly.

Oddly enough, she looked worried.

James must have thought so, too. "Is something wrong?" he asked, his voice hesitant.

"I never imagined it would be like this," Louisa admitted. "It's so grand, absolutely huge. James, you must be a very important fellow."

His relieved smile met her own uncertain one, and then he looked to Julia for her response.

"I think it's lovely," Julia reassured him, her heart lifting at his expression of relief. "It actually looks like it's in quite good repair. Was much done during your absence?"

"To tell you the truth, it wasn't as bad as I had feared," James replied, his tone now eager. "We've always had a few servants here to keep things from completely falling apart. The problem was, many of the unused rooms were shut up, and when the roof started to leak into some of them, no one noticed for a long time. But once the roof was repaired, the plasterers and woodworkers were able to come and work their magic. We're still under Holland covers in much of the house, but it'll come back into use, bit by bit."

By the end of this speech, Lady Irving was visibly bored by James's excited recital of repairs.

"Yes, yes, congratulations, dear boy. Your house is sound and that is an excellent thing, no doubt. Now, I'm sure there are other parts of the house you'd like to show us, too? Perhaps some . . . romantic places? That you and Louisa could go see while the rest of us have some tea?"

Julia rolled her eyes and tried to catch Louisa's gaze, but the taller girl was looking at the floor. Her face was expressionless, but her hands twisted together in agitation.

James seemed not to notice. "Lady Irving, I am surprised to say I think that a delightful idea," he replied, ignoring her huff in response. "In fact, why don't we all have tea? I'll have refreshment sent in at once and we can all have a seat in"—he peeped into a room off the entrance hall, and closed the door, shaking his head—"well, not in there. No furniture. Um, perhaps this next one?"

He opened the second door off the hall. "Yes, this one'll do." He gave an embarrassed smile to his guests. "Sorry, still sorting things out."

Lady Irving glanced around the damask-walled parlor. Its heavy, dark furniture created a gloomy atmosphere. "If all your furniture is like this, perhaps that other room would be an improvement. You'll have to get rid of everything for this parlor even to *begin* to be habitable."

"Aunt," Julia hissed, mortified. "I am sure his lordship is doing his best to be an excellent host."

James overheard her and shrugged. "I'm afraid I haven't done that well so far," he replied. "I've made you stand around with no tea, and didn't even know which room was ready to receive you. But as I've told some among you, I admit I have a lot to learn about running an estate in general, and about this house in particular."

He smiled at Julia, reminding her of their conversation of several weeks before. "Every day, some new part is torn up and put together again differently."

Then, turning his attention to Louisa, he said, "My dear, just for you, I made sure there were no holes in the floor for your visit." This finally drew a quick flash of a smile from Louisa.

Julia, watching them, was surprised to feel a twist of envy that shivered through her whole body when James called her sister "my dear." She wanted those words for herself, so badly she could almost feel them like a caress. Not from James, of course, for he could never be hers.

But perhaps from someone exactly like him.

Her attention was turned a moment later by Simone, who entered the room followed by a housemaid bearing the tea things.

Tea and biscuits—very good ones, Julia was happy to note—distracted them all for the next half hour; then James proposed a tour of the house before dinner.

"No, we would prefer to rest in our rooms," Lady Irving informed him. "Except for Louisa, of course. She would prefer to see every secluded corner you've got in this drafty old pile of stones. Wouldn't you, my girl?"

Louisa looked embarrassed and opened her mouth to speak, but Julia broke in before she knew what she was saying.

"Actually, Aunt, I would love to see the house, too." The words slipped out before she could consider her motivation. And it didn't really matter, anyway, because Louisa looked relieved.

James saw a rather grumpy Lady Irving and her impassive companion settled, then again offered both of his arms to the two sisters as they strolled down a long hall.

"This is very nice," he observed. "Peaceful at last, isn't it? I'm very glad to have the two of you here and show you the house. I expect you'll both be spending a lot of time here in the future. Louisa, especially you," he teased.

Louisa merely nodded. "What do you have in mind to show us?"

"I'm not sure," James admitted. "I haven't figured out the whole layout of the house yet. I hadn't been here for decades, you know, so I hardly knew the place when I saw it."

He paused in his walking. "Shall we just start opening doors? Or is there something you'd like me to try to find for you?"

"An orangery," Julia replied promptly.

"The library," Louisa answered a second later.

The viscount laughed. "There's no orangery here, Julia. If there ever was, it's dwindled away long ago."

Her request had been the impulse of a moment; she just wanted something to say to capture James's attention. And now that she had, she wanted to keep it, though she knew that was probably impolite.

"That's too bad," she began to blather. "I think oranges are really pretty. And good to eat, of course. I mean, that's why most people grow them. But I think they must make a beautiful sight as well, seeing the trees in their pots and all the bright fruits on them."

Louisa was looking at her as if Julia had an arm growing out of her forehead. "Where have you ever even seen an orangery?"

"I haven't," Julia confessed. "I've just read about them. But I've wanted to see one for a long time." Which was true, if you defined "long" as "at least a minute and a half."

"I'm very sorry not to be able to gratify the wish of a lifetime," James said with a friendly smile. Turning to Louisa, he added, "But your request I can satisfy, my dear. Nicholls does have a library, and I even know where it is. Shall we?"

There it was, that envious twinge again. Julia made a vow to leave the couple some time to themselves in the library. After all, if such a simple phrase as "my dear" could have such a strong effect on her, what must it do to Louisa?

In the library, James was gratified to see Louisa's face glow with appreciation. She looked around at the ornately carved shelves, the comfortably carpeted floor, stylish chairs and sturdy sofa grouped about the large room.

"Why, James," she said, a rare and beautiful smile lighting her countenance, "this room is lovely. Just lovely. Surely it wasn't like this before you began work on the house?"

Earning such a delighted smile from Louisa was a rare gift, and James valued it as such.

"It was not," he replied, pride welling up within him. "I started the renovations with this room as a surprise for you. I am so glad you like it."

She smiled at him again, but her expression was already absent as her eyes began to rove over the shelves. "It's wonderful. I love it. Thank you for your kindness."

An uncertain expression stole across her face, and she looked over at Julia. The fair-haired girl was sitting at the opposite end of the room, paging through a collection of maps with a look of great interest. James followed her gaze, and the familiar frisson of awareness shot through him. He might have conquered that initial attraction to her—well, mostly—but damnation, it was good to be around her again.

But Louisa—back to Louisa. "I never knew Julia cared for maps," she was musing. "Perhaps she's giving us some time to speak privately."

"If that's so, I'm grateful to her," the viscount said, ushering his fiancée to the room's most comfortable chair and then seating himself near her. "I hoped we would have time to talk."

She shot him that wary look again. He sighed and considered how best to explain himself.

"Louisa, I know talk of our marriage makes you uncomfortable. Please be assured, I don't intend to pressure you to set a wedding date or in any way take part in the next London season more than you wish to."

It was frustrating to have to be so delicate. Louisa had snapped up his offer so quickly, he'd been sure she would be willing to become his bride at once. Instead, months were passing, and he was no closer to the altar than he had been at the end of the season. For all he knew, the thin company that remained in London over the winter was still amusing itself by nattering at the expense of his sister's good name.

But apparently what he'd said was good enough, because Louisa's wary look at once dissolved into relief. James continued cautiously, "I just . . . thought it would be nice for us to have a chance to talk to one another. About life—our life. What we want to do after we are married."

Her pale cheeks colored at once and she bit her lip. James mentally berated himself for his word choice. The last thing his skittish bride-to-be needed to hear was anything that sounded like a reference to marital activities.

"I mean," he corrected smoothly, "where we will spend our time, how you'd like to see the house fitted out . . . things of that nature. I remember how you wanted the seashell-shaped bathtub, though I haven't commissioned it yet," he teased, attempting to lighten her mood.

"Well," Louisa reflected, "I'm willing to leave the choice of how the house will be furnished to you. The library's to my liking, and I may not be in many of the other rooms, so they really should fall according to your taste."

Disappointment seeped through James. He was trying his hardest to please her, and she was parrying his every attempt to strike at her heart, or even at her conscience. How could he provoke her into showing some enthusiasm?

"But . . . you'll be receiving guests. Your friends, your family," he prompted her. "And you'll have your own bedchamber—if you'll excuse my mentioning it," he added. "That should certainly be made the way you like it."

"Isn't it more important that *you* should like it?" Louisa replied, her smile an ironic twist.

James felt as if he were walking on a beach with quicksand somewhere nearby. Any misstep could land him in trouble, but he had no idea what such a misstep might be. He felt suddenly tense and frustrated.

"I want you to have things as you like them once we are married," James repeated carefully. "But if you honestly have no preference, then I'll do my best to guess, as I did in the library."

Louisa sighed, and looked up at him with eyes much older and more tired than her nineteen years. "James, I'm sorry. I do truly appreciate what you've done to make the library beautiful, and what you're doing to make a home for me. I'm just not used to thinking along the lines of how a viscountess would need to live. I shall try to do better."

Her beautiful, sudden smile burst over her face again. "I just heard those words come out of my mouth. Me, a viscountess? Oh, it's so ridiculous! I can hardly believe it. James, what were you thinking, asking me to marry you?"

He smiled back, relieved. At last, at last, he had broken through her shell of worry. "I was thinking, as soon as I saw you for the first time, glaring at me, that you would be an excellent hostess for the dinner parties I planned to throw every night for at least eighty-five people."

"Oh, stop," she said, laughing.

"And I could tell," he pressed, eager to take advantage of her change of mood, "that you would love to have sixteen houses in town, each bigger than the last, and a whole army of servants to command at each one."

She shook her head, giggling. "How well you know me. I'm astounded; you've penetrated to my very deepest desires."

"Ah . . . yes," James said, clearing his throat and trying not to think of *that* type of desire. He darted a look at Julia, of course just to see if she had been listening, but she seemed as absorbed in her maps as ever.

"Well, we'll leave the subject for now," he suggested, returning to seriousness. "But if you have any ideas about what would make you comfortable, you have only to say the word. In the meantime, I'll just focus on getting the place habitable. At least, what your aunt would consider habitable," he finished wryly.

"Not possible." Louisa shook her head. "If that's your standard, I'm afraid you might as well pull this beautiful old place down and rebuild it in the middle of Grosvenor Square. She doesn't care for much of anything outside of London."

"That could be asking a bit much. In Grosvenor Square? The rent would be scandalous," he bantered back.

Louisa smiled, and rose, her action matched at once by the viscount. "Thank you again, James. You're very patient with me. I . . . I'll try to do what you want me to. I do appreciate all your kindness."

She walked over to speak with Julia, who bounced up out of her seat at once and tossed aside the book of maps with a bit more force than would be expected for someone who was really enjoying their perusal.

James, left behind, again sank into his seat. Louisa

had seemed happy at the end of their conversation, but it still rang hollow somehow. He blankly watched the two sisters talking, seeing Julia draw more smiles out of Louisa in two minutes than he had been able to get from her in the past two hours.

A peal of laughter from the other side of the room broke into his thoughts, and he snapped from his reverie to see Louisa and Julia both giggling helplessly, Julia pointing at a plate in what he very much feared was an old human anatomy book.

Just then she looked up and caught his gaze on her. She turned red and instantly slammed the book shut, stowing it behind her back like a child caught in the kitchen with a handful of biscuits. Louisa laughed even harder at this, herself turning to look at James and shaking her head helplessly.

"Julia found something rather interesting on your shelves," she explained.

Yes, he thought bitterly; he could make his fiancée happy, as long as he didn't talk about anything serious. As long as her sister was around her to cheer and distract her.

He smiled at Louisa, but inside, he felt leaden.

Chapter 8

In Which Baboon Behavior Leads to Unfortunate Consequences

The visit at Nicholls was intended to last only for one week, but the following morning at breakfast, Lady Irving pronounced herself "completely unsatisfied" with the home's furnishings and arrangements.

"This is no fit place for a future viscountess," she stated. "It'll be at least a fortnight before I can bring the place into any semblance of fashion."

James raised his eyes to the ceiling in an expression of pained patience that he knew the countess would ignore. "Might I remind your ladyship that this is already a fit home for a viscount? I know it's not ideal as yet, but I'm working on it."

"Bosh," she replied. "You obviously need me to take you well in hand, Matheson. And I suppose you need Louisa to take you in hand, too, eh? You haven't even had any time alone together yet." She elbowed him. Actually *elbowed* him.

He eyed her buttery toast. He wondered if there was

any way he could swat it out of her hand and onto her livid green gown and make it look like an accident. Probably not, but the idea was tempting anyway.

"But, Aunt," Louisa replied, ignoring Lady Irving's last statement, "we must end our visit as planned; we packed only for a very short stay. And think of your parrot. Poor Butternut will be missing you as well."

"I'm sure Tom is taking good care of him," Julia interjected. "And surely this house is prepared for guests enough that we could stay longer regardless of our luggage. Good heavens, look at the breakfast they've made us."

James grinned to see her eyes widen with delight as another tray was brought into the room. She rose from her chair with shameless speed, and, finding ham and eggs under the cover, served a very unladylike heap of food onto what would now be her third plate.

As Julia reseated herself, she added, "Not that we mean to invite ourselves to overstay our welcome. At least, most of us do not. But in case you shouldn't mind it, James, we probably could. Not overstay, but stay longer. Oh, dear—but you won't be able to say you don't wish us to stay, even if it's the truth; that would be excessively rude of you."

"Rude I would never want to be, but as a matter of fact, I'd be genuinely happy to have you stay on," James replied. "No need for you to worry about being comfortable even with your small amount of baggage. I have a great deal of clothing here for young ladies, which was once my sister's. It's well over a decade out of fashion, but you're welcome to it.

"The only problem is," he confessed, his eyes limpid as he looked around the table, "that the options may be limited for you, Lady Irving. The only attire I have for, er, ladies of other ages belongs to the housekeeper and maids."

He blinked owlishly at the countess, trying to hold an expression of innocent worry. He probably shouldn't bait his future wife's aunt like this, but he still owed her one for that "taken in hand" comment.

Lady Irving looked sharply at him. "I'll wager I can fit into anything my nieces can, you young rascal. So you needn't try to send me packing at the end of the week by threatening me with a maid's costume."

"I would never try anything of the sort," James said, managing to hold a straight face despite noticing, out of the corner of his eye, Julia's desperate attempts to swallow a mouthful of eggs without choking herself on a laugh.

Faced with a string of several days and limitless possibilities for her enviable taste to find an outlet, Lady Irving determined after the meal to direct the long-suffering Simone and several of the Nicholls servants to re-arrange the furniture and pictures in one parlor that she found particularly offensive to the eye. This pleasing flurry of activity kept her occupied for the remainder of the morning, much to the relief of James and, he suspected, his other two guests as well.

Once Lady Irving's departure left them in relative peace, James wondered what Louisa and Julia would enjoy most. He was unsure of what to suggest or do next. It was an unfamiliar and unwelcome feeling for a man raised from birth to mix in the highest and most exacting circles.

In the end, although it seemed depressingly uncreative, he suggested that the three of them return to the library, where he would endeavor to point out some of the room's treasures despite his ignorance of most of the collection.

Julia trailed behind as Louisa eagerly came along with him, hooking her arm fondly into his and asking all sorts of questions about old and rare books that he found himself almost totally unable to answer.

No, he was pretty sure they didn't have a Gutenberg Bible.

Probably they had some things that were printed on vellum, but he couldn't say what those might be or where they were in the library.

No, he didn't *think* there were any books in Italian . . . but there might be, somewhere.

Finally, when she asked him if he had any examples of block printing in his collection, he threw his hands into the air.

"I have no idea," he exclaimed. "You're making me heartily ashamed of myself. I'm sure there are some wonderful gems in here, but my grandfather was the last serious collector. As far as I know, there's not even a catalogue of what we own."

"Then you really ought to have one made," Louisa said decisively. Her face lit up. "Oh, James, could I work on one? It would be my delight. I know our book collection at Stonemeadows so well, and as you might imagine, it's not often that I get the chance to look—*really* look—at another home's library."

"I would love to have you create a catalogue, if you would enjoy that," James replied. His nagging unease lifted a bit at Louisa's excited expression. "Actually, that's a fine idea. The library would be the better for your expert treatment."

"I'm hardly an expert," Louisa confessed. "Just a self-taught book lover. But I *would* like this, very much. I can make a beginning while we're here this week, and perhaps we can continue on here a while longer than we had planned."

"I'll help you," Julia offered. "We can start right now. I really want to climb around on that ladder that rolls along the edge of the shelves."

James followed her eager gaze. Good Lord, no. That ladder had to be twenty feet high. Well, fine, perhaps it was only eight or so—but it was still far too tall for a young lady to be climbing.

"Absolutely not," James answered. "Those are not playthings. They're for getting books down, not for pretending to be a baboon."

"A *baboon*?" Julia seemed much struck by the word. "I have no idea what that is, but it sounds fabulous. I'm climbing the ladder."

She at once began to step up the ladder, hitching up her skirt to her knees to get it out of her way. James averted his eyes, but not before catching a glimpse of a slim, well-shaped ankle and calf.

All right, so maybe he had waited to avert his eyes until after he had already gotten a good look.

His heart beat a little faster. He couldn't watch this—or, more accurately, *shouldn't* watch.

He coughed. "Far be it from me to diminish your enjoyment at all, but this is rather unusual behavior. While I am sure we both find it delightful, you may not want to do this at a party in London next season," he said formally, eyes firmly fixed on the floor. Away from her legs.

"Nonsense," Julia replied matter-of-factly. "I know perfectly well that libraries are the best places to meet handsome and eligible young men for the purposes of marriage."

He looked up swiftly; was she talking about him? She

had to be talking about him. Him, and the way he and Louisa had met.

What did she mean, referring to him as handsome and eligible? Was she teasing him, or was that how she really saw him? He shot a questioning glance at Louisa, but she didn't seem to be listening. She was already reaching her slender arms up for Julia to hand down several volumes into them.

Thus he missed exactly what caused Julia to fall.

He just heard Louisa gasp, saw the volumes tumble to the floor, saw Julia tumble on top of them. She landed awkwardly on top of a heavy folio, flat on her back, one of her legs pressed under her at a very odd angle.

Her face went white, and he was sure his own did as well. He went icy all over. He had killed Julia, he just knew it.

How could he have let something happen to her? In his own home, where he should have kept her safe? His skin prickled with shocked guilt.

Then she moved, and opened her eyes. Of course, of course. She was fine—or at least, definitely not dead.

He realized that he *might* have overreacted a bit. Thankfully, no one could read his thoughts.

"Oof," Julia said.

He and Louisa instantly bent over her, clamoring to know if she was all right.

"I'm fine," Julia assured them, her expression tight with pain. "Just a bit embarrassed. I can't imagine what caused me to fall. I'm not normally clumsy. Do you think it could be a problem with the ladder? Er, not that there's anything wrong with your ladder, James, I'm sure."

"Except for the fact that it nearly killed you," he said, still struggling to calm down.

Julia sat up cautiously and stretched out her legs in front of her, rotating her feet in slow circles. "It didn't do anything of the kind, and you know it. I was probably just overbalanced." She winced and stilled her right foot. "I suppose I landed wrong on that one. Drat."

Lady Irving bustled into the room, drawn by the noise.

"My, my," she exclaimed. "This is better than I would have expected from the rest of your house, Matheson." She gestured broadly at the untidy pile of books scattered on the floor. "Casual disorder is all the rage now, you know. Although I do think this is going a bit far with the concept."

"We're not being fashionable," Julia replied, struggling to stand. "I fell off this ladder and dropped the books."

Lady Irving looked at her in mock amazement. "What in God's name was a gently bred young lady doing scampering about on a ladder?"

"Aunt, Julia is hurt," Louisa replied in a quiet but firm voice.

"Oh, please, I'm fine," Julia insisted. "I'll just have to . . ." She shifted her weight onto her right ankle, and sucked in a pained breath. "All right, maybe I'm not exactly fine. But close."

She hopped over to the sofa so she could clutch at its back for support.

"Gently bred ladies don't hop either," Lady Irving informed her. "I can see you have a few manners to master before we go to London."

"Really?" Julia asked, diverted. "If you couldn't hop, what would you do if you hurt your ankle?"

"I'd use a cane, and swat at people with it, of course.

Much more fun. Besides, you look like a fool when you hop. Nothing personal, my girl; anyone would."

Julia rolled her eyes. "Well, I'm not going to hop in London. I just needed to get to the sofa."

James could see it was time to step into the conversation. "It's very ungracious of me not to help you," he said, and handed Julia gently onto the sofa. As she clasped his hand for him to assist her, his skin tingled with the physical thrill of it, and he drew his hand back as swiftly as manners would allow so Julia wouldn't feel him tremble.

"I'll get you a cushion so you can prop up your foot," he said gruffly, and found a small pillow on another chair. One all the way across the room, just to give himself time to calm down.

It must have been the surprise of her fall; surely that was it. He felt pulled to her; he wanted to touch her, hold her, kiss her until she forgot about the pain.

Again he averted his gaze. He shouldn't be looking at her like that. Not lying on a sofa, helpless, laid out quiet and lovely before his eyes like a gift.

Correction; he shouldn't even be *thinking* of her like that. He shouldn't be having any of these thoughts, for that matter.

What was wrong with him? Had twenty-seven years of an aristocratic upbringing taught him nothing about self-control? He had already chosen his wife. He might have chosen quickly and in a somewhat businesslike manner, but he had chosen well. Louisa would make a fine viscountess. For one thing, she would never clamber around on a ladder and make his heart stop with terror.

She would never make his heart stop at all.

He silently handed Julia the cushion, then left her side to rejoin the conversation between Louisa and Lady Irving.

"I think we should get her home as soon as possible," Louisa was saying to her aunt.

What? No, he had to put a stop to this talk.

"Surely she would be more comfortable as she is, staying here until she has a chance to recover," he suggested. His voice had only a *little* squeak of desperation in it.

"No, you're right, young missy," Lady Irving agreed with Louisa. "She'll do better in her own house. Closer to the surgeon's, for one thing, in case he should be needed. But also, no telling how long she'll be laid up."

The countess considered. "I can take her back to Stonemeadows, and you and Simone can stay here and complete your visit. Stay longer than we planned, even, if you like."

Louisa shook her head. "That will never do, ma'am. You know perfectly well you can't get along without Simone; you need her to arrange you every morning, and she makes you comfortable throughout the day."

"Very true," her ladyship acknowledged, running prideful hands over the bright green brocade of her gown. "I would never be able to trick myself out in style without her help."

James rolled his eyes. If Lady Irving's taste was in the common style, he was . . . well, he was a baboon.

"I suppose," Louisa replied, "we will all have to go home again." She fixed her eyes on James and looked genuinely disappointed. "I am very sorry, but I think it's for the best."

She cast a longing look around the library, over the pile of scattered books on the floor. "I wish I could stay longer."

James forced a smile to his face. "I'm gratified to hear it."

He looked at the small figure on the sofa, lying as flat

and still as if she had been ironed. She looked so pitiful; his heart turned over.

"I feel just terrible about your sister's fall."

"Please don't," Louisa assured him. "It was an accident, and she'll be fine. No power on earth could have kept her off that ladder once she decided it sounded fun."

"Well, I'm very sorry to have you go. But I have to say, I think she will be much more comfortable with you beside her."

Louisa's smile was sweet, her eyes a bit teary. "Thank you," she said, clasping his hands gently, "for understanding." She wrapped him in a quick, affectionate hug that surprised the breath out of his body.

Lady Irving was already summoning the capable Simone, who at once began to give orders to have trunks packed and the carriage brought round.

And that was that.

Before the afternoon was out, James saw them on their way, crammed into the carriage like tinned fish so that Julia's injured foot could be propped up on the opposite seat. Poor girl; she leaned hard on him to walk to the carriage, and thanked him sweetly although he could see she was in pain.

"I'll never be a baboon again," she promised.

He laughed, and apologized again to her, and to Lady Irving and Louisa.

The betrothed couple parted with a proper kiss on the cheek; honestly, he had been so distracted, he didn't even try to embrace Louisa in a more romantic way. He was too busy thinking of how he'd fallen short as a host, and as a future husband.

He had failed to keep them comfortable, entertained, and safe. He had failed even to keep them *there*. He didn't think they had taken it amiss . . . but still, would any of them want to come back, ever?

He remembered the warm, fragile feeling of Julia's body, leaning against his for support as she walked out to the carriage. He remembered Louisa's hug of affection.

He wished they would all come back, so he could try again, and get it right this time.

Chapter 9

In Which Portugal
Is Lost

To Julia's dismay, her ankle took weeks to mend.

The first week was unbearable. She spent what felt like every waking minute trapped on a sofa or lying in her bed. She could hardly believe her own stupid clumsiness, which had caused them all to leave Nicholls early and miss out on so much of James's company.

The second week began as badly, but then it brought a letter from James that Louisa read aloud to the family. The letter mentioned Julia's name twice and inquired very kindly about her health. That day actually went pretty well.

Weeks three, four, and five of Julia's convalescence brought more letters for Louisa. She no longer read them aloud to the family. She hummed through the days, wrote long letters to James, and seemed delighted when she received a reply—which she always did, promptly.

She happened to open one of James's letters once in Julia's presence, and Julia caught a glimpse of what looked like a list.

"Excellent," Louisa had breathed, skimming the missive.

"What's excellent?" Julia had been unable to resist asking.

Recalled to herself, Louisa flushed. "I just had some questions for James. Relating to, um, Nicholls."

Julia instantly lost interest. She didn't want to hear about Nicholls, about Louisa's and James's future life together. She couldn't bear the thought of Louisa leaving her, though she knew that was illogical and inevitable.

And maybe she didn't quite like to think of James married, either. Weren't they all content and happy as they were? Couldn't things just continue on like this? Why did everyone have to keep talking about him and Louisa getting married all the time?

It was six weeks and two days before Julia was able to test her ankle again. Six weeks and two days since she'd seen James, hurt herself, and left Nicholls.

Six weeks and two days of being a fool.

Usually she loved autumn, but this year, it seemed melancholy. She missed James's face, his voice, his smile.

She missed seeing him frown at her when she said something outrageous (usually unwittingly), or making him smile when she did something ridiculous (also usually unwittingly). She just missed . . . *him.*

Winter began early, with a biting cold that promised to be both long and severe. Julia's mood lifted somewhat when she was allowed back on her feet again in November, but as Christmas drew nearer, the coziness of the season didn't cheer her as it usually did.

She tried her best to wrap herself in glee, helping her small siblings poke silver trinkets into the plum pudding that would soak in brandy for the weeks until Christmas dinner. She helped the cook bake treats—and sample them: glossy jam tarts, Yule cakes, a gingerbread full of enough sweet spices to make an Elizabethan explorer swoon. She cut strips of paper for the children to paste into links, and laughed when they coiled so many paper chains around their father's favorite chair that it looked like a paper mill had spun a cocoon. Greenery was cut; the every-day tallow candles were exchanged for sweet-scented bees-wax, and warm, spicy smells filled the house.

But beneath Julia's smile, her gloom weighed on her. She was penned inside the house by the numbing cold; she missed the company of her sister, who spent much time in the library writing letters to James.

In between crafting amusements for the children, then, she paced Stonemeadows. She tried to walk away from her dull feeling, leaving it behind in some ne-glected attic or cellar, but it inevitably found her again. Lady Irving finally told her in annoyance that Julia only needed a set of chains to look like the home's resident ghost, wandering the corridors, muttering and pale.

But in mid-December, a letter arrived that changed everything. James had written another of his long lists to Louisa, who pored over it eagerly as usual. This time, though, when she read the end of the letter, her eye-brows knit in sudden displeasure.

"No," she said in a flat voice.

Lady Oliver and Julia looked up at her, startled, from the floor, where they were helping Elise, Emilia, Anne, and Tom put together a puzzle map of Europe. Tom was very little help, being scarcely past the age where he liked to put bright-colored objects in his mouth, and his sisters forbore his desire to work on the puzzle with grudging impatience.

"Is something wrong, Louisa?" Lady Oliver asked with concern, then immediately diverted her attention back to the four small children beside her. "Tom, don't eat

France; it's nasty. Can you help your sisters find where France goes? Emilia, can you show him?"

The girl sighed and shoved the offending country into place. Julia praised her, then looked up questioningly at Louisa.

Louisa pressed her lips together and was silent for several seconds, her eyes unreadable. "I've received an invitation that I don't wish to accept," she finally said.

"An invitation? Who on earth from?" Julia wondered. She realized that wasn't exactly tactful, and explained, "I mean, it's just that we are quiet here. I didn't mean people shouldn't be inviting you out all the time, because they should—at least, if there were many people around."

"I know what you mean," Louisa assured her. "It's . . ." She trailed off, then drew in her breath. "James's family wants me to spend Christmas with them in London."

"Wonderful!" Lady Oliver squealed, tossing the puzzle map's Portugal gleefully into the air.

Julia said, "Oh."

Louisa looked appreciatively at her sister. "I can see you understand, Julia. Mama, I don't wish to go. I've never spent Christmas away from home, and, honestly, I am terrified of James's family. I haven't spoken to them much and I'm quite sure they don't approve of me."

"Nonsense," Lady Oliver replied, distracted, as she began to look under furniture for the displaced country. "Portugal, where are you?" she crooned.

"I think it is a good sign that they want to have you there," Julia said bracingly. "It shows that they want to welcome you into the family."

"Maybe." Louisa looked doubtful. "But I had in my mind that I wouldn't have to go back to London until February at least. This is just so soon."

"But you want to see James again, right? You'll get to see him again?" Julia asked.

"Yes, of course. Yes, he'll be there," Louisa said vaguely.

Julia scrutinized her. What was she thinking of? How could she not want, with every fiber of her body, to go to London and see James and his family?

Granted, she had never met James's family, but if they were anything like him, she was sure they must be delightful.

"What if we go now?" Louisa finally spoke.

At the puzzled expressions of both Julia and Lady Oliver (who was still looking for the lost Portugal, ably assisted by her younger children, who were eager to finish their map), Louisa explained herself. "You and I, Julia. What if we could persuade our aunt to go to London now, and we could both go? I am sure you would be as welcome as I at Matheson House for Christmas. Would you like that?"

"Oh, yes!" Julia shrieked, clapping her hands together.

Louisa looked happier at once. Lady Oliver protested that she couldn't, just couldn't, let both of her girls go to London for Christmas; they would be missed too much. Who would hang the mistletoe? Who would lead the family in carols? But Louisa's expression turned stubborn, and when she informed her parent that she simply wouldn't go if Julia didn't go with her, then everything seemed to be decided.

It remained only to persuade Lady Irving, who at first described Louisa's idea of requiring her sister's companionship in London as "rot." But when presented with the alternative—Louisa not going to London, an irrevocable slight being dealt to a powerful family, the engagement being endangered—she had to recognize inevitable defeat.

"Well played, my girl," she acknowledged the maneuver. "You're getting more and more suited for the *ton* already." She sighed with dismay. "I do hate the greasy London winters, though. And one feels so unfashionable being there year-round."

"Viscountess Matheson never leaves London," Louisa pointed out.

"Yes, well, that began because of her husband's gout, and now it's due to sheer laziness," Lady Irving informed her. "I would rather be struck dead in my bed than have anyone think me too lazy to travel."

"Aunt, you are in no danger of having anyone think you the tiniest bit lazy," Julia replied truthfully.

"We'll have to stay through to the season." Lady Irving nodded, tapping her chin in thought. "Julia, you'll have to have an entire wardrobe made before you're fit for the young bucks to look at. And you, Louisa, have to put together a trousseau. *And* plan the wedding. Maybe even go through with the blasted thing, if one can be permitted to utter those words in this house," she grumbled. "Yes, it's quite a good idea at that. London's where you'll both need to be for the time being."

Louisa looked taken aback, but Julia hardly noticed. She could scarcely believe how much the world had changed today. This morning, months of cold, gray, quiet days had lain between her and the season. Now she was going to London, and better still, she would get to see James.

At last, Christmas cheer bubbled up within her.

Chapter 10

In Which a Friendly Embrace Is More Than It Should Be

Christmas Eve dawned crisp and lovely. However, none of the inhabitants of Lady Irving's stately town house were aware of the weather at dawn, as they were all still sleeping following a day of travel. In fact, Julia, exhausted from a sleepless night, only awoke when Louisa shook her gently and told her that James was downstairs.

She sat upright in an instant, sleep abolished. "What!" she shrieked.

Louisa laughed. "It's past noon. There's nothing very unusual about him coming by at this hour."

"Why didn't anyone wake me?" Julia frantically tossed her bedcovers aside and began hunting for something to put on. "*Where* are my clothes? Why the devil did I sleep so late?"

"Julia," Louisa gently reproved her.

"Sorry; of course I meant, 'why the deuce did I sleep so late,'" Julia dutifully replied, rolling her eyes.

She paused in her frenzied attempt to find where her

trunks were stowed, and took in Louisa's appearance. The tall girl's hair was glossy and well dressed; her pale primrose gown was simply cut but elegant, and trimmed with intricate silk knots and a row of bugles.

"Why, you look wonderful," she squeaked. "Even for you. I mean, your general appearance has a pretty high level of wonderful, but today it is especially so."

To her surprise, Louisa blushed. "Oh, well, thanks," she said dismissively, but she smiled all the same. "I . . . I suppose I didn't want to be a discredit to James when I met his family. Actually, *we* are going to meet his family."

Louisa's expression turned guilty, and she admitted, "I've never met the viscountess before, but I know James thinks she's rather intimidating. So if you don't mind, we'll all go together. I feel I could use the support of your presence. James has already agreed that it sounds delightful. And of course it would be nicest to spend Christmas Eve all together, don't you think?" Her voice sounded hopeful, wheedling.

Julia didn't need to be wheedled at all. "Of course! I'm absolutely rabid to meet the woman who was girlhood friends with Lady Irving." She grinned mischievously. "Do you think they'll have a fight while we're there?"

She was only teasing, but Louisa looked worried. "I hope not. I want our visit to go as well as possible. Do you think my aunt would be offended if I asked her to be calm and not provoke anyone?"

"Not a bit, but she'll probably decide to be on her worst and most flamboyant behavior if you do," Julia decided. "Better not to say anything. She wants this to go well, too, you know. We all do," she added self-consciously.

Louisa nodded her understanding, and then looked around the room. "They can't have unpacked your clothing without your hearing, can they?" She looked in the wardrobe, and was greeted by a neat arrangement of garments.

She shot a skeptical look at Julia. "I know Simone is very good at what she does, but no one is *that* good. How could you not hear her unpacking you?"

"What? Those can't be my clothes." Julia came over to examine them. "Well. They are my clothes. I'll be—"

"Julia," Louisa said again, reprovingly.

"I'll be *delighted*," Julia finished. "Actually, I really am pretty delighted to see them unpacked. And I'm surprised. I guess I was sleeping more deeply than I realized."

She shooed Louisa out and asked her to send in Simone to help her dress and make herself presentable. "Don't let James leave until I see him," she warned.

"Silly." Louisa smiled. "We'll be over there for an early supper and will see him all evening."

"But I don't want to wait that long," Julia exclaimed. Then, embarrassed at her unguarded tongue, she busied herself sorting through her dresses for something fit to wear to meet a viscountess.

More quickly than she would have imagined possible, Simone's deft fingers had teased the snarls out of her hair and selected one of her myriad white gowns.

"This is nothing special," the Frenchwoman explained dismissively of the garment as she helped Julia into it, "but at least it will not offend the fashionable. When we are able to visit a *modiste*, then we will choose beautiful garments for you."

At Julia's look of interest, she clarified, "They will naturally be dresses that are also appropriate for a young woman who is not married. Yes, I know that expression of *joie*; you are truly your aunt's niece. You must trust in Simone for *couture*, if you please."

Julia looked at herself in the glass. Pale, plain, boring.

Lank hair. White dress. Circles under her eyes. Cheeks flushed from hurry. It was all rather discouraging. But James might get tired of waiting if she didn't appear downstairs soon.

"Can I at least wear ostrich plumes with the dress?" she asked hopefully. "Louisa said they are shockingly expensive, so they must be all the rage."

"They are very wrong for today, when you are to spend Christmas Eve with one who is like a relative," Simone explained as she coiled Julia's hair into a simple, neat chignon.

"How do you do that?" Julia breathed, gingerly touching the roll of hair. "I always have to use about a hundred pins to make it stay in place."

"That is why I am I, and you are you," Simone replied in her light accent, with considerable pride. "Go on and see your man now."

"He's not *my* man," Julia corrected, feeling her face turn a treacherous red.

"I am sorry, I did not express myself well," Simone said with a small smile. "Go and see the man who is here to visit you all."

Julia nodded uncertainly and headed downstairs to the drawing room.

And there he was.

She'd waited so long to see James, and there he was at last. His light brown hair was shorter, his clothes finer, his build a bit leaner than the last time she had seen him. She noticed every difference even as she savored the sight of him.

She was a fool, she knew, but she was a willing one. It was just so *good* to see him, to have him around again.

Overcome, she grinned and launched herself toward him. Forgetting where she was or who was watching, she dashed up to greet him with an embrace as she would a member of her family—then skidded to a stop, suddenly recollecting herself when only a step away from embarrassment, and bobbed into the most awkward curtsy she'd ever managed. James, for his part, reached out a hand to shake hers, then began to bow, then reached out in response to the beginning of her attempted hug, then collected himself and bowed again. As they both straightened up, they were aware of Lady Irving and Louisa staring at them, puzzled, and Julia's chagrined blue eyes met James's green gaze.

They looked ridiculous, they both realized at once, and they burst into laughter. James wrapped Julia in a friendly hug, holding her so tight he actually lifted her feet off the floor.

"It's wonderful to see you," he said gruffly. "Happy Christmas."

My dear, she thought. *Call me "my dear."*

He didn't, of course. He never would. But held close to him, Julia's heart pounded all the same. She felt short of breath, and not because he was holding her so tightly. He was here, and he was holding her, and just for a second, she wiped from her mind that nagging awareness that he wasn't here for her.

Just for that precious second, she allowed herself to rest her head on his shoulder, allowed the feel of his arms to imprint her body with their heat and strength.

But just for one second. Then she pressed her arms against his chest as a signal to set her down.

He did at once, but she remained standing next to him, too close for propriety, but unable to step away. The warmth of his arms still soaked through her, heating her whole body and, she knew, turning her face pink with awareness. She felt such joy at seeing him, she could hardly contain it. And yet she had no words of greeting; no words at all, which was a shock for her to realize. Usually words spilled out of her unbidden. But for James, she had nothing. Perhaps there was nothing she needed to say.

She became suddenly self-conscious and realized that she was behaving in an improper fashion. She took a giant step backward and clasped her hands behind her back to keep them from treacherously reaching out for James again. She glanced at Louisa, who seemed to be amused. Lady Irving, fortunately, was digging distractedly through her reticule by now. To Julia, seeing James again after weeks apart seemed the first sun after a long winter; to Lady Irving, it was just the beginning of a dinner engagement.

Noting Julia's unease, James covered for her hesitation with the smooth presence of mind of the nobility. "Now that we are all here, shall we go? I'm sure my mother's impatient for her dinner. You know how it is, ma'am, when you get to be a certain age."

This last remark, unmistakably directed at Lady Irving, broke the spell of silence that was making Julia feel so discomfited. The barb was tempered with a mischievous smile that drew an unwilling cough of startled amusement from her ladyship.

"You young rogue," she replied in cheerful tones, and allowed him to escort her downstairs to the front door.

"Here goes nothing," Louisa murmured to Julia as they followed behind.

"Not at all," Julia replied, attempting to hearten her sister. "Here comes a delightful Christmas Eve dinner with your future family, who will love you at once. It's going to be marvelous."

If only she had been right.

Chapter 11

In Which
Plum Pudding
Is Vulgar

Matheson House, in Cavendish Square, was large, cold, stately, and formal. The chill in the air came less from the sharp temperatures outside, which were tempered by a roaring fire in the drawing room, than from the dismissive expression on the Viscountess Matheson's face as she greeted her guests.

The room was elegantly trimmed with holiday greenery. Julia felt somewhat cheered as she glanced around, taking comfort from the familiar freshly cut mistletoe, laurel, and holly.

They'd be cutting those now in the country, she realized. She could almost imagine her mother and young siblings running around the house in excitement to decorate it. Her father, she thought, would carefully consider which goose the family would eat for their Christmas dinner. Ultimately, she knew, he would decide he couldn't part with any of his beloved animals, and would beg his wife to spare them all and order cheese for the family dinner. Then Lady Oliver would speak to the cook later, one of the geese (it didn't matter which) would be killed and delectably roasted, and tomorrow Lord Oliver would enjoy the Christmas feast with gusto, never thinking about the source of the delicious meat served to him.

Imagining the comforting family rituals, Julia felt very distant indeed from their home in Kent. A wave of nostalgia hit her with surprising force. Louisa had been right; they were a world away from that now. Why on earth had she come here?

She reached for Louisa's hand for support, but just then James spoke, and she remembered why she had come.

That's right, she recalled; it was for Louisa. And, were she to be honest, for herself, too.

James presented the visitors very properly to his mother and to his elder sister Gloria, a widowed viscountess herself, whose lovely face was stiffened into an expression of extreme hauteur. Gloria still wore the dark crepe of half-mourning, and James explained that Gloria and her young daughters now lived with his mother since her husband's heir, the new Viscount Roseborough, had acceded to the title several months before and taken possession of the ancestral property.

"Everyone is happier this way," he explained. "My mother and sister truly enjoy each other's company." He smiled encouragingly at them.

"I can see that," Julia murmured into Louisa's ear, noting the unresponsive faces of James's female relatives. "They both look simply ecstatic."

Louisa didn't respond aloud to her comment, but a nervous smile tugged at the corners of her mouth.

James hadn't been exaggerating when he said his mother would be eager for her dinner. The unconventional party of James and the five ladies ("just an intimate dinner," the elder viscountess explained with a syrupy smile, "so we can all get well acquainted") progressed downstairs to the meal almost as soon as introductions had been dispensed with.

"I'm sorry about the short notice on this," James offered in an aside to the two young women. "It was, ah"— he shot a quick glance at his mother—"a bit difficult to get everyone's plans figured out. I'm so glad you could come anyway; I think this will be a very good opportunity for you to become comfortable with one another."

His voice was hopeful. Already, Julia was less so even than when she had arrived.

It was through her dinner that Viscountess Matheson demonstrated the Christmas spirit, not with gladness of heart or generous statements of welcome, but with slices of tongue and generous portions of food. Besides the tongue—which Julia couldn't bring herself to eat, being just a bit too cognizant of its source due to all the time she had spent with Lord Oliver's livestock—their hostess provided the party with several lavish courses, including a succulent roasted goose, rabbit, pheasant, and quail.

This surfeit of dishes was accompanied by very little conversation. James's sister spiritlessly picked at her meal, while the elder viscountess selected and consumed her food with single-minded relish. She spoke mainly to James, and even then talked only of titled young women with whom she would like him to become acquainted.

"Lord and Lady Alleyneham will be in town soon after the new year," she informed him, forking up a wafer-thin slice of quail. "I believe they're planning a ball to open the season in early spring. I'm sure it will completely eclipse their ball at the end of last year's season.

"That affair proved to be rather lackluster, wouldn't

you agree, my son?" she asked, flashing a sweet smile at James. "But Charissa Bradleigh—that's the earl and countess's third daughter, you know—is a simply lovely girl. I am sure you would like to see her again and get much better acquainted."

Louisa was cowed completely into silence by this barely cloaked insult, for it was at the previous season's Alleyneham House ball that she and James had met.

James, for his part, seemed to miss the hidden meaning of his mother's words. He simply replied that he had very much enjoyed every ball the earl and countess had put on, and expected this next would be much the same.

As the cloth was removed in order that dessert could be served to the silent party, Lady Irving finally came to welcome life at Julia's side.

"It's no wonder the late viscount suffered from gout, eh?" she stated, just quietly enough that their hostess could pretend not to hear, and just loudly enough to ensure that she *did* hear. This remark drew an answering sniff from the viscountess, but her attention was immediately distracted by the arrival of a variety of sweets, including syllabub, tarts, and a mince pie.

Julia had a nearly irresistible urge to shout "hell" at the top of her lungs and shove a tart into the arrogant faces of the two viscountesses. She knew this wouldn't be the most auspicious time to try out particularly unconventional behavior, but still—how had a man like James come from a family like this?

She felt annoyed at his relatives for being so unwelcoming to Louisa, a future member of their family. In comparison to that, their cool disinterest in Julia herself seemed unimportant. Louisa had been nervous before the visit; now she almost looked ill from distress. Julia wondered desperately what she could do to help her sister feel more comfortable.

Thus it was that Julia blundered. Her mind distracted, her eyes blankly cast over the desserts laid out on the table, and they noticed something missing.

"No plum pudding?" Julia's disappointed question slipped out before she thought.

Oh, dear. She'd done it again.

She met Louisa's dismayed gaze, stricken at her carelessness, and then bravely turned her eyes to the viscountess.

Lady Matheson looked her over coolly for a long moment, then returned her attention to the selection of sweets. "Pudding is vulgar," she informed Julia.

Julia flushed, but raised her chin. "Really? I was unaware that such a popular tradition was vulgar. I must be dreadfully common, if so."

"I find that very possible," the elder viscountess replied matter-of-factly.

A shocked silence fell over the table. After a moment, James broke it. "Really, Mother; that's very impolite."

"So is a guest who questions the spread laid before her by her hosts," her ladyship replied, unperturbed.

"That's utter nonsense, Augusta." Lady Irving verbally shoved her way into the conversation with the familiarity of a long-lost girlhood friendship. "If you don't have a pudding when you invite guests over on Christmas Eve, you're positively un-English. And if you insult your guests, you're positively rude. Now, shall we try this exchange again? I am sure you're eager to welcome us, seeing as how your summons was so urgent that we left family Christmas in the country in order to spend time with you instead."

Her voice was calm, but her eyes were steely. Julia felt

a whirl of excitement in her nervous stomach. Her aunt was often irritable, always opinionated, but rarely angry. She was a force to behold at this moment, tall and stately in her chair, the inevitable ostrich plumes adorning her crown of hair, sherry-brown eyes boring into those of her old acquaintance as she awaited a response.

Lady Matheson stared back at her, mouth slightly agape. Her eyes, as green as James's, goggled a bit. Lady Irving had, quite simply, flayed all the arrogance off her, and all that was left was surprise.

She wasn't an aristocrat for nothing, though; after a minute she recovered her composure. She drew herself up in her chair and ignored everything that had just passed. Almost.

Her stony face almost seemed to crack as she said in a carefully neutral tone, "I believe we've been at our dining long enough. If you would care for some dessert, I will have sweetmeats brought into the drawing room. Miss Oliver, you and your aunt may join me for some cards. Gloria, you will make up the fourth."

It wasn't a question. Lady Matheson rose at once and made her way back upstairs to the drawing room. The others dutifully followed her, though Julia hung back to whisper to Louisa, "That's a good sign, right? To join her at cards?"

Louisa threw a skeptical look back at her. "Who knows?" she whispered back. "At least we know Aunt Estella can control her." Her mouth twisted. "James obviously can't."

"Since when did any mother, even a kind one, ever pay the least heed to what her son said?" Julia defended him in a furious whisper that made Lady Irving turn to look back at her expectantly.

Louisa nudged her. "You and your loud whisper!

Come along; we have to join them. At least we'll be able to go home soon."

The card table was set up for the four players in front of that lovely, luxurious fire, and the players prepared for a rubber of whist. James was at first occupied with settling Louisa and mediating between the two elder women. Lady Irving considered playing for Lady Matheson's suggested low stakes sadly flat; it was hardly even worth playing at all on those terms. Gently, James reminded her ladyship that they were at his mother's home, not in a gaming hell, and perhaps a family card game on Christmas Eve need not involve the exchange of large sums of money.

Idling nearby beside the fire, Julia overheard this, as well as Lady Irving's subsequent bark of laughter and her capitulation. *Notice that, Louisa,* she thought. *Maybe James tries to ignore his own mother's rudeness, but he won't let our aunt test him.*

Temporarily left alone, she meandered around the large room, but found it chilly at the edges. She soon returned to the fire and sat as far away from the card players as she was able while still remaining warm. In her chair, she absently folded up her legs and wrapped her arms around them as was her wont at home.

She idly watched the two older women, partnered at whist, chatter spiritedly and with increasing warmth as they sipped at sherry. They clutched at James's sleeves to keep him with them—Lady Irving for Louisa's sake, Lady Matheson for her own. Louisa and Gloria, also partnered, played mechanically and with little spirit and even less conversation.

Julia was content to sit alone, but to tell the truth, she

was growing a bit bored. She was relieved when a governess hesitantly entered the room with two young girls who appeared to be around eight and six years old.

She hopped up at once, interested in the young arrivals. The group at the card table took longer to notice them, but Gloria instantly rose when she did see them. With real, warm affection, she went over to the children and led them forward to meet the rest of the party.

"These are my darling girls," she said with unmistakable pride in her voice. "Anne and Sophia."

She introduced each of the other members of the party to her daughters in turn. Julia, last to meet them, watched in amazement to see the frosty widow thaw into eager life in the company of her children. Gloria, dowager Viscountess Roseborough, was positively transformed. Freed from her willful silence, she appeared a young and beautiful woman. Her daughters, in turn, clung excitedly to her as if they loved to be at her side.

Julia crouched to their level when they came to greet her. "Hello," she said warmly. "I'm so glad to meet you both. I have sisters almost exactly your age, and I've been missing them very much today."

The children were instantly fascinated by this adult who bent to speak to them from their own height. They asked her who her sisters were, and where they lived, and if they were in London now, and seemed disappointed to learn they were far away in the country. Anne, the elder, was very gratified to learn that one of the sisters in question shared a name with her, and both girls expressed so much eagerness to meet the Oliver children that Julia suspected they were starving for friendship.

"I would love to have you come visit us in the country sometime," Julia offered, looking questioningly at Gloria to see her reaction. To her surprise, the young widow gave her a small smile and unbent a bit toward her.

"That's a very kind offer," she murmured. "Thank you. Now, come, girls; you mustn't bother Miss Herington. Back to the nursery with you."

"Oh, no, please," Julia blurted before she could stop herself. "Could they stay? I . . . I really do miss my young sisters, and I'd be happy to play with them if you'd like to return to your card game."

Gloria looked doubtfully at her, but then nodded and agreed. Before she stepped away, while the girls were still distracted and capering about in glee at getting to remain with the adults, Julia asked her if she might give the girls each a coin. "For their Christmas boxes," she explained.

This time Gloria's smile was real and warm. "Thank you, Miss Herington," she said. "I think they would be delighted."

She bit her lip and looked anxiously at her mother. Lady Matheson was consulting her cards and looking impatient for the game to resume. "Thank you for thinking of my girls," she added in a rush, and with a nod, returned to the table.

Julia grinned back at her, pleasantly surprised. James had once said he had little in common with his sister, describing her as excessively proper. Julia had expected her to be reserved and haughty, and so she had seemed throughout dinner. But she clearly had a heart to be touched; she loved her children so much. Her chill manner, Julia thought, had probably been made worse by the recent loss of her husband, and by having to live with her terrible mother—who, so far, seemed to have no such warm heart as her daughter.

Julia dug into her reticule to find half crowns for each

girl. Naturally, they shrieked with delight and thanked her eagerly, over and over, as she wished them both a happy Christmas.

In the flurry of movement, James broke away from the card table and came over to join Julia. He crouched with her to greet his small nieces.

"Well, so these rascals are staying with us for a bit?" he teased, ruffling the hair of the adoring young girls. They clutched at his coat and clamored to be hoisted into the air, and he at once obliged them.

Julia watched, wonderingly, at his comfort and happiness with the girls, so like his sister's own joy in them. "So this is how you knew so well how to play with the children at Stonemeadows," she reasoned.

"Hmm?" James said, distracted by small fists pounding him in the shoulder as Sophia begged to be lifted up again. "Oh, well, maybe so. Your four there were a bit much for me to keep up with sometimes, but I like children. And I do love these young ladies," he said, lowering his voice. "They lost their father very suddenly, and they had to leave the country for London, so they lost their home, too. No dower house for them on the Roseborough estate."

He swooped Sophia in a wide circle as she shrieked with laughter, drawing an irked stare from Lady Matheson that James and Julia both ignored.

"London's no place for children, not year-round. I can say that from my own experience. I'd like to get them back to the country someday. That's part of the reason why I'm interested in restoring Nicholls," he explained. "I hope my sister will send them to live with me."

Julia's heart warmed at his affectionate words. It was so like him to be warm and welcoming—and like him, too, to be a bit impractical. He seemed not to have thought of the one major flaw in his plan. She hated to say it, but it needed to be said. "James, I don't think your sister would part with her children. She loves them so."

He looked surprised. He opened his mouth to speak, but first laid the giggling Sophia over his shoulder, and picked up Anne with his now-free arms.

"Oof." He pretended to have trouble lifting the older girl as she collapsed bonelessly into giggles. "You've grown so much, you must weigh eighteen stone."

Nieces momentarily assuaged, he returned his attention to Julia. "What do you mean? Gloria never cared for the country."

"Maybe not," Julia replied, "but she cares for her girls. Why, she lit up like a, a"—she searched for an appropriate simile, and finished—"like a Franklin stove when they came into the room."

"Very poetic," James congratulated her with mock gravity.

"I'm serious," Julia insisted. Then, recollecting herself, she continued quickly in a hushed voice pitched low for his ears, "I've only met her this once, and you've known her your whole life, so of course I don't know her as well as you do. But she wasn't all that welcoming at first. I mean, she was welcoming, but not really *welcoming*, if you know what I mean? But then when her daughters came in, she was much more comfortable and she was actually quite kind and lovely."

James blinked at her and set down his nieces one by one. He sent them off to their governess and bedtime with one last hug apiece, then looked back at Julia.

"I see. Ah . . . well . . . thank you for letting me know what you think."

Julia flushed. "James, I'm sorry," she assured him in a rush. "It's not my place to say anything about your family.

What I meant was, I think they're lovely children, and your sister obviously cares about them very much."

"I'm not at all offended," he replied mildly. "I suppose I'd better invite them all."

He darted a glance over at the card table, and, once assured that the four players were all occupied in their game, confided, "My sister and I have never been particularly close, and our parents led us toward very different lives. She married very young, and I . . ."

He trailed off, then admitted, "Well, I never had to do very much with my time, so I ran in, er, some different circles from those in which I was raised. Anyway, it's been quite a while since Gloria and I have dealt much together. Perhaps it's time I get to know her again." He smiled and rested an encouraging hand on Julia's shoulder.

Julia smiled back, relishing the feeling of his hand. She wished she had just a bit more courage—with only a bit more, she would touch his hand with her own; she'd entwine her fingers with his.

She felt lucky to be a party to his plans, to be standing here with him, enjoying his company. The last time she'd felt so happy was . . . well, probably when she'd seen him earlier today. And before that, not for quite some time.

But here, in this moment, with him, there was nowhere else she would have wanted to be, and she was glad, *glad*, that she'd come to London for Christmas.

The intimate moment lengthened, and as so often happened, she spoke without thinking. "What happened to her husband? He must have been very young when he passed on."

James's mouth tightened, and he dropped his hand from her shoulder. Julia realized she must have blundered terribly. "I'm sorry, I don't mean to pry." She crossed her arms tightly across her chest, wishing she had a fan to flap around to occupy her hands, which felt awkward and heavy.

James sighed and rubbed a hand across weary eyes. "It's all right," he replied, dropping his voice even lower. "Your aunt would probably tell you eventually, though it's not really fit for the ears of a young woman."

Julia bit her tongue, hard, to keep from hurrying James along. This promised to be quite interesting. She had long been convinced that some of the things most worth hearing were those deemed unfit for the ears of young women.

"How much Latin do you know?" James asked, fixing her with a piercing gaze. His green eyes were hard and tired.

She didn't know the right answer, but suddenly this didn't seem amusing anymore. She wanted to lift that terrible look from his face. She'd say anything to ease it; she'd caress the furrows from his forehead and kiss the sorrow from his mouth.

But all she said was, "Not much, I'm afraid. No more than most women."

James nodded, as if this was the answer he expected. "Do you happen to know the phrase *in flagrante delicto*?"

Julia's mouth fell open. That was one phrase she *did* know, though she'd never have admitted it to her mother.

"I see that you do," James continued in his grim near whisper. "That's how the rat died, with a mistress my sister didn't know he had. A mistress who ran out into the street, screaming for help, wrapped in only a bedsheet, for all the *ton* to see and hear."

"Good God." Julia forced her mouth closed, but she couldn't think of what to say next. Poor Gloria, to suffer a loss and betrayal at once, and then be sent to live in this cold pile of a house with her even colder mother.

"God had nothing to do with it," James said. His mouth tightened into a hard line she'd never seen before. "Her fool of a husband all but made her a laughingstock, and our family by extension. I wish . . ."

He trailed off, and looked over at Louisa, who sat unawares next to a woman who, Julia now knew, hid a great wound with her haughty expression. "I had hoped to marry soon, and thereby be in a position to help undo the damage. With a wife at my side, and Nicholls restored, I could offer them respectability and a real home in the country, away from all of this."

He closed his eyes for a long moment, but Julia could have sworn she saw bright unshed tears in them before he did. He gestured to the stairway up which his nieces had vanished. "For their sakes, you know. For all of us, but especially for those girls, I hoped to marry as quickly as possible and give our family a chance to be decent and happy again."

The reminder of his upcoming marriage affected Julia with the physical force of a horse kick to the stomach. She nearly choked on the sudden shock of it.

"Yes, of course," she managed to say.

What was she doing, heating herself up with thoughts about James? She was such a fool. He might enjoy her friendship, but there was another lady here with a much greater claim on his attention. Why, his very expression became wistful as he looked from her to Louisa. He wished to be with Louisa now.

Of course he did; that only made sense. But she still ached to think of it, and she was relieved when the party broke up soon afterward.

They all wished each other a happy Christmas again, and Lady Matheson was as glacial as ever in her farewells.

But when Julia spoke with Gloria, the widow clasped her hands with genuine warmth.

"Thank you again for your kindness to my daughters," she offered. "I'm so very glad to have met you."

"And I you," Julia replied with equal candor, stammering under the weight of her too-deep understanding. "You have lovely daughters. I'm . . . I'm delighted to have met you all."

She took her leave from James with a friendly handshake, then turned away in order not to see whether he kissed Louisa good evening. All the way home, she remembered his wounded eyes, and she could swear she still felt the warmth of his hand on her shoulder.

Chapter 12

In Which Her Ladyship Recarpets the Morning Room

Julia didn't really want to think or speak about the evening once they all got home, but Louisa sought her out in her bedchamber later that night as she was completing her preparations for sleep. She had already changed into her nightdress, and the knock on the door sounded just as she was splashing her face with water.

"Go away," she grumbled, and Louisa immediately walked in.

"Sorry, what did you say?" Louisa asked. She seemed nervous and distracted, so Julia took pity on her.

"Nothing, nothing. What's going on? Are you all right?"

The tall girl sat carefully on the edge of the bed to avoid creasing her dinner gown. "How do you think it went?" she asked hesitantly.

"Oh, it was fantastic," Julia replied at once with her brightest smile.

Louisa's dark eyes bored into her. "You're a terrible liar. Was it disastrous, or just merely bad?"

Julia flung herself onto the bed and wiggled her feet thoughtfully, sighing as she considered her answer. She didn't know whether Louisa wanted lies or the truth.

She settled for ambiguity. "I don't exactly know. It definitely wasn't like a cozy Christmas Eve at home. But I don't think there's anything you could have done differently to make it go better. Does that help?"

Louisa blew out a breath between thinned lips. "Maybe a bit. But the fact remains, they don't really want me to marry him, do they?"

"As long as he wants to marry you, what does it matter?" Julia replied.

She knew that was dodging the question, but she didn't really want to talk about this. She felt uncomfortable, even a bit envious. Which was ridiculous, she knew, since her season would begin soon and she would have her chance to find the same happiness Louisa had.

Except Louisa didn't seem happy right now; she still seemed worried. "I suppose it was kind of them to have me join their game, but then they excluded you, which again seemed impolite to me. Not very hospitable. Do you agree?"

"Yes, and Lady Matheson was very rude to me at dinner, too," Julia said. "I could hardly believe she called me common."

Just the thought of it made the desperate annoyance wash over her again. Although . . . then James had come to her defense. And then he had told her his future plans and family secrets. Had he told them to Louisa? Or had Julia somehow earned a special confidence?

The thought cheered her, although the memory of James's bleak eyes was as painful as a wound.

"So, doesn't that seem like a problem to you? If they

aren't willing to accept my family as well as me?" Louisa pressed.

Julia struggled to focus on her sister's worried words. "It won't bother me a bit, as long as it doesn't matter to you," she replied honestly. "I probably won't meet up with them often. Though I did like James's little nieces. I meant what I said about inviting them to Stonemeadows."

Louisa was insistent. "But we should all have good relationships, shouldn't we? Do you think James should marry without the support of his family?"

Now it was Julia's turn to blow out a breath impatiently. She knew she should be giving Louisa her full attention, but she just wanted to stop thinking about the whole situation. "Louisa, he can do whatever he chooses to. He is a grown man who's already come into his title and estate. He's what, almost thirty years old?"

"Twenty-seven."

"Fine, twenty-seven. Anyway, he's self-sufficient. And if he wants to be engaged, which he *does*, his mother had better get used to the fact. She may be too top-lofty to notice anyone below her own rank, but it would be the devil of a scandal if she tried to break things up."

A scandal. Julia could almost laugh, if it wasn't so sad. It was precisely that, a family scandal, that James was trying to suppress through his marriage. Now that he was engaged, his mother ought to be more judicious about suggesting other young women for him to run off with.

Louisa acknowledged these pragmatic words with a miserable half smile. "That may be true, but what kind of life would it be for his wife if she couldn't get along with his mother?"

"Why are you speaking in hypotheticals?" Julia demanded. "You're the woman in question; you're going to be his wife. And then you'll be a viscountess, too, as well as the mother of his heirs." She thought for a moment. "Actually, if she's too much of an evil cow to you, you could simply refuse to have any children but girls."

She almost smiled at the mental image of the dowager viscountess being presented with a squalling baby granddaughter.

But the idea of James, the father of another woman's child—that thought was enough to wipe any smile from her face.

"Evil cow," Louisa repeated, much struck. "She was a bit, wasn't she?"

"More than a bit," Julia agreed. "She's lucky our aunt wasn't in an attacking mood tonight. I wasn't either, really, but I wished they'd been more friendly."

Louisa stared forward and nodded. "Yes, definitely that. A woman like that can put a lot of pressure on someone."

Julia looked at her curiously, but Louisa seemed to be in a reverie.

"Well, I don't mean to bother you," she said, standing abruptly. "I just wasn't sure what to make of the situation."

She still looked uncertain, and Julia felt ashamed of her own reluctance to talk. If she had sensed unfriendliness in the air that evening, how much more so must Louisa feel it?

"I'm sorry," she said at once, reaching for her sister's hands. "Stay, talk as long as you need to."

"No, I'm fine," Louisa assured her, managing a more sanguine expression. "I just have a lot to think about, I guess." She squeezed Julia's hands. "Happy Christmas."

Julia responded in kind, and relaxed back onto her bed. It hadn't really been much of a happy Christmas Eve, but there was still tomorrow to come, and pieces of the evening had been pleasant nonetheless. Eating a large, delicious dinner. Playing with two young, shrieking children. And, of course, seeing James. Feeling the warmth of his trust in her.

It took a while, but she eventually drifted off into a troubled sleep, dreaming of her sister's betrothed husband.

She was awoken the next morning by a gentle scratch on her forehead. Her eyes snapped open, expecting in the fog of half-sleep to see a man with green eyes peering down at her.

Instead, Louisa grinned at her and waggled a sprig of mistletoe across her face again. "Happy Christmas, Julia. Put on your wrapper and come see what our aunt has done."

Julia yawned and shuffled after her sister, struggling toward wakefulness, away from the lingering threads of disturbing dreams. "Was it necessary for you to swat me awake with a plant?"

"You're lucky it was I," Louisa replied. "It's mistletoe, you know. Our aunt wanted to send a footman in to embrace you awake, but I convinced her that would be vulgar."

Julia choked. And then, when she entered her aunt's morning room, she choked again. The sharp scent of evergreen slapped her fully awake in an instant.

"Did a pine forest anger our aunt?" she murmured to Louisa. The entire morning room was carpeted with evergreen branches; the ornate chandelier was twined with mistletoe and holly. Pine garland swooped around the delicately plastered walls and snaked around the legs of the chairs and sofa.

Julia crunched slowly across the room, wishing she'd

donned her slippers. "Happy Christmas, Aunt Estella. What—"

"It's Christmas morning, is what." Lady Irving, festive in a men's red brocade banyan and a bright apricot turban, rose from her perch on the morning room's sofa. "I know you girls like to have your holiday folderols about you, so I've done my best. As you can't go tramping about a forest in the heart of London, I've had the forest brought to you."

As Louisa thanked their aunt with the pretty manners that always made Lady Irving demur with gruff pleasure, Julia sank onto the bed of pine and laced her fingers through the fragrant branches. Their waxy texture was fresh and pleasant, needling her into an awareness of the difference between last night and this morning.

Her aunt had turned her house into a holiday bower to please her nieces, knowing they would miss Christmas in the country. James's poor nieces would have no such warm greeting this morning from Lady Matheson.

Aunt Estella interrupted Julia's thoughts by shaking a string of nuts in her face. "The queen covers a pine tree with candles," she said. "Rubbishy idea, if you ask me. One of these years, she'll burn down half the City with a scheme like that. Still, I thought you girls would like her idea of almond garlands. Eat."

Julia was always willing to obey such an order. She took the nuts and nutcracker her aunt handed her and began to tease the almonds free from their string, handing every other one—well, every third one—to Louisa.

Lady Irving rearranged herself on the sofa near her nieces. "Perhaps we ought to have invited your young rooster over, Louisa," she mused. "Think he'd like to meet you under the mistletoe, my girl?"

Louisa scrabbled for the end of the almond garland,

her cheeks reddening. "I'll see him a little later. His mother invited me for Christmas dinner, you know."

So James would not come here. Julia tugged her wrapper more closely around her suddenly chilly form. "Atonement, I hope?"

"Or she wants to dangle the promise of a better bride in front of James again," Louisa said in a resigned voice.

Lady Irving raised her eyebrows. "You paint such an attractive picture, I'm tempted to stow away in your reticule and take part in the evening."

"Louisa, I'm sure you'll have a grand time at Matheson House," Julia added. "We'll be having plum pudding here, which I've been told is dreadfully common."

Not even this mild joke lifted the discouraged expression from Louisa's face, and her sister's dilemma clanged through Julia like a caroler's bell. Not yet a wife, Louisa must balance her own family's needs with those of her future husband's. This included trying to make peace with a woman who had no desire to make peace with her.

"If you have to go, I understand," Julia said stoutly. "James will love to see you on Christmas. And I'll save you a slice of pudding as big as the smile you can make right . . . now."

Such nonsense teased a small smile from Louisa.

"That's not big enough for two bites," Julia scoffed. "Give us a big false one."

Laughing, Louisa opened her mouth in a huge yawn, and Julia poked an almond into it before she could close it, sputtering.

"Much better," Lady Irving agreed. "Now that we're falling all over each other, we've a proper celebration under way. Breathe your fill of evergreen, girls, and then we'll get ready for church."

They obliged, then pounded back upstairs to dress for Christmas morning services.

All the trappings of the holiday surrounded them, and for that, Julia was deeply grateful to her aunt. But she was divided all the same. Though her body stood in Grosvenor Square, her heart went out to the girls caught in the chill of Matheson House, and to the hopes and plans of their uncle.

Especially to their uncle.

Chapter 13

In Which Serious Damage
Is Done to the
Contents of Pocketbooks

Christmas night passed quietly. Boxing Day was spent at home, too, since Lady Irving had an aversion to, in her words, tipping the entire City of London. But the following day, Julia and Louisa were to venture out upon the City at last.

That morning, Lady Irving breakfasted on a tray in her room and didn't emerge downstairs until the highly fashionable hour of eleven o'clock. By that time, Louisa and Julia had both woken up, dressed, eaten breakfast (with Julia seizing the welcome opportunity of her aunt's absence to eat an enormous and definitely unladylike amount of food), collected their wraps and reticules for the planned outing to Bond Street, and kicked their heels for almost an hour waiting for her.

Unusually for them, they waited in near silence. Louisa didn't seem upset, but she wasn't much inclined for conversation. Despite herself, Julia felt horribly curious about how the previous evening had gone, but she took her cue from Louisa's quiet, thoughtful expression and decided not to press her.

"Country hours," Lady Irving sniffed when she saw them ready and waiting. "Don't let it get about that you were up before eleven."

She summoned Simone, and then her carriage, which drew an inquiry from Louisa.

"Can't we walk, Aunt? We've hardly gotten any exercise since we arrived."

"Packages," Lady Irving barked. "I like fresh air as much as the next person, but if you think I'm going to stumble through the snow with my arms full of packages, you're a candidate for Bedlam."

She thought for a moment, then corrected herself. "Actually, I suppose it'd be Simone carrying everything. How would you feel about that, my girl?" She elbowed the maid jocularly in the ribs.

"I would much prefer to take the carriage," Simone said calmly.

With what her aunt deemed vulgar curiosity, Julia pressed her nose to the carriage window and studied the London streets as they rolled by. The latest dusting of snow had already been ground into the macadam by the constant churning of carriage wheels, but shop roofs were as delicately frosted as queen cakes. Shop windows had been denuded by parents and lovers hunting Christmas gifts, but greenery and garland swung invitingly across doorways. It was still the season for joy and remembrance, after all.

The sweetness of the sight, the sharp joy of the novelty, banished some of the chill Lady Matheson had imparted to the season.

Too soon, the carriage pulled up at the discreet, elegant shop of Madame Oiseau, *modiste.* Unlike so many of London's "French" dressmakers, who were actually Englishwomen with put-on accents, Simone assured them that Madame was *vraiment française*.

"She is simply the best," the maid explained. "I assure you, you will be transformed." She bit her lip in an oh-so-French gesture of uncertainty, and added, "If she will see you, of course."

Julia was skeptical of *madame's* skill at first; the shop was small, and she saw not a stitch of clothing or fabric on display. It was scrupulously clean and looked to have been recently plastered and painted, so at least it was cheerful. But what was all the fuss about? She and Louisa and Lady Irving seated themselves and waited while Simone eagerly darted back into the private portion of the establishment.

Several minutes passed, and Julia's hesitation grew. Surely they were wasting their time; they had better go. When she began to ask her aunt a dubious question, Lady Irving quickly shushed her, staring raptly at the small woman who suddenly came forth from the back of the shop, followed by a beaming Simone.

A flurried interchange in French followed between the lady's maid and the dressmaker, a thin woman in late middle age who was simply and elegantly dressed in a dark blue silk gown with slashed sleeves. They both looked Julia over as they spoke—Simone in a rushed, excited voice accompanied with flamboyant hand gestures, and Madame Oiseau in a more subdued fashion punctuated with many nods and shakes of her head.

Julia's French wasn't fluent enough to follow their conversation, but they were unmistakably speaking about her. She straightened in her seat and tried to look nonchalant, but her stomach was twisting with apprehension and she couldn't keep from fidgeting. She had no idea what was being discussed, but she could tell from her aunt's reactions that this would be momentous. Lady Irving seemed to be hanging on their every word, nodding eagerly whenever *madame* did, and leaning back in disappointment whenever she shook her head.

Finally, Simone's gesticulations ceased, and she turned to face her employer, her usually unperturbed countenance beaming with pride. "She says she will accept to dress the blond *mademoiselle*," she informed her observers, her accent thickened from a frantic conversation in her native tongue.

"Excellent!" Lady Irving crowed, hopping to her feet. "Nice work, my girl." She clapped Simone soundly on the back, which fazed the lady's maid not a bit, but drew a startled stare from Madame Oiseau. "Sylvia Alleyneham, with all her money, couldn't get Oiseau to take on her girls. Earl's daughters," she trilled with gleeful triumph. "You should consider this an honor."

"Indeed," Louisa breathed in the ear of the now-nonplussed Julia. "She wouldn't dress me last year; our aunt certainly tried to persuade her."

Surprised, Julia darted her sister a quick look, but the elder girl's face was smooth and untroubled.

Several excruciating hours followed, hours of pinning, measuring, cutting and piecing of fabric, and frequent conversations in hurried, emphatic French between Madame Oiseau and Simone, on whose opinion the dressmaker seemed to place no small reliance. The older woman was clearly a *modiste* of formidable talent, but the lady's maid also came into her own in this environment, with an unerring eye for measurement and flawless taste in choice of fabric and color. It must be a great sorrow, Julia realized, for her to work for a woman with such violent taste in clothing as Lady Irving.

Lady Irving, for her part, looked as excited to watch the fitting as Julia would have been to be faced by a platter full of cream pastries, especially after she had been standing for several hours. Julia thought wistfully of her long-ago breakfast as she stood surrounded by billows of fabric. She should have eaten an extra piece of toast, or perhaps even stowed one in her reticule.

After long discussion, her ladyship finally settled on three ready-made frocks that had been hastily altered to fit Julia—and even so, they still fit better than anything she had ever owned. They also placed an order for a half dozen day dresses in assorted pale colors, a few evening gowns suitable for going out to small events, plus a stunning ball gown in ivory silk.

Lady Irving decided to defer the order of a court dress for the time being.

"Silly garments," she huffed. "But I suppose we'll have to have one made eventually so we can present the girl properly to the queen."

"Not in white," Madame Oiseau had declared boldly, refusing to allow any of Julia's gowns to be made in this traditional color. "She should never wear white. *Les blondes*, they are so light, they need some color in the gown."

"How much will all of this cost?" Julia wondered quietly to her aunt.

"It's vulgar to ask," Lady Irving informed her. "And besides, if you have to ask, you probably don't want to know the answer."

She chucked Julia under the chin as they prepared to leave at last. "It's all right, my girl. I'll help you out with this one. Consider it a Christmas present. Your parents have simply no idea what it costs for a young lady to look her best."

At Julia's answering protest, Lady Irving countered, "Very well, then, it's an investment. An investment in you, to make sure you take this year."

Julia stared at her aunt. She wasn't sure if she should be grateful or offended by her aunt's combination of generosity or mercenary honesty.

"Be honest with yourself, Julia," the countess continued. "You haven't got a title, and your dowry is just this side of pitiful. But you do have looks and spirit, which are not unimportant. And you have me to look out for you, which is an undeniable advantage. And now you have Oiseau, too. With all of us on your side, we'll have you suitably matched before the season's over, I guarantee it."

Julia nodded somewhat weakly at this recital. She hadn't realized her aunt was approaching the season with so much planning and foresight.

She decided to be grateful, but reserve the right to be offended later on.

"Rich, titled, fills out his breeches well." The countess ticked off the essential male qualities on her fingers. "That's what we'll be looking for. Mind you, girl, there aren't a lot of those fellows around, and there's a great deal of competition for them. If we find one starts sniffing around you, we shall snap him up at once."

And with that decisive statement, the party left the shop, extracting from *madame* a parting promise that the finished gowns would be delivered in a few weeks.

In the meantime, Lady Irving explained, Julia would make do with her shockingly bland wardrobe, comforted by the knowledge that London was terribly thin of company this time of year. As there would be hardly anyone to see her looking so dull, her chances to make a social success during the season would hardly be blighted at all.

Once they made a few more stops for "essential pieces"—gloves, slippers, bonnets, and more silk stockings than Julia had owned in her whole life—they were ready to head home at last. Julia was exhausted, ready to eat an entire Cornish hen, and reeling from the amount of money that had exchanged hands in the last few hours. Lady Irving was still in a talkative, exuberant mood that had only been heightened by the rash of spending that followed their time at the dressmaker's.

Good Lord, didn't the woman ever get hungry? Julia thought irritably as Lady Irving continued to exult.

"Now that you're on at Oiseau's, we can come back anytime and have more dresses made up. But I think I may wait until I cross paths with Sylvia before I start planning that one. Perhaps I'll talk to her about the court dress, just to drop the Oiseau name."

As it turned out, their paths were to cross sooner than she expected, for the Countess of Alleyneham had left her card during their absence.

"Damme, I didn't even know she was in town," Lady Irving exhorted. "One of her girls must have taken ill. I can't think why they'd be so contrary as to bring her back from the country."

Louisa disappeared as Lady Irving mused aloud about the best time to return the call, but Julia wasn't about to go hungry any longer. She served herself a large plate from the cold collation that had been prepared. The simple slices of ham and chicken seemed the most delicious things she had ever tasted after long hours of being jabbed by pins.

Hungry though she was, she'd had enough of her aunt's company for a while. As soon as Lady Irving sat down for her own repast, Julia decided she'd eaten enough. Craving a bit of quiet, she reflexively headed for the library, where she knew her aunt seldom trod.

As she entered the room, she saw Louisa, and hot shame flooded through her. Her dear sister had sat and waited for hours, with nothing to do as Julia was fitted by a dressmaker so exclusive that she had refused point-blank to wait upon Louisa herself the year before. Julia's attention had been diverted by her aunt's eagerness and the attention of those fashionable Frenchwomen. She'd forgotten about her sister, waiting patiently, probably wishing she were anywhere else.

This was what she had come to, after only four days in London. No wonder Louisa thought it a wretched place.

Louisa didn't seem to think Julia a wretch, though. She was as calm as ever as her eyes skimmed over the spines of Lady Irving's books.

"Did you have a good time?" she asked Julia. "Goodness, I do believe I've read all of these at least twice already."

"I'm so sorry," Julia blurted, rushing over to her. "They took so long, and I was so excited at first, and then I was so hungry I couldn't even *think* about anything else. Which is obvious, because I didn't think of you and how boring it must have been for you, and I do hope your feelings weren't hurt, and I think it was very impolite of Madame Oiseau to refuse to take you on."

"Slow down," Louisa admonished and squeezed Julia's hand, a quiet half smile on her face.

"Don't worry about it," she continued. "If you had a good time, I'm happy I went. My aim is to do what I can to help you shine even more than you usually do.

"Although," she added, her delicate brows furrowed in consideration, "I'm not sure I actually helped at all. They didn't exactly consult my opinion in the matter of the fitting, not that I would have dared disagree with them anyway." She smiled, a real smile this time. "Perhaps I should have just stayed home with a book?"

"I'm so glad you didn't," Julia said eagerly. "The whole time they were looking me over, I felt like I was a horse being trotted out, only I had no idea what they wanted from me."

"You need to work on your French," Louisa said. "Simone was talking about how much spirit you had, which was apparently clear to them both from the way you were fidgeting in your chair."

Julia gaped at her. "Fidgeting? That's what impressed the illustrious *madame*?"

"That, and the fact that she thought you were extremely beautiful," Louisa said, pinching Julia's nose affectionately. "She thought you lacked polish, but Simone convinced her that it was charming, and her beautiful clothes would be all you'd need to be the talk of the *ton*."

"I *am* charming, in my own way. And I don't want to be the talk of the *ton*," Julia protested. "I just want one nice man to fall in love with me."

One specific man . . .

Yes, she was indeed a wretch, and it wasn't London's fault.

"Well," Louisa replied, oblivious to Julia's deeply terrible and wretched nature, "you'll be wearing Oiseau, so that just got a lot more likely. She has a gift for making women look their loveliest."

"I'll probably be glad for the help," Julia joked feebly. "I nearly screamed when I saw how much silk stockings cost here."

"It's all right," Louisa said. "The shopkeeper probably would have regarded it as a compliment."

"Seriously," Julia tried to return to the subject from

earlier, "I am very grateful that you came today. I would have felt even more horribly intimidated than I was if you hadn't been there, and it was just me with our aunt and those energetic Frenchwomen."

"What a shining example I am," Louisa teased. "What are the qualities that brought us through this grueling experience? *Je ne sais quoi? Joie de vivre? Eau de vie?*"

"My French may not be the greatest, but I know perfectly well that last one means 'brandy,'" Julia replied, stifling a giggle. "By the time we were done, we probably all could have done with a brandy, don't you think?"

With that ridiculous comment, Louisa started laughing, too, and Julia felt that, in some small way, she'd made things right with her uncomplaining, ever-patient, must-be-so-bored sister.

She hadn't made things right with herself yet, but this would do for a start.

Chapter 14

In Which Sapphires
Are Ever So Tempting

James, Viscount Matheson, walked aimlessly down Bond Street, considering whether he ought to buy a belated Christmas gift for his fiancée.

It seemed like the kind of thing an affianced man should do. He couldn't be sure, of course; he certainly had never been engaged before, and neither had any of his friends. Good Lord, his old crony Xavier had practically spit out his brandy when James had first told him of his engagement to the Honorable Louisa Oliver at the end of the previous season.

"You're making a mistake," the dark young gentleman had informed him after he recovered from the shock. "I never thought you were a fool, Matheson."

Naturally he had resented having this description applied to him, and he demanded that Lord Xavier explain himself. Xavier was a good fellow at heart, but he could have a rough tongue at times.

In this instance, however, the younger man had

backed down and assured James that he wasn't serious;
that Louisa Oliver was no doubt an excellent choice for
a wife; and that he would endeavor to assure the viscount
again of this opinion if he ever met the lady in question.
Xavier even managed to exert himself to extend his congratulations, which, when you considered how unyielding the man could be, was like receiving a bag of gold
from a miser. Or, James now thought as his mind
roamed for an unlikely simile, like holding an utterly
conventional, not at all shrill or embarrassing conversation with Lady Irving.

All of which was to say, he didn't have much guidance
in the area of how a man should behave toward his fiancée, especially if she seemed to be the retiring sort. His
father wasn't around to enlighten him, and his mother
certainly wouldn't be of any help. She had been margin-
ally friendlier when Louisa came to dine on Christmas
Day, but she was still clearly against the match. He supposed he could ask Gloria, who had actually been rather
pleasant upon meeting Louisa for the second time. Even
as a grown man, though, there was something that rankled about asking his older sister for advice.

So here he was, peering doubtfully into the window of
a jeweler's shop, wondering what might be an appropriate gift for Louisa. He hadn't gotten her anything for
Christmas yet, although in his defense he hadn't expected to see her then, and the holiday had never been
made much of in his family anyway. Christmas gifts were
really mainly for children.

Louisa hadn't given him anything either, true, but
he had a nagging feeling that the burden of gift-giving
(for a burden was exactly what it felt like) should fall on
the engaged party with the greater discretionary income.
Which would be he.

Besides, a gift could possibly help Louisa feel more comfortable during what had turned into an awkward holiday season for them both. She seemed to be reluctant for their marriage because of all the changes it would bring to her life—but maybe, just maybe, if he showed her that the changes would be good, she would be more eager. As a viscountess, she would certainly have more money at her command, and more jewelry, than she had ever owned as a baron's daughter. Many women would find that very exciting, though he knew, deep in his heart, that Louisa wasn't one of them.

He sighed. Would diamonds be too much? He didn't want to overwhelm her; that would have precisely the opposite of the desired effect. Which was, quite frankly, to have a fiancée who seemed to give a damn when he was around.

His eye caught on a sapphire set—just a trumpery set without any real precious stones, but it was simple and lovely. He knew that blue as well as he knew his own face; he realized at once the jewels were the precise shade of Julia's eyes.

Julia.

He smiled just to think of her, causing a female passerby who saw his grinning reflection in the shop window to shriek and give him a wide berth.

He barely noticed, though. He kept his thoughts so tightly marshaled these days that it was seldom he even allowed himself to think about Julia, but he let her wash over him now. She was just so . . . so *herself*, all the time. Climbing a ladder. Teasing her aunt. Cramming handfuls of biscuits into her mouth. The first time he'd met her, she'd showed him what she was really like, and he'd wanted to get to know more. He'd been fascinated.

He'd tried to tell himself for quite a while that that

was just because he was eager to get to know Louisa's family, and he'd been happy to make a friend among her relatives. But now, he knew, that was not the full truth. When he'd seen her again after several weeks' absence, when she'd catapulted herself into his arms, he had felt such longing that he had had to make a physical effort to let her go. It had been one of the most difficult things he'd had to do in a long time.

Therein lay the problem. Therein lay the reason he didn't often permit himself to think about Julia anymore, and the reason he frequently reminded himself of what Louisa's fine qualities were.

She was elegant, self-possessed, thoughtful, and startlingly intelligent. He admired and respected her enormously. He hadn't been in love with her when he offered marriage, true, but he hadn't expected to fall in love with anyone else either.

Love? Was that what he felt for Julia?

Surely not. But he wondered how much that little sapphire set cost.

Despite himself, he turned from the window to the shop door, preparing to head inside and inquire about the sapphires.

At that very moment, a female voice called his name.

He jumped as if he'd been shot, or caught with his breeches off. He knew that voice. He had been about to buy sapphires for that voice.

But it wasn't Julia alone. She was, most unexpectedly, walking with Lady Charissa Bradleigh. He hadn't even known the Earl of Alleyneham had brought his family to town, or, for that matter, that Julia knew any of them.

He greeted them with habitual civility, turning his attention first to Lady Charissa as the highest-ranking lady present. This gave him a few seconds to return his thoughts to their usual order, or at least some semblance of it.

He had been caught off guard, true, but it might be for the best. The encounter kept him from making what probably would have been a horrible blunder, buying those sapphires.

Now that she was here, he realized the sapphires wouldn't have done her eyes justice anyway.

Then he realized that was precisely the type of thought he ought to be trying *not* to have, and he ruthlessly squelched it. His face all politeness, he inquired after Charissa's family.

"I wasn't aware you were in town," he explained, "or I would have been by to offer my respects to your parents."

"Oh, Lord, don't worry about that!" Charissa replied with a laugh. "We only just got here on Boxing Day and we haven't seen many people. Audrina's fallen ill, you see—that's my youngest sister," she explained for Julia's benefit. "Anyway, my lord, it turns out your mother knew a very good doctor here in town, and recommended we all come back for Audrina to be treated by the best."

She looked up at James under flirtatious lashes. "She made a point of telling us *you* were here as well. And . . . something about a Twelfth Night masquerade? I can't remember, exactly." She dimpled at him roguishly and waited for a response.

He'd once heard Lady Irving dismiss the Bradleigh daughters as "whey-faced," but an honest appraiser would judge Lady Charissa quite a lovely girl. She had clear skin, russet hair, and pleasant, regular features, including a pair of large, lovely, and provocative gray eyes. She was also a bit chattery, though, which could be the reason she hadn't yet snared the duke her rather fatuous mother seemed adamant she should marry. That, and the fact that there were very few unmarried dukes to go around.

Seeing her smile up at him, James thought fleetingly of the differences between the young women in front of him. How could one be impish and talkative and leave him utterly cold, while the one at her side shared the same traits and he thought them the most appealing thing on earth?

Curse it, there again was one of those thoughts he ought not to be having. *You fool,* he chastised himself, and shook his head to turn his mind in another direction.

Julia responded at once to his unconscious gesture. "There's not a masquerade?"

"What?"

"You shook your head. Is there not a masquerade, or are you not present in London? You must have been disagreeing with one statement or the other. Or else you weren't attending to us at all, which would be incredibly impolite of you. I mean, not that you're impolite in general; just that in this particular it would be, you know, less than your usual level of politeness."

There it was, that sheepish smile that showed him she knew she'd been running on too much; it positively made his insides flip.

"Er . . ." He struggled to respond normally. "I believe I was shaking my head in disbelief at my mother's level of interest in various people's activities."

Both young women were perfectly willing to accept this explanation, so James quickly asked when they had met, in order to get them talking on a different topic from that of his unexplained gestures.

They both started to speak at once, laughed, and each told the other one to go ahead. Finally Charissa began.

"We met a few days ago through my mama and Julia's aunt, who have been friends since girlhood, you see. Lady Irving came to pay a call and brought her two nieces with her. Of course, I already knew your enchanting fiancée from last year," she acknowledged with another roguish smile, and he bowed to acknowledge the compliment. "But I was simply delighted that Lady Irving had such an excellent friend for me with her this time! For my sisters, you know, are really no fun at all," she finished, drawing her pretty mouth into a moue of mock dissatisfaction.

"Yes," Julia continued eagerly, "I was so glad my aunt introduced us, and Charissa has been kind enough to allow me to use her Christian name already. She has been showing me all around town. She knows it so well, and I wanted to see all the things Louisa told me of, like the Tower of London and Hookham's library. Charissa's been kind enough to show me there *and* to places I didn't even know of. We even went to a musicale last night, and saw an opera singer. I've never seen one before."

Her excitement abated for a moment as she admitted, "He was much . . . *louder* than I thought he would be. But I enjoyed it very much all the same," she hastily assured her friend.

"How nice for you," James replied, struggling for the usual polite responses.

It was difficult to speak in trivialities to these two women, when all he wanted was to wrap Julia in his arms and put his tongue in that little hollow above her collarbone. And when he also wanted to smack his head against a shop window for even thinking such a thing.

Damn it all, there were only so many competing ideas a man could hold in his mind at once.

Luckily, the earl's daughter was oblivious to most

things outside of her own well-coiffed head. She rolled her eyes affectionately and linked her arm in Julia's. "Sweet girl, she has barely gotten a start on learning where everything is. Someone has given her the flattest idea of what there is to do in London! Hookham's; honestly, I declare I've never been there before in my life. But I knew where it was; it's close to the most stunning jeweler's. Right here, you see?"

She gestured at the shop window James had just been lurking in front of. Julia's eyes widened as she took in the gemstones on display, and she nodded in acknowledgment of the truth of her friend's words.

James thought he heard a faint, faint whisper of "Hell's bells" as Julia's amazed eyes roved over the jewels.

"Anyway," Charissa concluded, oblivious to any epithets that may or may not have been spoken, "we are just coming from Hookham's now." She gave a tiny shudder, but added kindly, "I'm very glad I went to see it. It really is quite a lovely place, and it has the most interesting smell."

"It did have an unusual smell," Julia confirmed, wrinkling her nose thoughtfully. "I suppose it was all the bindings. You know, James, your library had rather a similar smell, now I come to think of it."

"It did?" James was taken aback to have his home drawn into the discussion of odors. "I'm sorry to hear it. I hope it wasn't unpleasant."

"No, there's nothing at all wrong with it," Julia hastened to explain. "It's the smell of bindings, some of them old, some well handled and in need of care. For a library, it's a lovely scent. It shows that you care about your books, that they have a history."

Lady Charissa seemed surprised at the intellectual bent of this speech, then discarded it from her notice and reacted only to the kernel of information that interested her.

"You've seen his library? At his country house, I suppose? He hadn't been there in, oh, years and years, but then all of a sudden it caught his fancy again. Last summer, I declare, we hardly saw him at all, he was so in love with the place!"

At the word "love," she darted another of her roguish looks at him, and James began to feel distinctly uncomfortable. What if Julia should think he was flirting with this young woman, right in front of her? That would be discourteous to Louisa. And, well, he also didn't want Julia to have that impression of him for her own sake. He might have sown a few wild oats in the past, but he'd never been much of a flirt.

He changed the subject again. "Where are you heading now? May I accompany you somewhere?"

"Oh, yes, let's walk together," Julia said. "It's a little too cold to be standing still outdoors. Charissa, where do you want to go next?"

The young lady seemed undecided at first, but when James offered her an arm, she was perfectly willing to walk with him and Julia. They decided to head in the direction of St. James's Square, where the town residence of the Earl and Countess of Alleyneham was located.

As they walked, much conversation flowed on the topic of Lord Xavier's planned masquerade, most of it from the mouth of Lady Charissa Bradleigh, who was cheerfully dropping name after name of the people who might possibly be there, if they were in town, and Julia would simply *have* to get to know them; they were the *dearest* creatures. Julia, unable to contribute to this speculation about people she had never met, simply bobbed her head agreeably in response to Charissa's words. She looked rather like a child's nodding toy, James thought, deriving great amusement from the sight but trying not to display it.

As an older acquaintance, Charissa inevitably directed much of her conversation to James as well as to Julia. By the time they finally reached the door of Alleyneham House, the earl's daughter had extracted from James a promise that yes, he would be at the masquerade, and yes, he would certainly be honored to dance with her then. After this last promise, he looked with some small degree of anxiety at Julia for her reaction, but she only smiled and pressed his hand in farewell.

"I'll see you at Lord Xavier's, then," she assured him. "I'm really looking forward to it." Her voice grew confidential. "I've never been to a masquerade before. It sounds very exciting. Will there be secret identities, and intrigue in dark corners?"

He laughed hollowly. Intrigue in dark corners. She'd never have dared speak the words to him if she could read his thoughts.

He forced his voice into a light, joking tone. "Secrets at Xavier's? They'd better not, if they don't want it in the *Ton Bon-bons* scandal sheet. The man can't keep a thing to himself."

"Oh." Julia sounded disappointed. "Are you going to wear a costume?"

This was too much for Charissa, who, through giggles, entreated him eagerly to wear something historical. "Perhaps something with tights, like Henry the Eighth! Oh, wait; he's rather too fat. Although you could wear padding."

"No," James said firmly, quashing that idea at once. "I'm sorry to disappoint a lady, but I will *not* wear a costume. That's never required," he explained to Julia.

"There are always masks for those who come in ordinary evening wear. I'll probably just wear a cape or something simple like that."

"A cape? He's going to go as a coachman!" Charissa exploded with laughter.

She bobbed a farewell curtsy to James, and with a waggle of her fingers, headed into her house. Julia gave James a helpless smile, and followed her friend, looking, James thought, a bit overwhelmed.

Yes, Charissa Bradleigh could do that to a person. He wondered, as he absently strolled in the direction of his own residence, how she and Julia had become friends so quickly. He rather had the feeling that the young noblewoman had seized upon Julia as a novelty and was now running the life out of her. Julia had formidable energy, but she wasn't used to town hours, town manners, and the intense but fleeting nature of many town friendships.

He wondered, too, how it was affecting Louisa to have her sister seized from her all the time. He thought with a pang that he ought to call on her and see if she needed any cheering up.

And that was when he realized, standing a good half mile from where he'd started, that he'd taken his carriage out today and had left it behind him in Bond Street. *And* that he never had chosen a gift for Louisa.

Chapter 15

In Which Both Dinner and a Husband Are on the Menu

"This Twelfth Night masquerade is scarcely worth the trouble of getting gussied up," Lady Irving opined, "except for the fact that the three of us will all rip each other's throats out if we stay home any longer. It's a shame that London is so shockingly thin of company still, but that's the way it always is in winter. Ah, well. We'll still get our last little gasp of holiday revelry."

A mischievous smile slid across her face. "I am *very* glad the Bradleighs are here now. What are the chances I could persuade Lord Xavier to notify all of his other guests to come in formal dress, but tell Sylvia to come in a costume?"

She snorted. "Imagine her coming as a shepherdess, and everyone else in their lovely evening dress," she hooted. "Why, she wouldn't know where to stick her crook, if you know what I mean."

"I'm very glad that I do *not* know what you mean," Louisa said firmly. "And I think it would be unkind of you to play such a trick on your old friend."

"She'd love it," Lady Irving insisted, then relented. "All right, fine, fine, I'm the one who would love it. It would be hilarious. But I won't say anything to Xavier."

"He probably wouldn't do it anyway," Julia chimed in. "James said there probably wouldn't be any scandals at the masquerade. I was disappointed," she admitted. "I'd love to see a real scandal taking place, wouldn't you?"

Lady Irving shook her head. "They're not as much fun as you think, my girl. Now, which of you wants to be Helen of Troy, and which wants to be the fortuneteller?"

In the end, Louisa got the gracefully draped Classical costume, and Julia garbed herself as the fortuneteller in Lady Irving's brightest red silk gown, matching turban, and heavy gold jewelry. Her aunt had been somewhat offended by the idea of having her finest clothing used as a costume, but Julia had won her over by explaining that she had no idea what a fortuneteller actually looked like, and if anyone couldn't guess who she was and had to ask, she could just say she was going as a countess.

"Make it a duchess," Lady Irving had corrected her. "That's one of my best gold sets you're wearing."

As for the countess's own costume, she covered her green gown in a black silk domino and called it complete. "Costumes are for ninnies," she scoffed, then, seeing her nieces' crestfallen faces, corrected herself. "Ninnies, and the young."

James was to dine with them before the masquerade, then escort them to Lord Xavier's home for the event. As the time for his arrival drew near, Julia found herself growing unaccountably excited. Well, not really unaccountably—it was her first real *ton* event, after all. Her aunt could belittle it for being small and informal, but to Julia, this was her real debut into London society.

When she thought of it like that, it was actually a bit

nerve-wracking. She was glad she already knew all of the Bradleigh daughters and had made a friend in Charissa. And, of course, she would gain courage from walking in with her aunt, her sister, and James.

James. She hadn't seen him since they'd crossed paths in Bond Street several days earlier. It had been so good to see him, better even than she had expected, though she had been a bit dismayed to be able to talk so little with him. She'd felt self-conscious speaking to him in front of Charissa, afraid that her friend's sharp gray eyes would see things they shouldn't, or that she herself would say something she ought not. It was getting harder and harder to keep that proper friendly tone with James; to keep everything light and casual and show him no hint of what she was really feeling. Which she knew she shouldn't be feeling anyway.

She actually had been thankful that Charissa had dominated the conversation with James. That was often the way when she was around Charissa, actually. On the positive side, you never had to think of anything to say, which might come in very handy tonight if she was faced with an intimidating crowd of the wealthy and titled. But when Julia was with James, she always had something she wanted to say. Often too many things.

Her mind was jittery and full, returning always to Christmas. She had thought so often of his hand on her shoulder, his deep green eyes heavy with the weight of his family's good name, that the memories had become threadbare. Since then, he'd given her no other sign that she was special to him. He'd happily listened while Charissa nattered away about nothing. He'd never tried again to speak to her alone, to return to the confidence they'd shared while their relatives played whist by the firelight.

But why should he? And why should she continue to hope and wish?

Trying desperately to turn her mind to a different topic, she paced around the house. Perhaps if her feet moved fast enough, her thoughts would stand still. She must have stomped through every room in her gaudy red gown, but if anything she only felt more agitated. She finally wound up in the library, where she sat in a chair opposite Louisa.

Louisa looked wonderful, as always. The clean lines of her belted toga emphasized her long, lean form, and her carefully coiled Classical hairstyle was only a few curls away from her usual stylish coiffure. Next to her, Julia felt like a tomato.

They were going to the masquerade as Helen of Troy, the most beautiful woman in the world, and a little puffy red tomato.

"I'm a tomato," she grumbled.

"Sorry?" Louisa looked up from her book, puzzled.

"I said, I'm a tomato," Julia repeated. "You look beautiful. I look terrible. And I'm the one who's supposed to find a husband." Her stomach churned at the very idea.

"You don't look terrible," Louisa assured her, laying aside her book at once. "You look lovely. I've never seen you in red before, but it actually suits you quite well. The turban's not my favorite," she admitted, "but it's a costume, after all."

"I just want everything to go well tonight," Julia replied, swinging her feet with nervous energy.

"It will, I promise. Please try to relax and not worry too much about this evening. It's really not a big event."

"But it is," Julia said anxiously. "What if my future husband is there tonight, and he thinks I look like a tomato, so he doesn't even try to obtain an introduction?"

Louisa raised a skeptical eyebrow at Julia and fixed her with a what-on-earth-are-you-going-on-about expression. So Julia tried to explain. It was difficult, since she couldn't tell Louisa the truth about her feelings, and she could barely make sense of her own thoughts anymore these days.

"It's just . . . I've seen how well things worked out for you, and how you met this wonderful man and you're going to get married, and that's why you came to London. And I came to London to make that happen, too. We didn't expect to come so early, and most people aren't here yet, but some people are, and you never know who the right person will be. And I sort of think I would just *know* when I saw my future husband, but he might not know me, and I just feel like I really ought to be looking my best and having everything go well tonight. And looking like a tomato is not the way to do it," she finished breathlessly.

Louisa considered her words. "All right, I can understand what you're worried about. But I think you're romanticizing this far too much."

"How can I romanticize *courtship* too much?" Julia asked, incredulous.

"Courtship?" Louisa said with a dry laugh. "Is that what you'd call it? I suppose *technically* that's what it is, when a gentleman determines a young woman is the appropriate combination of brains, beauty, and money— not necessarily in that order. I suppose it's *technically* courtship when he then pays several rigorously supervised visits, brings suitable gifts, and eventually, after an appropriate amount of time has elapsed so that he is no longer a total stranger, makes an offer. But there is really not very much of romance in the process at all."

Julia stared at Louisa, thunderstruck. She felt as if

Louisa had slapped her; she'd never heard such acid in her sister's voice. "Is that really what it was like for you?" Her voice came out in a choked whisper.

Louisa immediately looked contrite. "No, no. Of course not. I mean, James and I weren't a love match, but we certainly were able to make our own decision. I agreed to marry James because it's what I wanted to do at the time."

The full import of these words took a moment to sink in, and Julia's skin prickled as if touched by ice. "You mean, you don't love him?"

Louisa sighed, her lovely face shuttered. "I doubt very much if most *ton* marriages involve love at the time they're contracted. But I do like him very much, and I respect and admire him. I believe I will come to love him someday. And even if I don't, we'll deal together well enough."

She bit her lip. "I'm sorry if I said too much. I shouldn't have dampened your excitement. Believe it or not, I meant to be reassuring."

Julia was still reeling, trying to take in all of Louisa's admissions at once. "Reassuring?" she repeated in disbelief. How was she supposed to feel reassured, when Louisa and James—positively the best woman and man in the world—were engaged to one another, and Louisa's heart was no more touched than if she were buying a horse?

Louisa nodded. "Yes; you know, to tell you that there's some logic behind the process as well. It isn't all passion and thunderbolts. There's careful thought involved. Which means, if your future husband's there tonight, he'll want you even if you look like a tomato." She smiled. "Which you don't."

Julia nodded back to show her acceptance of her

sister's explanation, but disappointment weighed on her even more than her dratted turban had been weighing on her head. "I suppose that makes sense. I just . . . was hoping for some passion and thunderbolts, that's all."

Louisa stood and hugged Julia where she sat in her chair. "There may well be for you. I hope you'll have it all."

She seemed suddenly struck by an idea and sat back down with uncharacteristic haste. "What *would* you like in a husband, Julia? Maybe we can be logical about it, too, rather than just waiting to see which men come your way. Think of the qualities you'd like, and James and I can help to sort possible suitors for you."

Julia shook her head furiously, heedless of her carefully placed turban. "I don't think I'd feel comfortable having James know what I want in a husband."

All the qualities she wanted instantly came to mind—kind heart, clever eyes, ready laugh, sandy hair, loving with children—and she clamped her lips together tight in case any of the treacherous words should try to leak out.

"Nonsense; who better?" Louisa insisted. "He knows everyone in London, he knows you, and he likes you and will have an eye out for your best interests. Now, what would you like?"

"You make it sound as if I'm ordering dinner from the cook," Julia muttered, but settled back in her chair to think. She supposed she could at least humor her sister for a few minutes. Otherwise Louisa might wonder why Julia was being so obstinate.

"Well," she began slowly, choosing her words with great care, "I'd want him to be kind, of course. He must be kind. And financially solvent. I don't mean wealthy; just not in debt, and not with any rakish habits like gambling problems. And I'd like him to have a sense of humor, and be good-looking, and like children. Oh, and be punctual."

"Punctual?" Louisa teased. "Up with the chickens every morning?"

"No, not exactly that. I guess I mean reliable. I want him to be there for me when he says he will. Literally as well as figuratively."

A knock sounded on the door of the library, and Simone peeped her head in to announce the arrival of "the young viscount fiancé gentleman."

Louisa smiled bracingly at Julia. "There we are, perfect timing. Ready to eat?"

"Absolutely," Julia replied promptly, rising. "Always."

It was a lie; her stomach still roiled with nervousness, but it wouldn't do to tell Louisa about that. If she wasn't in the mood for a meal, Louisa would instantly suspect something was wrong.

"And are you ready to place your order for a husband?"

Julia shook her head. "That I feel less ready for."

"Come on," Louisa pleaded. "Please let us help you. I want you to have all the fun I wanted for myself last year and didn't have. I want lovely men to flock to you."

"All I want is one," Julia replied.

At the familiar twinge of guilt and longing, she paused in her walk, thinking. She felt as if she were on the edge of something important.

If she agreed with Louisa's scheme, she would start something new. She would open her eyes to a new world, full of potentially exciting people. But she would also close off the possibility of something else, something deep and comforting and real. Her ideal; her chosen love.

But that had never been a possibility anyway. It was time to let that go.

Even though Louisa had admitted she didn't love him.

Julia nodded desperately to clear that thought from her mind. "Very well, I'll do it."

"You mean it?" Louisa clapped her hands together in excitement.

"Yes," Julia said, covering her uncertainty with a shaky laugh. "Let's order a husband for me, and let's find him."

Chapter 16

In Which the Viscount Is Unhelpfully Helpful

James, ever appreciative of the absurd, showed what he thought was a very reasonable amount of delight when Julia and Louisa informed him, on the way to the masquerade, of the "husband order" they had determined to place for Julia. He promised, dutifully, but with a rebellious twinkle in his eye, to help root out someone first-rate for her.

This casual attitude offended Lady Irving.

"I think it's a very sensible idea," she barked. "Julia's got her eyes open. A young miss *ought* to have her eyes open when she's sorting through a lot of riffraff, which today's young men are." After a long pause, she grudgingly added, "Present company excluded, I suppose."

"How charming you always are, my lady," James said with a grin. "Such great age brings great wisdom as well."

And thus, with the score tied one to one between the

countess and the viscount, the party entered Xavier House.

Lady Irving ran on ahead, crowing about finding Lord Xavier and getting together a "spirited" and "fun" game of whist for "real stakes," which her relatives now knew was likely to involve some shockingly deep play. For James, the fun began not with cards, but when his old acquaintance Freddie Pellington darted up to the remaining three members of the party and pumped the viscount's hand energetically.

"Dash it, old boy, it's dashed good to see you. Damme, I didn't know you were back in town. Thought you'd run off to the country for good. Back in London already, though, ain't you?"

"Yes, here I am, as you see," James replied patiently, accepting Pellington's energetic clap on the back. Freddie Pellington was a kind enough young man, but definitely not the brightest fellow of his acquaintance.

And that's when his brilliant idea struck.

He couldn't say he had relished the idea of helping Julia find a man. The idea of systematically searching for a husband had seemed amusing enough when she and Louisa had first revealed their scheme, but it hadn't sat all that well with him once he had a chance to mull it over. He was just supposed to help sell her off? Never mind that it was to be to someone who was kind, funny, handsome, wealthy, warm-hearted, et cetera, et cetera. If such a paragon existed—which was doubtful—why on earth would James ever want to spend any time around him? He would feel positively inferior, and honestly, he would probably want to slug the fellow in the teeth for making eyes at Julia.

He couldn't just refuse to cooperate with his fiancée's request, though. However . . . he realized now that he could honor the letter of the request, if not the spirit. He would find Julia exactly the type of man she had requested in a husband. No less, but certainly no more.

He felt better already.

"My dear Louisa—Julia—please allow me to introduce the Honorable Frederic Pellington," he said triumphantly, then introduced the ladies to the young man in return. With a speaking look to both women, James added, "He's a very *kind* man. Aren't you, Freddie?"

"Charmed, charmed," burbled Pellington as he made his bow to the ladies. "Any friend of Matheson's, you know. Friend of mine. Happy to meet you." James's words seemed to sink in just then, and he continued, "Dash it, Matheson, no need to go on about me. Always try to be kind and whatnot, but you know, definitely a man of the world."

James nudged Julia significantly and nodded to drive the point home unmistakably. Her eyes widened in surprise, and she darted a quick look at him, as if to say, *Really?*

He supposed he couldn't blame her for being suspicious. Perhaps he'd stretched the limits of her credulity too much by presenting her with Pellington right off. The man was usually a positive pink of the *ton*, but tonight he had gone all out for the masquerade in what appeared to be the makeshift costume of a pasha. He was wearing a gold waistcoat with an untucked shirt under it for modesty's sake, extremely baggy purple trousers, and—most unfortunate of all—a scarlet turban exactly like the one Julia was wearing.

Oh well, it was worth a try to throw the two together. If Julia gave him the slightest opening, Pellington would talk her ear off all evening and she'd never have the opportunity even to look at another man. And then she'd be safe from suitors for the night, because, honestly, there wasn't a chance in the world she'd take that rather dim fellow seriously as a possible husband.

Finally, Julia replied to Pellington, and James knew she had taken the bait. "How . . . how nice to meet you," she faltered, making her curtsy. "I think your costume is very interesting."

Pellington's eyes blinked wide open, and a bright smile spread across his face. "Do you really? Dashed kind of you, I must say. I wasn't sure about it myself, but Xavier insisted on fancy dress. Never fond of a costume in the common way, but decided I'd get a bit creative this time. All among friends here, you know; just a very small gathering."

"Pellington's wealthy, too," James added ruthlessly. "*And* he's fond of children."

"Are you really?" Julia replied weakly, shooting another are-you-sure-about-this look at James, which he met with his brightest, most open smile. All right, maybe it was more of a grin.

"Oh, well, dash it, Matheson," Pellington replied, blushing. "Haven't got any children myself, of course; not that type of a fellow. But someday, you know, and all that. Always liked them. Seem like nice little creatures. Have quite a knack with them, actually."

A memory struck him. "Did you know you can soothe a baby with brandy? I mean, it always works to settle me, but I wouldn't have thought a baby would have a taste for it. But I tried it on my brother's baby when he was fussing—the baby, I mean—and the little fellow took to it dashed fondly."

"You . . . gave brandy to a baby?" Julia said weakly, unable to entirely suppress an expression of horror from her face. She looked even paler than usual under her shocking red turban, the heavy weight of which was already beginning to shift to one side. Blinking in agitation, she shoved it back into place absently, wreaking unwitting havoc on Simone's careful hairpinning.

Louisa, meanwhile, used the cover of the long, gauzy folds of her Classical dress to grind one delicately slippered foot onto James's boot. His boot was thick enough that he could hardly feel it, but he still got the idea. All right, time to salvage the situation.

"Pellington was just joking, weren't you?" He shot a significant look at the costume-clad gentleman.

"What? Joking? No indeed," that young man replied, completely missing the sub rosa meaning of James's glance. "Mind you, didn't give the baby very much. Only a few drops. Although," he confessed, "his mother caught me at it, and she was dashed angry. Made me swear not to do it again. Can't see why, because it worked like a charm. But promised her anyway."

He smiled ingenuously. "Always want to keep a female happy, you know.

"I say," he continued, another thought seizing him, "have you met our host yet? I'd be dashed glad to introduce you, if you'd permit me the honor."

He seemed to come back to an awareness of his surroundings then, and added, "Dash it, Matheson, would you mind if I took Miss Herington off your hands? I'd consider it quite an honor. Love to show her around and take her to Xavier and whatnot."

Without daring to look at Julia for fear his face would crack into a laugh, James nodded and waved the pair away. "I leave her in your capable hands, Pellington. It's very *kind* of you."

Julia looked back at them once, desperately, as Freddie Pellington bore her off. James could overhear him saying, as they walked, "Went to school with Matheson, you know. Dashed good fellow. Bit of a stick, though. Didn't even come in costume. So you really do like mine?"

That had worked better even than he had hoped; James reflected that he must have more of a talent for machinations than he'd known. There was absolutely no way Julia would be meeting any potential husbands tonight. He supposed the thought ought to make him ashamed, since it went against the express wishes of the two gently bred ladies who had asked for his help.

But it didn't. He felt positively triumphant. And maybe a bit jealous, too; after all, Pellington still got to bear Julia away and keep her company for the evening.

James's reverie was interrupted by another surprisingly hearty stomp on his foot by his fiancée.

Oh—his fiancée. He realized he'd been impolite to Louisa, more even than she knew, and his sense of satisfaction melted into chagrin.

"Really." Louisa looked at him reproachfully as soon as she was sure Pellington and Julia were out of earshot. "That was unkind of you, James."

"Un*kind*?" he repeated, unable to resist. "All right, maybe he's not exactly the type of man she's looking for. But he really is everything she asked for in a husband."

Louisa continued to stare at him as if he were an idiot.

He folded his arms and looked back at his fiancée defensively. "He *is*. That's what she gets for not specifying intelligence." He knew it was a childish response, but he was feeling a bit childish right now.

Louisa rolled her eyes. "Fine. Please add 'intelligence' to the list of qualities Julia is looking for in a husband."

James sighed. She had him cornered there. If Julia had ever managed to escape Pellington's verbal cage, he'd had a string of vapid young time-wasters in mind to keep her occupied throughout the evening. Now he might have to think of someone she might actually like, or Louisa would see through him in a second.

In fact, she already seemed to be seeing through him with uncomfortable clarity. "What are you doing, James? You know perfectly well Pellington isn't the sort of man who'd make her a good husband. Why even encourage her to spend any time with him, beyond a courteous introduction?"

"He's not a bad fellow," he replied, somewhat lamely. "And she seemed interested in him."

"She was being *polite*," Louisa replied, smiling sweetly for the sake of appearances in case anyone might be watching them, but with gritted teeth. "Which, by the way, is the only quality that is keeping me from kicking you behind the knee and making your legs buckle, right here in the drawing room of Xavier House."

At James's startled look, she explained logically, "Well, I can hardly kick you in the shin. My slippers are far too soft; I'd hurt my foot more than I'd hurt you."

"Your point is taken," James said calmly. "I promise to introduce her only to the finest men in England from this point forward."

Inside, however, he was seething *just* a little. Why should Louisa assume that he'd be willing to go along with this harebrained scheme of theirs? Who ever heard of ordering a husband like a Christmas dinner, anyway? He felt like he was the poor goose in question, pursued, caught, and roasted. These women were using him.

To be fair, Julia was to be family, so he supposed they thought his close relationship to her would make him willing to help with any favor they deemed necessary. And it should; it really should.

Except this one was difficult for him. Unexpectedly

difficult. He knew it shouldn't be. After all, he wasn't permitting himself to think of Julia in anything but the most friendly, casual way. Usually.

He decided to drop that line of thought and just try to enjoy the rest of the evening. He tossed the end of his cape over one arm—despite Pellington's assertion, he *had* come in a costume, albeit a cursory one of a domino over his usual evening clothes—and offered Louisa his arm. He might be a goose, but he need not act like a pig as well.

"Come along, my dear. Let's see who else is here."

Louisa came with him willingly enough, and over the next few hours they spoke at least a little with nearly everyone at the gathering. Lord Xavier was the first person they sought out, of course, to pay their respects.

This young gentleman, dressed as a Georgian of their grandparents' generation in powdered wig and knee breeches, with a black mask over his eyes, was regaling a group of bachelor friends with a decidedly improper story involving an opera dancer, a bottle of champagne, and a pineapple. James was interested in hearing the ending of it, but the young man stopped the tale as soon as he saw Louisa.

"Ah, you must be the Honorable Miss Oliver," he transitioned smoothly, making his bow and kissing her hand. He lifted his mask to his forehead to remove any obstruction to his vision. "How enchanting to meet you at last. Or should I call you"—he cast his eyes up and down her form, taking in the details of her costume—"the goddess Diana, perhaps?"

"Lord Xavier." She curtsied. "The honor is all on my side. And Helen of Troy was the intention, though I suppose that's a bit presumptuous for any woman. Diana is equally flattering and will certainly do very well."

She smiled knowingly, skeptical of his flattering tones, and James felt proud to be escorting her. She *could* hold her own socially, he knew it. See how the young men who had been speaking with Xavier were now looking at her? They gaped at her, dazzled by her Classical beauty, as if she truly were the goddess he had called her.

"Xavier," James acknowledged his friend. "Thank you for the invitation tonight. Are you portraying our ailing, lamented king in his youth?"

"The Sun King, rather, I think," Xavier drawled. "Our George never enjoyed wine, women, and song nearly so much as did Louis the Fourteenth. You could hardly expect me to portray a *dull* creature, now could you?"

He smiled, slow and dangerous and lewd, and Louisa drew in her breath sharply. Was she indignant? James, mindful of his duty to safeguard her from impropriety, nodded to his friend and thanked him again, drawing her away from the group of men.

"I don't suppose he would do for Julia," Louisa whispered in his ear, casting a dubious glance back over her shoulder as they walked away. "That look he gave me— I felt positively undressed. It was very uncomfortable."

"No," James said shortly. "He wouldn't do." Behind him, he heard the Sun King resume the tale about the pineapple. He looked back to see his old acquaintance's eyes still on Louisa, thoughtful and dark, even as he held his friends spellbound with his bawdy story. "He definitely would not do at all."

"He's a friend of yours, though?" she asked doubtfully, a worried crease between her brows.

"Yes, he is," James replied. "We grew up together, as Pellington and I did. I don't know that I've got all that much in common with either of them anymore. Xavier's a bit younger than I, and still very wild. He came into an enormous fortune at an early age and seems to be doing his best to run through it in any number of creative ways."

"He's quite handsome, though," Louisa mused. "And obviously very intelligent."

Handsome, James would grant, though it seemed odd to think that about another man. But he knew the lean, dark looks of Alexander Edgware, Lord Xavier, appealed to many women—as did his air of barely curbed wildness. And he was intelligent, too; he could read people with uncanny swiftness, he always rose the winner from a game of cards or chance, and he could be very quickwitted, even uncomfortably so.

However . . .

"He's not kind enough," James informed her. "Not for Julia. Of the two, she'd be much better off with Pellington."

Louisa shuddered. "Then we obviously need to find a third possibility for her."

As it turned out, Julia found that third possibility herself. Pellington had steered her around the room and into a smaller side salon, introducing her in his fractured, enthusiastic style to several of his acquaintances. At the moment James and Louisa reencountered them, they were speaking in the smaller room with Sir Stephen Saville, a baronet in his mid thirties.

"Damnation," James said when he saw them, ignoring Louisa's gasp at his unguarded language.

Pellington was hovering around Julia and the baronet as they sat on a sofa, interjecting frequent comments that were mostly ignored by the other two. Sir Stephen, wearing a simple black domino with its accompanying mask flipped up atop his head rather than over his face, was staring spellbound at Julia, holding onto her every word as if it were a gem, plying her with questions whenever her conversation wound down. Julia, for her part, was chattering away merrily to the older gentleman, darting occasional replies to Pellington and frequently shoving her slipping turban back into place atop her now-untidy hair.

"This looks much more promising," Louisa commented in James's ear. "Who's that with Julia and Pellington?"

"Sir Stephen Saville," he replied shortly, unable to keep all his annoyance out of his voice. "Widower. Childless. Lives in Surrey much of the time. Known to be on the lookout for another wife."

"Kind?"

"Yes, if you like stuffiness."

"Intelligent?" Louisa asked, ignoring his editorial comment.

"Yes, I suppose. We're looking together at a parcel of land near his estate; I rather thought I could learn something about hog farming from him," James admitted.

"Really," said Louisa, and James could almost hear the wheels turning in her head. "So, financially solvent, too."

"Yes," James reluctantly admitted. "He is."

"Well, then, I think our search is over. Probably the best thing you or I can do is leave them alone," she decided.

"I want to hear what they're saying," James protested, and tugged Louisa's arm. He couldn't help himself. What was Julia saying that had the older man so transfixed?

"A kitchenmaid or scullery maid only wants a bit of kindness," she was telling the baronet at the moment they drew closer. "I do understand that the poor creatures can tend to be skittish, but a housekeeper or cook who shouts will only make matters worse. Why, we haven't had a single broken dish since we gave the cook a raise in wages and added an extra scullery maid at Stonemeadows. The cook is so much happier now, and the maids are, too."

All right, James thought with relief; so at least it was hardly romantic.

Sir Stephen, however, reacted as warmly as if Julia had stripped off her clothes right in front of him. (There was another of those thoughts he ought not to be having, James reminded himself; not even when thinking in similes.) More warmly, in fact, considering the man's well-known sense of propriety.

"Really?" the baronet replied, astounded. "So you take quite an interest in the staffing of a household, then?" He looked at Julia as if she were delicious, and he were starving. (There, nothing improper about that simile, James thought to himself.)

Unable to help himself, he cleared his throat loudly to draw their attention to his presence, ignoring another of Louisa's discreet stomps on his foot.

Julia turned at once, and beamed at him. "Hello there," she said. "I wondered where you'd got to. Have you two met Sir Stephen Saville?"

"Indeed, I have had the honor of long acquaintance with his lordship," the baronet explained, standing to acknowledge the arrival of the domino-clad viscount and Helen of Troy.

James took his cue to present Louisa, who responded to her introduction to Sir Stephen with more warmth than James had almost ever seen her display. She was almost . . . effusive.

Lady Charissa Bradleigh bounced up just then, saving

James from having to decide how to respond to what seemed to him a horribly obvious attempt on Louisa's part to throw Julia together with a man who was patently much too old for her, and much too dull. Even if he did, technically, have all the qualities she was looking for in a husband—well, damn it, the fellow simply wasn't *right* for her.

Charissa demanded all their attention at once. "Oh, do come," she gasped, without greeting or preface. "Lord Xavier has *promised* that we may have dancing, *and* that there will be a waltz!"

In fact, couples were already beginning to trickle into formation for a country dance, right there in Lord Xavier's drawing room. James sighed with annoyance; this was just perfect. Sir Stephen would ask Julia to dance, and his regard would be absolutely cemented once he had her all to himself for another half hour. Any man's would be.

His sigh drew Charissa's large gray eyes to him. "Ah, Lord Matheson!" she burbled brightly. "Don't you intend to dance?" She batted her eyelashes at him with what he supposed was meant to be appealing flirtatiousness.

"Yes, of course," he said hurriedly, with a speaking look to Louisa. Without a word, she accepted his hand, and he led her to the bottom of the forming row of couples.

"Thank you for that," he said in a low tone as they waited for the dance to begin. Sure enough, Julia and Sir Stephen were right behind them, followed by the determined young Lady Charissa dragging a cheerfully protesting Freddie Pellington by the elbow.

"For what?" she asked, puzzled.

"Coming to dance with me," he prompted. "Getting

me away from . . . ah, you know," he indicated Charissa with an incline of the head. He didn't add, but thought to himself, that perhaps he did owe the energetic earl's daughter a debt of gratitude for interrupting the world's coziest conversation between Julia and Sir Boring. Sir Much Too Old for Her. Sir Stick in the Mud.

The fact that such thoughts were beneath the dignity of a grown man, and a viscount no less, did nothing to temper his desire to boot the baronet out of Lord Xavier's house.

Louisa replied to his thankful admission with a quiet smile. "Isn't it my duty to follow where you lead?" she replied wryly.

And before he even tried to wrap his head around what *that* might mean, the music began, and the dance separated them.

The night ended late, with much more dancing followed by a spirited and not precisely proper game of charades. Lord Xavier had apparently determined all the clues with the help of several other eager young gentlemen, because the company found itself acting out "Madame de Pompadour," "Mrs. Fitzherbert," "Nell Gwyn," and a series of other royal mistresses. Lord Xavier's eyes glittered with amusement at the young ladies, especially, as they attempted to create a tableau that would reveal the answer without compromising propriety.

James thought this not quite well done of the man, but had to admit that he himself seemed to be the only gentleman, besides Sir Stephen, of course, not laughing uproariously and having an excellent time. Good Lord, he had never expected to be in company with Sir

Tedious. Maybe he really was sobering up now that he was an engaged man.

Thinking of his engagement, as his party began hunting for Lady Irving in preparation for their departure at the end of the night, he had the uncomfortable feeling that he might not have done right by Louisa on this evening. She had asked him for his help, and he had given it only grudgingly. She hadn't seemed to think his behavior odd, but he wondered if *she* wondered why he'd acted that way.

Honestly, he wondered why as well. Why couldn't he just let Julia go, to find a kind, intelligent, et cetera, et cetera man who would treat her well, as she deserved? Didn't she deserve to be as happy as Louisa?

Ah, as happy as Louisa.

Now how happy was that? He couldn't help but wonder, as he watched her calm, expressionless face, her eyes searching the crowd in the drawing room for her aunt's familiar bobbing ostrich plumes. He had absolutely no idea how happy she was. But he certainly hadn't helped matters with his reluctance to fall in with her husband-finding scheme. He hoped she wouldn't look too deeply into his reasons, and he would try not to either.

Lady Irving made her appearance from a second side salon, followed by several other card players. She was holding the corner of her black domino in front of her to create a makeshift pouch for her winnings.

"Forgot my blasted reticule," she explained. "Look what I've won, though; I skinned Sylvia Alleyneham alive tonight. The poor woman's never had a head for whist," she added gleefully.

"Aunt," Julia said sweetly, coming up next to James, "isn't it *vulgar* to display your winnings like that?"

James grinned, unable to resist Lady Irving's non-plussed expression. After a frozen moment, she barked, "For you it would be. Don't you worry about me, though, young miss. I'd like to see the person who would call *me* vulgar."

"I think you just did," James replied. Her ladyship's annoyed harrumph of reply was more beautiful in his ears than any music could have been.

That was why he didn't want to introduce Julia around. Fulfill her list of requirements though he might, Sir Stephen would never, never appreciate her sense of humor.

Not like he did.

Damnation, there was another one of those thoughts.

Chapter 17

In Which, Alas, There Is No Man-Tree

Louisa sat musing in the library, heavy-eyed from lack of sleep, the morning after the masquerade. It was barely eight o'clock, and the party had only returned to the Grosvenor Square address five hours before. It was so early, in fact, that the tentative winter sun barely cast any light into the room. Louisa hadn't bothered to ring for a fire to be lit, so the room was dim and quite cold.

She didn't mind the weak light, and she hardly noticed the room's temperature. She sat in a huddle on her aunt's swooping Grecian sofa, lost in thought. She had, she realized, a great many things to think about.

First and foremost, she was beginning to see that Julia didn't need her here, after all. Perhaps she hadn't given her sister enough credit. Perhaps she'd drawn too much upon her own miserable experience in London and assumed that Julia's would be the same.

But good heavens, Julia hadn't needed her help with anything. She'd gotten the most desirable *modiste* in town to dress her, without even trying; she'd made friends, even if they were a bit silly; she'd seen more of London already than Louisa had seen in her entire season.

And now, it seemed, she had a kind, handsome, intelligent, reliable, and financially solvent man—a man who was everything she said she wanted—displaying honorable interest in her. It was why Julia had come to London, to find such a man, and the season hadn't even begun.

So much for Julia. What about James, then? Louisa mused, curling herself into a smaller ball as she considered the other person for whom she had come to London.

Well, what about him? She had told Julia that courtship was a matter of logic, so she might as well be logical about this.

James was unfailingly gentlemanly to her. She saw him often. He liked her family quite a bit, and he certainly gave their aunt tit for tat, for which Louisa thought Lady Irving rather admired him.

His family had become more polite as well; Louisa even had a standing weekly engagement to take tea with them. The invitation had been extended by his sister, who was thawing out noticeably. Given time, Louisa thought, she and Gloria might come to be friends.

But time—time was the problem. How much time did she have to give? Or *want* to give, for that matter? How much time would she give herself to feel right about her decision to marry James? Was she ready to give a lifetime?

Families aside—how did she and James *really* feel about each other?

She tried to curl up even more tightly, but she had reached the limits of how small she could make her long form. She wasn't ready to think about the answers to those questions, especially not the last. She might read a lot of novels, but she had always tried to be a sensible girl, and it would hardly be sensible to jeopardize her standing as one of the luckiest girls of last year's season.

If she just wasn't so tired, maybe everything would make more sense. And so, very sensibly, she went back upstairs to her bedchamber, and did her utmost to fall asleep, until she heard others moving about the house and could get up again.

Naturally, Sir Stephen called later that day, bearing a bunch of snowdrops "as fresh and dainty as are you, Miss Herington, if you'll permit my saying so."

Julia was willing to permit this statement, although it seemed a bit . . . well, *flowery*, to be honest. But she couldn't help being flattered; she'd never had a man give her flowers before.

She had liked talking to Sir Stephen the evening before. He'd been interesting to talk to, unlike Freddie Pellington—who, though she supposed he really was as kind as James had promised, couldn't seem to make anything come out of his mouth that didn't involve at least two "dash its" and one "old fellow." But Sir Stephen had talked with her about household management, and actually seemed to care about what she said and thought. He'd listened, which she knew from long experience with her head-in-the-clouds stepfather Lord Oliver was something that many men just didn't do. James did, of course, but James was unusual.

Anyway, she was glad to see Sir Stephen again, and he was just as interesting to talk to as he had been the evening before. Julia could talk for any length of time about household matters or her family, and she was delighted to be encouraged to do just this by a new acquaintance.

True, there was that one hitch in the conversation, when she made a mild joke about her young siblings running her down to within an inch of her life. Sir Stephen had blinked at her in concern, and asked if she were "able to apportion herself sufficient time to recuperate from her charges' enthusiastic behavior, in order to maintain her good health."

Then it was Julia's turn to blink, and reel through the lengthy words to figure out what he had asked her.

"Oh," she finally replied after she had parsed the sentence. "Yes, it's fine. I, ah, didn't mean it literally."

"Ah," Sir Stephen said, enlightened. "You were being hyperbolic." He smiled appreciatively. "I understand perfectly."

Julia just nodded, puzzled. Didn't the man understand a simple figure of speech? Well, he did now—he knew she was being "hyperbolic." But still, it was odd to be taken so literally. So *seriously.* A girl appreciated the attention and everything, but there were limits.

However, she brushed it aside, and they passed the remainder of a very proper twenty-minute visit under the lax chaperonage of Lady Irving, who kept "forgetting" items that she needed and leaving the room to retrieve them.

Sir Stephen commented that it was a shame to have her ladyship's industry so often interrupted, and he did hope it didn't make Julia feel uncomfortable to be left alone with him even momentarily. He even offered to stand outside the door until Lady Irving should return to the drawing room. Julia assured him this wasn't necessary, after which statement he looked at her with concern and said that he only had her reputation in mind.

"Yes, well, I certainly appreciate that," Julia replied patiently, "but I assure you, my aunt will return in just a moment."

After that they fell silent, a bit constrained. When Lady Irving did return, the baronet stood and took his very proper leave of both ladies. He asked if he might call again, and before Julia could even reply, her ladyship jumped in with a dazzling smile.

"But of *course*, Sir Stephen, we'd be simply *delighted* to have you. Please come *anytime*."

And with that reassurance, their male caller left with a smile on his face.

Lady Irving turned at once to Julia and hissed, "Next time, make good use of the opportunity when I leave the room. Wealthy, single gentlemen don't grow on trees, you know."

Julia rolled her eyes. "Yes, I *know* that, Aunt. There's no man-tree for husband-grubbing maidens such as myself. I know why I'm here, I promise. But what would you have me do, jump in his lap? Honestly, I think he'd leave in terror." Not to mention she didn't really want to jump in his lap.

As soon as the words left her mouth, she knew they had been a mistake. Lady Irving always considered even the most outrageous "hyperbolic statements" with the same level of seriousness she gave to the selection of her silk turban each morning. Which was a surprisingly high level of seriousness.

"Jumping into his lap . . . it's not a bad idea," the countess now replied thoughtfully. "Good girl. I wasn't sure you had it in you. Mind you, though, I'm not saying that's right for Saville. He's keen on propriety, and it might put him off. But if he doesn't come up to scratch, that would work like a charm with most other young gentlemen."

"Wouldn't it make them think I was fast? You know, like a lady bird?" Julia asked doubtfully.

"Don't say 'lady bird,'" Lady Irving admonished. "It's vulgar. Where did you ever learn about lady birds, anyway?"

Julia had to think about this one. "Maybe I heard you mention them?"

"Hmmph." Her aunt looked skeptical. "Possible, but it's unladylike to talk about. For a young miss, that is. I can say whatever I want. Just you keep in mind the difference between an unmarried lady and a widow, my girl— especially a wealthy widow."

Julia dutifully promised to keep the difference in mind, though she wasn't exactly sure why there was such a large gulf between what was permitted for a lady unmarried and a lady married. Wasn't a maiden allowed to have a brain in her head? She was beginning to wonder. Her aunt had certainly told her that any number of her phrases and behaviors were vulgar or unladylike since coming to town. She'd have to watch herself carefully, she was beginning to realize, especially when the *ton* started streaming back to London in greater numbers to begin the season in earnest.

She sighed. She couldn't help missing Stonemeadows when she felt London pinching away at her like this. And sure enough—

"It's unladylike to sigh," Lady Irving replied automatically. "You'll be wanting to avoid that type of thing when you're around Sir Stephen."

No, actually, she wasn't sure that she would.

Several weeks trickled by, weeks in which James and Sir Stephen were frequent callers at the Grosvenor

Square address. Sometimes both of them came at once and squired her and Louisa around the city. During these outings, they inevitably began with Louisa and James paired, leaving Julia to accompany Sir Stephen.

She supposed he was nice enough, but his intense seriousness began to pall on her, and his eager interest in her every word was intimidating. She felt she had to weigh each word with care lest it be misinterpreted, which was an undeniable hardship for a girl used more to speaking in paragraphs than sentences.

Whenever she could, she tried to break the stride of the foursome as they walked out together—by stumbling, staring into a shop window, whatever it took—so that she could try to switch their grouping around and walk with James. She felt a tiny bit guilty leaving Louisa with the baronet, but Louisa never admonished her for it. And anyway, Louisa got to see James all the time, while Julia did not.

In truth, Julia hardly ever saw James anymore, since she was out so much of the time with Charissa Bradleigh, or paying the requisite morning calls with her aunt. Between the efforts of those two aristocratic ladies, she was learning more and more about the ins and outs of London society as the wealthy and titled, bit by bit, straggled back to town from their country estates.

She had never expected to be kept so busy, and with such a series of inconsequentialities. Some days she came home late, exhausted, and couldn't think of a single memorable thing she had done. She didn't mind it, she supposed, since she knew it was the reason for her being in London. But more and more, she understood why Louisa's spirits had been lowered by the relentless social beating each day brought. Julia *liked* talking to a lot of people, and still, it was tiring.

So, she and James rarely crossed paths now. No one seemed to think it at all necessary that she should ever get to spend any time in the company of her sister's fiancé. It was much more important that she meet powerful strangers, or undergo yet another dress fitting, or be seen driving out in Hyde Park with someone or other, by someone or other.

And she supposed it wasn't such a social necessity that she see James . . . but she missed him, anyway. He was a necessity to *her*. Even though she'd promised to look for a husband, she thought about him more than she cared to tell anyone. It felt like a secret she ought to keep, even though she couldn't think of the last time she'd kept a secret, especially from Louisa. The knowledge of her hidden fixation preoccupied her, putting a feeling of distance between her and Louisa.

So passed the remainder of January, and the grayness of February. The weeks flew quickly, and Julia could recall little of them after they had passed. The delivery of the first batch of Oiseau dresses was, perhaps, Julia's favorite day of that time. She realized it was probably very shallow and vain of her to enjoy them so much, but she couldn't help it. She'd never had such beautiful clothes before in her life, and while the thought that they were only just *beginning* the season, after having been in town for two months, was daunting—well, it helped a bit to think of getting to wear her lovely new gowns.

At the end of February, Charissa Bradleigh excitedly called to tell Julia that there would be a ball at Alleyneham House in a few weeks, to begin the intense and unrelenting whirl of gaiety that made up the London season.

"Lord, it's going to be absolutely amazing!" the young aristocrat exclaimed. "We've never had a ball so early in the season, but I suppose Papa and Mama are keen on getting us married off this year. They've been planning this one almost since the last one was over with."

She laughed unconcernedly. "What care I why, though? A ball is a ball, am I right? Except this one will be grander than any we've ever had before. Why, everyone who's *anyone* will be there."

"Really?" Julia replied with interest. She couldn't help herself; she just had to ask. "You'll be inviting ... say ... Viscount Matheson?"

"Oh, good heavens, of course!" Charissa replied cheerfully. "I expect we'll be inviting about four hundred people or so; maybe even more. So he'll be included, I'm certain." She smiled insinuatingly. "He is a handsome gentleman, isn't he? I'm sorry he's engaged, but that doesn't stop a girl from looking!"

Julia realized she'd blundered, and hastened to cover her mistake. "Er—of course, he's a nice-looking man. I mean, I haven't really thought about it, but I suppose he is. But, you know, he's marrying Louisa, and so of course, if we're to go, then I wanted to make sure he would be there. For her sake. Since, um, she feels better when he's around."

And so do I, she thought, but she certainly wasn't going to say *that* to her friend. She'd already said more than enough.

Fortunately Charissa wasn't of a contemplative turn of mind, and she cheerfully agreed that she supposed Louisa would like having James with her.

"After all," she dimpled, "I rather like having him around myself. I know he's hands-off, no-touching," she assured Julia, "but he's nice to look at, and so witty, I declare!" This drove her into a peal of giggles.

Julia tried to share her friend's laughter, but it felt false. Charissa's words woke all sorts of feelings that she'd tried to quash over the past weeks. She ached with the desire to talk more about James, and the pain of the knowledge that she shouldn't.

So instead, she asked Charissa all about the ball, and the earl's daughter happily prattled about the decorations, the food, the number of extra servants they would have to take on for the evening, the sad crush—also known as a social triumph—that it was sure to be.

As her friend talked on, eventually, Julia's discomfort began to melt away. Charissa's excitement was so vivid and contagious that she couldn't help beginning to share it. After all, the ball at Alleyneham House had been a turning point in Louisa's life less than a year before. Now she would have a chance to attend the same type of event, only—if Charissa could be believed—even larger, grander, more exciting, more elaborate, more *everything*.

Maybe, just maybe, it would be a turning point for her as well. Somehow.

Chapter 18

In Which Julia
Comes to Appreciate
French Sartorial Genius

"Please sit still, *mademoiselle* Julia, or I will burn your ears off with the curling tongs."

Julia sighed and tried once again to hold still. It wasn't the first time Simone had admonished her to stop squirming. Though she didn't think the capable maid would really burn her, she didn't want even so much as a single singed curl tonight.

Tonight, of all nights, she had to be absolutely perfect in every regard, for tonight was the grand ball at Alleyneham House.

The very thought of it made her insides quiver, as if her stomach were full of butterflies—or perhaps something less pleasant, like snakes.

Despite her best intentions, her fingers began to tap again. She shrugged her shoulders, trying to find a comfortable seated position.

Simone sighed theatrically and drew back her hands, saving *mademoiselle*'s ears once again from a tragic burn.

"I'm sorry!" Julia cried. "I'm just rather nervous, I suppose." She hadn't been able to eat anything since breakfast, and her head spun with jittery fatigue.

Simone frowned at her charge. "And why is this?" asked the maid skeptically in her lilting accent. "Have you not been to a ball before?"

"Of course I have," Julia replied, biting her lip. "But this one is special."

Simone continued to stare at Julia with expectant raised brows, and Julia tried to think of an appropriate explanation.

Louisa met James at Alleyneham House last year, and I want to meet someone like him at the ball this year. Because I want someone exactly like him. Him, in fact.

No, the truth would never do. But it weighed on her like an albatross, ill-fated and undeniable, sinking her mood. There was only one James, and he was already engaged. How could she go to a ball and dance with other men, encouraging them to desire her, court her, and marry her?

She didn't know, but somehow she had to. She had promised she would. She had promised herself and her family, and even James.

"This ball will be such a grand event," she managed at last. "So many glittering people. It's practically the height of the season. I'm worried I'll be a wallflower."

Well, that part was true enough.

Simone seemed to accept this excuse. She abandoned the curling tongs and poked a pearl-headed pin into a coil of Julia's hair.

"I find that to be unlikely," she replied. "Certainly the viscount and the baronet Sir Stephen will dance with you."

"Certainly," Julia agreed miserably. So what if they

did? She was still a fool, living a lie that could only hurt herself and her family. A stupid, simple, country fool.

The full import of the event hit her suddenly, with all the impact of a runaway coach and four. What was she doing, anyway, hoping to ensnare wealthy men at a *ton* party? She, Julia Herington, didn't belong with the likes of the Earl and Countess of Alleyneham. She belonged in the nursery at Stonemeadows Hall, reading her young sisters and brother a story.

She felt as if her tight bodice was squeezing the air out of her chest, preventing her from drawing breath. She doubled over, light-headed, and moaned.

"You are disarranging your gown," Simone informed her calmly. "You will not appear your best if you do not sit up straight at once."

It wasn't exactly a sympathetic statement, but it was as sobering as a bucket of cold water. Julia sat bolt upright and allowed Simone's clever fingers to tuck and pull the fabric of her gown back into order.

She noticed these deft movements only vaguely. Her mind still spun ahead to the inevitable consequences of her stupidity. She'd fail to find a husband; her parents' money would be wasted. She would have to return home and would languish away, an intolerable burden on her family for the remainder of her life. Unless she could somehow persuade Louisa and James to take her in at Nicholls.

Perhaps she could serve as governess for their children.

"I feel sick," she whispered. Her vision grew dark around the edges.

Simone grasped her shoulders and shook her. "Look at me."

She waited to continue until she had fixed Julia's

wide gaze with her own sloe eyes. "Breathe deeply, *mademoiselle*. Calm yourself and do not think these things that are bothering you. Are you or are you not Lady Irving's niece?"

"Yes," Julia replied automatically. "Well, only by marriage, but technically, yes. I believe she thinks of me as a niece. I think of her as an aunt, after all."

Simone ignored this babbled explanation. "Then you will do nothing wrong. If you appear confident as does your aunt, everyone will believe you are so, and no person will question what you do."

She paused for a moment, then admitted, "That is not perfectly correct. Your aunt does some things a young lady should not. But still you should be calm. Think of how your sister always appears, so possessed of herself."

Julia breathed in and out, slowly, concentrating on the movement of air through her lungs. Simone was right. Why should everyone be watching her to see how she behaved? If they were, they would take their cue from her own demeanor. They would assume that she was fashionable and confident and eager, and that her heart was as untouched as her body.

Suddenly Simone's final sentence sank into her consciousness. "Simone, where's Louisa? Why hasn't she been in to join us yet? Doesn't she need your help, too?"

"Do not unquiet yourself again," Simone said calmly, running an expert eye over Julia from head to foot. "*Mademoiselle* Louisa will be very well. Stand, please, and permit me to observe you. I believe you are very nearly ready to descend."

She adjusted a final pin in Julia's hair, and with a nod of satisfaction, offered her hand to assist the younger woman to rise.

Julia stood obediently and turned in a slow circle for

Simone's inspection. The maid's usually impassive eyes widened, and she drew in her breath sharply.

"Nom d'un nom," she breathed out. "I am a genius, truly."

"What? Why? What do you mean?" Julia was puzzled.

A slow smile spread over the Frenchwoman's face. "You look wonderful, *ma belle.* You have never looked finer. I say again, I am a genius. I shall ask your aunt to pay me more money."

Julia laughed unsteadily, then moved across the room to peer at herself in the glass.

It was her own self . . . but she had never seen herself look like this. Her anxiety melted into astonishment at the very sight.

Wispy curls framed her forehead and face, while the long mass of her fair hair was held back by two fine pearlescent Grecian-style bands. Behind their restraints, Simone had coaxed her hair into a neat chignon style, but with additional twists that made of Julia's hair a glossy pile of sophisticated coils. Even when Julia prodded them with a curious finger, their perfection remained unmarred.

"Amazing," she breathed. Her hair had never looked so tidy and stylish in her life.

Below the mass of her hair, her skin glowed pale and rosy next to the ivory triumph of Madame Oiseau's first and most elaborate creation. The delicate silk fell in a lustrous sweep from the low-cut neckline down to Julia's slippers. The skirt of the gown was gathered at the back into folds that just swept the floor in a suggestion of a train, and the dress's net overlay added a gold-tinted shimmer. Long ivory gloves and delicate pearl jewelry completed the sweetly sophisticated ensemble.

Julia turned and stared at herself in the glass, and

turned back and stared some more. When she met her reflection's eyes, they were still disbelieving. This young woman was . . . beautiful? Elegant? How could this be?

Simone had worked a miracle, for the woman in the mirror looked like she could do anything. She could be fascinating and charming, and she would never take a false social step. Men would fall at the feet of this woman. If her heart was hurt, no one would ever notice, because she would tilt her head back proudly and smile.

Julia tilted her head back proudly and smiled. The woman in the mirror smiled, too, right back at her.

It made her feel better. She tried again, and this time the smile was even real.

"Oh, Simone, how did you do it?" she finally said, touching the glass one last time. "I look . . . I look like a real town lady." She choked on the words, and turned to face the maid.

"And so you are, when you are at a party," Simone replied. "Especially this night. Remember that people know only what you want them to know about you. And in this"—she wagged a dexterous finger at Julia's ensemble—"they will know that they should admire you and be charmed."

She smiled at the younger girl. "So, feel your most charming, *ma petite*. You are enchanting. You cannot fail to please."

Julia's throat caught. She grasped Simone's hands gratefully and managed a watery smile. "Thank you," she whispered.

"There, child, no crying." Simone patted her hands, then opened the bedchamber door for Julia to exit down to the drawing room. "I am very wonderful, I know, but how much will it help you to cry and undo the magnificence that I have created?"

As Julia passed through the doorway and headed for

the stairs, the maid added too softly for anyone else's ears but her own, "*Il va craquer, je suis sûr.* He will never resist her when he sees such a beauty. I am a genius, *vraiment.*"

She permitted herself a small smile as she watched Julia begin, with an expression of great concentration, to descend the stairs deliberately, holding her skirts away from her feet. Then, with an anxious glance at Louisa's closed bedchamber door, Simone returned to Julia's room and began to tidy up the litter of leftover pins, curl papers, and other evidence of her undeniable brilliance.

James waited downstairs in the entry of Lady Irving's house for at least one of the ladies to make her appearance. He had been perfectly punctual, though he should have known that women preparing for a ball tended not to keep to a scrupulous timeline. He hadn't been able to keep himself away any longer, though. There was nowhere else he wanted to be.

Given a few unexpected minutes of quiet, he idly paced back and forth, his cloudless face giving no hint of the hectic buzz of his thoughts. Despite himself, despite his years of experience with the *ton*, he found himself anticipating the night's ball with as much pleasure as if it were his first.

Something wonderful was going to happen tonight, he had a feeling. By gad, his very fingers were tingling.

His mouth crooked into a wry smile as he regarded himself in the decorative pier glass of Lady Irving's fashionable entryway. He had wanted to look especially well tonight, for whatever happened, and he'd let his fastidious manservant arrange his cravat. Delaney's standards were amazingly high, and they'd wasted eight starched neckcloths before the valet had been satisfied. It was ridiculous, of course, but the effect was rather good, if he did say so himself.

"Drat." A voice from the bottom of the staircase broke into his reverie.

James's smile broadened. He knew who that had to be. Without turning to look, he said, "Hello, Julia."

She gasped, and he turned to face her, grinning at her surprise. "James! I didn't see you there."

He opened his mouth to offer his usual friendly, joking reply, and then he just left his mouth open.

She was luminous.

She was herself, of course, but more beautiful than he had ever seen her. Was it the elegant sweep of her gown? No, her sophisticated clothing was but the gilt on the lily. She herself made it shine. Her skin glowed; her hair was bright; her lips were rosy.

She was the loveliest creature he'd ever seen.

He sagged against a wall. He needed to get hold of himself. This would not do. This would *not* do.

He closed his mouth and drew in a deep breath through his nose, and felt somewhat normal again. At least, if you were comparing him to someone who'd just been hit on the head with a club, run over by a carriage, and then been committed to Bedlam.

He was quite certain at that moment that there was indeed a God, because Julia didn't notice him gaping at her like a schoolboy seeing his first nude statue.

All right, that wasn't the type of thought that was going to help him get hold of himself.

He shook his head again to clear it, and noticed at last that Julia was behaving rather oddly. She was turning in slow circles, wrenching her head to one side. She looked as if she were having a tooth drawn by a set of clock gears.

"Er—is everything all right?" he managed.

Julia continued to turn in that odd way. "I'm not sure," she said over her shoulder. "Simone had me all prepared like a perfect town lady, and then I was trying to be so careful as I came down the stairs, thinking that I mustn't miss any of them, that I concentrated too hard instead of just going down normally, and I forgot how to move my feet properly. So I actually did miss one of the steps and my foot slid onto my hem, and now I'm afraid I've ripped it."

She stood straight at last, flushing the embarrassed pink he knew by heart. "Could you check it? It's the part in the back just next to the train. I can't twist around quite far enough to see it."

"Of course," he replied. He crouched at her feet like a supplicant, his eyes not seeing her dress. The position gave him another welcome few seconds to hide his face for fear of what his expression would show her.

He took another deep breath, then cleared his throat as he stood slowly. "Your gown is fine. You look very nice."

He still couldn't trust himself to say more, or even to meet her eye. He pretended to check the arrangement of his cravat again in the glass.

At the edge of the glass, he could just see Julia's reflection. She lifted her chin and smiled at his lukewarm compliment, cool and proud, looking for all the world like a princess.

"Thank you," she said, sounding not quite like her usual self.

He turned to face her again, his face schooled into what he thought was a look of normal, friendly interest. "Why were you so worried about your dress?"

She grinned at him—her regular, everyday Julia

grin—and its brightness hit him like a punch in the gut. He pitied the poor bachelors who would soon be vying for her hand.

"I'm just nervous," Julia admitted, the self-deprecating grin still on her face. "It's my first real ball, you know." The grin crumpled, and she shuffled one of her dainty slippers on the floor. "Even so, I suppose I've let myself dwell too much on things I shouldn't."

James allowed himself to place one finger under her chin and tip her face up to his. Even through his glove, he could feel the heat of her smooth skin. "I know the feeling you mean," he whispered huskily.

Her lips parted as if to reply—and of course she had a reply, because she always had a reply—and he drew his fingertip up to cover her lips for a moment. He'd never allowed himself such a liberty before, and he swore to himself that he never would again.

Probably.

"No protests," he said, using mock seriousness to hide his deadly earnestness. "I simply must have a dance tonight."

"Of course," Julia replied softly, her eyes wide and fixed upon his. "As many as you like."

She blinked and laughed suddenly. "In fact, please watch over me throughout the ball, and come to rescue me with that dance if I prove to be too unpopular. I would hate to be a wallflower, tonight of all nights."

It was too much. She was actually asking him to watch her all evening and seize her for dance after dance. Good Lord, he wasn't a magician who could just . . . not be made of flesh for several hours. He had obviously gone soft in the head, and how he was going to get through this evening without making an utter ass of himself, he wasn't sure.

Luckily for his presence of mind, Lady Irving marched down the stairs just then and drew all attention to herself. Her ladyship was resplendent in ruby satin and sporting an unusually garish brocaded, bejeweled, and ostrich-plumed violet turban on her head.

"Let's go," she commanded, thumping James on the back with an imperious hand. "I want Lady Alleyneham to see me with this . . . this *thing* on my head before my curls are completely crushed."

Noting her niece's gaping mouth, she explained, "Ever since we were girls together, Sylvia has copied me in everything, so I must have my bit of fun. I'll take this off as soon as we greet her, but ten to one the silly creature will be sporting a plumed violet turban for her next at-home."

James was amazed to see her literally rub her hands together in anticipation, and he couldn't honestly call her laugh anything but a cackle.

"Will Louisa be ready soon?" James asked smoothly, pretending he hadn't heard a word.

Guilt stabbed through him. Once again, he knew there was a God, because there wasn't a mind reader in this house. No one but he would know what a cursed fool he was.

"Oh, she's not coming. Didn't you know?" Lady Irving said distractedly, gazing at her reflection in the much-used pier glass and prodding at the arrangement of her ostrich plumes. "Sick headache, or some such nonsense. If you ask me, all that girl needs is a good—"

She broke off suddenly, darting her gaze at James, then meeting Julia's puzzled eyes in the glass, and said, "Well, never mind what she needs. Anyway, we're free to leave anytime. Is your carriage waiting, Matheson? Come, Julia, my girl; gather your wrap and things."

"But I should go to Louisa," Julia interjected. "I didn't know she wasn't feeling well. Maybe I should speak to her, or even stay home with her tonight if she's ill."

Her expression was so worried that James's heart turned over in sympathy. Feeling even guiltier that he hadn't spoken up first, he, too, made an offer. "Certainly we can spare all the time needed for you to run up to your sister. In fact, I'd like to speak with her myself. She seemed well the last time I saw her. I hope it is nothing serious."

"Don't bother," Lady Irving said, as she collected her wrap and began to walk toward the street door. "Either one of you. She told Simone that she was going to lie down, and she didn't wish to be disturbed at all this evening. By anyone, and that includes both of you. *And* she said to have a wonderful time and not worry about her."

She noticed neither James nor Julia was following her, turned on her heel, and looked expectantly from one face to another. "What are you two waiting for? An order? Very well, I order you to follow me, get in the carriage, and come have a marvelous time this evening. Heaven knows, if Louisa is ill, she will have a much better time here at home than getting overheated in the middle of a crowd of shoving nincompoops. And if she doesn't want company, which she doesn't, then *you* will have a much better time at the ball than you would fluttering around her, plaguing the life out of her, and getting no thanks for it."

Faced with such logic, James allowed some of his guilt to melt away. Louisa should be here at his side. He knew that. But if she didn't want to be there, he still could accompany her relatives. It was perfectly proper to do so.

He met Julia's eyes and shrugged. "Cinderella must go to the ball," he joked lamely, willing her to agree.

Julia bit her lip nervously and glanced upstairs toward Louisa's chamber.

"It feels wrong," she murmured.

James said something sympathetic as he took her arm and led her out to his carriage, but he wasn't sure if he meant it.

He was too far gone. The only thing that felt wrong, at all, was how right it felt to have her hand on his arm.

Chapter 19

In Which the Viscount Eventually Dances

The turban was an immediate success.

Lady Alleyneham, Charissa's mother, stared with covetous eyes at Lady Irving's dazzling headdress. Lady Irving pretended not to notice, patting her violet monstrosity absently as she made Louisa's excuses.

"Of course, she'll call on you at your next at-home to deliver her regrets in person," Lady Irving said with a feline smile. "As the season's begun in earnest, I'm sure you'll have new garments for the occasion, if I know you, my dear. You are always so elegant."

Next to her aunt, Julia reeled. Lady Irving had spent the entire carriage ride to Alleyneham House nattering about The Affair of the Turban, as Julia now thought of it. Now that her ladyship had triumphed over her foes— or more accurately, her friends—Julia hoped she could be left alone in silence for a few blessed seconds. Just enough time to come to terms with the fact that Louisa wasn't here.

And James was.

But before Julia could slip away in search of a quiet place to think, her aunt seized her by the elbow and began steering her into the ballroom, hailing a series of friends and acquaintances as she strode.

"Might as well get all the use I can out of this creation," she muttered, giving her plumed turban another pat as she nodded to an elderly nobleman. "Good evening, Haverley. Am I not looking ravishing this evening?"

The countess turned to James with a dazzling smile. "Well, we'll see you later on, Matheson. Perhaps at supper. I'm sure you want to find the card room, or whatever it is that unnecessary young gentlemen do during balls when they're not dancing."

Julia's mouth dropped open. James was her lifeline; her aunt couldn't send him away. James looked taken aback, too, and seemed about to reply, but Lady Irving waved a dismissive hand at him and began to drag Julia away in her talon-like grip.

"He can't do you any good this evening, my girl, as he's already taken," she explained in a voice that was not nearly quiet enough, considering the number of people pressing against Julia and carrying her away from James. Two dozen perfect strangers, at least, could hear Lady Irving barking out orders. "We need to find Sir Stephen for you at once, or perhaps that Pellington fellow. Remember what I told you—rich and titled. You've got to keep your eye on the prize."

This was utter humiliation. Julia's thoughts were still in a tumble from Louisa's sudden illness, and now her aunt was telling half of London that she was on the hunt for a husband.

She began glancing at her surroundings, trying to

pretend she didn't know the strange and magnificent woman prodding her in the arm. It was difficult to see much of the ballroom around the crowd of people. Truly, this event would achieve the triumph of being called a mad crush with no exaggeration whatsoever. The size of the room alone was imposing; to Julia's unaccustomed eyes, there seemed to be hundreds of people milling about within its walls.

Peering through the crowds of hot, jostling, elegantly dressed people, she could catch glimpses of a polished dance floor already occupied by what looked like dozens of couples winding their way through the ball's opening minuet. A thicker crowd at one end of the long ballroom indicated the probable location of the refreshments.

The nervousness she'd felt earlier in the evening began to twist through her body again. It choked her throat, made her stomach clench, and caused her feet to feel heavy and clumsy as her aunt pulled her around the ballroom in search of someone with a fat bankroll. James had long since vanished in the crowd, and Julia couldn't spot Charissa either. Without friendly faces around, the crush and the crowd and the scramble for partners lost their magic and excitement.

Simone had been wrong this evening, completely wrong. Julia couldn't hold her chin high and pretend that she loved it here. She was just one of a surplus of inexperienced girls in fancy dresses, and she was hardly the richest, prettiest, or wittiest of the bunch. Yet here she was in London, tasked with finding a husband, grasp and scuttle though she must.

Just as she was beginning to wish she were back in the Grosvenor Square house with Louisa, she felt a gentle touch at her elbow. The one *not* currently being wrenched by her aunt.

She twisted in Lady Irving's grasp to see Sir Stephen's smiling countenance behind her.

"Sir Stephen," she greeted him, curtsying. This drew Lady Irving's attention, and the countess again switched on her most dazzling smile.

"Sir Stephen," she echoed, and gave him her hand to kiss. "How delightful to see you. Are you just arrived? Have you had the chance to dance yet?" She raised her arched eyebrows expectantly and looked back and forth from him to her niece.

Julia could have sworn the ostrich plumes on Lady Irving's turban bobbed from one of them to the other as if colluding in her aunt's effort to throw her at the baronet. She supposed her aunt *could* have been more obvious if she had commanded Sir Stephen to dance with, ravish, or wed Julia on the spot (all would probably do equally well, in Lady Irving's mind), but really, this was embarrassing enough.

Fortunately, Sir Stephen picked up the unmistakable hint. "Indeed I have recently arrived, and have only just finished greeting our host and hostess. I have not yet had the opportunity to dance, but would be most grateful if Miss Herington would do me the honor of accompanying me in the next set."

His eyes turned from Lady Irving to Julia herself. His smile was kind and genuine, as always. Dependable and reliable; that was Sir Stephen.

She wished she could feel as excited about the proffered dance as her aunt apparently did; Lady Irving was practically quivering with her eagerness to throw Julia at the baronet's feet.

Ah, well; it would be nice not to be dragged around by her aunt in search of male prey for at least half an hour.

Ruefully, she rubbed the arm that Lady Irving had just

released. "I would be delighted to dance with you, Sir Stephen."

She smiled back at him and was gratified to watch his amiable face light up. He really was a handsome gentleman, although the crinkles at the corners of his eyes never failed to remind her how much older than she he was.

She took his arm and allowed him to lead her into the dance, her smile growing as excitement began to bloom within her again, as he complimented her on her appearance and swooped her into the line of dancers.

Perhaps she could find something to be proud of, after all. She lifted her chin, just as Simone had shown her.

Standing only yards away, James was manfully restraining himself from throwing a punch at one of Sir Stephen's eyes. Every male gaze that turned Julia's way rankled him, but the baronet was the worst. He was looking at her so intently, he might as well have been peeling off her gown in front of hundreds of people.

James's fist clenched at his side. Julia *had* asked him to keep an eye on her, after all. He'd already trekked all the way around the ballroom after her, unnoticed by either her or Lady Irving, no doubt cutting any number of acquaintances without even realizing it. He couldn't help it; he was in a fog, drawn after Julia, a moth to her flame.

Perhaps he could intercede if Sir Stephen seemed to be too demanding. And yet he knew the purpose of Julia's season was to contract an honorable marriage.

Even if she'd be better off contracting malaria.

He glowered at the dancing, laughing pair throughout their country set before slinking off to the card room at last for an hour of fruitless play in the company of men he barely knew and never cared if he saw again.

Following his time in the card room, James returned to the ballroom, and the evening began to seem endless. Hours passed, and James noted—like a good friend and protector—everyone who led Julia onto the dance floor. Far from languishing as a wallflower, it seemed she scarcely had the chance to reach the edge of the ballroom with her previous partner before another young man asked her for a dance. Xavier, Pellington . . . good Lord, it seemed practically every man in London had an eye on her this evening.

Of course, Sir Stephen was the worst of them. Really, could the man not keep his hands off her? For someone so attentive to propriety, it was a positive scandal how he looked at her, and how he asked Julia to dance again and again. The man even monopolized her during the supper dance so he could lead her into the meal afterward. Really, it was too much.

Immediately following the supper, which James bolted down while standing in a corner of the room from which he could keep a strategic eye on that Saville fellow, he followed the pair as they headed back toward the ballroom. Unable to restrain himself any longer, he touched Julia lightly on the arm to draw her attention to him.

She turned to see who was summoning her, and when she looked into his eyes, her cheeks took on the rosy pink he knew as well as his own face.

"James," she breathed, looking flustered. "Where did you—I've been—that is, I haven't seen you this evening. Have you danced much?"

Was that anxiousness in her eyes? He smiled reassuringly, and took the arm not being held by Sir Stephen.

"I've been around. No, I haven't danced much." In truth, he hadn't danced at all, but surely he could be forgiven this small lie. "I've been in the ballroom enough to notice you've hardly been a wallflower. Still, I would like to claim that waltz you promised me, if I might?"

He darted a glance at Sir Stephen out of the corner of his eye, counting on the older man to bow out.

Indeed, the baronet did just that, surrendering Julia's arm and kissing her hand lightly as he took his leave. He thanked her very correctly for the honor of their dances and the supper together, and was pleased to leave her in the hands of her dear friend.

James would have rolled his eyes if that wouldn't have been incredibly rude. Honestly, the fellow was like an etiquette textbook. But since he knew his share of etiquette as well, he only nodded his acknowledgment of the older man's words and began to lead Julia toward the other dancers, who, following the supper, began at once to collect again near the musicians and the center of the ballroom.

As the instruments were tuned, James took Julia's hand in his and touched his other to her slim waist. It would be a few minutes before the dance started, but he couldn't help himself. He would have sworn he could feel the shape and warmth of her body through the delicate fabric of her dress. The tingling in his fingers began to return.

Julia drew a startled breath at the unexpected contact of his hand. His usual good humor now returned, he rather enjoyed Julia's response to his touch. "Haven't you waltzed before? I know you have permission."

"Yes, I have," she said, blushing again. "It's just . . . I forgot what it is like." She bit that delicious full lower lip and smiled hesitantly at him. "I suppose I sound old-fashioned, but it's almost shocking that such a thing is permitted in public, is it not? I mean, it doesn't feel so when one is practicing in the nursery with one's sister, but this is rather a different matter."

"I should hope so," James replied, stifling a laugh. "But it can't be improper for us, since I am to be your brother."

Her brother. He shuddered; the very thought was repugnant.

He realized that this was the first time he'd thought of Louisa, even indirectly, since entering the ballroom. And realized that the feeling of Julia's waist under his hand was arousing in him a response that was decidedly unbrotherly.

In his arms, Julia was oblivious to these revelations. She was staring fixedly at the floor.

"Is something wrong?" James asked.

"Not at all," Julia replied, her voice slightly muffled by her proximity to his chest. She was so close to him; only a breath away from an embrace. His heart began to pound treacherously fast.

Then she explained prosaically, "It's just that I wanted to see how you placed your feet. I can't remember how we start this dance, and it would be horrid if I trod on your toes in front of all these people."

James mentally shook himself for his foolishness. He managed a laugh and responded as lightly as he could. "For the sake of my feet, I would prefer you not to tread on my toes regardless of the number of people watching. But this is false caution; I know you to be an excellent dancer. Here, the music is about to begin—follow my lead and we'll do splendidly."

She met his eyes and nodded her readiness. The tune began, its pulsing three-four rhythm sending the eager dancers into whirling motion around the floor. James spun Julia in concert with everyone else, the pressure of his hand at her waist subtly guiding their movement.

With Julia in his arms, the room came alive. Myriad candles glittered off the polished marble of the floor, the heavy pier glasses on the walls, and the cut crystal of the chandeliers hanging from the high, ornately plastered ceilings. Flame upon flame, reflected and multiplied throughout the room, glistened on the pearls at Julia's throat, burnished her fair hair to gold, and added points of light in her eyes.

The dance picked up momentum, and Julia smiled at James, then began laughing as they whirled faster. The clasp of her hand tightened in his. Looking down at her elated face and her starry eyes, winking and lovely in the low light, James felt his heart turn over, and he knew that he could never let her marry Sir Stephen.

Julia's whisper broke into his thoughts. "Do you know what I've wanted to do, ever since I came to London?"

Her warm breath heated his face, and his insides felt tight and eager as he replied in the negative. What was her secret desire, hidden for so long?

"To say 'hell' in a crowded ballroom," she whispered, and pulled back delightedly to look at his face. "And I just did! James, I said it in front of all these people, and they didn't even know!"

Once again, the feeling of heated tension broke. James threw back his head and laughed, as much at himself as at Julia. He was such a fool; she had her mind on the dance and nothing more, which was as it should be. "I'm so glad you've realized your heart's desire," he offered. "I won't tell a soul about the depths of iniquity you've plumbed here in this very ballroom."

"My heart's desire," Julia repeated, blinking at him

owlishly. All at once she looked much more serious, and she opened her mouth as if to speak again.

James didn't want to travel that line of thought any further. "How are you enjoying the ball so far?" he asked, sounding less nonchalant than he had hoped.

Julia was effectively diverted into a babble of small talk about the grandness of the home and the astounding number of beeswax candles the earl and countess had lit. And, because she was Julia, she told him all about what she'd had for supper and how she hadn't been able to eat nearly as much as she wanted.

"I was too nervous to eat earlier, and I'm ravenous now," she explained. "But at least I've been dancing enough to avoid Aunt Estella, so she hasn't been able to call me vulgar or inflict any of her horrid advice on me. Although I'm sure I've done quite a few things she'd consider vulgar, without meaning to. Somehow I always do."

"I can think of one." James hadn't meant to say it; it slipped out. Damnation. He really must keep better control over himself.

Julia couldn't have looked more stunned if James had actually slapped her in the face. Her eyes were wide and hurt as she asked in a small voice, "Really? What did I do?"

Her expression made James feel like the lowest sort of dog. He wouldn't have hurt her for anything. But since she was asking, and since he'd already said too much, he might as well have it out. "I saw Sir Stephen dance with you twice this evening already."

Julia's wounded face turned puzzled. "But there's nothing wrong with that. Twice is no scandal, is it?"

"In an etiquette handbook, perhaps not." James struggled to explain. "It's more the *way* he danced with you.

He's been singling you out above all others throughout the evening, in fact."

His voice became stiff, the I-am-a-viscount voice that his father had always employed to gain instant obedience. James had always hated that voice, but it seemed he'd inherited it anyway. "Just take care that you do not give him the wrong impression and lead him to hope for more than you wish to give."

Julia stared at him for a long moment, then rolled her eyes. "Oh, please," she scoffed. "Sir Stephen is a very nice man, but I'm sure he never thinks of me as anything special. See, there he is across the floor now, dancing with Lady Caroline Bradleigh."

James felt a little calmer at this reply, but he judged it safer to stop talking for now. What did it matter if the man singled Julia out or not? Good heavens, Sir Stephen was exactly the sort of man James and Louisa had plotted together for her to meet.

They whirled in silence for a while, one-two-three, one-two-three, and James became increasingly aware of the curve of Julia's waist beneath his hand. For her part, she seemed unconscious of his inner agitation; in fact, she looked relaxed and happy in his arms, her eyes half-closed as she gave herself over to the sway of the music. He had never seen anything so beautiful as her joyful face, and his heart was wrung. He had no right, none at all, to hold her or even think of her, yet he wanted nothing else.

The dance finally ended, none too soon, and James led Julia swiftly from the floor. "Now, what can I do for you?" he asked, taking care to keep his voice friendly and polite. "May I take you to speak with a friend, or find your next dance partner?"

"Actually, I'd like something to drink," Julia confessed. "Well, what I really want is a haunch of pork, but

I don't suppose there's one in the saloon. Would you mind getting me some lemonade?"

"Not at all," he said, bowing over her hand with strict formality. He made his way into the saloon, which he was dismayed to see was damnably crowded as these things always were. He grew increasingly irritable as he was elbowed by a series of young bucks, who all flashed insolent and insincere grins of apology.

Minutes dragged by before he was finally able to shove his way through the mob to gain possession of a glass of lemonade for Julia. By the time he returned to her—with half the glass sloshed onto the floor due to the jostling of the crowd—he saw that he was too late. Freddie Pellington had already seized hold of her and found her some sort of beverage. The two were laughing merrily about something, and Julia's smile didn't fade even when James grouchily thrust his hard-won cup at her. "Here is your lemonade; I'm sorry some of it spilled."

"Oh, that's all right," she said. "Mr. Pellington has brought me something to drink as well, you see, and it is delightful!"

She shifted the glass to her other hand and accepted the cup from James as well, smiling broadly at both men. "My goodness, I am lucky, aren't I? I know how trying it is to make one's way through the crowd to get hold of something to drink. So I shall save these both and treasure them *immeasurably*."

She nodded emphatically to punctuate her words, and Pellington, that fool, tittered and copied her lead. "Just so," he said. "Dashed glad you like it. Special recipe and whatnot."

James looked at both of them skeptically, but mentally shrugged. Julia seemed a bit off, but perhaps she was just hungry and excited. And Pellington was a harmless enough fellow. There was nothing wrong with him, after all, that a few more pounds of brains wouldn't fix.

Naturally, Pellington led Julia out for the next dance, which James was relieved to see was a country set rather than another waltz. Knowing that no one would be groping Julia for nearly a half hour, he sought a quieter place to think.

He made his way out of the raucous ballroom and into the comparative quiet of the hall outside the library. The blessed silence was punctuated only by the occasional giggle of a private *tête-à-tête* behind one of the hall's several closed doors.

He couldn't help thinking of the last time he had been here for a ball, the night he met Louisa. He'd been reeling from his quick summons to London and the weight of his responsibility as the head of his family. A responsibility that had driven him to propose marriage to the first woman who gained his trust and respect, so that he could set up a household with his wife and provide a secure home for his shamed sister and her children.

He'd taken the step of engagement so lightly; it seemed logical at the time. And now his choice seemed a lifetime ago, and the woman he'd chosen had never made it to the altar with him. His best-laid plans had grown stale, his elegant fiancée was a mystery to him, and his own sense of honor—the honor that had driven him to protect his family—was merely a sham.

Alone with his thoughts, he couldn't deny the truth. He was a dishonorable fool.

He had fallen in love with his fiancée's sister.

He leaned against the wall and closed his eyes. How could this be? How had he let this happen? He had no answers, but the knowledge of his love for Julia pulsed through him like a heartbeat, inevitable and true. He knew this love, deeply and with certainty, though he'd never allowed himself to realize it before.

How seeing her always made him smile.

How he loved to hear her talk, and make her laugh that lovely, unfettered laugh of hers.

How he grew warm around her, and his thoughts roamed into furtive and passionate places.

Yes, he loved her, and part of him was sorry for it. He'd come into this family both too soon and too late, for his own good and the good of everyone else.

But he would not act with dishonor, even though it riddled his thoughts. He would abide by his engagement to Louisa. He would marry her whenever she was ready, and he would make her as happy as he possibly could. She would never guess the truth. She was a good woman, kind and true, and she deserved as much as he could give her, and more besides.

And Julia—well, someday she would marry Sir Stephen Saville, or someone very much like him. Until that time, he had better stay as far away from her as he could, within the bounds of family politeness.

That is, after he checked on her in the ballroom one last time. Just once more . . .

Chapter 20

In Which Pellington's Special Recipe Figures Prominently

James's newfound resolution to keep his distance from Julia lasted for approximately thirty seconds after he reentered the ballroom.

He spotted her immediately, just as Freddie Pellington deposited her, a glass again in her hand, in a chair at the edge of the room. As soon as Pellington turned away, Julia leaned her head back against the wall and shut her eyes.

James's heart seemed to stop with sudden concern. Heedless of the vow he had made to himself in the hallway, and of the masses of people between them, he at once pushed his way over to where she sat.

"Julia, are you all right?" he demanded.

Her eyes opened lazily, and she smiled slowly, a seductive smile that lifted one corner of her mouth and made it dimple. He caught his breath at the sight, and, with all the willpower he could muster, just barely resisted the urge to bend over and kiss her.

"Oh, James," she breathed. "I'm very tired. But I feel *wonderful.*" Her head lolled to one side, and her eyes drifted closed.

His brows knitted, perplexed, and he leaned closer to her. "Are you sure? You look as if you're—"

She hiccupped. Her eyes flew open wide in surprise, and she quickly straightened up and covered her mouth. She hiccupped again.

James drew back, stunned. "You're foxed."

"I beg your pardon?" Julia said indignantly. *Hic.*

"You're three sheets to the wind. You're—well, I'm not sure how one says this to a lady. You're . . . you've . . . you seem to have imbibed excessively of alcoholic beverages."

"I have not!" Julia answered hotly and just a little too loudly. James shushed her, and she continued in her loud whisper, "I have *not.* I haven't had any alcohol at all. The last thing I drank was the lemonade that you gave me, and those glasses of punch Mr. Pellington gave me before and after our dance." *Hic.*

Realization dawned on her face, and she gasped, "Oh, Lord, the punch. What was in that punch?" She gaped at the empty glass in her hand and thrust it away from her in mortification. *Hic.* "He said it was a special recipe, didn't he? Oh, dear, this is embarrassing." *Hic.*

James shook his head, not sure whether to be amused or angry. "Heaven knows what was in that punch, but apparently it was quite spiritous." He smelled the dregs in the glass in her hand, and recoiled at the powerful scent. "Yes, quite."

As Julia hiccupped again, looking shocked, James decided to feel amused. Anger could wait until later, when he could get his hands on Freddie Pellington. What had that silly ass been thinking, giving spirits to a lady?

James remembered dimly that Pellington had mentioned once giving brandy to a baby, so he supposed he shouldn't be all that surprised. But still, the situation called for quick action.

"We've got to get you home before someone notices your, ah, condition," he explained, helping Julia to rise. "Are you all right? Can you walk?"

She nodded her assent, but leaned against him bonelessly when he started to move, and he realized they needed to leave the ballroom at once. Making his way with her toward the door, he signaled to a footman and asked to have his carriage brought round.

"Stay here," he admonished Julia, propping her against a wall. She nodded sleepily.

He looked doubtfully at her lolling head. How were they going to get out of here without anyone noticing her condition? He coaxed, "I will tell your aunt Estella to give you all the breakfast you want in the morning if you can pick your head up and smile normally at everyone who goes by for the next three minutes."

It was the right thing to say. Instantly Julia's head snapped up, and her eyes flew open. "Do you mean it?"

"Yes, I mean it. Ham, eggs, porridge—if her cook can make it, you can eat it. Now, stay right here and just nod and smile if anyone speaks to you. I am going to take our leave of Lord and Lady Alleyneham, and I'll leave a message for your aunt."

She nodded her comprehension, but he still felt skeptical about her ability to hold herself up, and he dispatched his errands with his host and hostess as quickly as he could. He found Lady Irving herself, too, playing whist with friends in the very card room he had left several hours before. Her bright violet turban was upended on the table next to her to hold her winnings, denuded of its plumes, which she had stuck down into her bodice for safekeeping.

On receiving his assurance that Julia was "just tired," she nodded distractedly and said she would be home later, if he would just send the carriage back for her. He left the room accompanied by her gleeful shouts, her friends' groans, and the bobbing of those blasted plumes as she reached forward to rake in another pile of winnings and, crowing with triumph, drop them coin by coin into the turban.

Swiftly, he made his way back to Julia, finding her just as he had left her. "I was *wonderful*," she assured him, wobbling slightly as she pushed herself upright, away from the wall. "I smiled at *everyone* and no one suspected a *thing*."

"That's excellent," he soothed, and retrieving her wrap from a waiting servant, he led her away from the crowds and out into the blessed coolness and quiet of the night air. The sounds of gaiety receded behind them as they left the house, and the slam of the carriage door shut them into a silent world.

James breathed a sigh of relief at their just-in-time exit from the party before becoming uncomfortably aware that, despite his vow to keep his distance, he was alone with Julia.

In a closed carriage.

At night.

And she was tipsy.

Oh, Lord.

Chapter 21

In Which a Carriage
Plays Host to
Unexpected Revelations

James shut his eyes in despair. Why? Why did this have to happen to him? Why should he be thrown into this situation—to have temptation rubbed in his face, practically? He tried to be a good person. He *was* a good person. Well, except for the whole loving-his-fiancée's-sister thing.

His clothes felt uncomfortably tight and hot, and he shifted as far away from Julia as he could. Staring at the carriage floor, he pressed his lips together, determined not to speak. He would hold still and remain silent, for as long as it took. The ride would be short, and then it would be over and he would be out of danger once more.

But a snarl of carriages blocked their way, and James could hear the coachman shouting oaths at the other drivers whose masters and mistresses were still inside, not yet ready to leave the crush indoors to create one outdoors. He shook his head in despair. This would take a while.

Well, it didn't matter how long it took. It could take seven years, and he would not speak. He would hold still. For as long as it took. Surely he was capable of that much.

Maybe if he thought it over and over again, it would become true.

"What's wrong?" asked a soft voice from the other side of the carriage.

"Pardon?" Damn. He'd sworn not to speak. But he couldn't ignore a direct question.

"I could see you shaking your head. Is something wrong?"

"Oh. No. The carriage has to wait before it can leave."

"Oh," Julia echoed. After a pause came her voice again. "Well, that's all right, isn't it? I like waiting with you."

James felt even hotter, and he tugged at his neckcloth. "Err . . ." was the only sound he could force out of his mouth. Not his finest reaction ever.

"Let me help," said Julia, sliding toward him on the carriage seat. "I know you are very stylish, but there's no need to be uncomfortable now that we're alone. And it must be so scratchy to have that giant cloth around your neck all the time." Small hands ministered to him, deftly undoing the intricate knots and folds of his neckcloth, and James groaned.

"Did I hurt you?" Julia asked, concerned. "Did I strangle you or something? I really didn't mean to strangle you."

"You didn't," James replied, his voice sounding very strangled indeed.

"Oh, good," she said. With a laugh, she admitted, "I've never removed a gentleman's clothes before."

He cleared his throat and tried to speak, but no sound came out. He swallowed, then tried again. "Julia, that is not a proper comment for a young lady to make."

"I was just joking," she said, sounding defensive. After a pause, she continued, "Well, not really. I mean, it really was a joke in that I said it for humorous purposes, but it is also literally true."

James sat in silence, trying desperately not to think of clothes being removed. His clothes, her clothes, his clothes being removed by her, her clothes being removed by him . . . no, it was no use; he simply couldn't get the images out of his head. He groaned again.

The small sound, which he tried to stifle, seemed to inspire Julia to continue.

"I hope you know I would only say that to you."

"Yes, well, I feel very comfortable making amusing comments around you as well," he said stiffly. It was a lie, of course; he felt anything but comfortable. When was this cursed carriage going to get on its way? Desperately, he looked out the window, and the slanting moonlight showed him that he was still caught in a great snarl of traffic.

Wonderful. He obviously must have done something terrible without knowing it, because the Fates were tempting him viciously. He shifted as far away from Julia as he could.

But she spoke on, her words weaving a quiet spell. "No, I mean . . . I would only want you to hear me say such things. Things that are improper."

Even in the moonlit darkness, he swore he could see the hot color rising in her cheeks. His groin tightened. What was she saying? Good God, how could this be happening to him? It was like a dream and nightmare at once, as her hand found his fingers and then his knee. And then began moving up his leg.

"You don't know what you're saying or doing," he said

huskily, removing her hand from his thigh but keeping it held in his clasp. "That's the punch acting on you."

"No, it's not," she insisted, her enunciation overly precise.

"Well, maybe it is a little," she admitted, "but only because it let me tell you what I've been thinking for a long time." She began to laugh raggedly. "I can't believe I said that, though. Or touched you. I'm going to be so embarrassed in the morning."

Her laugh trailed off, and she looked straight into his eyes. She withdrew her hand from his to press it firmly against her other hand, it seemed for courage.

"But right now I don't care. I know I am just a silly country girl who says the wrong thing, and eats too much to be ladylike, and likes *ton* parties because they use beeswax candles, and gets impressed by stupid things like new gowns, and—oh, God—and you're going to marry my sister."

Her intense gaze dropped, and she rubbed her hands over her face impatiently. "I know you love my sister, and you're going to be married. But I love you, and I think of you all the time, and I think of you in ways that I shouldn't. And I didn't intend for you ever to know, but it was just bursting inside me, and now I am glad I told you."

"Julia," he said softly, and his voice broke. He couldn't go on. He had no idea what to say, anyway, so he simply took her hand back again, savoring the feel of her slim fingers in his. He felt as if his heart were breaking and being remade anew, both at the same time.

He tried again to speak. "Julia. I care for you very much. More than you know—"

She cut him off with an impatient gesture and again drew her hand back from his. "I know you do, but I don't want brotherly love. I want *real* love. The kind of love that men and women are supposed to have for each other. The love people have in novels. Love like a husband and wife should have, and that I have for you."

In a small voice, she added, "Louisa doesn't love you like I do. She told me so. I probably shouldn't have told you that either, though."

"You don't know what you're saying," he repeated, unable to think of anything else in reply. Surely she didn't know what she was saying. She didn't, *couldn't*, know what she was saying.

But she *had* said it. She loved him? And Louisa didn't love him?

But . . . Julia did?

He had to take hold of himself.

"It doesn't matter," he continued in what he hoped was a firm voice. He strove for formality to keep a grip on his emotions.

"I am very flattered by what you say, of course. But Louisa has agreed to marry me, and that decision is irrevocable on my part regardless of my own feelings. I believe we will be compatible. And naturally, I have tried to make her love me, and I will continue to do so."

There, that sounded good. He hoped.

"Oh, James," she said, shaking her head, and he could see in the faintness of moonlight that her eyes were soft, her gaze so liquid and deep he felt as if he were sinking into it. "You didn't even have to try to make me love you. I think I loved you the first time I met you, when I horrified you over the tea and biscuits at Stonemeadows and you teased me so kindly. It took me a while to realize it, but I have loved you always."

Her words poured over him like a healing rain. He sat, stunned, his thoughts scattering in different directions. She loved him. He loved her. They could be together. . . .

No. There was one thing he had to remember and hold on to.

"I have promised to marry Louisa." He swallowed, but the lump in his throat wouldn't go away.

"But do you love me?" she asked, her eyes huge and beseeching, and he felt the carriage jerk to a start at last. Its jolt echoed through him. His heart pounded as her eyes sought his in the moonlight, and heat spread throughout his body. He couldn't stand this anymore; she was torturing him. It was sheer agony, yet it was the finest feeling he had ever known.

"Do you?" she asked again, leaning closer.

"Yes," he whispered. "Yes."

That was all she needed to hear, and all he needed to say. They slid toward each other on the seat as if drawn by magnets, and Julia eagerly reached to touch his face. She ran light fingers over the planes of his cheeks, his jaw, and she pressed feathery kisses onto his forehead. He shut his eyes in ecstasy, letting her do what she wanted with him, and his hands found the light folds of her gown and pulled her closer.

"You love me," she repeated in wonderment. "I never dared hope."

Then, being Julia, she began to babble. "I mean, I always hoped, but I tried not to. I tried not even to think of you in that way." She sighed. "But I couldn't help it."

She kissed his eyelids, his cheeks, his neck, and the light touch of her hot mouth raised a flame inside of him. As his breathing began to quicken, he caught her chin in his hand, and finally, finally kissed her lips.

Her kiss was unpracticed but pure, and in it, James felt her love for him, and he poured all of his own. As her lips pressed softly against his, she moaned, and it was the most seductive sound he had ever heard. He swiveled to face her fully on the carriage seat, taking her face in both of his hands, and her lips parted under his to deepen the kiss. He sank into it, returning all her passion, willing her to feel all of the emotion he had bundled up and tried to hide for so long. The kiss intensified and held; his tongue stroked the inside of her lips lightly, and he felt her shiver.

He slid one hand down her back, pulling her whole body to him, and he felt himself hardening as her breasts pressed against his chest. She moaned again as he pressed kisses down her neck and into the hot hollow of her collarbone. She leaned her head back to expose more of her neck to his kiss, and his feeling of need became almost unbearable as he took in the sight of her eager face, her willing form.

He couldn't touch her enough; he couldn't stop kissing her. He kissed every square inch of skin he could see, all over her face and her neck, and the sensitive skin of her inner wrists. She shivered and laughed, and he smiled at her, sending her all his heart in his eyes. He kissed her lips again, and this time she knew exactly what to do. The tip of her tongue stroked his, and she twined her fingers in his hair to deepen their embrace as his arms tightened around her in a thrill of excitement.

Good Lord, he had never felt such pleasure, even as a green boy. He was stunned by the force of it; he wanted more. He kissed and licked his way again down her neck, and she moaned again as his tongue reached the tops of her breasts. With just a little encouragement, he thought he could—he tugged lightly at the low neckline of Julia's gown, and a whole, pearly breast peeked free. Julia drew in her breath sharply as his eyes hungrily took her in, and James was suddenly terrified she would ask him to stop.

"Do you want me to stop?" he asked. It killed him to ask, but he asked.

"Never stop," she whispered, staring him full in the eyes, and the love in her gaze struck him right in the heart.

He bent his mouth to her nipple, warming it first with his breath, and he smiled to himself when she shuddered with pleasure. He gently took the rosy tip into his mouth, licking and nipping lightly. She squealed at first at the unaccustomed sensation, but when he licked again, she relaxed.

"Oh, that's lovely," she said wonderingly, and this time he met her eyes as he smiled.

"It gets better," he assured her, then hungrily, his mouth returned to her skin, savoring its silkiness, as he breathed in her scent. Again he drew her nipple into his mouth and flicked it lightly with the tip of his tongue. As it puckered under the caresses of his lips, her breath grew unsteady, and he began to enjoy the effect he was having on her. He focused all of his pent-up love and desire onto that nipple, rolling it between his lips, mouthing it softly, sucking it lightly until she arched in his grasp, gasping.

He continued to lick and suck her dainty skin, enjoying his effect on her. As she moaned, gripping his hair in her hands to hold him ever closer to her body, he was dimly aware of his own desire, that it had never, never been like this before. Never had he felt such joy, such love, such longing.

Suddenly, he awakened to himself. He felt as if he had been dashed with cold water, and a wave of shame washed over him.

He had to stop. He couldn't do this. Not to her, and not to Louisa.

Regretfully, so regretfully, he pulled his mouth away. He averted his gaze as he tugged her gown back into place, though he wanted more than anything to drink in the sight of her skin one last time as he did so.

He shook his head, his thoughts still clouded with desire, but one idea was quickly coming into focus. He met her gaze, and the hazy look of arousal in her face was almost enough to break his resolve.

Almost.

"I'm so sorry, Julia," he began, hating to see her expression change at once to one of hurt surprise. "I forgot myself. But I have to stop. I can't do this with you. I shouldn't have done any of this."

She looked stunned, as if he had kicked her, and he hastened to explain.

"I love you so much," he said, his throat tightening, his eyes lingering on her glowing skin and pale hair in the hints of moonlight that peeped into the carriage. "I never expected to fall in love, or to feel it so deeply. But I can't be other than who I was raised to be, either. I have betrothed myself to Louisa, and I can't go back on that promise."

He drew in a deep breath to calm his pounding heart, and he continued, "And it would be dishonorable of me to compromise you, Julia. I can't believe what I just did to you; I'm so sorry. You are a young lady of quality, and if I were free to marry you, I would rightfully propose to you this instant. But I must marry someone else, and eventually you must, too, and I musn't take anything that rightfully belongs to your husband. I've already done far too much."

His throat closed at the idea of Julia married to someone else. Kissing someone else. In bed with someone else. He felt sick.

Julia's expression softened into one of resignation. "I understand, of course," she murmured. "I knew it couldn't be any different."

Her voice broke, and she seemed to continue only with a supreme effort. "I'm glad I told you I love you, and I'm so glad to know you love me. But I always knew it couldn't be any different. I . . . only hoped so. Somehow. I forgot myself, too."

Her voice trembled at the finish. Slowly, she let out a deep breath, and added in a more normal voice, "Thank you for being a gentleman. If you were other than you are, I wouldn't love you as I do."

"We musn't say those things to each other ever again," James said desperately. "You have to forget I said that."

"Oh, no," Julia said, and now there were tears winking in the laughing eyes he loved so well. "I'll never speak of it again, but I'll never, never forget it."

The carriage drew to a halt, and she heaved a shuddery sigh. "Home. Perfect timing, I guess."

He strove for normality. "Would you like me to see you in? This late at night, it seems only right that I see you in."

She smiled sadly at him and grazed his cheek with her fingertips. "Always a gentleman. Very well, see me to the door."

As he helped her out of the carriage, James felt as if he were leaving a cocoon, another world. Already the embraces and the words that had passed between them seemed unreal as he breathed the cool night air again.

But it had been real.

But he couldn't think of it.

But, he thought to himself, glowing just a little inside, it had been real. She loved him. She wanted him.

He smiled as he reached for the door knocker. He smiled as he wished Julia a very proper good night in front of the sleepy-eyed servant who opened the door to her. And he smiled all the way home, and through all of his preparations for bed, and until he was in his bed.

And then he realized again that he was smiling because he was in love with his fiancée's sister, and he groaned.

Chapter 22

In Which Julia Must, Unfortunately, Face the Day

Morning seemed to Julia to dawn earlier and brighter than usual. When she awoke, her head felt heavy, and the sun glared into her eyes with unaccustomed harshness.

"Mmmph," she groaned, holding her hand ineffectually in the path of the sun's rays, and then putting a pillow over her face.

Ugh, she felt terrible this morning. She remembered James telling her she had drunk too much punch last night—was this what men felt like all the time after parties? Oh, her head pounded. She swallowed beneath the protective darkness of the pillow, trying to relieve the dryness of her mouth. She felt so tired. How had the ball at Alleyneham House gone last night? She couldn't summon it to mind right now. She wished Louisa had been there so they could talk about the ball as they always did afterward.

Afterward . . .

She sat bolt upright, the pillow and the sun forgotten

as she suddenly remembered what had happened after she drank the punch. And after the ball, in the carriage. The kisses, the touches . . . James had . . .

No, actually, she did *not* wish Louisa had been there last night.

She groaned again, clasping her head in her hands, and the pounding in her temples took on a new urgency. How could she have said those things to James? How could she have *done* those things with James? With *James*, who was going to marry Louisa?

Despite herself, she shivered to remember the carriage ride home. It all began to come back—what she had told him, and how he had kissed her and told her he loved her.

He loved her. James, who was going to marry Louisa.

Julia shook her head. This was not good. This was the complete opposite of good. She hated to think of it as a bad thing, that the man she loved returned her feelings, but—honestly, with him engaged to her sister, what else could she consider it?

And what should she do now? She couldn't possibly tell Louisa; it would crush her. No, the best way she could reward her sister's trust was never to break it again. Which meant simply ignoring the fact that James loved her.

Was she really better off than before she had known?

"I have always been so, so stupid about him," she mumbled to herself. "Stupid, stupid, stupid."

A perfunctory knock sounded on her door, and Simone entered at once and dropped an equally perfunctory curtsy. "Good morning, *mademoiselle*," she tossed over her shoulder as she began to tidy the post-ball clutter of clothes and hairpins around Julia's room.

"No, it's not a good morning, Simone," Julia groaned. "And I'm not awake yet. Can you come back later?"

Simone continued tidying as if she had not heard. "I heard you talking; I knew that you were awake. I came in to arrange you before you speak to your sister. You should put on a dressing gown, too."

Icy dread washed over Julia, and she felt the blood drain from her face. "Why should I speak to Louisa?" Surely she couldn't know anything. Could she?

"And why should you not? You go to a ball last night; she wants to hear about it."

"She . . . wants to hear about it?" Julia repeated feebly.

The maid turned and stared at Julia with a gimlet eye. "Why should she not?" she pressed. Then, noticing Julia's stricken expression, she relented.

"I saw you come in last night, *mademoiselle*. I helped you into your bed. I know that something happened that was not ordinary, but your sister does not know. And if you do not want her to know, you need to look your most normal, but in the best possible way. Neat and well clothed. The mind follows where the appearance leads."

"That is *so* French," Julia muttered, rolling her eyes.

Despite herself, she had to smile at Simone's reasoning. It was just possible that she was right. "Very well, what do you suggest? Not that you're right about anything happening last night, but, you know, a lady always wants to look her best."

"I will fix your hair to be pretty, and you will put on a dressing gown," Simone decided, retrieving the garment in question from the wardrobe.

"Louisa won't care if I'm wearing a dressing gown," Julia protested.

Simone looked sharply at the younger girl. "Does your sister know you better than anyone else? I think she does. You need to know what you will say to her, and you cannot do that if your hair is all a mess and you wear no dressing gown. Come, I will fix you up."

She sighed as she looked at Julia's tangled hair, and added to herself, "*Mon Dieu*, it would be better if we were to wait for this speech until you are dressed. But we need to be as normal, so this will have to do." She stepped out of the bedchamber for a moment and Julia heard her ordering morning chocolate from a housemaid.

Suddenly Julia felt exhausted and very nervous. When the maid stepped back into the bedchamber, she shut her eyes against the still-sharp morning light and Simone's insistent voice, and passively allowed the Frenchwoman to minister to her. When the chocolate arrived, she sipped at it as Simone's deft fingers untangled her hair and her own mind whirled fruitlessly. What would she say to Louisa? She needed to act natural. But how could she possibly act natural after what she'd done? She was a terrible person.

In a very few minutes, between the chocolate and Simone's ministrations, Julia had to admit that she looked much better, even if she still had no idea what she would say to Louisa.

"You can thank me later, when your vocabulary has returned," Simone said pertly, and Julia rolled her eyes again as the maid left the room. Would anyone but Aunt Estella have a servant more arrogant than half the *ton*?

Well, maybe it was for the best. Simone had at least distracted her. Now that she was alone again, she felt a sickness that had nothing to do with the aftermath of Freddie's punch. How was she going to hide the truth from Louisa? She had never hidden anything from Louisa in all the years they had known each other.

Of course, it helped that she'd never had anything to hide before.

She allowed a feeling of despair to creep over her for one minute, but only one. Then with a supreme effort, she forced it down. Despair was self-indulgence. She mustered all her determination that Louisa should never know what she had done; it would hurt her sister too much.

And for her own part, she would never be tempted again. She would never speak to James again; she would never hide anything from Louisa again. She believed, and hoped, that she meant all these things, for Louisa deserved nothing less.

But she swore she could feel the heat of his hands on her skin, his lips on her lips. She let the pleasure of the memory wash over her for just a moment, unable to resist, then pushed it aside again.

At the thought of her sister—her loving, unknowing sister—part of the knot in her chest dissolved, and she was able to school her face carefully in preparation for Louisa's entry. Even so, she jumped when the knock came on her door.

"Julia, can I come in? Simone said you were awake."

"Thank you *so* much, Simone," Julia grumbled.

At a normal volume, and in what she hoped was her normal voice, she added, "Yes, of course, come in."

Louisa came in, looking cool and elegant as usual in a morning dress of primrose muslin. She seated herself in a chair opposite Julia's bed, and looked expectantly at the younger girl.

"So? How was the ball last night?"

Despite herself, Julia felt her face grow hot. Her stomach clenched. "I had a very nice time."

"I know you danced, because you always do," Louisa said, smiling. "Who did you dance with?"

"Sir Stephen Saville, of course, and Freddie Pellington, and Mr. Cosgrove, and Mr. Milligan, and Lord

Xavier, and . . ." She desperately tried to think of someone else, without mentioning *his* name. "Lord Alleyneham?" she finished weakly.

"Didn't James ask you?" Louisa said with some surprise.

"Oh, yes, that's right. I suppose I did dance with him, too," Julia replied with forced nonchalance, feeling herself grow even redder.

Louisa seemed not to notice her discomfort. She fixed her gaze on the wall several feet to the right of Julia's face, and said, "I'm glad you had a nice time. And I . . . believe it was for the best that I wasn't with you. I didn't really have a headache; I needed some time to think. I did a lot of thinking last night while you all were out."

After the silence had spun out for almost a minute, Julia realized Louisa wasn't going to scratch her eyes out. Clearly something was bothering her greatly, though. "What were you thinking about?" she prodded, relieved to have something to talk about besides herself.

"About . . ." Louisa trailed off, then collected herself and met Julia's eyes. "Well, there's no other way to say it except bluntly. I've decided to break my engagement."

Julia didn't have to feign her shock at all. "What? You are—what? Are you serious?"

"Yes, I'm perfectly serious."

"Does James know? Is it something he did? Or, er, that anyone else did?" Guilt washed over her, and she prayed that it wouldn't show in her treacherous face.

Louisa frowned, considering. "I don't think he knows I was considering this step, but he might not be surprised when he thinks about it. It's certainly not because of anything that he did or didn't do. He couldn't be kinder to me."

"Then why are you doing it?" Julia had to ask. The wash of guilt became an ocean.

Louisa sighed, and despite the freshness of her appearance, her eyes looked tired. "It's the idea of being engaged, I think. At least, being engaged to him."

She smiled ruefully, dropping her gaze to her fingers, which she began twisting together in her lap. "I suppose I ought to feel very fortunate, and I did at first. After all, I had come to London to meet someone just like him, and get married, and become part of his world."

She sighed heavily, seemingly from the very soles of her feet. "Julia, I can't do it. I can't go through another season, and I can't go through with the marriage. I'm not ready; I don't love him."

Tears welled in the corners of her eyes. "You were right about courtship; it *should* be romantic. We had a business transaction, not an engagement, and that's not what I want for myself. I don't want a marriage of convenience, and I don't want to be a viscountess, and I never, never want to come back to London again."

She looked up at Julia, and Julia had never seen such pain in her sister's eyes before. "Julia, I've failed. I failed our parents, and Aunt Estella, and I failed James, who is an honorable man."

"What do you mean, you failed?" Julia's face went white. Surely Louisa hadn't . . . ? "Did you . . . ah . . . you know . . . with someone else?"

Louisa gave a sad half-smile. "Nothing like *that*. I just couldn't do what they needed me to. I couldn't be the carefree young miss who made everyone fall in love with her. I couldn't be Evelina Anville, or Marianne Dashwood, or any of the other enchanting young women we used to read about. I couldn't become a part of this glittering, busy world. I could barely even speak to people.

"Every time I went to a party, I thought, this time it will be different. I know how to act, I know who these people are, I know what they want from me. All I need to do is smile and speak. That's all. But I could never do it, and people stopped noticing me."

"Oh, Louisa," Julia said softly. "I had no idea you had felt that way."

"I was ashamed; I didn't want to tell anyone," Louisa admitted. "I suppose I'd gotten used to being good at everything I put my hand to. I just didn't realize I'd never tried anything I didn't have an inclination for. I'd never been away from everyone I loved. It was a desperate feeling, and when James asked me to marry him, I thought—yes, this is it; this is my way out of this desolate situation."

Julia's throat closed; all she could do was nod her understanding as Louisa continued.

"But it wasn't a way out. Do you see? Life with him would be the same world. Maybe not all the time, but every year he would want to come back to London. He knows this world, and he's comfortable in it, and I never can be."

Louisa shook her head. "He's a kind man, and he wants a true companion in his wife. And he deserves to have that. I couldn't make him happy in marriage, and he couldn't make me happy. I know I'll be branded a jilt because of this, but I think it is the only thing to do."

Her voice was hollow as she added, "It will probably get me the most attention I will have received since my come-out. An added bonus."

"But you wrote so many letters to him when you were apart during the autumn, and they seemed to make you very happy. Didn't that help?" Julia pressed.

Louisa's smile was mirthless and swift. "Those letters

were my favorite part of our engagement. But for the most part, I was asking him questions about his library, and he was providing me with book titles and information about their condition. For the catalogue I was so excited about working on."

She met Julia's eyes. "That's the romance of every girl's dream, isn't it? I suppose I should have tried harder to work things out, but inside I must have always known I hadn't made the right choice."

Tears pricked at Julia's eyes as she realized the depth of her sister's discouragement. Surely she could have made this better. She, who knew Louisa better than anyone, should have known something was wrong and done something to fix it. "Louisa, I am so sorry. I neglected you once we got here, in my own excitement. I didn't realize how you felt. I'm so ashamed of myself."

Fleetingly, she thought of James, and her sense of shame deepened. There was no more she could say. Except—"What would make you happy? What can I do to help you?"

Louisa twisted her hands again. "I really don't know. I always wanted more than our life at Stonemeadows. I never could resist all the books in which an insignificant country girl like me found happiness and wealth by going to London and making an excellent match. But when I got the life those book girls wanted, I didn't want that either. It was so alien to me."

Her shoulders slumped. "Maybe I'm not fit for either of those worlds."

"Don't say that," Julia said, wrung at the sight of her elegant, proud sister brought to such a level of dejection.

What could she say? How could she comfort this girl she thought she had known so well, who had hidden such misery? Julia remembered hints, of course; Louisa had spoken of her loneliness in London. But Julia had not known the sadness went so deep or back so far, that Louisa hadn't felt happy for so long.

She got up from the bed and went around Louisa's chair to wrap her arms around her sister where she sat.

"You're fit for anywhere you want to be," she insisted. "You're the finest person I know."

Still hugging the older girl, she rested her chin on Louisa's head and continued, "You came back to London for my sake, and I can never thank you enough. It gave me advantages you didn't have."

She smiled, hoping her expression warmed her voice so Louisa could hear it. "You brought our home with you, and I never had to feel alone as you did. I've never had to do anything without you since we met as children, except for the year you were in London alone—but then I was safe at home with everyone else.

"You came back here for me, and it has made all the difference to my season. You and James helped me feel comfortable right from the beginning. And now"—she straightened up and moved around the chair to face Louisa, who looked up at her with bleak eyes that quickly shuttered closed—"I am going to help you however I can. I've been selfish."

Oh, God, how she had been selfish. Louisa must never know. A guilty memory of James, smiling at her with love, flashed into her mind and she ruthlessly suppressed it. She repeated, "Yes, I've been selfish. I came to London to enjoy myself, and I never thought of what it was costing you to be here."

Desperate to engage Louisa's eyes, to bring warmth into her face, Julia grabbed her hands. "You are the dearest person in the world to me. Is there anything I can do to help you? I would do anything to help you find happiness."

Louisa lifted her eyes, and fragile hope shivered in them. "I know. I know you would."

She took a deep breath. "I didn't mean to tell you all this. I meant to come in and ask you about the party, and perhaps say something about my engagement."

Warmth was flickering back into her expression as she went on. "But I couldn't go on without telling you. I finally had to tell someone how I really felt. It's the only secret I've ever kept from you. I hadn't wanted to say anything, because I so wanted you to be happy."

"I have been," Julia rushed to assure her. "You helped make it so."

"Well, I'm glad you know the whole truth, if no one else ever does. I don't know what would make me happy, but at least I know what won't."

She smiled her self-deprecating half smile and began to look like herself again. The crisis seemed to be ebbing.

"Actually, there is something I would love you to do for me," Louisa added.

"Anything. Anything at all."

Louisa looked embarrassed. "Could you send for James and give him a letter for me? It will tell him everything I've told you, though of course not in quite the same way. I know I should do this in person, but I can't quite bring myself to face him after all his kindness. And perhaps by being there, in case he's shocked, you could be a comfort to him, or help to explain things. There may be no way around it, but I would not want him to think ill of me. At least, no more than necessary," she finished ruefully.

"Give a letter? And talk to James? For you?" Julia

repeated, trying to wrap her mind around the idea. It sounded like a very, very bad one.

"Yes, could you? As soon as possible." Louisa's expression was anxious.

"I really think you should do it yourself. You know, talk to him in person," she coaxed.

Louisa shook her head vehemently. "It must be this letter. It says exactly what I want to say. There's no way I could do that in person. I'd probably lose my courage and wind up setting the wedding date instead of calling the whole thing off."

Her eyes beseeched Julia. "Will you please do this? For me?"

Julia gulped, nodded, and put what she hoped was a warm smile on her face. "Of course I will."

Chapter 23

In Which the Second Letter Is More Significant

The morning after the Alleyneham ball, James also awoke with a pounding head and a sickening feeling in his stomach—though, unlike Julia, he could not attribute any of these sensations to having overimbibed the night before. Rather, he was all too aware that he had been terribly, terribly sober when he . . .

No, he didn't want to think about it. He shouldn't.

But despite his best intentions, he allowed his thoughts to turn to the carriage ride home. He felt a twisting mixture of delight and pain, remembering how he and Julia had admitted their love for each other.

And then how he had taken advantage of her admission to act in a way a man betrothed never should. Even if his engagement was more akin to a contract than a love match, his fiancée deserved better from him. He felt sick with self-loathing at having betrayed Louisa—and also at the fact that he wasn't, deep in his heart, one bit sorry for it.

He knew it could never happen again, and that made him all the gladder it had happened, just that once.

He lay in bed, pondering the complicated ebb and flow of his feelings about the night before, when he was interrupted by his manservant's knock on the bedchamber door. Without waiting for a response, Delaney entered with an even smugger smile than usual.

"Good morning, my lord." He smirked as he wrenched the room's curtains open, letting a blast of late morning sun hit James's bleary eyes. As he winced and averted them (for a viscount could never go so far as to pull the covers over his head in front of a servant), he could practically feel his manservant's impish glee.

"My apologies, my lord. Were we out late last night?"

James sighed. "*I* was out late last night, as you well know, although it was not particularly late for a ball. As you also well know." Under his breath, he grumbled, "Since you bloody well know everything that goes on here."

"I beg pardon, my lord. I did not precisely hear what your lordship said. Does your lordship have instructions that I might carry out?"

"No, curse you," James said, his good humor beginning to return as they started their old familiar sparring. "I was just saying you're too nosy for your own good."

He stretched luxuriantly, accepting that it was time for his day to begin. "Any post? I can go through it with my coffee. If you'll take my hint."

Delaney's knowing smile widened. "As a matter of fact, we received a very intriguing letter by messenger this morning. I did not take the liberty of opening it, since it appears to be from a correspondent of the feminine persuasion. I shall bring it up directly with your lordship's coffee."

He left the room on the promised errands as James began piling up pillows to prop himself up in bed. He wondered whom the letter could be from. If it was from his mother or sister, Delaney wouldn't have made a special point of mentioning it. And Louisa had never once sent him a letter since arriving in London.

He couldn't imagine who else could be writing to him, unless it was some old flame from the depths of the past. But surely that wasn't it. Though it almost seemed more likely than the only other possibility he could think of.

He hardly dared allow himself to entertain the thought that *she* might be writing to him. But as soon as he saw that flowing hand on the thick folded missive Delaney brought him, he knew it was from Julia, and his stomach flipped. He would have known that handwriting anywhere. Somehow, in the months since meeting her, he'd come to pick up those details about her without even realizing it, until now he felt he knew her better than anyone in the world.

Even so, the contents of this letter were a complete mystery to him. She wouldn't have written about their wonderful but foolish behavior of the night before, would she? His head was suddenly clear and curious, the coffee service unneeded. He unsealed the letter eagerly, waving the obviously curious Delaney out of the room so he could read it in peace.

Once he had it open, he realized its bulk was due to the fact that it enclosed another sealed missive. Julia's own correspondence was just a brief note of explanation. Still, he greedily drank in every word penned by her hand:

Dear James,

   Louisa has asked me to deliver this letter to you as a friend, but under the circumstances, I thought it might be best for you not to receive this from me in person. Please accept my sincere apologies, and do let me know if there is anything I can do as a friend to ease any displeasure you might have.

                                   Sincerely,
                                   Julia Herington

Well. That wasn't *quite* what he had been expecting. And once he read the note through several times to be sure he hadn't missed any hidden crumbs of meaning, he became slightly annoyed. It was so formal and impersonal. So she didn't want to see him, did she? Even though her sister had asked her to give him . . . something? He had no clue what this talk of displeasure was, but figured from the tone that Louisa didn't know what had taken place the night before.

Then there was that phrase "as a friend," which she had repeated twice. "As a friend." Well, if he hadn't been a friend to Julia, what had he been? True, last night had been an unforgivable lapse in propriety—and yet she *had* forgiven him, and even seemed to regard him as well-as ever when they parted. And before last night, he had shepherded her gently along the rocky path of London society and manners for weeks so that she would be a credit to his family when he and Louisa were married. Good Lord, he'd even helped her look for a husband of her own. How many other friends would have done as much?

At least, helping her become a credit to his family was how it had started out. His feelings had changed along the way, as they both now knew, but still. He didn't have to be *reminded* that they could only be friends.

He shook his head in puzzlement and "displeasure," to borrow her own term, and unsealed the letter that had been enclosed within the folds of Julia's note. This one was from Louisa. The first real letter he had ever gotten from her, and somehow he didn't think it was going to turn out to be a love letter, based on Julia's brief note of explanation.

Dear James,

I have hesitated for a long time about writing this letter, or about communicating at all the feelings that I have at last decided to reveal. However, I believe I owe you the same candor and courtesy with which you have always treated me, and so I must own the truth.

You must have known for a long time how unhappy I found myself in London, but what you cannot have known—and what I did not know, myself, until I granted myself time for reflection last night—was that I cannot see myself ever taking part in the life you lead here. It is too foreign to me, and I am ill suited for success in it. In a sense, therefore, I became engaged to you under false pretenses, though it was unwittingly done. I know that you need a wife who can share fully in the social and economic responsibilities of your life, and even perceive them as joys. I also know that I can never do this.

I therefore release you from our engagement. I believe that you will be happier, and I hope that I will, too, though this statement is certainly not intended as a reflection on your behavior toward me. You have always treated me as a gentleman should, and my greatest regret is that my action must necessarily prevent our families from interacting in the future. I know my own family has come to value you greatly. I trust that if you can find it in your heart to forgive the embarrassment I must be causing you, you will not allow it to affect your feelings toward them.

In time, perhaps, you may forgive me as well. I hope to forgive myself someday for putting us both in this untenable situation, although that day has not yet arrived.

With my sincerest regard,
Louisa

He reread this letter several times as well, to be sure that he understood it. Louisa was breaking their engagement . . . because she was unhappy?

He was stunned.

It was like the answer to a prayer, considering his own growing ambivalence, and yet it hurt more than he would have imagined. He was shaken, embarrassed, stung. It seemed unbelievable that he could have failed so utterly to notice how dissatisfied she felt.

Of course he had known that she didn't enjoy *ton* parties. They had, after all, met because she'd fled the Alleyneham House ballroom. But he could hardly understand it, all the same. How could she wish to give up everything he was offering her, just to avoid the social circles in which he had to move? His name, his fortune, and—if he did say so himself—a fairly even temperament, liberal mind, and not unhandsome appearance should make him a reasonably agreeable husband by anyone's standards. Why was he not enough for her?

Hmm. Thinking about it like that, it did seem rather cold and businesslike. He might have seemed right to her when she considered him on paper, so to speak, but . . . well, if she couldn't enjoy living in London at least part of the time, spending time with his family, even hosting events, she would frequently find herself unhappy. He had assumed their different temperaments would work themselves out, but it now seemed that hadn't been realistic. And it wouldn't be realistic for her to expect him to change everything on her account, either; a viscount couldn't just drop out of society unless there was a major scandal attached.

As these thoughts ran through his head, he began to understand Louisa's motivations a bit better, and the hurt began to abate. It wasn't personal, she had made clear. And his own loss, while great, was not the loss of a love match.

Excitement bubbled up in him.

He was free.

He was free, and Julia loved him, and now he could pursue her.

Except—no, he really couldn't.

The realization clanged down onto his excitement like a hammer onto an anvil. (Where did these pastoral analogies keep coming from, he wondered. It must be from all that time spent in Lord Oliver's blasted stables.)

No, if there was any woman he couldn't pursue now, it was Julia. Louisa was correct; there would be social repercussions from their broken engagement. Oh, it wouldn't exactly be a scandal, but a jilted viscount would be the talk of the *ton* for a while, and it would certainly be difficult for Louisa herself to reenter society should she ever choose to.

Not to mention the fact that it would cause a shattering amount of gossip if he took up at once with the sister of his former betrothed. He doubted his own family would ever deign to speak to Louisa or any of her relatives again, since a broken engagement would, in their eyes, be taken as a huge slight.

Yet he had meant well, from the beginning. He had tried to do right by his family, and by Louisa. They had *all* meant well. Funny how such a lot of well-meaning people could wind up at cross-purposes.

He laid his letters from the two sisters in front of him on the bed and sighed from deep within. If there was one thing worse than being engaged and unable to be with the woman he loved, it was being *un*-engaged and still unable to be with the woman he loved.

He rubbed his hands over his face, then straightened up and set his feet on the floor. It was time to face the day. It was going to be a long one.

It seemed likely that they would all be long ones, for a while.

Chapter 24

In Which Julia Is, for Once, at a Loss for Words

Julia tried not to laugh. She knew it would be absolute disaster if she did.

She had never received a proposal before, so she hadn't exactly known what to expect. Still, she had always imagined it would be dignified and touching, even romantic and passionate. But this—this was just *ridiculous*.

Sir Stephen Saville meant well, she was sure, but filling her aunt's drawing room with flowers and referring to her as "the flower of his heart, and he hoped, his hearth" as he ardently clasped her hand to his chest was just too much, even for a girl who enjoyed a good novel.

That was the problem, actually. She enjoyed a *good* novel, and this was like something out of a very bad one. The flower of his hearth? As she thought of it again, her cheeks dimpled despite herself, and she tried desperately to school her expression into a serious one while Sir Stephen still gripped her hand.

"You are smiling," he noted. "Can it be that my

proposal meets with your approval? Will you make me the happiest man in the world?"

Oh, good Lord, the man needed an answer right away, and she had no idea what to say.

Here it was, the proposal that she was supposed to angle for throughout her season, from a man that even James had recommended to her as kind and good. Now that the moment was here, though, she was startled all the same, utterly without the right words, which was a terrible feeling for her.

Why hadn't they prepared her for this, her aunt and James? She knew everything else about how to act in polite society, from when to use a fish fork to how to curtsy to the queen. But she had no idea what to say when she received a proposal.

Or maybe she did; at least, she knew what she wanted to say. She thought of the letter that Louisa had asked her to deliver, breaking an engagement to a man who was otherwise perfect, but whom she didn't love. She couldn't do what her sister hadn't been able to do: marry where she ought rather than where she longed to. Especially not after last night.

Images of James, the revelation of the carriage ride, and her note to him that morning bobbed into her mind and sobered her at once. No, she couldn't marry Sir Stephen, no matter what her aunt Estella wanted her to do, or what her parents—or the whole *ton*, for that matter—might be expecting.

What could she say to him, though? What did girls always say in novels? She thought desperately and seized on a vague thread of memory.

"I am honored by your proposal," she began.

Oh dear, that couldn't be right. He looked far too happy all of a sudden. "But," she quickly continued, and his face fell at once. "I cannot accept your offer. I am so sorry."

The baronet inhaled sharply as if punched, then seemed to shake off the blow with an effort. He took her hands in his, peering closely at her face to gauge her reaction.

"Have I done something to offend you? Perhaps I danced with you an insufficient number of times last night, or I did not bring enough flowers with me today? I have tried to make my regard for you clear, and let me assure you I will make you a most devoted and steadfast husband. It will be my delight to meet your every need."

Julia smiled again, this time in genuine appreciation for his kindness. It was a shame he was wasting it on her, really. It wasn't his fault she wasn't reacting as she ought.

She tried to lessen the blow, responding in like manner to the quiet formality of his words. "Dear sir, you have not offended me in any way. You've always treated me with great respect and warmth, and I feel the honor of it. But . . ." She trailed off, losing courage, and dropped her gaze. "My heart is already engaged, although not in any formal sense. I feel it would be wrong to promise myself to you under the circumstances."

She nodded in satisfaction as she finished speaking. That sounded like something out of a novel, definitely.

He squeezed her hand gently, then dropped it from his clasp. His voice was still hopeful as he entreated her once more.

"I'm very sorry to hear it, for my own sake," he said. "You have, of course, my best wishes for your future happiness. Will you at least allow me some hope, and promise me that you will still consider the possibility of marriage with me? If not now, perhaps at some point in the future?

I am sure my own wishes shall remain unchanged, if yours ever do."

Oh, good heavens. Now she *really* didn't know what to say. How did one decline a man's proposal twice when—in his view and the view of one's rather pushy aunt—there was no earthly reason to do so? How could she possibly let him know that no, there was no way she could ever marry him, because she could never get over James, but she could never have him, because he'd just been jilted by her sister, so she could probably never get married at all to anyone, ever?

Right. She'd just spill all of that out to Sir Stephen.

Suddenly mortified, Julia settled for what she hoped was a timid-looking nod. "Thank you," she offered. She knew she ought not even to have said that much, but she wanted to put an end to this interview as soon as was humanly possible. She was too agitated to be more insistent with the baronet at this time. Vague though she had been on the details, she thought she had probably been remarkably tactless to bring up another man during his proposal anyway.

A man with whom she had precisely no chance of a future.

And yet, she wouldn't take it back, she mused, as she vaguely heard Sir Stephen making his proper good-byes to her and, on his way out of the house, to her aunt (who had suddenly reappeared from the nonexistent errand that had caused her to vanish from the room upon his arrival). She couldn't take back her no. She just couldn't marry out of obligation, ever, and she could never marry someone else while her heart and mind were so full of James.

She sat stunned for a few minutes, nervous energy coursing through her body. She wanted to go somewhere else. She needed to talk with someone about Sir Stephen's proposal, and what she had said, and why, and about what—or more precisely, who—was really weighing on her mind.

But today of all days, she couldn't talk to Louisa about engagements of any sort. And she knew what her aunt would say, should she explain the situation to her. Lady Irving would call her an idiot and insist that she summon the unlucky gentleman back so she could accept his proposal at once. She could still remember the feeling of her aunt's talon-like nails gripping her arm and dragging her around the Alleyneham House ballroom in search of Sir Stephen.

No, there was only one person she could talk to about all of this.

She had to act quickly; she knew she had only a few moments before her aunt came in and demanded a full account of what had passed. Alive with purpose, she peeped out of the parlor, and finding no one around, quickly retrieved Simone's cloak. The capacious garment was the best she could do to disguise her appearance. It wasn't much, but anything that would keep her from being recognized would help, since she was going to do a thing a gently bred young lady ought never to do.

She was going to James, to see him at his home.

Alone. Now.

Chapter 25

In Which More Than One Proposal Is Discussed

James's bachelor lodgings were in Stratton Street, not far from her aunt's fashionable Grosvenor Square address, but Julia felt as if she were walking for hours. The delicious, unfamiliar freedom of leaving her home unaccompanied was almost overcome by her anxious desire to see James and her nervousness about being spotted by someone she knew. The wide square's crisscrossing pathways had never seemed so long nor so crowded. She could have sworn every eye was on her, that everyone knew where she was going.

When she finally reached James's door, she paused before knocking. She inhaled deeply to try to calm herself. In. Out. In. Out. Then, overcome with nerves, she tapped on the door with the large brass knocker. Her hand seemed to jitter out of her control, striking a quick, incessant staccato with the knocker until, after what seemed like at least a week, that arrogant servant of James's opened the door with his brows lifted skeptically.

Despite her anxiety, Julia was gratified to see Delaney's supercilious expression change to one of surprise. His mouth gulped open and closed again silently.

"Miss Herington," he finally managed, looking behind her for the presence of a maid. "Er . . . welcome."

"No maid with me," she replied to his unspoken question, feeling her self-possession return a bit. "Could I— that is, I would like to speak with Lord Matheson."

"Of course," Delaney responded at once, slipping back into his proper servant mien as if there was nothing remarkable about her showing up unannounced and unescorted. He showed her up to the drawing room and, when she declined refreshment, promised to notify his master of her presence directly.

She plumped herself down onto a sofa in the quiet room and waited, feet tapping, for James to come in. What was she going to say to him? She hadn't thought this through. Her sister had only just today decided to break off the engagement, and Julia was now going to start talking about having turned down a proposal.

"What was I thinking?" she muttered. For all she knew, James hadn't even read the letter yet from her *or* from Louisa. He might not know anything had changed. Good heavens, he might not even be awake yet, for all she knew. In which case it would seem as if she was just here to throw herself at him. Again.

Humiliating.

Though . . . the thought actually sounded more appealing when she toyed with it a bit. She remembered the luscious pleasure of his kisses, the heat between her legs, the longing such as she had never felt before. Maybe throwing herself at him wouldn't be such a bad idea after all.

But this wasn't the time; she still had that proposal looming over her. The thought of Sir Stephen was a dash of cold water, sobering her in a second. Yes, that was why she had come; she needed someone to talk to about Sir Stephen. In truth, it had been very sensible to come. If for no other reason than to escape Lady Irving's wrath for a short while.

She began to feel antsy again, so she got up and began to pace around the room. Despite her preoccupation, she was curious about James's house. Had he put anything of himself into it, as he was beginning to at Nicholls?

She hoped not, actually. It was so *bland*. The paper was plain, the furniture of good quality but without color, and a bit out of date in its mahogany heaviness and formal arrangement against the walls. It was an impersonal, humorless room. The only sign of character was the positive riot of books and newspapers on a few side tables. Curious about James's taste in reading, Julia picked up a volume and opened it to the title page.

Mansfield Park, volume 1. A copy of the book he had given Louisa when he first began to court her last season.

She felt a twist of sadness in her chest. Just then, she heard the door open and James's footsteps enter.

"I don't like this room," she said without turning around.

"Neither do I," said the familiar voice, without missing a beat. "But then again, this isn't really my house."

She turned in surprise to look at him, and he continued, "By the way, hello to you. I can't say I think much of your new greeting style."

She ignored this last statement. "What do you mean, this isn't your house?"

"I mean, it's a rented house, and rented furniture," James replied. "I didn't choose any of it, but it suffices for now. I live here when I am in town, but that's very little. Someday when Nicholls is completely restored, I flatter myself that you and your family will be able to walk into a room without telling me how much you hate it. Although," he added, his face pensive, "your aunt may never come to that point, considering her reaction on first seeing the place."

Julia goggled at him. He looked untroubled, and he was talking about her family as if everything were normal. Had he not read the letters yet?

James stared her right back in the eye and cocked a skeptical eyebrow at her. "Not that I think you came to talk about interior design. What *did* you come for? I have to admit, I am surprised to see you after the very interesting set of letters I received from your household this morning. *As a friend.*" He laid heavy stress on the last few words, then folded his arms, looking at her expectantly.

Ah. So he *had* read the letters. She scanned his face intently for a hint of his feelings, but his expression was shuttered and unreadable.

Her nervousness was back again in full force, and she twisted her gloved fingers together as she searched for words. "I . . . I just . . . there was something I wanted to talk to you about," she said lamely.

He continued to stare at her, arms folded, eyebrow raised.

Julia squirmed under the chill of his gaze, then blurted, "Sir Stephen asked me to marry him, and I told him no, but then he asked if he could still hope and it seemed unkind to insist, and I just wanted him to leave me alone, so I said he could. But I don't want him to hold on to any hope, and I don't want him to propose again. And I can't tell my aunt because she'll be so angry, and I can't talk about this with Louisa, especially not today, and I really needed to talk to someone because I'm not sure if I did the right thing."

James's eyebrow lifted even higher. "Not sure if you did the right thing? By saying no, you mean?"

She was getting tired of this haughty nonsense. "No, you ass," she replied, and was pleased to see his cold expression crack into one of shock. "Of course I'm sure I was right to say no. What I mean is, I don't know if I did right by leaving him with any hope. Because really, I will never want to marry him. Only it's the first proposal I ever received, and I don't know how these things are done. How does one make a gentleman understand that one's response is irrevocable?"

James seemed not to have heard her explanation. He was still reeling and gaping at her. "What on *earth* did you call me?"

"Um, nothing." Julia felt her face growing hot with embarrassment. "I didn't call you anything. I just, um, explained the situation and why I had come, and why I was feeling, um, a bit at sea. But, um, I'll be going now." She sidled toward the door.

"Not so fast." In a flash, he darted a hand out and caught her arm in a gentle grasp. She looked up at him, worried, then to her relief noticed that he was smiling.

An answering smile spread over her own face, and then they both started to chuckle. Her very heart seemed to warm, and she wanted desperately to hold him. She even began to reach for him with her free arm.

So when he dropped her arm from his grasp, still shaking his head with laughter, she felt lonely. He was right there, but so far away. Why *had* she come? What could he possibly tell her that would help? What could either of them do now?

"Sit down," he said, still chuckling. With a graceful bow, he directed her toward a very hard horsehair chair, and he sat on another facing her that looked just as uncomfortable.

He shook his head again. "That's my Julia. Two minutes in my house, and she tells me she hates it and calls me an ass." He started laughing once more.

"That's not what I meant," she tried to explain, but she didn't feel the need to justify herself too much. He had read the letters, and yet he laughed with her. Maybe he had been angry, but he was laughing now and he had called her his Julia. *His.*

Her feeling of isolation eroded a little, and she relaxed. As much as she possibly could relax in such a cursedly hard chair, that is.

"So." James slapped his hands against his knees. "The man finally came up to scratch, and you said no."

"Yes," she replied. "I had to."

She searched his face, looking for some sign of ardor or excitement, or even of acknowledgment that something significant had happened. But the familiar, loved countenance remained open and expectant.

So she continued talking. "I know you had told me that he would be a good person to marry, but I just couldn't say yes. But then he badgered me, and I caved in and agreed that he could still hope, which I now regret. I don't really know what to do next. I suppose I should plan to avoid his company as much as possible so he won't get any false hopes."

Now it was her turn to look at him, waiting for a reply. He puffed out all of his air, and shook his head again. "God almighty, what a ridiculous couple of days we've had."

She bristled. "What do you mean, ridiculous?"

He must have noticed her displeasure, for he hastened to explain. "Only this: Two days ago, I was engaged and thought I would be so indefinitely. I knew my fiancée wasn't the most enthusiastic bride-to-be, but I had no idea that she was miserable, or that her sister loved me. I wasn't even fully aware that, over the past several months, I had fallen so jealously, crazily in love with that same sister that I would forget myself as I never had before. And that when precisely the kind and eligible gentleman I urged her to marry finally proposed, it would make me so much more jealous that I would contemplate throwing him through a window, even though she said no."

"Not *quite* no," Julia corrected, though a beaming smile was breaking across her face.

"True, not quite no, and not 'no' enough for me," James continued. "I don't think I'd be satisfied unless you had told the fellow you never wanted to see him again, and spat on his boots as a finale. I still want to throw him through a window." He stood up and looked around the room. "Where's my coat? I know where he lives. He has big windows; they'll look positively amazing shattered to bits."

"Oh, stop it," Julia said, half laughing, and put a hand on his arm. "I didn't come to tell you to make you feel jealous. Although it is a nice bonus."

"Why did you come tell me then, minx?" He crouched down in front of her and took her chin in his hand. He stared intently at her, a roguish smile on his lips, his gaze hopeful.

The yearning in his eyes unsettled her, heated her, made butterflies flit through her whole body.

"I was so confused," she faltered. "I knew what I wanted to say, but not what I should say. And now that I'm here with you, I know what I want to say again, but not what I should say."

"Why not?" His clear gaze fairly burned her.

"Well, I know it would cause a nine-days' wonder if it became known that Louisa had jilted you," she began.

"It would," he agreed, still looking at her intently.

"And also if anyone found out that I had rejected Sir Stephen's suit. Especially if I then took up with you," she continued.

"A positive scandal," he agreed, drawing her face closer to his. The heat of his gaze was twisting her stomach into an excited knot.

"And I know your family's very proper, and they would be mortified to be a part of a scandal," she added. "Especially considering what your poor sister has already been through. Not to mention they wouldn't be all that delighted to have you throwing yourself away on an untitled girl with no more than a passable dowry."

"They are indeed, very proper," he agreed, leaning forward to press soft kisses along the long line of her neck. She closed her eyes, focusing all her attention on the feel of his lips, the whisper of his breath. It warmed her through to her very core.

She drew in a gulp of air at the quick flashes of pleasure he awoke in her, then strove to continue. "And . . . I . . . you . . . you know, we . . . um . . ."

Her head was foggy from his kisses. Her neck began to feel so pliable, her head so heavy, that she simply had to tilt it back to allow his mouth better access.

"Something you wanted to say?" he murmured, a laugh in his voice as he kissed his way down her neck to her collarbone and began to toy with the edge of her bodice.

"Oh, for heaven's sake, I can't think straight when you do that!" Julia exclaimed.

Obediently, James drew back and watched her patiently, still crouching in front of her chair. She felt disappointed and cold, and she impulsively held out her hands to him.

He grabbed them at once and raised them to his lips. "You said you didn't know what you *ought* to say," he reminded her, "but you knew what you *wanted* to say when you came here."

His bright green gaze bored into her eyes, seeking the corners of her very soul.

"Why did you come? What did you want to tell me, Julia?"

She faltered. "I . . ." She lowered her eyes, embarrassed. She had tried so hard to be a proper town lady, and she knew a proper lady would never, *never* say what she wanted to say.

"Julia," he whispered, catching her chin again and bringing her face up to meet his eyes again. "Darling. You can tell me anything."

There was such hope in his eyes, and his endearment was like a kiss in itself. She drew up her courage and told him.

"I don't care about the scandal. I don't care about anything else that might happen. I want you, in the way a woman wants the man she loves."

It was all he needed to hear. He leapt to his feet and scooped her up into his arms as if she weighed less than nothing. He kissed her fiercely and then, still carrying her, strode quickly to the door.

"What are you doing?" she said, laughing shakily, hoping she knew the answer.

"You said you didn't like this room," he replied, nudging the door open. "I think it's time you saw my bedchamber instead."

Chapter 26

In Which Julia Realizes She Hadn't Known What to Expect, After All

"Now this room I *like*," Julia said wonderingly as James, still carrying her, booted open the door of his bedchamber and afforded her a first glance at the room.

It at once impressed her as warm, comfortable, and masculine, with red and gold pin-striped paper on the walls and a cozy chair in the corner. The room was dominated by a rather large mahogany-framed bed, its counterpane and hangings also in muted red tones. Rather . . . passionate colors.

She gulped despite herself. Her nervousness had returned, though now it was a pleasurable tingling of anticipation. She didn't quite know what she had gotten herself into, but she was ready to find out.

James set her down gently on the bed and sat on its edge next to her. "I'm very glad you like it," he finally replied. "I tried to make this room comfortable and warm. I . . . I hope you'll spend quite a while here."

"I would like that," she answered shyly.

He looked sharply at her. "Julia, do you know what you're saying? No, you can't possibly know."

He stood up at once. "I need to be very clear about this," he went on, his teeth slightly gritted. "It's very hard to bring myself to say this considering the way I am feeling right now, but I owe it to you. If we go ahead and . . . you know . . ."

"Couple?" Julia suggested, now enjoying his discomfort. Oddly, it seemed to be more physical than emotional discomfort, judging from the look on his face.

He groaned at her reply. "If we *make love*, it will be irrevocable. You will give me a precious gift that you can never then give to any other man."

"I wouldn't want to," she assured him. "You are the only one I could ever want."

He groaned again. What was the man's problem? Now she noticed, the front of his pants was bulging suspiciously.

Her eyes widened. Of course; it made sense now. She knew how the act worked from seeing the livestock mating, but she hadn't quite realized that people had the same type of . . . equipment.

Or that the pleasure of anticipation could be so great.

She leaned back onto the bed and arched her back slightly, instinctively. "I told you I know what I want, and it's you. Don't you trust me to know my own mind?" she teased.

He yanked off his top boots, heedless of their fine craftsmanship, and tossed them into the corner of the room.

"Throwing your boots around? Your valet will be distressed," Julia observed, smiling.

"Curse the man," James replied just as cheerfully, climbing onto the bed and covering her small form with his long one. He propped himself up on his forearms and looked down into her eyes.

"I want this more than anything," he began. "But I have to ask again if you're sure about this. About me."

"Of course," Julia replied at once, stroking his cheek, the face she loved. "I trust you. And I want it, too." Then she added conscientiously, "Although to be honest, I don't really know what I'm talking about. I mean, I know the basics, since I grew up on a farm. I've seen animals coupling many times. And I can tell you have the same male parts, because of the way your pants are bulging."

He snorted with laughter and silenced her momentarily with a kiss.

"But," she finally managed, her lips still just a breath away from his own, "it never seemed to hold much pleasure for the females. And I feel such pleasure already."

James laughed again and buried his face in her hair. He kissed her ear, and said, "My ridiculous darling. This is only the beginning."

"It is?" she breathed wonderingly, as he continued to press kisses onto her face. She felt his hands beginning to roam her body, caressing and shaping her breasts, and she inhaled raggedly at the sudden wonder of it.

"Yes," he confirmed, "and I'll thank you not to make any more comparisons between us and animals. What you've seen is nothing, *nothing*, like what happens between people who love each other. Especially not between you and me."

"Why especially us?" she couldn't help asking, though her desire to speak was, admittedly, dimmed quite a bit by his long fingers, which had slid beneath the fabric of her bodice and were now stroking and toying with her nipple, driving her to distraction.

"Because," he answered, "of what I'm going to do to you with my tongue."

"Oh," she answered, her thoughts reeling confusedly. What was he going to do? Was he going to . . .

And then . . . *"Oh."* She understood, as he tugged down the bodice of her dress to reveal her breasts and, as he had the night before, began to lick and lightly suck at her nipples. "Oh, that's lovely."

"If you're able to talk, it's not lovely enough," he growled against her pale skin.

She hated to feel him draw his mouth away, although it was only to raise himself off her and begin searching for the fastenings of her clothes. Obligingly, she turned onto her side so he could reach the buttons at the back of her dress. She had to laugh at his fumbling inability to slide the small beads from their openings.

"I'm not usually clumsy," James said in his defense, a look of intense concentration on his face. "I just really want this dress off you this second. I can't keep my hands steady."

Julia was, she had to admit, a bit proud of this proof of her appeal. She had made a grown man forget how to work buttons! But she savored the feeling for only a moment. She had no idea what he was going to do next, but she was as impatient for it as James seemed to be.

Her gown loosened and lifted over her head, her slippers tossed after his boots, her stays unlaced, she soon lay before him in only her shift and silk stockings. He divested himself of his coat but remained dressed in his pantaloons and now-rumpled shirt.

"Why are you still wearing so many clothes?" Julia asked, her voice innocent but her eyes winking at him.

James seemed to choke, and he stared at her in

what seemed like awe. Again he seemed in physical discomfort—yet he seemed almost happy about it?

"I wasn't sure if you were ready to see me," he admitted. "And I felt I needed to give you one more chance to tell me to stop, if you want to."

"You keep asking me that," she pondered. "Don't you want to make love to me?"

His only reply was a low growl of laughter as James pounced back on the bed and again covered her now-thinly-clad form with his own. He kissed her deeply and she savored the feel of his lips against hers, the tender warmth of his tongue lightly touching her own. One of his hands began to stroke her thighs, raising shivers that ran up and down her body. Yet if she shivered, why should she feel so warm?

She didn't realize she had spoken the words aloud until James replied teasingly, "You're warm, you say? Then we need to take off more of your clothes."

He smiled and began tugging at her shift, trying to work it up over her head.

"Let me." Julia stopped him. She stared him straight in the eye, daring him to touch her, to worship her with his gaze as she sat up and slowly rolled the light garment up over her head. With a smile of instinctive mischief, she tossed it after her slippers into the beleaguered corner of the bedchamber. She sat before him on the bed, calmly nude except for her stockings and garters, as he gaped at her in wonder.

"Interesting," she said. "I thought I might feel self-conscious, but I don't. Is that strange?"

He shook his head dumbly. "You're so beautiful," he told her, his voice almost cracked with strain. "You have nothing to be self-conscious about."

She smiled and began to toy with the collar of his shirt, relishing his groans of protest as she swatted his eager hands away from her breasts. "It's my turn to fumble around and be completely unable to unfasten your clothes," she teased.

She reached for the front placket of his trousers, enjoying the moans he was unable to hold back as she searched out the shape of his body with her fingers. "This is interesting, too," she said, feeling gently up the length of his hardness. "It's very big. How does it all fit in your clothing?"

"It doesn't, right now," he choked. He tried to seize her hand. "Julia, please, you don't know what you're doing to me."

"True," she admitted. "But I want to learn."

Her hands lightly explored his body, roaming not just over the bulge in his trousers, but also up under the fine linen of his shirt, across the smooth, strong planes of his chest. She found his nipples, and remembering how much pleasure he had granted her, she lightly stroked them.

His muscles twitched under her fingers. Quickly, he lifted his shirt over his head and faced her again, his breathing unsteady.

She squealed with delight. "I made you jump! I made you strip!" She touched his nipples again with the softest graze possible.

This was too much for James, who seized both of her small wrists in one of his larger hands and again pressed her back onto the bed. Leaning over her, he said with voice husky and warm, "It's my turn again."

"But I want to keep touching you," she said.

"I want to touch you, too," he replied, tugging off her garters one by one and, with infinite slowness, rolling her stockings down her legs. His touch was a whisper against her skin, promising gratification of a kind she had never known.

"How do you do that?" she wondered. "How can you make me feel so good with your hands?"

"This is nothing," James said, parting her knees and settling between them. "I still haven't shown you what I can do with my tongue." His smile was positively wicked.

"Yes, you di—oh!" The words were surprised right out of her as James's hot tongue licked her *there*. She was shocked, as if she had been shaken awake by the sheer force of the pleasure of it. "James, are you allowed to do that?"

"If you allow it, I'll do it," he murmured, and his delicious, devilish tongue dipped into her core to taste the very heat and heart of her womanhood.

No one else had ever, ever touched her there. But somehow it seemed right and fitting that James should be her first. Her only. She could never imagine being so vulnerable for anyone else, or permitting anyone else to see her so exposed or touch her so intimately.

And then she stopped thinking, and just let the pleasure wash over her.

His tongue lapped and tasted her, his lips kissed her, his warm breath heated her through. Those clever, strong hands found her breasts, her nipples, and stroked them even as he continued to lick at her delicate folds. She clutched for his shoulders, seeking to release the pleasurable pressure building in her, but as he continued the play of his fingers and tongue, she gave up and let her arms fall to her sides, boneless.

She moaned and shivered under his touch, feeling as if she were being drawn inevitably toward something, but she had no idea what it was. And then he moved his tongue just a bit, *there*. The intimate stroke was all she needed to push her over the brink, and she simply shattered, shuddering and crying out from the intense, unaccustomed joy of it.

As the shivers of pleasure subsided, she felt herself drawn back to the present as if from a long distance. Tingling, vibrant life came back into her limbs, and the space between her legs was warm, sensitive, and eager.

"Oh, James," she breathed. "That was the loveliest thing I've ever felt."

He smiled, this time with tenderness and none of the mischief of before. "I'm so glad, my love," he said simply.

His love; that was much, *much* better than having him call her "my dear." She felt the difference in her heart; she knew the truth of it.

He kissed his way up her stomach, her collarbone, her neck before again kissing her lips. "My love," he said again. "We can stop now, or we can go on."

"There's more?" she asked, amazed.

"Yes, so much," he said, and now there was a bit of a laugh in his eyes. "My darling, we haven't even . . ."

"Ah. Coupled?" she again suggested helpfully, laughing at his growl of mock annoyance that she quickly stifled with a kiss. As she lifted his head from hers to look into his eyes, a smile spread across her face, a smile that was more knowing than that of only a few minutes before. Now she understood the pleasure that could happen between men and women, and she wanted more of it. She wanted to feel it, with him.

"I'm ready," she told him, gazing deeply into those green eyes. She felt as if she could fall into them, as if she was falling now.

Eagerly, James stripped off his remaining clothes. As he stood before her, naked, Julia's eyes widened; she thought she had known what to expect, but this was simply unbelievable. His male parts were just so . . . *large*.

"Um, actually, maybe I'm not ready," she admitted.

James looked so disappointed, she at once regretted her words. "I take it back. I might be ready."

"No, no, tell me the truth," he said, through teeth gritted with physical tension. "I don't want to do anything you aren't completely comfortable with."

"Well, I thought I was ready for . . . the rest. But you look so big, I just don't believe it'll fit. I don't even know if it will fit in my hand."

To prove her point, she gently wrapped her hand around his shaft. "Oh, I guess it can fit." She gently stroked him, intrigued at his responsive shudder.

"Let's wait a while on that," James said through an increasingly tight voice. "I'm not made of stone, you know."

"I know exactly what you're made of," Julia teased, eyeing his nude body up and down. Her voice softened, and she added, "Inside and out, I know."

She relaxed back, and reached for his shoulders. Blue eyes to green, their gazes met and held. His eyes searched hers intently, and she felt as if he saw all of her, her eagerness and her love. "I really am ready, for everything."

Finally, James needed no more encouragement. He climbed onto the bed and covered her body with his own, clasping his arms around her. He gently nudged her knees apart, and with one swift thrust, he pressed into her slickness, drawing a shocked breath from her.

"Are you all right?" he asked at once, raising himself onto his forearms to look at her face.

She nodded, an undecided look on her face, and wriggled. "I feel very full, but it doesn't hurt."

"That's because you were so ready for me," James said thickly, holding himself very still.

"I like it," Julia decided. "How long do we stay like this?"

"We don't," James said. His words were a promise

immediately fulfilled, as he began to thrust with slow, gentle strokes that raised the heat between Julia's legs again.

It felt different this time; more intimate, less fervid, as hands clasped, lips pressed, and bodies met in the deepest of embraces. With each thrust, Julia felt James enter farther into her passage. The gentle friction was unaccustomed and fascinating to her. She savored every sensation, parting her legs wider to welcome him deeper and deeper.

He was part of her now. They were one.

Just as she was beginning to settle into a warm, loving glow, James's thrusts began to grow faster and even deeper. Julia's body knew intuitively how to respond, her hips rocking to match his increasing urgency. This was a whole new sensation, still deeply intimate but now with a flickering heat of . . . was this what passion was? She felt such longing, it was almost unbearable, and she grasped at James's hips to hold and pull him more closely into her.

He responded electrically to her touch, stroking with deep, quick measured movements, playing his hands over her face and breasts.

"I can't touch you enough," he gasped.

"I'm all yours," she replied, smiling for a second before a faster stroke, a gentle kiss on the sensitive skin of her nipples stole all thought from her. The feeling of longing and need was building to such a pitch, she wrapped her arms tightly around James and let him carry her away with the force of his body.

And when they both reached the wild joy of a shuddering, moaning climax, she held on to him afterward just as tightly, and she knew that she never wanted to let him go.

Chapter 27

In Which Things Aren't Strange, Then Are

"I don't feel a bit awkward around you now," Julia mused as the two lay lazily entwined in James's bedsheets.

"Good," James said, drawing a finger along the line of her chin. "That's the way I would certainly prefer things."

"No, I mean it, James. I feel as comfortable around you as ever, even though we have no clothes on and I'm in your house. In your *bedchamber*."

"Well," he replied, dropping a kiss onto her nose, "if we didn't feel extraordinarily comfortable around each other to begin with, I don't think we'd be in this type of situation." He nuzzled her hair and wrapped her in a hug, but she barely noticed, still trying to puzzle through a train of thought.

"Shouldn't I feel somehow strange, or different? Since what we did was so strange—well, not precisely strange in the sense that it's never been done before by others. Actually, I wouldn't really know. Did we do anything very unusual?"

"Not especially," James answered, amused. "Though I'd like to think we did it particularly well."

"All right, so we did something that in itself wasn't strange or unusual, at least not on a global scale. But on a personal scale, for me, it was very strange. I mean, I've never done anything like that before, and it was rather significant. As you know. Since you practically tried to talk me out of it."

"I'm very glad I didn't succeed," he said, his hands now beginning to wander her body again.

Despite the distraction of her mind, her body began to respond to his touch, and her thoughts grew fragmented. "I am, too—that is, I didn't know what it would be like. But now that it's over"—she paused and shook her foggy head to clear it, as he circled her breasts with one teasing fingertip—"I know what it's like, obviously, and I realize that it was more significant even than I thought."

"You're babbling," he mumbled, kissing her neck. "I like it."

"Oh. Well. Anyway, it was amazing, and I just feel *right* about it," she finished in a rush. She let her head loll back, relaxed and enjoying his touch.

"That's wonderful," he said, his fingertips now brushing against her nipples and raising them to peaks. "Because we'll be doing a lot more of this when we're married."

He brought his lips to hers for a kiss, but she pressed him back to look questioningly at him.

"Was that a proposal?"

He raised his head, glassy-eyed, and looked confused for a second. Then his expression became chagrined. "Yes, of sorts. Not a very good one, though, apparently. Sorry."

"But did you mean it?" she insisted.

"Of course I meant it. You can't think I would do *this*"—he gestured widely at their bodies, the bed, the heap of discarded clothing in the corner—"and not intend to marry you."

Now she *was* embarrassed. "You aren't just proposing to me because of what we did, are you?"

Her face grew hot. Blasted face, always showing her feelings so easily. She felt suddenly conscious of her nakedness and of the enormity of what she had just done. "My God, James, I gave myself to you. I can never marry anyone else."

"You wouldn't want to, would you?" He sounded hurt.

"No, of course not," Julia hastily replied. "I love you and I would never want to marry anyone else." The words were true, she knew they were true, but they tumbled out in a hurry and sounded awkward on her lips.

They lapsed into a self-conscious silence, the budding passion of a moment before now cooled into caution.

"I believe you," James said carefully, "but you don't sound very glad about it."

"I am," Julia insisted. Then she corrected herself. "Well, right now I guess I am not quite glad about it, since I'm embarrassed and I sort of feel like you are bringing up marriage out of a sense of obligation."

James looked indignant. "How can you say that? Don't you remember what we said to each other last night, and just a while ago? You knew I wanted to be with you if I were ever free. I didn't think that would happen, even after I got Louisa's letter this morning—but then you came, and it was the greatest gift of my life."

Julia was mollified somewhat by this speech, until she

dissected its full meaning. "Wait—you weren't going to pursue me even after you got the letter?"

"I didn't think I had the right. I knew it would be a huge scandal. And after what Gloria's already been through in the last year, I didn't want to add to my family's notoriety."

"And now?" Her voice was accusing.

"It will still be a scandal, of course. But now we have to marry, and I'm glad for that because it's what I wanted." His voice was defensive, belying his loving words, and now Julia felt stung.

"I didn't try to manipulate you, you know," she retorted.

"I didn't think you did," he replied, brows knit as he searched for the right explanation. "I'm used to young women throwing themselves at me because of my title, but I can certainly tell the difference between that and the way you've always treated me."

"Oh, that's right," Julia said, a chill in her voice. "I had forgotten I was with a *viscount*."

James blew out his breath between exasperated lips. "Maybe I didn't put that very well. But please understand my intention, which is honorable. Lawful marriage. It may be the right thing to do, but it's also what I want to do."

Julia watched him carefully for a few seconds, but his expression was neutral and waiting. "Well," she replied. "All right."

He blinked. "So you'll marry me?"

"No," Julia replied without thinking. James looked shocked, and she hastily explained. "I mean, I might. Probably. Yes. But what I was really answering was your statement about understanding your intention. And I meant, all right, I understand your intention."

"So you'll only *probably* marry me?" he said in disbelief.

"I think I need not to talk about this right now," Julia answered. "I know I love you and you love me, and it makes sense for us to get married, especially now, et cetera."

"'Et cetera'?" James repeated, his voice yet more incredulous. That haughty eyebrow was cocked again, as if what Julia was saying was the stupidest thing anyone had ever said since the dawn of the English language. Which it probably was, since her thoughts were in such a tangle that she hardly knew what she was going on about.

"Right, well, anyway," she hastened to finish, "I need some time to think and let all this settle in. Since I woke this morning, I've had two proposals, helped my sister break her engagement, and lost my virginity. It's been quite a day."

James laughed at her recital. "When you put it that way, it is rather a lot to think about all at once. Fair enough."

Julia smiled back at him, relieved. "We'll talk about this again later?" she asked, sliding off the bed to retrieve her clothes from the corner of the room.

He slid after her and began to help her sort out her clothing. "Yes, of course we will. You'll never be able to get rid of me. I'll propose over and over again. I'll harass you about it every time I see you."

He handed Julia a stocking. "By the way, when will that be next? I assume I'm no longer invited over to dine with you and your family tonight."

"Oh. Yes, probably it would be best if you didn't come, for Louisa's sake. She'd find it very awkward." Julia considered. "What if I send you a note when I know of our next plans? I don't know what Louisa will want to do, or what my aunt will consider proper under the circumstances."

"Well, don't wait too long," James said, a twinkle in his eye as he helped her roll her second stocking back onto her leg. "Otherwise I'll come after your aunt myself and tell her about how very improper we've been, to force your hand so you'll have to marry me."

"Ha." Julia acknowledged his joke with an affectionate roll of her eyes, standing up and shaking her rumpled garments into place. "Don't worry; I'll write as soon as possible. I want that as much as you do."

She twisted to look over her shoulder. "Is it completely obvious just what I've been doing?"

"Not at all," James assured her. "That is, not if you wear that big cloak again."

She wrinkled her nose at him and gave a wry smile, comfortable again now that she was dressed and had earned some time to think.

Well, she wasn't *entirely* comfortable; he was still disconcertingly, unabashedly nude. It was quite distracting.

She averted her eyes and kissed him on the cheek. "I'd better go."

He found a dressing robe in his wardrobe and wrapped it around his lean form. "I'll see you out."

Strolling thoughtfully downstairs, with James wrapping his arms around her from behind, Julia tried to enjoy the present moment. In the back of her mind, though, uncertainty about the next step niggled at her. What was she going to tell her aunt, and how, and when? Or her parents? Or Louisa, for that matter? Each confession seemed more daunting than the last.

At the door, she raised her lips to James's, and the viscount dropped a gentle kiss onto them.

"Be careful as you go home," he warned. "After everything you've gone through, I wouldn't want you to come to any harm. In fact, if you'll wait a moment, I'll make myself decent and see you home myself. I think that would be best."

"Not necessary," she scoffed. "How would I explain you to my aunt? She would never believe that we just happened to cross paths while I was out walking alone, or that I had a good reason for filching Simone's cloak."

He shrugged. "Why shouldn't she?"

She smiled. He was so dear; she loved how protective he had become, even if it was foolish. "No, it'll be fine. I'll see you soon." She kissed him again. "I do love you."

He held her tight for a moment. "I love you, too."

He drew back out of the entryway, and Julia opened the door and stepped out of the house.

And bumped straight into Lord Xavier, who was standing on the stoop, about to knock on James's door.

The force of the blow caused the breath to whoosh out of Julia's body, and she stumbled backward.

"Steady, lass," the tall nobleman admonished her as if she were a servant, taking hold of her cloak-clad shoulders to keep her balance from being overset. Then he saw her face, and his cool gray eyes widened with recognition. He instantly took in her startled expression, her swollen lips, her rumpled clothing.

"Well, well, well," he mused, inclining his head in greeting. "Miss Herington. This is a surprise. But how enchanting you look! It is truly delightful to see you."

She bobbed a quick curtsy, her cheeks flaming. "Lord Xavier. It is delightful to see you as well."

"I imagine not, actually," he replied, then noticed the half-open door and James's dressing robe–clad form still standing in the home's entryway. His mouth quirked.

"Interesting," he said, and pushed the door open all the way. "Very interesting. Greetings to you, Matheson."

James gaped at him for a second. "Xavier. How—What—Did you—" He cleared his throat, but was unable to finish his sentence.

"I was stopping by to see if you wanted to go to White's for a bit," Xavier replied smoothly, eyes glinting with unreadable emotion. "But I seem to be too late with my invitation. It appears you have already found other . . . entertainment, shall we say?"

"It's not what it looks like," James said hastily, with a quick glance at Julia. If anything, this only made her feel worse, as if she was complicit in something shameful and secret.

Which, she supposed, she was.

"Really? I imagine it is exactly what it looks like," the younger man drawled, his eyebrows raised in skepticism. "But I am dreadfully thick-witted sometimes and do not always know what I am looking at. Perhaps I shall have to have it explained to me."

"Come in, come in," James said hastily. "For God's sake, man, we can't stand out here in the street talking like this."

"Indeed not," Xavier replied, stepping into James's house.

"Good afternoon, Lord Xavier," Julia interjected quickly, preparing to make her escape.

A slow, lovely, dangerous smile spread over his face. "Indeed it is, Miss Herington. Indeed it is."

Chapter 28

In Which
Her Ladyship Finds Out

By pleading a sick headache, Julia managed to keep to her bedchamber for the remainder of the day. She couldn't face her relatives until she had figured out what to do. Whatever that might be.

It wasn't that she thought she had done wrong, precisely, and it certainly wasn't that she regretted being with James. But she knew Louisa would be crushed if the truth were known, and her aunt would be disappointed, and *that*—the embarrassment and sorrow brought to two people who had given her so much—was what she couldn't figure out how to avoid, though she would have given the world to do so.

She knew that word would get around, and she was only postponing the inevitable. She remembered James's cautionary words from the Twelfth Night masquerade: If anyone caused a scandal at that event, Xavier would spread it all over town. Now she feared the truth of those words. What on earth had James said to Xavier after she'd left? What would Xavier do?

As it turned out, the storm, when it came, was even worse than she had imagined.

She knew she was in for a reckoning when Simone came to summon her to her aunt's presence the following morning. The maid's customarily serene countenance was worried, and Julia felt a sense of foreboding that was justified as soon as she stepped into her aunt's bedchamber. Lady Irving was still in the bed, an untouched cup and pot of chocolate on a tray in front of her, a copy of the *Ton Bon-bons* scandal sheet in her hands. Her stare, when Julia dared meet her eyes, was nothing less than livid.

"Do you know what I had awaiting me with my morning chocolate today?" she barked, shooing Simone out of the room with a sharp gesture.

"No," Julia replied warily, drawing a chair up to her aunt's bed and seating herself. She didn't trust her trembling legs to hold her up. *Good Lord, how bad must it be?*

"*This.*" Lady Irving slapped Julia on the head with her rolled-up newspaper.

"Stupid girl," she said, her voice like ice. "Stupid, stupid, girl. Most of the *ton* hops from bed to bed, but *no one speaks about it.* No one looks, no one asks, no one tells. And now you go and throw this type of behavior in everyone's face. I've obviously taught you nothing."

She thrust the paper at Julia in disgust, averting her eyes as if she couldn't bear to look at either the newspaper or the girl at her side.

"Read the column of *crim cons.* The first item, naturally." Her voice was thick with scorn, laying heavy stress on the last word.

Julia's eyes blurred with anxiety, but she forced herself

to focus, drawing a deep breath and finding the item in question on the periodical's front page.

> The peace of Lady I——'s household must certainly be disturbed this morning, as it has come to the attention of the editor that young Viscount M——, recently engaged, was encountered in a state of déshabille with the lovely Miss H——. One wonders if this has any bearing on the contemporaneous end of the viscount's engagement to the Honorable Miss O——, sister by marriage of the young lady (?) in question.

It was bad. Very bad. As bad as she had feared, and then some.

Julia gulped. "They could be referring to anyone," she said lamely.

"Don't be an idiot," Lady Irving replied witheringly. "I know exactly who they mean, as does everyone in London. So what I want to know is, what did you do, and how did you get caught?"

Julia raised her eyes to meet her aunt's. "It's not as bad as they made it sound."

"It usually isn't, but that doesn't matter since this is the account people will read and believe. I repeat, what did you do?"

Julia had never truly been afraid of her aunt before, but the anger in the older woman's eyes made her feel like cowering in a corner. Or better yet, running back to Stonemeadows Hall, and never even thinking of London again.

She forced herself to straighten her back and maintain eye contact with her aunt. "Yesterday morning, Louisa let me know that she wished to break her engagement with James. She asked for my help."

"Whaaaaaat?" Lady Irving's eyes fairly goggled out of her head.

Gaining a small amount of courage from her aunt's surprise, she continued. "Yes, she let me know that she's been very unhappy, and she wished to end her engagement. She had written a letter to James explaining everything, and she asked me to deliver it since she knows James and I are friends."

Her face grew hot with self-conscious shame, and her voice quavered on the last word. Lady Irving was still gaping at her, so she plunged on despite her burning face.

"I decided instead to send it to James by messenger with a covering note, since I thought it would be unwise to go to his home or summon him here. Er . . . so that's the story of the broken engagement."

Lady Irving shook her head, her eyes turned heavenward. "I can't believe it. I literally cannot believe it. Why did you both put yourselves in my hands and come to London? Wasn't it to trust me to help you get suitably married, or am I losing my mind? Rich, titled, fills out his breeches well. That is all you need. My mind simply cannot comprehend the fact that Louisa would break an *engagement with a viscount.*" Her voice rose to a high, shrill pitch on the final words.

"It's true," Julia said, relieved to have the focus of her aunt's anger removed from herself. "She was afraid to tell you. Though I certainly can't imagine why."

Lady Irving darted her a quick, sharp glance from the corner of her eye. "This is no time for jokes, miss. Is that the whole story? This isn't so bad; I think we can fix things with a word or two in the right quarter. I can speak to Lady Matheson, perhaps. This may yet be undone."

"Well, actually, there's a bit more." Julia steeled herself. "As you know, Sir Stephen came by yesterday afternoon, and . . . well, he made me an offer."

"Aha!" Her ladyship barked in triumph. "I thought he might. Better and better. Excellent."

"I declined his proposal," Julia admitted. "But he asked if he might still hope, and I couldn't bear to tell him no again, so I let him leave with that understanding, but then I was confused and wanted someone to talk to. So I did go to James's house after all," she finished miserably.

"What." It wasn't a question. It was a cold, flat statement of angry disbelief.

"You see, James is my closest friend—besides Louisa, of course," Julia tried to explain. "And I wanted to talk to him. I . . ." Her voice trailed off.

"Speak up, girl," Lady Irving commanded.

"I love him," Julia whispered, eyes downcast. "That's why I said no to Sir Stephen."

She looked up warily, in time to see her aunt throw herself violently back onto the pillows of her bed. The chocolate pot teetered, and Julia hastily removed the tray from Lady Irving's bed lest the hot liquid spill and ruin the bed coverings. Her aunt didn't need anything to make her even angrier this morning.

"This I *really* can't believe," Lady Irving said with measured calm, lying prone with her hands pressed over her eyes. "You love your sister's affianced husband. Why not? So you turn down a perfectly eligible match. Even better. And she also throws away her chance of a match.

Certainly, it all makes perfect sense up to that point. But then *you go to his house*."

She removed her hands from over her eyes and turned her head to look at Julia. "There you lose me. Because I cannot imagine why you would do such a thing."

"I wanted to be with him," Julia answered in a small voice.

"I'm not even going to ask if you mean what I think you mean," Lady Irving said, her voice sounding defeated. "Judging from your now-understandable reluctance to face us yesterday evening, and the comment in the newspaper about the state of *déshabille*, I assume you mean *exactly* what I think you mean."

She sighed and raised herself up to a seated position again. Her eyes, when they met Julia's again, were now filled with sorrow rather than anger. She reached out for Julia's face. Julia flinched, expecting another swat, but Lady Irving only grazed her cheek gently with her fingertips as if memorizing her features.

"Foolish girl," she said, her voice choked. "Foolish, foolish Julia. I'm very sorry for you."

She sighed again. "I can't blame you too much; probably not as much as I should. We all love. We're all human. Those among us who are luckiest love their spouses; others find love elsewhere."

Her eyes watered with emotion, and she dashed an impatient hand across them. When she moved her hands, she looked older and very tired, and Julia realized that her aunt was speaking from her own decades of experience.

Her voice choked, her gaze unfocused, the countess explained, "Did you think I loved Irving? Of course I didn't. He was much older, and he wasn't handsome, and he couldn't dance or speak prettily, which was what

I cared for as a girl. But my mother reminded me that, as the daughter of a mere baron, I could do much worse than wind up a countess. And thus the Honorable Estella caught herself an earl, by sitting attentively next to him when he talked about his cursed hunting dogs and horses, by allowing him to kiss her with his loose mouth, and by agreeing with everything he asked of her."

She looked Julia pointedly in the eye. "Everything."

As Julia stared at her aunt in amazement, the countess continued in a stronger voice, "Being his wife was the price I paid for being a countess, for having a social freedom and financial independence such as I had never known as Miss Oliver. And when I say social freedom, I mean it. I could say what I wanted, be with whom I wanted, go where I wished. I wouldn't trade that for anything." Her mouth quirked wickedly. "Especially since an apoplexy carried him off only five years after our marriage.

"Still," Lady Irving returned to the subject at hand, "the *ton* follows a set of unyielding rules by which we must abide. I followed them until I was wed; you haven't. It may be unfair, but there is an unbreakable rule that a young woman, unlike a young man, must engage in no scandalous behavior before her marriage. Nothing that smacks of impropriety, or of being too fast. And certainly no carnal acts."

She stifled the beginnings of Julia's protest with a raised hand and a shake of her head.

"No, you *must* listen to me. What you have done is not quite so wrong as the paper made it seem, since there was no infidelity involved. Still, I am afraid there will be no recovering from this. I must take both of you back to the country at once. In time, Louisa may overcome the scandal, though I am afraid it will be at your expense.

All the world currently believes the engagement was broken as a result of your behavior."

The countess mused for a moment. "If you are willing, we will allow that impression to stand. I believe you owe it to your sister to give her whatever help you can at this time."

"Of course," Julia agreed eagerly. Her sense of chagrin, of having wronged her sister, was so great that no atonement seemed too great. Louisa *should* recover. She *should* have another chance for happiness.

Lady Irving nodded her approval, and continued. "Very well. As for you, I am afraid your social life is over. You will never be able to come back to London. Possibly you will never be able to marry at all."

These words fell onto Julia's ears with the heaviness of stones. Dumbly, she nodded her understanding.

"Unless . . ." Lady Irving was struck by an idea. "If Matheson will marry you, all will eventually be forgiven. There will be a scandalous amount of talk at first, but soon enough it will be replaced by the next *on dit*."

"He did offer for me," Julia replied, feeling a spark of hope. "I left him with the understanding that I intended to accept."

At her aunt's skeptical expression, she explained, "I was . . . um, a bit overset by the events of the day. But I am sure he has the impression that I would *like* to marry him. I believe I was clear enough about that."

"Then we must confirm that impression," Lady Irving said with decision. "The sooner the better. If a notice of your engagement can be placed in tomorrow's *Post*, we'll be well on our way to dealing with this unfortunate situation."

She paused, then continued in carefully measured

tones, "Of course, if we can't achieve that, we will need to leave town. I hope you understand."

Julia nodded. James would agree, happily. He'd said so himself. "Yes, but I am sure there will be no problem."

Lady Irving motioned for Julia to bring her lap desk and drew out paper and pen. "For all our sakes, I hope not. Would you like to write the note, or shall I?"

"I will," Julia offered. She quickly composed the following note, her handwriting large and untidy with agitation:

> *My dear James,*
>   *I am sure you know of the scandal that has broken this morning concerning us all. This may be remarkably forward of me, but I hope you won't mind if I tell you that I would dearly love to accept the offer you made me yesterday.*
>   *I am sure you know that that is my fondest wish, regardless of circumstances, although currently our situation makes a speedy betrothal (and wedding) desirable.*
>   *Please let me know, as soon as possible, your answer. I rely on you, and hope to see you very soon.*
>
>   *Yours, with love,*
>   *Julia*

She showed it to her aunt, who nodded shortly and folded it up within a blank sheet of notepaper to hide Julia's message before sealing it. "It'll do. I'll have it taken to his home at once. If he's a gentleman, which I believe he is, we should hear back within the hour."

Chapter 29

In Which
Louisa Finds Out

Julia's penance continued as soon as she left her aunt's room. She felt she owed it to Louisa to tell her everything before her sister should find out from someone else.

Louisa already knew, though; Julia could tell that as soon as she entered the library and saw her sister sitting blank-faced on the sofa, leaning over with her elbows resting on her knees. She looked up at Julia when she heard the door open to admit her, and her expression instantly changed to one of worry. She stood and rushed over to Julia, wrapping her in a tight hug.

"My poor darling," she said in a soothing voice. "I'm so, so sorry. I blame myself."

Julia gaped at her for a second, stunned at this response. "What . . . *what?*"

Louisa pulled back, her hands still on Julia's shoulders. She looked guilt-stricken as she explained, "Simone brought me a paper this morning and I saw that terrible item. I know it's all a misunderstanding, but it's all my fault. If I hadn't asked you to give the letter to James . . . oh, dear. I know you only went because I was so insistent and you wanted so badly to help me."

She sighed, her eyes defeated, and sat down hard again on the sofa, slumping. "I didn't imagine you would go over to his home, but how were you to know that isn't exactly good *ton*? So they've put this terrible insinuation into that scandal rag, when it was all perfectly innocent. It's ridiculous, but it will sound very bad to anyone who doesn't know the truth."

She straightened up and took Julia's hands in hers, looking determined. "I promise you, I will do whatever I can to straighten things out. I'll take all the responsibility upon myself, and will tell everyone I meet the truth."

Her voice faltered as she added, "That is . . . I haven't spoken to Aunt Estella yet, but I swear she shall be the first to know. Perhaps she can undo everything; she has powerful friends. I only hope this unfortunate item will not affect your relationship with Sir Stephen Saville. I know he's rather a stickler, but I'll explain the situation to him as well." She offered Julia a watery smile. "He may not ever forgive me my social trespasses, but he won't think the less of you."

Julia simply stared at Louisa through this whole impassioned recital, swaying with shock where she stood. She simply couldn't believe what she was hearing. Louisa had put entirely the opposite construction on everything that had been intended by the scandal item. She blamed herself, she trusted Julia, she thought only of how her own supposed faults might have hurt others.

It made Julia feel much, much worse than if Louisa had refused to speak to her. Or yelled at her, or slapped her.

But that simply wouldn't be like Louisa to react in that way. Louisa's way was always to look out for Julia, and to protect her however she could, regardless of her own inclinations. That's what she'd done since they were children; that's why she'd come to London. And that's what she was proposing to do again now—to sacrifice herself so that Julia could recover socially.

Not for the first time, Julia was struck dumb with disbelief at Louisa's selflessness. She was too good; Julia wasn't worthy of a sister like her.

But she would try to be.

Louisa still sat looking at her anxiously, awaiting Julia's response to her apologies and assurances. Oh, dear. This was going to be really difficult, but it had to be said. Her sister deserved the truth.

Julia sat on the floor in front of Louisa and leaned her head on her sister's knee, so she wouldn't have to look her in the face or trust her own legs to support her as she spoke.

"It's not your fault," she began, then took a deep breath for courage. "Louisa, the item is true, in everything it implies. It's not your fault. It's ours—mine and James's. And that ass Xavier's," she couldn't resist adding.

A pause succeeded her words; then Louisa said blankly, "Xavier's? What has he to do with anything? I don't understand."

Julia explained the situation as quickly as she could—how she'd sent the letter, how Sir Stephen had proposed, how she'd wanted to talk to James to work through her confusion, and how he'd read the letters and come to accept Louisa's decision. She left out the part about how she and James had already admitted their love for each other on the previous night; it might be cowardly, but she justified it with the thought that it might hurt Louisa further.

Instead she said, "And when I was there, it just . . . just *happened*. It wasn't planned, but I wasn't sorry for it. The only thing is, as I was leaving, Lord Xavier saw me, and apparently he's blabbed everything to the papers. Not that it's any of his business, damned scandalmonger," she grumbled.

For once, Louisa didn't admonish her for her language. She simply began stroking Julia's hair slowly. Julia waited for an agonizing minute for her to say something, but when Louisa remained silent, Julia raised her head to look at her sister's face.

It was nothing like what she would have expected. Louisa's gaze was far away, her expression quiet and considering, but a small smile played about the corners of her mouth.

"Louisa?" Julia asked hesitantly.

The older girl's eyes snapped into focus and turned toward the face of her seated sister. "I'm still trying to believe it," Louisa said. "It's all rather ridiculous, wouldn't you say?"

Ridiculous? That was the word James had used too, and Julia was no less surprised this time.

"I mean," Louisa mused, "you loved him all along, didn't you? I should have seen it; I should have been able to tell. And here I was pushing you toward this other man you couldn't care a pin for, when all the while I was becoming certain of how wrong it is to marry without love. To marry for logic, and propriety, and security. It's just not enough, is it?"

She rested her hand on Julia's head again, and Julia felt all the healing of her sister's understanding and forgiveness.

"He loves you, too, doesn't he?"

Julia nodded hesitantly, and Louisa continued. "I admit, I'm surprised at what you did—at least, what I presume you did—but if you really love him, I can't fault you for anything."

She smiled ruefully. "I only wish I could have felt the same way, but I never did. He just wasn't right for me, and I certainly wasn't the one for him. He was my escape; he was never my destiny."

"You're not angry with me?" Julia asked, scarcely able to believe it.

Louisa sighed. "If this damned item hadn't been in the paper—yes, Julia, I know those words as well as you do, and this is absolutely the time to use them—I would be unreservedly happy. I was afraid I had ruined our family's relationship with James and that I would embarrass him terribly. I knew he didn't love me and wouldn't be hurt on a personal level, but I thought his pride would be touched. I'm . . ." She shook her head. "It's a good thing you have each other."

Louisa began absently to tease tangles out of Julia's hair in their familiar way. "I'm not sure what to do about the situation, though. The paper implies that my engagement was broken because of you, which is quite wrong. I would like to see that corrected."

Julia straightened up and looked Louisa directly in the eye. In this way, at least, she could show herself worthy of Louisa's trust. "No, I won't allow it."

Louisa looked taken aback. "What? What do you mean?"

"I mean," Julia explained, "as it stands, you are innocent in the eyes of the *ton*. You have every chance to walk away from the situation unscathed and find happiness with someone else. It would be madness to do anything to change that."

"Madness? I hardly think that," Louisa protested. "Julia, it's not right. I won't have you protecting me."

"Yes, you will," Julia insisted. "For once, you'll let me shield you. It's the least I can do. Louisa, I feel as if I haven't done right by you, even by allowing myself to think of your betrothed husband in a romantic way." *Or by acting on it,* she thought, ashamed once again about the encounter in the carriage.

She added, "Thank God, he's an honorable man and he's offered for me. Eventually, we will be married, and it'll all be forgotten. We'll spend time in the country for a while, and we'll come back when everything's blown over. We'll be fine." She tried to smile bravely. "A viscount can get away with a prodigious lot, you know."

Louisa gave a short laugh. "Yes, I know that well enough." She bit her lip, looking uncertain. "I just don't feel it's fair to you," she said again.

"Trust me on this," Julia said. "It's more than fair. The least I can do, to help you through this situation—which wouldn't even exist if it weren't for me—is to make sure that you come out of it unscathed."

"But if you hadn't gone to James's house, all the world would know the truth about me. That I'm a jilt," Louisa insisted.

"You aren't," Julia replied. "You only agreed to marry James out of a sense of obligation to our family, and to him. If anything, this is more like . . . an annulment," she decided.

"Now *that* is the most ridiculous thing of all," Louisa said, smiling, and Julia knew she was beginning to come around.

"So you'll let it stand?" Julia pressed. "You won't say or do anything to counter the story?"

Louisa sighed and waved her hands in capitulation. "Fine, fine. I'll allow you to throw yourself to the wolves—well, one wolf—in order that I might seem innocent and have a chance at finding another potential husband."

"James isn't a wolf," Julia protested, but she was smiling now, like her sister. Thank heaven this conversation had gone so well. Thank heaven above, Louisa was a generous and forgiving person. Thank heaven Louisa loved her—and *didn't* love James.

"All the same," Louisa added, "I would like to leave London for a time. A long time. I think it will take me a while to come to terms with all this. I'm not angry," she assured Julia, "but I feel like I've got to start over. I have to decide what I want, and who I want, and this certainly isn't the place to do it."

"Well, Aunt Estella plans to take us back to the country very soon if James and I can't pull off a hasty wedding," Julia said. "Honestly, even if we can, I'd like to leave, too. I think we'll all need to get away from the wagging tongues for a while.

"Besides," she admitted, "if I ever cross paths with Lord Xavier, I'm sure I will haul off and punch him in the face, and you know that would cause a scandal of its own."

"Ah, yes; as Aunt Estella would say, that would be both vulgar *and* unladylike," Louisa replied. "So our aunt knows, then?"

Julia rolled her eyes. "She summoned me this morning and nearly flayed me alive. And she hit me on the head with her newspaper."

Louisa gasped, and covered her mouth to suppress a startled laugh.

"Go ahead, laugh—" Julia waved a hand airily. "I

deserved it. She was very angry, but I think she's less so now. By the way, it was her suggestion to let the impression stand about your engagement being broken as a result of, ah, the events of yesterday. I do completely agree with her, of course. But I just wanted to let you know in case you tried to pull any self-sacrificing tricks."

Louisa gave her sister a small, knowing smile. "After all the fun you got to have? I suppose I'll agree to both your wishes, so I at least have a chance of such fun in the future."

"It was *wonderful*!" Julia squealed. She blushed at once. Had she really just said that aloud?

Louisa only laughed, so Julia hastily covered her discomfiture with a change of subject. "Come, let's speak with our aunt. Perhaps she's gotten word back from James by now."

Chapter 30

In Which a
Note Passes through
Several Hands

James had lain awake into the early hours of the morning, savoring the feel of the bedclothes against his nude body, thinking of Julia and how she had so recently been here with him.

Julia. What changes the last day had brought. He could finally allow himself to love her, to long for her, to touch her. Good Lord, he wanted her even more now that they had been together and he knew what lovemaking with her was like. *Would* be like—for they would be doing that all the time once they were married, he would see to that. It had been amazing, transcendent; it was a pleasure he had never felt before, not with any other woman. He had grown hard just thinking of it, and wished mightily that she were in his bed so he could demonstrate to her just how greatly she affected him.

He'd gone to quite a bit of trouble the previous day to procure a special license, as soon as Xavier had left him. He was looking forward to bearing Julia off as soon as the clock struck a decent hour of the morning, making her his wife, traveling to Nicholls with her, and having a spirited repeat of their activities of the previous afternoon. Or more than one repeat, preferably.

Needless to say, he'd had trouble falling asleep in such a physical state.

His mind wasn't entirely untroubled, either, which didn't help a fellow drift off. He had been feeling uneasy about that whole conversation with Xavier. Of all the damned coils, to have *that* man, of all the men he knew in London, come by at such a time. Xavier, who missed nothing, and—if James remembered their schoolboy days rightly—withheld even less.

Xavier had come in off the street while James was still in that cursed dressing gown, drunk James's best brandy while he waited for the viscount to dress decently, and smirked at his host when James rejoined him and tried to explain that there was nothing in it, simply a family visit related to his engagement.

That had been a mistake. It would have been better to say nothing at all and just fill the man with so much liquor that he was too stupefied to recall what he'd seen. Instead, at the mere mention of James's engagement, Xavier's clever features had perked up like a hound scenting the fox. He had plied James with questions that the viscount simply refused to answer, but it was too late. The young earl had already seen more than enough to draw his own conclusions.

By the time the sun rose in earnest, the viscount had only just drifted off into a troubled sleep. Unfortunately, he was soon awakened abruptly by a flood of sunshine.

He squinted, startled awake, and gasped at the sight of his mother standing in his bedchamber, one hand still gripping the curtains that she had just wrested open.

Good Lord, that was an unwelcome sight. She'd never before come to visit him at his lodgings, and now she had plowed her way past Delaney into his most private room.

"What are you doing here?" he demanded, still blinking in the sudden brightness of the room.

He drew the bedcovers up to his chin and tried, as his mother began to rant, to absorb the fact that she was standing in his bedchamber. Something must have happened. Something dreadful, judging from the fire in the dowager's eyes.

She said something about "how sharper than a serpent's tooth" as well; James distinctly heard that even through the clammy fog that clouded his brain once he saw what was in his mother's hand. In the hand that wasn't scrabbling at his curtains, she held a newspaper.

It was dreadful, all right.

James snatched the paper from his mother's hands and read the item she jabbed at with a furious forefinger.

His whole body went cold, as if he'd been plunged into icy water. The words were there on the page in front of him, but he still could hardly believe this.

He'd expected Xavier to bandy the news about in his club. He had expected lewd ribbing from friends, and probably even anger from Julia's family.

What he had *not* expected was that the news would be printed in the *ton*'s favorite scandal sheet for all to see, or that it would reach the eyes or ears of his mother before he was safely removed to the country with Julia as his bride.

Some might call that a cowardly hope, perhaps; James had preferred to think of it as sensible. His mother wasn't going to change his mind no matter what she said to him, and he knew she was going to be livid whether she spoke to him or not. So, he reasoned, he might as well save his time—and hers—by sparing them both the annoyance of a confrontation.

Unfortunately—disastrously—none of it had worked out that way. Here it was, in the paper, for the whole *ton* to read and judge him. And to judge *Julia.* And here was his mother, ranting at him from the foot of his bed as if he were six years old and had rolled in horse shit.

She'd already said the bit about the serpent's tooth more than once; did the woman have no other way to call him ungrateful than by relying on Shakespeare? She also called him a rake, a disgrace to his illustrious name, and unprincipled, vulgar, and ungentlemanly. This last string of epithets almost made him smile despite the seriousness of the situation; Lady Irving would probably be proud of her old crony's vocabulary.

"Don't you dare smile, young man," Lady Matheson fumed, seeing his mouth curving. "You have dragged our name through the mud once again. Through filth, I say! Yes, filth is the word for this entire situation. At least Gloria's debasement was Roseborough's fault and not of her own choosing. Your engagement was bad enough, but I stood it, because your motives were honorable, and at least it was respectable—although barely so. Throwing yourself away on a baron's daughter with a mediocre dowry!" She sneered.

These inflammatory words blew away James's lingering sense of shock. A trickle of anger began to fill him instead, slowly but mountingly. How dare she barge into his home and insult him and his decisions? She had no right, and he opened his mouth to tell her so—but her ladyship was hardly finished with her tirade.

"Then you splash our name in the papers as if we were the vulgarest sort of *cit,* with no idea what was due to the sensibility of gently bred persons. And for what? A quick tumble with the daughter of nobody knows who? To slake your lusts with some upstart who hopes to entrap you into marriage! Was it worth it? Because you've disgraced us all. You are even worse than Roseborough. You *disgust* me," she spat. "There are *whores* for that sort of thing."

Her words stung, as much as if she had raked her nails across his face. And just as if she had struck him a physical blow, he felt almost overcome with anger, hearing her insult not only Julia but the nature of his feelings for her. This was going *much* too far. The woman might have given him life, but he wasn't going to stand this, even from her.

James took a few breaths to keep himself from exploding at the viscountess, coiled up his rage into a small, icy ball, and let it burn his throat into hoarseness as he spoke.

"Get out of my bedchamber at once, or I'll remove you by physical force, regardless of my state of undress," he began in a quiet, dangerous voice.

"I will receive you properly, as a guest in my home, in the drawing room in fifteen minutes. At that time I will speak to you about Miss Herington, my *future wife*, in civil and logical terms. If you are at all insulting to me or to her, you will leave. And, I might add, you will also leave Matheson House, which I currently allow you to occupy as a courtesy, and you may draw on your jointure to find yourself other lodging. Is that absolutely clear?"

Truth be told, he hated the drafty, dark family town house, and he'd never live there himself. But he was certainly of a mood to boot his mother out of it if she abused Julia one more time. He seldom flexed the power that his title gave him, but he would do so now, and she knew it. Lady Matheson had been rooted to the Hanover Square house since the early days of her marriage, and as he stared at her white-angry face with his own hard eyes, he knew he'd struck home with his threat.

She narrowed her eyes at him until they were livid slits. Green gaze to green gaze, heated to icy, mother and son stared at each other for several long seconds. Then, without a word, Lady Matheson spun on her heel and marched out of his bedchamber and down the stairs.

James relaxed a bit as soon as his unwelcome visitor left the room, and he blew out a breath he hadn't even noticed he was holding. Quickly, fired with the energy of righteous annoyance, he dressed, washed his face, and finger-combed his hair into a semblance of order. Without the help of his valet, however, he took a bit longer than he'd thought. Oh, well; it wouldn't kill his mother to wait twenty minutes rather than fifteen. Especially because he wanted to take one more look at that newspaper her ladyship had left behind.

Yes, it was as bad as he'd thought. He shuddered. He supposed he couldn't blame his mother for her anger; the shock she'd felt upon reading it must have been terrible. But that did *not* excuse her insults.

He made his way downstairs, drawing a breath to steel himself before entering the drawing room. The viscountess had probably gotten even angrier while she waited for him, and she was sure to have another tirade ready as soon as he appeared. He pushed the door open, prepared for another confrontation, and ready to make good on his every threat.

But to his surprise, his mother was sitting demurely on a sofa, her lady's maid flipping through a bound volume as if preparing to read to her.

James was instantly suspicious. Why on earth would she be so *calm* all of a sudden?

Before he could even say a word, Lady Matheson

noticed his arrival. "My dear boy," she said, rising in greeting. "Do come join me."

Her voice, if not precisely warm, was at least no less cool than her usual formal tones. She stepped forward to take hold of his hands and guide him to a seat next to her. As she clasped James's hand, he felt that hers held a note, which she attempted to thrust aside. "Perhaps some coffee, if you haven't had yours yet? It is rather early in the day, isn't it? I am sure it will do you good."

James ignored this overture. "What have you got in your hand?"

"This? Oh, it's nothing," she replied, a small smile playing over her face. "Just a little billet that arrived for you while you were upstairs."

Wordlessly, James held out his hand for it, and the viscountess sighed and placed the letter into his grasp.

"The seal's broken," he said, again suspicious. He scanned his mother's face as she blew out a dismissive breath and told him it had come that way. "It's probably a mere nothing," she said, her expression disinterested. "The messenger must have dropped it, that's all."

But it wasn't a mere nothing. It bore Lady Irving's seal; he could tell that even though the wax had been split, and the message the paper bore was short. Short, but momentous.

My Lord:
   You have dishonored my nieces, and you have dishonored me. I assume you know to what I refer. We leave for the country at once. Please make no attempt to see, write, or speak to us.

                                        Estella Irving

James felt as if he had been physically struck. As if a horse had kicked him in the head. As if his heart had been torn from his very body. What *was* this?

How could Lady Irving react in this way? Hadn't Julia let her know that he had proposed marriage? Didn't Lady Irving *want* him to marry Julia?

"Something amiss?" Lady Matheson asked in a syrupy voice, and the world righted itself in a moment as soon as she spoke. Of *course* her anger had vanished by the time he'd come into the room. Somehow, she'd written this note, and she was pleased with herself.

That had to be the answer. This couldn't possibly be from the Grosvenor Square house. Lady Irving *couldn't* think this; she couldn't want him to stay away from Julia.

"This is a fraud," he said flatly, thrusting the note back at his mother. "This isn't from Lady Irving at all. *You* wrote this."

"But, dear boy," she replied with a shake of the head, glancing at the paper James had handed her, "that's not my handwriting. Surely you know your own mother's hand? And besides, where on earth would I have gotten that dear creature's seal from?"

As she quickly read the contents of the brief letter, that small, tight smile quivered onto her face again. "Oh, *dear.* How very unfortunate."

She crumpled the missive and dropped it on the floor. "Well, least said, soonest mended, wouldn't you say? If you'll take my counsel, you'll simply let them leave, and that will be that. The whole affair will soon be nothing more than the mildest of unpleasant memories, to be forgotten entirely in the joy of a suitable match."

"You're mad," James said. "I don't care what the letter says. I'm not letting them leave without a word of explanation."

He retrieved the note from the floor, smoothed the paper, and read it again. He still couldn't believe it. Was this really from Lady Irving? Was she so insulted as to wish to cut ties completely?

No; it couldn't be true. Something strange was going on here. "I'm going to marry Miss Herington," he insisted.

"You can hardly do so if she is unwilling, which she apparently is," his mother replied in a sugary, soothing voice, her eyes steely and exultant.

James had had about enough of this. He had no idea what was really going on, or who had written that letter, or what Julia really wanted—but he was desperate to find out.

Which meant that it was well past time for his mother to leave.

"Allow me to show you out," he said, rising and attempting to pull his mother to her feet after him. "You can't possibly wish to say anything more to insult me or my intended bride. I don't believe you truly wish to hunt for rented lodgings, do you?"

As his mother stood unwillingly, he thought he saw a tiny shadow of . . . was that fear in her eyes? He felt a flash of remorse; he really wasn't cut out for this whole threatening-women-with-homelessness business. And after all, the woman *was* his mother, and it really *wasn't* her handwriting. Maybe she had done nothing worse than unseal and read his mail.

Still, he was more than ready to leave, and he certainly wasn't going to allow her to stay behind to wreak havoc in his house at her leisure. More gently this time, he tugged—well, call it *guided*—her arm toward the door.

Just then, Delaney entered with a tray of coffee. "Is her ladyship leaving?" he asked ingenuously.

"Yes," James barked. "We're both going out, almost at once."

His mother looked surprised, though she quickly covered it, and then reseated herself as swiftly as he'd ever seen her move.

"No, indeed I am not, dear." She turned wide, innocent eyes to him—an expression he thought sat ill on her shrewd face. "Surely you wouldn't deny your own mother a cup of coffee? After coming all this way to see you, in chill weather?"

"I didn't ask you to come," he replied ungraciously, folding his arms.

Her wide-eyed expression vanished at once, replaced by a look of annoyance. "Very well, so it was an unsolicited visit. Is there any reason why I can't visit my son?"

"Can't. Shouldn't. Haven't. There are hundreds of reasons," he answered, eyebrows lifted in a hurry-up expression.

"Well," her ladyship said primly, serving herself some coffee, "be that as it may, I intend to fortify myself with a hot beverage before venturing back outside."

James turned away from her. "Be my guest," he said. "I'm leaving." He didn't want to wait any longer; he would just have to trust that Delaney could keep an eye on his mother during his absence.

"James," the viscountess said, and this was a new voice. It was soft and beseeching; it held traces of the affection she must have once felt for him. It was a *mother*'s voice, not a noblewoman's voice. He hadn't heard that voice for a long time. "James, my dear boy. Please . . . stay with me."

He turned to face her, and her expression was pleading. "Just one cup. Drink one cup with me, and then I'll go. And then you can do whatever you want, and marry whomever you wish, and I won't say another word against it."

This earnest mood was surprise enough, and James was struck by the novelty of it. She seemed sincere. Had he really hurt her feelings? If so, that would be the first time since his childhood that he'd managed to reach her heart in any way. He only felt sorry that it had to be for this reason, at this time of all times.

Hers was an offer worth considering. It would be well worth a few minutes of his time to win her promise to stop hassling him and hold her peace about his choice of a bride.

"Just one cup?" he said doubtfully.

"One will be plenty," the viscountess replied with a small smile, giving her son's hand a squeeze as he sat down across from her.

"Just one," he agreed with a sigh, and poured out a cup of his own. One cup, and then he would go to Julia. Surely these very few minutes wouldn't make a difference?

Chapter 31

In Which Proposals Are Rescinded

The inhabitants of the Grosvenor Square address passed an anxious hour waiting for James to reply to the pleading note Julia had sent. The minutes piled up with unbearable sloth, until Julia's jittery pacing around the drawing room had driven both her and Louisa to the point of snapping at each other.

"Please be *still*," Louisa begged her sister from an uncomfortable chair near the fire. Her own back was ramrod-straight and her face quiet and calm, but her hands twisted anxiously in her lap, belying her nervousness.

"I can't," Julia replied, sitting down and beginning to beat her heels against the legs of the chair. "I have to move. It keeps me from thinking. At least, as much as I would if I were sitting still."

Kick, kick. Kick, kick. Louisa sighed heavily in annoyance, and Julia jumped up at once and began pacing again.

"Why doesn't he write? Why doesn't he come? What's the matter?"

She stopped pacing, struck by an idea. "I should just go to him and speak to him in person."

This elicited a strong reaction from Louisa. "No!" she cried, rising from her chair to stand between Julia and the door. "Absolutely not. You must see that that's impossible."

"Why?" Julia replied petulantly. "What on earth could it matter now? The worst is already done."

Louisa rolled her eyes. "We are far from having had the worst happen. If you go to him now, your reputation as a loose woman will be confirmed in everyone's minds. You may never recover, even if he does marry you. But if the next news related to you is marriage, people will soon forget. They may enjoy a good scandal, but everyone knows that things are usually not as bad as they sound. They'll let it go."

Julia felt mulish, and she folded her arms. She was desperate to do something. As she stepped forward again, Louisa spread her arms wide to block the doorway. "Julia. You must stay. We can do nothing else that does not strictly comply with propriety." She swallowed and added, "If you won't regard that for yourself . . . will you think of me?"

Julia threw her hand up in capitulation. She had to give Louisa credit for not playing the "do it for my sake" card until she had to—but her sister had known that would absolutely work. Julia had been thinking only of her own impatience and apprehension, but of course Louisa was going through the same emotions, with an added dash of humiliation to leaven the mixture.

Julia dragged herself back to a chair and dropped into it spiritlessly, not even bothering to swing her heels against the chair legs this time. Why bother kicking? It wouldn't make James come for her any sooner. Why try not to think of it? How could she possibly hope to distract herself from something that would dictate the whole future course of her life? She *should* be thinking of it, unbearable though the suspense was.

Thankfully, a message came from James soon afterward, relieving both young women. Julia ripped open the sealed missive and read it, almost before Louisa had dismissed the servant who had brought it in.

She scanned the letter eagerly, but her hopefulness changed at once to stunned pain.

"No," she whispered, turning white. "I don't believe it." Her head felt light, as if all the blood had drained from it. With boneless legs, she sagged to the floor, drawing deep breaths to keep her vision from going black with terror.

"Good God," Louisa gasped, staring at Julia in amazement. "What does it say?"

Julia squeezed her eyes shut and shoved the paper along the floor to Louisa. She heard the other girl pick it up and read it softly aloud.

> *Miss Herington:*
> *Thank you for the honor of your letter. I regret that I am unable to oblige you in the matter you requested.*
>
> > *Sincerely,*
> > *Matheson*

To hear this read aloud was an agony that Julia had never known before. She would have rather had her hand cut off than receive this chill, formal rejection. She was so stunned that she had nothing to say.

If it hadn't been so terrible, she might have thought

it was rather funny. She, Julia, had finally been brought to the point of silence.

She wished she could vanish. Just blink out of existence, away from seals and notes and broken promises.

"What is this? Is this some kind of a cruel joke?" Louisa finally asked.

Her eyes still shut, Julia replied flatly, "How could it be a joke? It bore his seal."

She opened her eyes and looked up at Louisa from her huddle on the floor. "What did I do? Why did he change his mind?" She could barely manage to whisper, her voice was so choked with pain. "Doesn't he love me anymore?"

"I don't believe in this," Louisa said decisively, slapping the note against her palm. "Remember, I know James's handwriting, and this isn't it. And this doesn't sound like him, does it? He would never be so cold."

A flicker of hope stabbed through Julia. "He didn't send that?" Then she thought of another possibility. "Perhaps he just had his valet write it." A lump rose in her throat. "If he really didn't care."

He'd already bedded her, after all. Perhaps that was all he had ever wanted from her. She couldn't really believe that of him, even now, but here was the terrible written evidence right before her, bearing his seal.

Such was the word of a viscount. A bitter laugh escaped her.

Louisa crouched down to look Julia in the eye. "You are overset. You know that can't be true. He loves you deeply." She mused for a moment. "Perhaps he's not at home, and some guest took advantage of his absence to send this."

"Who would do such a thing?" Julia said lifelessly. "Who bears me such a grudge? Not even Xavier. He didn't seek to single me out; I was just unluckily at hand when he came by."

"I don't know," Louisa said. "But it can't be from James. Let's show this to our aunt and see what she thinks."

Lady Irving entered the room just then, drawn by the commotion of doors opening and closing. "Is he here?" she asked eagerly as she swept through the doorway. Then she noticed her two nieces sitting on the floor, a rumpled piece of paper between them.

"Ah." She paused, drawing swift conclusions from the scene before her. "I wouldn't have thought it of the fellow," she said, heavy scorn in her voice. "How bad is it?"

Wordlessly, Louisa handed her the paper and rubbed Julia's back. Lady Irving skimmed the message, then crumpled it and threw it in the fire. Despite herself, Julia gasped, and reached fruitlessly out for the burned paper.

"That was the last note I will ever have from him," she whispered. She knew even as she said it that it was a pitiful thing to wish for. Why should she want such a dreadful message? But it had his name on it. She loved that name.

"Rot," the countess snorted. "If you think that message was truly from Matheson, it's time to pack you off to Bedlam. The only thing is," she mused, "how would someone have been able to send a note under his seal?"

"That's what I was trying to think," Louisa chimed in. "Perhaps he's not at home, and some caller took advantage of his absence? Though I cannot imagine who."

"We'll sort this out," Lady Irving replied grimly. "I'll send Simone over to his place for a look about. If he's gone, we'll leave another message for him. And if he's home . . ." A martial light glowed in her eyes, and she finished, "Well, he won't treat my girls like this. I'll have his manhood for it."

Both girls gasped in shock, and Lady Irving turned a sharp eye on them. "What? Let the punishment fit the crime, I say. Now get up off the floor and make yourselves presentable. Very likely we'll be having a wedding today after all."

Her face relaxed into an affectionate smile, and she helped Louisa and Julia to their feet and into chairs. "There you go, my girls. This is all rather fun, isn't it?"

Fun? Julia stared at her aunt in amazement, and saw a similar expression of disbelief on Louisa's face.

Before she could even reply, a footman announced Sir Stephen Saville and at once ushered him into the room.

Oh, Lord. As if they were any of them equipped to deal with a caller at this time. Especially *him*. Why in heaven's name had he come? Julia wondered with a sudden prickle of apprehension if his chivalrous urges would lead him to "save" her from the distressing situation by renewing his proposals of the previous day.

Had it really all happened in only a day? Unbelievable.

Well, she hoped with all her might that he would say nothing of the kind. Her mind whirled even as her voice mechanically made the proper greeting and her head inclined for a curtsy, and she saw her relatives doing the same, their faces as bemused as hers must be. If he should offer for her again, what should she say? If James truly refused to marry her, this could be her only hope for social recovery. For a family of her own.

No, even so, she still couldn't do it. She *must* trust that things would work out with James.

Somehow.

From her position next to Lady Irving, Julia saw her aunt draw aside the footman who had shown in their guest.

"Fool," her ladyship hissed in an undervoice. "We are not receiving callers at this time."

The footman gulped, but replied, "My apologies, my lady. You had told me that Sir Stephen might be shown up at any time he called."

With an expression of annoyed dismay, Lady Irving dismissed the servant and turned to their guest with a bright, false smile. Fortunately, Sir Stephen had noticed none of this exchange, as Louisa had directed his attention toward the choice of a comfortable seat and ascertained that he needed no refreshment.

"I fear this is not entirely a visit of pleasure," the baronet intoned, "although of course it is always an honor to be in the presence of ladies."

He nodded at Lady Irving and Louisa, and Julia felt a gnawing sense of doubt begin to grow in her stomach. What did *that* mean? Was he referring to the fact that Julia was the only untitled woman here, or . . . was this about that cruel news item that cast doubts on her respectability?

She couldn't think of anything to say, and apparently neither could her aunt and Louisa, because all three women just stared at him, waiting for him to come to the point.

"Yes, well," he continued, looking a bit discomfited at having three steady gazes on him, "what I have to say is somewhat personal, for the ears of Miss Herington. I deem it only appropriate that you remain here as chaperone, Lady Irving, but I would like to give Miss Herington the opportunity to select the audience for this conversation."

He cast his eyes from one woman to the next. Nobody budged.

Finally, Julia replied in a wooden voice, "Anything you have to say to me may be spoken in front of my aunt and my sister." She couldn't imagine what was coming, but she knew it wouldn't be good.

"I see." Sir Stephen hesitated, then began, "This is difficult for me to say, but I am anxious that there should be no confusion between us, Miss Herington. My proposals of yesterday, and my regard for you, were based upon an apparent misunderstanding of your character and proclivities."

Julia gasped. The nerve!

Sir Stephen continued, "I am sure you understand to what I refer—the unfortunate, ah . . ."

"Yes, we know," Lady Irving broke in crisply. "Come to the point, man."

Sir Stephen cleared his throat and looked uncomfortable. "Ah . . . very well. I, ah, wanted to let you know that I will not be renewing my proposal of marriage to you, Miss Herington. I do condole with you and your family for this very public embarrassment, but I am sure you understand that I am looking for a wife of moral uprightness."

Julia stood, and her relatives echoed her movements at once. Sir Stephen looked doubtfully at them, and then slowly rose himself, as was proper.

Always, what was proper. Julia couldn't blame the man for being horrified, but *honestly*. Couldn't he have given her credit for enough tact not to run to him for a haven after she was publicly condemned for being with another man?

"Thank you for your extremely enlightening message, Sir Stephen," she replied in a cool voice that fell just short of courtesy. "I assure you I had no intention of pressuring you into a renewal of those proposals you extended to me yesterday. As I mentioned then, and as must be abundantly clear to you now, I care for another."

Sir Stephen flinched at her chilly reply, and pressed on inexorably, his eyes worried. "I meant no disrespect, Miss Herington. I do feel for you, most sincerely, to be used and cast aside by one whom I had regarded as a friend to us both." He shook his head in sorrow. "I had thought Matheson would at least act honorably after exposing you to such public condemnation, but I fear I was mistaken in his character."

"What do you mean?" Lady Irving asked, her eyes narrowing. "Matheson's offered to marry her. We've just received a note from him to that effect." The lie tripped off her lips smoothly.

The baronet looked taken aback by this statement. "Is that so? I am happy to be wrong, then. Only I just paid him a visit to commiserate on his public misfortune, and he said nothing about it. I was most distressed at his detachment from the whole affair."

"He was . . . at home?" Louisa asked, her eyes wide and startled. She looked quickly from Julia to Lady Irving.

"Why, yes," Sir Stephen replied. "Very much so. He was taking coffee with his mother when I arrived. They seemed most convivial. His mother was even speaking of plans to attend some type of a musicale with Lord and Lady Alleyneham."

Lady Irving swiftly moved to the door and opened it for the baronet. "Thank you very much for your call, Sir Stephen. You've been most enlightening. We need not keep you any longer."

Their guest nodded his understanding, and with a last stricken, sorrowful look at Julia, he bowed his farewell.

He had looked genuinely sad for her. For them all. Julia wondered if he had loved her, after all. If so, it must have been a terrible shock for him to read that morning's scandal sheet.

But she had bigger problems to consider now than the degree of Sir Stephen Saville's disappointment. Eventually, he would overcome it. But she . . . she wasn't sure she would get over hers.

Because James was at home.

He was home, and he was talking about going out and about publicly with her *friend* Charissa Bradleigh, while she was here waiting for him to show up and marry her so she wouldn't be ruined. He must have sent that note—or, if it wasn't his handwriting, then he must have had someone else send it for him.

She didn't understand, but she didn't have to. Waiting around was intolerable, and waiting around with the entire *ton* ready to pity her, judge her, and give her the cut direct was even worse than intolerable. If there was such a thing.

Julia looked up to meet the eyes of her aunt and sister. They were both staring at her, open-mouthed, stricken, waiting for her reaction to Sir Stephen's revelations.

"I still don't believe it," Louisa insisted quickly, but her eyes were wounded and doubtful. Lady Irving said nothing, only shook her head.

"It doesn't matter," Julia said in what she hoped was a calm voice. "Well, that's not true. Of course it matters. It matters more than anything."

She choked for a second, and with an effort, held back angry tears to explain. "Whether he wrote that terrible note or not, he's not *here*. He didn't come when I said I needed him.

"Maybe it's all a misunderstanding; maybe not. I can't

imagine that he wouldn't marry me after he promised to." She darted a quick look at Louisa, remembering too late that her sister had, only two days ago, been the lady engaged to the viscount in question. "But I can't wait around anymore to see what he'll do, or when. I can't just do nothing and wait for him to save me. I want to leave; I want to go home. That's the only thing I *can* do, unfortunately."

"I'll second that," Louisa said. "I'm ready to leave here for good."

She wrapped Julia in a tight hug. "I'm so sorry. I can't believe it either. Maybe we can write to him again when we get home," she suggested.

Lady Irving shook her head. "It's for him to make it right." For the first time in Julia's memory, the countess looked spiritless. Seeing her vivacious, sharp-tongued aunt brought low was, in Julia's mind, the most shocking development of all. If her aunt no longer believed in James . . . maybe that was that, then.

"We'll leave today," the countess decided. "As soon as we can be packed."

"Need we wait for that?" Julia pleaded. "Simone could follow with the trunks, couldn't she?"

She searched her aunt's doubtful countenance, begging with her eyes for understanding. *Please, please, let us go now. Please let us get out of this terrible situation. Please let us go home.*

"Very well," Lady Irving assented at last, her voice regaining some of its strength. "We'll go as soon as the carriage can be brought round. I'll have the knocker removed from the door at once." She grimaced. "We certainly don't need anyone else coming by to throw their pity in our face."

"But what if James comes by?" Julia asked. She couldn't help wondering, or just a little, still hoping.

"If *he* comes," her ladyship said scornfully, "I don't suppose the simple fact of the knocker being off the door would stop him from finding you."

Within twenty minutes, they were in the carriage and on their way back to Kent. James had not, after all, come for her.

Chapter 32

In Which Julia
Receives a History Lesson

The family, the servants, and probably even the assorted livestock of Stonemeadows Hall were surprised to see Lady Irving's crested carriage drive up without any notice late that afternoon. And they were even more surprised to see the carriage disgorge three very harried-looking and travel-worn women who carried not a single bandbox between them.

Lord Oliver greeted his sister and children warmly, happy as always to see his relatives. He then drifted away, musing aloud to himself about some essential aspect of estate management or cow breeding.

Lady Oliver, however, did not simply take the arrival of the countess and her charges in stride and flutter on with her day. Only the least astute observer (which Lord Oliver decidedly was) could fail to notice that something had gone seriously and suddenly awry.

"What on earth *happened*?" she asked, plying Lady Irving, Louisa, and Julia with tea and biscuits as soon as they could settle themselves in the drawing room. "Are you all right, all of you?"

Lady Irving opened her mouth to speak, from sheer force of habit, but then seemed to think better of it. She looked at Louisa, Louisa looked at Julia, and Julia looked back blankly at the two of them.

"I don't know how even to begin to tell her," Julia admitted. The very thought was too daunting. All through the brief journey home, she had tried to keep her mind away from James, but it had taken all her willpower. Now that they had arrived, she wanted nothing but to sob onto her mother's shoulder.

If her mother would let her, knowing the truth of what Julia had done.

"Everything is fine, Mama," Louisa said, easing most of the apprehensive look from Lady Oliver's face. "At least, we are all unharmed."

Lady Irving snorted. "Physically, perhaps. But let me tell you, Elise, your girls have had a rough emotional time of it. That *viscount* doesn't have the slightest idea how to behave toward persons of quality. He has used both of your daughters extremely ill. And probably he kicks puppies, too," she added for good measure.

Lady Oliver was taken aback by this outburst. "Puppies?" she asked blankly. "I don't understand. Did you keep a dog in London?"

Julia shook her head. "Aunt, you are only cluttering the issue with hyperbole." A memory flashed into her head, of Sir Stephen Saville gravely informing her that she had been "hyperbolic." Poor man. It seemed as if it had been years ago.

Well, for all the similarity her future life would bear to her life in London, it might as well have *been* years ago.

She took a deep breath, and looked at Louisa for

permission to tell her mother everything. At her sister's nod, Julia spoke as quickly as she could, trying not to consider her words too deeply for fear that she might choke on them.

"Louisa broke her engagement to James due to unhappiness. I love—loved—him, though, and he loved me in return. We were involved in a scandal and this morning he sent a note saying that he refused to marry me. So we left. And here we are."

She looked anxiously at her mother, waiting for a reply. Lady Oliver shut her eyes for a few seconds, then opened them, and they were full of sympathy.

"Oh, my dear girls," she said softly. "My dear sister." She reached to gather them all in a hug at once, which involved a lot of uncomfortable bending and squishing together as three grown women tried to scoot within the grasp of one.

To Julia, however, this seemed not the smallest bit ridiculous. She felt intense relief that she'd been able to clear the first hurdle of telling her mother without, first of all, crying her head off, and second of all, provoking any type of enraged reaction (Lady Irving's outburst about the puppy-kicking notwithstanding). True, she'd given only the vaguest outline of what had happened, but it was enough. Her mother wanted to hug her, not boot her out of the house.

So. She deserved to know the rest of it. And maybe . . . maybe it would help Julia to say it all again. Maybe the whole sad ending of the affair would become a little more real, and maybe she could stop grasping at the faint hope that it would all work out in the end.

But it wouldn't be easy to tell it all.

Julia spoke next to her aunt and sister. "Would you mind leaving us alone?"

Lady Irving began to protest, not wanting to miss the chance to add her considered opinion of the viscount and his moral flaws, but Louisa rose at once to leave the room. The countess looked after her reluctantly for a moment, then also stood.

"Very well," she agreed. "We'll wait in the breakfast parlor or some such nonsense. But I'm taking the biscuits. I need fortification after what I've been through today."

Julia rolled her eyes at this statement. She could have done with a biscuit herself, or perhaps a dozen. But she supposed she should just be glad to have her other relatives out of the room. She didn't want to listen to her aunt rail against James, even though he had failed her. And she didn't want to talk about the situation in front of Louisa's bruised eyes. If there was a good side to this at all, it was that Louisa had been able to come home as she wished. Still, Julia couldn't help feeling that she had added to Louisa's misery, even though her sister had not only forgiven her but given her blessing for Julia to be with James.

Once she was alone with her mother, Julia again drew a deep breath for courage. She looked at her mother's sympathetic blue eyes, so much like her own. It was hard to know where to begin. She had always told her mother everything, and her mother had always understood—but then again, nothing had ever really *happened* to Julia before. She'd lived her life in the country, seeing the same small circle of people over and over again. She'd certainly never been in love before, or publicly humiliated, for that matter.

"My girl," Lady Oliver began with a soft smile. "It's good to see you again, no matter what the cause for your return." She put her arm around Julia's shoulders and added, "You don't have to tell me anything else if you don't want to."

This permission, this graciousness, freed Julia's tongue at last, and she was able to tell her mother everything. She spoke for what seemed like hours, as Lady Oliver listened quietly and sympathetically.

She told her mother how she had fallen in love with James almost at once; how guilty she had felt, knowing he belonged to Louisa; how she finally realized she must try to forget him and seek a match with someone else. She described Sir Stephen, how he had pursued her and proposed to her. How Louisa had enlisted her help in delivering the news of the broken engagement. How Julia had gone to James's home to talk to him.

The next part was more difficult to tell. "I spent time with him in his home, Mama. Of an intimate nature," she admitted. "And then, as I was leaving, we were seen together."

Lady Oliver read between the lines. "Oh, dear," she replied. "That was quite a step to take."

Julia looked nervously at her mother's face. "Are you angry with me?"

Lady Oliver shrugged, her expression as untroubled as ever. "It's not a good idea for a young woman, because of the risk of a baby. But in this case, he wants to marry you, so I think all shall be well, even if there is a baby."

"A baby," Julia repeated. She felt numb. She hadn't even thought of the possibility of a baby.

Lady Oliver noticed her daughter's thunderstruck expression. "Why are you so worried, my girl? What does it matter if the baby comes a week or two earlier than it might have if you waited for your marriage? Babies always come in their own time; no one will ever know the difference."

"But, Mama," Julia insisted, "he *won't* marry me." In a flat voice she assumed to hide her growing terror—dear God, if there would be a baby, how would she care for it, all alone in the world?—she told her mother about the scandal item in the morning paper; the messages sent and received; Sir Stephen's rescinded proposal and the information about James's whereabouts.

"So he must have felt that he had been disgraced, and he changed his mind about marrying me, which I *thought* he had only suggested in the first place because of what we had done, and I felt uneasy about it. And as it turns out, I was right to feel that way, because he never came for me, and I shall have a baby and be a disgrace to you and be cast out alone into the world," Julia finished. She was wrung out at the end of her tale; she could do nothing but gasp for breath and stare at her mother with haunted eyes.

Lady Oliver stared back at her for a moment, absorbing this frantic stream of words. And then she laughed.

And she kept laughing, for what seemed to Julia like minutes on end, her loud peals of amusement finally simmering down into giggles, but breaking out again periodically into another hearty chuckle.

"Oh, my goodness," Lady Oliver said, wiping at her eyes, as her daughter gaped at her in hurt shock. "Oh, I'm sorry to laugh at you. But you are just so *funny*."

"Funny?" Julia was insulted. "What part of my tragic tale was *funny* to you?"

"Julia, my girl"—her mother smiled fondly, cupping her chin—"I think the world of Louisa, but she has obviously encouraged you to read far too many Gothic novels. You are allowing your imagination to run away with you."

She looked her daughter full in the face as she ticked

points off one by one on her fingers, still smiling. "First of all, you are loved; that can never be a tragedy. Second, if there should be a baby and no marriage, you will always have a home here with us. Third, that will never come to pass, because there will be a marriage, because the viscount is head over ears in love with you."

Julia stared at her, a faint, eager optimism beginning to grow inside of her. "Why do you say that? Are you just repeating what I told you he said in the past, or . . ."

"Please," Lady Oliver scoffed gently, "allow that your own mother has eyes in her head to see what's going on in her house, even if your father tends to be, er, a bit too distracted to notice. I was very eager for Louisa's match to take place, but when I saw how reserved they were with each other and how comfortable James was with you and you with him, I thought there might be a change of bride at some point."

Julia was stunned. She had had no inkling that anyone else had ever observed her feelings for James. "You thought that all along?"

Lady Oliver smiled again. "It would hardly have been tactful to say anything while Louisa was still engaged to him, would it? I only hoped that, if it should not work out, it would not be a disappointment to Louisa. But she's stronger than even she knows, and she's seen to her own happiness in this case."

"She's been wonderful," Julia blurted. "She forgave me in an instant. Once she had given James up, she was more than happy that I should . . . well, be happy."

"So?" Lady Oliver looked at her daughter expectantly. "Are you going to be?"

Julia shrugged. "I don't know. My aunt says it is for James to make things right at this point."

"Bosh," the elder woman replied, and looked startled

at her own response. "My goodness, I must be taking on your aunt's personality."

She blinked in surprise, then explained, "If you want something, you must go and get it. It may not be precisely the conventional thing to do, but it's the only way to be sure you'll have no regrets. If you love him, you must pursue him, and if he loves you in return, then all will work out for the best. And if by some impossibility, he does not—I know, dear; no need to shudder, for it won't happen—then you will have tried your utmost, and you need never wonder about what might have happened."

Julia considered her mother's words. She had been so hurt by the note James had sent—well, it couldn't *really* have been James who'd sent it, but still, perhaps it had come on his behalf—that she hadn't thought about anything beyond escaping from London. She had been devastated. Crushed. Mortified.

She had no desire to experience any of that again. Her mother's encouraging words had cheered her at first. But now she was being told to take a risk, a very bold and unladylike risk, and take the chance of experiencing another, worse pain than before.

She felt grouchy. What did her mother know about it, anyway? Her mother had a perfect marriage and a husband who loved her even more than he loved mucking about with his animals, which was truly saying something. All right, perhaps she had been a little melodramatic talking about her "tragic tale"—but still, it was too much to ask that Julia risk humiliation again.

"Who would actually pursue a man in that way?" she grumbled. "Women aren't allowed to do anything. We just have to wait for the men to ask, and then we simply have the choice of yes or no."

Lady Oliver raised her eyebrows in surprise. "But my

dear, that's not true at all." She brought a considering forefinger to her cheek. "Did you never wonder why you were named Julia, rather than being named Elise for me?"

Julia hadn't been expecting *that* response. "Um . . . no. No, I never thought about it, I suppose."

"Well." Lady Oliver sat back and folded her hands over her knee, as if settling in for a long tale. "It was, of course, expected that I would name you for myself, as my oldest daughter. But you are named instead for your father."

Despite the passage of time, the baroness's eyes grew misty with remembered fondness. "I was only eighteen, even younger than yourself, when I met Julian Herington. I was the daughter of a country squire, and he was the curate."

Her voice turned confiding. "He was the handsomest man I'd ever seen, positively golden, and so kind and intelligent. I would stay after services every week just to talk to him. My father was delighted with my devotion to the church."

Julia smiled back at her mother, encouraging her to go on, but she was puzzled. She'd never heard any of this before. She supposed she'd never even thought to ask, since as far back as she could remember, there had been no father—and then, when she was still a young child, there had been Lord Oliver. She'd never thought about the man who had been in her mother's life before.

Lady Oliver spoke on, telling her daughter about how she managed to provoke the curate into admitting that he loved her, but he felt he did not have the right to marry her because she was so far above him.

"So far above him." The baroness shook her head. "As if there could ever be such a thing, when such warmth and wit were involved. However, my parents agreed with his view of the matter, and hoped to match me to a baronet, or a knight at the very least. I was quite the heiress, you see." She smiled mischievously. "So I simply took matters into my own hands."

Julia's eyes were round with amazed interest. She'd never known *any* of this. It wasn't hard to think of her lighthearted mother as young—but this willful woman, in love and determined, was a revelation. "What did you do?" she breathed.

Lady Oliver turned pink, and hesitated before speaking. "While I was talking with him alone, I pulled the bodice of my dress down just before I knew some women would be coming in to decorate the church."

She coughed, remembering the old scheme with slight embarrassment. "Naturally, they were horrified by his scandalous conduct, and he was forced to marry me at once. I hadn't foreseen that he might also be removed from his position as curate, but so it was. I did regret that part."

Her smile grew warm and her eyes distant. "But the marriage—ah, that was wonderful. My father used his influence and my dowry to buy Julian a living in Leicestershire, and we went to live there following our marriage."

She looked her daughter straight in the eye. "It was the most wonderful time of my life, and it would never have happened if it weren't for my own determination. When we discovered you were on the way, it made our happiness complete."

Julia hardly dared ask what had happened next, knowing that the idyll must have soon ended.

"Yes, it was very soon over," Lady Oliver replied, her eyes downcast. "Your father was killed in a carriage accident three months before your birth. He never even saw you."

She choked on her next words. "Despite my grief, I thanked God for you every day, for you were a little piece of him. I longed to hold you, to keep any connection with him that I could. So of course I had to name you for him."

She reached out to stroke Julia's hair with a hand that trembled. "You look like me, but you have his smile. His smile could warm you in winter, just of itself."

Her wistful expression brightened. "So there you have it, my darling girl. You are here on earth because I was a rather bold and improper young lady. We women may not have the right to ask, but we can still get what we want, even if for just a little while."

Her smile broadened. "Actually, I must correct myself. I've been very fortunate to have what I wanted for years. My early loss was terrible, but some years later I met Lord Oliver."

Her expression turned considering. "We met at Tattersalls, you know. I believe I was the only woman there looking at horseflesh. Naturally, I drew his eye at once. I wasn't thinking of marrying again, though I did like him very much. But when I learned he had a daughter also— *well.* Then I wanted to know him better, and in time I came to love him. Just as much as I loved your father, though not in the same way, of course. Lord Oliver is a very unique person, you know."

"Yes, I'm well aware of that," Julia replied with an understanding quirk of the mouth.

"And when you and Louisa met—you just fit. You were meant to be sisters. You healed each other, and I hadn't even known that you needed healing."

She gave a pensive sigh. "Oh, Julia. How fortunate you are. You, who could have all the approval and congratulations of the world for joining yourself with a titled gentleman, have nothing to risk but your own heart. And that, as I have told you, is already his, as his is yours."

Lady Oliver stopped speaking, and she fell into a reverie, her mind dancing back nineteen years to her first love. Julia saw her mother's face turn preoccupied, and she considered her own situation anew.

She felt heavy and sorrowful, thinking of her young mother's terrible loss, with an unborn baby on the way. If that had happened to her—if she had lost James so swiftly and irrevocably—it would be unbearable. But never to see him again, while he lived, would be even worse. It would be a waste. A loss that need never be.

She blinked her eyes wide open, understanding at last. Her mother's sorrow had all been worth it, despite the short duration of her first love. That's what her mother was trying to tell her. It was worth the risk of grief to pursue that bold delight. For if you caught it . . .

Lady Oliver had been fortunate enough to find a second happiness, but she, Julia, would never even have existed if her mother had not pursued her first.

Well. She could do the same, could she not? She felt she owed it to her mother to pursue her own heart's desire—but also, of course, she owed it to herself. And to James. Good heavens, hadn't she already done something similar, forcing the next step by going to his house alone? She had always known within herself, or hoped, what would happen if she did.

So now that she was home and away from London's prying eyes, what did she really want? Despite the long, momentous day and her physical exhaustion from worry and travel, the answers were clear.

She wanted James. She loved him, and she wanted to marry him.

She did *not* want to go back to London for some time.

She did *not* want to see Sir Stephen Saville again for quite a while, either.

And she didn't want to listen to her aunt. She didn't want to wait and see if James would come after her. She wanted, as her mother had said, to do all she could to find him, clear the air, and make him hers.

"All right," she said with determination. "I'll do it. I'm going to get James."

Lady Oliver blinked back to the present, and took in Julia's words slowly. Then she beamed a bright, delighted smile at her daughter. "That's wonderful! I'm so happy for you. And for him."

Julia smiled back, allowing a sense of relief and glee to fill her. She knew what to do. She didn't have to wait for anyone to decide her life for her. She would take the next step herself, and handle the consequences that came.

Then a sudden doubt seized her. "Mama, what should I do to find him? I don't know if he knows where I am, and I don't know if he plans to stay in London either."

"Hmm." Lady Oliver pondered this. "We're a day behind in getting the London papers here. Tomorrow we'll receive the one with your, ah, news."

Julia shuddered. "Could we dispose of that one, please?"

Her mother nodded. "I'll just tell your father that Manderly scorched it with the iron when preparing it to be read. Your father won't think twice about it."

"Poor Manderly," Julia said, thinking of how the starchy butler might react to having his skills impugned. Oh, well. She couldn't bear to have her father, or her siblings, or the servants thinking ill of her after reading that scandal item. It was only a matter of time before word got around from the neighboring estates anyway.

Unless she married James, of course. Just another reason to make that happen; she could add that to the hundreds she had already thought of. First of which was, of course, that she desperately wanted to.

"Anyway," Lady Oliver went on, "by the following day, there may be an item if he has decided to leave for the country. Then you'll know if you should write him in town, or visit him at Nicholls."

"That makes sense," Julia said, nodding. More waiting; it seemed endless. "But I want to leave at once." Never mind that she didn't even know where she ought to go.

"I understand," her mother soothed. "But—and you must forgive me for once again sounding like your aunt—you'll appear to much better advantage if you rest and bathe before embarking on another journey."

"Oh." This sensible remark put a sudden stop to Julia's feeling of desperate longing. She ran a tentative hand over her hair, and could feel the snarls and prickling pins of an untidy coiffure. She looked down at her dress, and admitted the creases in it as well. And now that she thought of it, she wasn't sure she was exactly at her cleanest after a long and traumatic day that involved a close and frantic carriage ride.

"Very well," she sighed. "I'll wait until I appear to be a decent human being again. Simone will be here sometime soon with the trunks, I hope before nightfall. So I'll take your advice and wait another day—but not a bit longer than that," she said, a warning light in her eyes.

"I think that sounds delightful," Lady Oliver said cheerfully. "Now, what's this I heard about you getting some Oiseau gowns? I would love to see them."

Despite the uncertainties pressing on her mind, this comment provoked Julia into a laugh. "Yes, Mama, I do have the most beautiful dresses. And they look absolutely nothing like Aunt Estella's!"

Chapter 33

In Which
Simone Gets Lost

This newspaper is distressed to report the sudden departure of Viscount M—— for his country estate. The *ton* will certainly be sorry to lose one of its shining stars, especially one who has provided so much recent interest for the clucking tongues of society matrons. One wonders if he intends also to make a visit to the home of Miss H——, the interesting young female so recently involved with the erstwhile viscount?

So. He was back at Nicholls. And Julia could answer quite decisively, if anyone had cared to ask her, that the "erstwhile viscount" had *not* made a visit to her home.

That meant she would go to his, then. She had already packed her trunk, just in case, and had notified her relatives that she might be leaving again at very short notice. Lady Irving was the only one who had raised any demur to this plan, although after Lady Oliver had taken her aside and talked to her for a solid forty-five minutes, even the countess had finally agreed that Julia might as well "try to bag the rascal" after all. She made Julia promise to take Simone with her if she went anywhere, however, since, she said with a meaningful lift of the eyebrows, it hadn't gone all that well for Julia the last time she went running off to a man's house without the supervision of a maid.

Actually, Julia thought, it had gone rather *too* well, but there was no need to argue with her aunt on this point. She agreed to the company of the French lady's maid, knowing that Simone would be a sensible and efficient traveling companion.

Louisa offered to come along as well, but Julia declined, not wanting to give rise to the polite world's most awkward situation since Miss Lettice Hopston's bosoms had tumbled out of her court dress while curtsying to the queen. Which was to say—since she didn't know how the meeting was going to go, she thought it would be better to have fewer witnesses, and to have none of those witnesses be the viscount's former fiancée, even if that lady also happened to be one of her favorite people in the whole world.

Julia and Simone left for Nicholls within an hour of reading the newspaper with the information on James's location. Lord Oliver was nowhere to be found at the time of departure, and thus had no idea what historic events might be about to take place. But Lady Oliver, Louisa, and Lady Irving all hugged Julia farewell and sent her off with a unique parting message.

"Don't get married away from home, mind you," Lady Oliver reminded her daughter. "Have him bring you back here once all is settled between you, and we'll read the banns in the Stonemeadows church if he hasn't got a special license."

"If he hasn't got a special license," Lady Irving muttered, "he won't be a functional male any more after I'm through with him." She grumbled on for a few minutes, with only the words "scapegrace" and "the honorable thing" audible to Julia's ears. Finally, with a hard, quick hug, the countess released Julia, adjuring her to return swiftly since she couldn't get along without Simone.

Louisa simply gave Julia a long hug, her dark eyes shining. "Take care," she whispered. "I hope all shall be well."

"It shall be," Julia assured her, "one way or another."

She expected that the journey would seem unbearably long, but it passed more quickly than she could ever have hoped. Simone could tell that Julia didn't wish to speak, and the gentle rocking of the carriage lulled the travelers into a state of quiet contemplation.

What was on Simone's mind, Julia couldn't even guess. Her own thoughts spun in circles as she wondered what she would say or do when she saw James. Different scenarios flitted through her mind. Should she be demure and wait for him to apologize? Should she be cold, and allow him to beg her forgiveness? Should she fling herself into his arms? Should she act as if nothing were wrong?

They made only a brief stop at a posting house to change horses and have a quick meal, arriving at Nicholls in early afternoon.

"How do I look?" Julia asked her traveling companion as their carriage pulled into the sweep of the Nicholls drive—which, she noticed vaguely, was now well-graveled and entirely devoid of the terrible ruts that had jostled the carriage on their last visit.

Simone cast appraising eyes up and down Julia's face and form. Wordlessly, she retrained a few curls, adjusted a few hairpins, and brushed at the fabric of Julia's dress, then leaned back to examine her charge.

She nodded, approving her work. "It is not so excellent as I would like," she admitted, "but it cannot be helped after travel. I think you will do very well for your *monsieur.*"

Julia rolled her eyes and accepted this less than enthusiastic approval. As Louisa had once told her, what seemed like ages ago, her future husband wouldn't mind what she looked like, even if she were wearing a tomato-like costume.

Besides, she knew James so well that she probably *could* dress like a tomato, and it wouldn't affect his response to her. At least, not once he was done laughing.

So. Now it was time to find out what that response would be. She and Simone disembarked from the carriage and were ushered into the house by a butler so correct that he showed absolutely no sign of surprise that two young women, without a bit of baggage, were there to see his lordship. He offered to show them into either the drawing room or into his lordship's study.

Here the dignified servant's mask slipped a bit, and he suggested with a significant twinkle in his eye, "Might I show you into the study? It has been recently refurnished and will be much more comfortable for a discussion of any significant length or import."

Julia gratefully accepted this suggestion, and the butler deposited the two visitors in the room in question, promising to send in some refreshment to them.

Julia sat down blindly on the first seat she saw and buried her face in her hands. She still had no idea what to say to James. Good heavens, she was going to see him in a very few minutes, and the whole course of her future life depended on what she was going to say to him. Her breathing grew shallow and quick. She was taking such a chance here, and what if it should come to nothing?

"If you will excuse me, *mademoiselle,*" Simone said, tapping Julia on the shoulder to get her attention, "I shall find the *salle des bains* for use after the journey." Her face neutral, she added, "I do not perfectly recall where any chambers are in this house. It is very possible that I will wander for much time before I am able to return to you."

Julia smiled at her implied assurance. Her nervousness didn't entirely disappear, but this hint from Simone did dissipate most of it. So she was to be left alone with James, was she? That did make things easier. She could talk to him—oh, *how* she could talk—until everything was understood between them. Until she knew what had happened, and why, and what would come next for them.

It was beginning to feel rather exciting, actually.

"Thank you, Simone," she replied gravely. "I do hope you don't get too lost, but I am well aware that this is a very large house."

With a curtsy of agreement, the maid left her alone. Alone to kick her heels against the chair legs as was her wont, waiting impatiently for James to arrive.

"Why am I always having to wait in some stupid chair for him to come to me?" Julia muttered, and at once rose from the chair to pace around the room.

Once she had worked out a bit of her nervous energy, she began to look at her surroundings.

"Why, this is lovely," she whispered. Here James had finally been able to make the comfortable home for himself that he had never bothered to do in London; here she could at last see his taste given free rein.

And she *liked* it. The walls were painted a warm, muted blue, while a deep-piled Aubusson carpet in rich tones covered most of the dark wood floor. Comfortable chairs and a long sofa provided plenty of space to sit. The room was dominated by a mahogany secretaire, the cabinets of which held an assortment of ledgers and volumes, and the desk of which was covered with a litter of notes, bills, crumpled papers, and a sealed letter. The style of it, and the room's other furnishings, was clean but sturdy, simple, and masculine, with lines lovely to behold.

Rather like their owner, actually.

As Julia was reflecting on this similarity, the door opened behind her. Before Julia could even turn around, arms wrapped around her from behind, and the beloved voice breathed her name in her ear before pressing a kiss onto her neck.

Well. That decided that, she supposed, tilting her head to allow James to kiss her neck again. She need not muck around with some elaborate plan to make him feel guilty, or to trick him into revealing his feelings, since those were abundantly clear.

He was delighted to see her. He must love her.

A breath of relief hissed out of her. She felt as if she'd been holding it for days and could at last relax.

So, she could be dignified and elegant with him. They could discuss the situation calmly and dispassionately, as mature adults.

She whirled furiously about and stomped on James's foot.

"How could you *do* that to me?" she demanded, struggling to get out of his embrace. "How could you send me that terrible letter, and then just *leave* me like that?

Didn't you know what people would think of me? Didn't you care anything about me at all?"

All right, so much for dignified and elegant. But at least he understood what she really thought.

Well, maybe he didn't understand. He looked astounded at her sudden reaction and rubbed his injured foot absently behind the calf of his other leg.

Julia struggled to keep from melting back against him. Even flabbergasted, he was the most beautiful person in the world to her, and she wanted to jump into his arms again and never leave.

She turned her thoughts back to the issue at hand with an effort and tried to glower at him, waiting for a response.

"What are you talking about?" James still looked thunderstruck, but at least he put down the foot Julia had stomped on. "I never sent you any letter. All I got was one from your aunt, saying that I shouldn't call on you or write to you ever again. I didn't think you had changed your mind about me, but I thought she had been humiliated by the public attention to our, ah, time together, and wanted to keep us apart."

Now it was Julia's turn to be shocked. "She sent *what*? Impossible. *I* sent you a letter, telling you to please come for me, for I thought we should be married at once. And," she added with embarrassed primness, "because it was what I wished for anyway."

They stared at each other, equally confused and hurt, and then they both spoke at once.

"But it bore her seal—"

"It wasn't your handwriting, but you had sealed it—"

And then, together: "How could you ever think I would send such a thing?"

They glared at each other for a few seconds, and then

James's mouth quivered. Julia saw his stern expression crack, then warm into a smile, and then he was laughing, and she was laughing right along with him.

He gathered her into his arms again and dropped a kiss onto the top of her head. "Obviously we have a few things to straighten out," he said, "but I'm just so happy to see you, I can't help myself."

He tipped her head back and kissed her gently, with the uncertain tenderness of a man who isn't sure whether he has been forgiven. And Julia—the dutiful daughter of the former Elise Crawford, who had compromised herself into gaining the marriage she longed for—took James's face in her hands and kissed him back with a fervor that assured him that not only had he been forgiven, but they had a lot of catching up to do.

James broke off the kiss after a long, heated moment. "My God."

He stepped back and reached a hand out to Julia. "We'd better have a seat and talk things over before we go on like that. I'm about two seconds away from losing all control, and I know that's not what you need right now."

Julia allowed him to show her into a chair, but she couldn't resist asking, "What would happen in two more seconds?" She thought she might know the answer, and it brought an impish smile to her face.

He shook his head at her in amazement. "If you keep looking at me like that, you're going to find out."

Julia covered her mouth, but was unable to suppress a laugh. "Does it involve being unclothed?"

James looked at her sharply. "Yes," he said, shifting uncomfortably in his chair. "Extremely unclothed."

Julia's face flushed warm; the heat spread, light and tingling and aware, through her whole body. To be with James again, in that so intimate way—was that why, once again, she had come to his house?

Perhaps it was, in part. Now that she was thinking of it, she longed to see him again, naked and proud, and she longed to have him touch her and wake those primal, ecstatic feelings.

But they *did* have other things to talk of; James was right. How had their letters gone awry?

With an effort on both of their parts, they turned their attention from the sensual to the logical, figuring out the timeline of messages sent, messages received, visitors, and departures. For the most part, it was a calm process, except for when Julia described for James the contents of the letter she had sent, and the one she had received back in his name.

"My dear," he whispered, reaching for her hands. "My poor love. You sent me that, and you got back—what did it say? No, never mind; don't think of it. If I'd truly gotten the message you sent, I wouldn't have been able to stay away from you for a second."

He drew his chair nearer to her, his expression urgent. "I wasn't yet dressed at the time your message came, but if I'd seen it, I would have sprinted over in my dressing gown, special license in hand." He sat back to smile at her wickedly. "As soon as we were married . . . well, there would have been less to take off that way."

Julia smiled back at him, but absently; she was still trying to sort out the chain of events in her head. What had happened to her letter? It must have gone astray sometime while he was upstairs. It was the only possibility.

"Oh, no," she realized with dawning horror. "It was your mother."

"What?" James looked confused.

"It was your mother," Julia repeated more firmly, beginning to feel angry. "It had to be. Don't you see? She was alone for what, fifteen or twenty minutes? She must have intercepted my message, and . . ." She thought for a moment. "I believe Aunt Estella had enclosed my letter in an extra sheet of paper for privacy, since I wrote so large that I covered both sides of the paper."

She was unable to keep all of the bitterness out of her voice as she recalled that measure, intended to be so helpful. "Your mother must have broken off the seal when she saw who it was from, read my letter, and used the blank sheet with the seal to write one of her own."

James shook his head. "No, that can't be. I'm sure it wasn't her handwriting."

They both looked crestfallen for a moment. Then James snapped his fingers, seized by a sudden memory.

"She had her lady's maid with her," he recalled. "Some poor creature who was probably terrified of her. She must have had the maid write the letters for her."

James looked so livid as he said this that Julia felt a bit nervous—not for herself, but for Lady Matheson, should that unfortunate viscountess happen to cross her son's path. He rose from his chair and began pacing around the room—Julia knew that urge well—kicking at the legs of every chair in his path, and muttering something about Matheson House and eviction.

It was rather amazing, actually, but the angrier he seemed, the calmer Julia began to feel. Her anger, her sense of having been wronged, began to melt away. What, after all, had she lost? Merely a couple of days with James, and perhaps the good opinion of people she didn't care about anyway, and might never meet again in her life. But what had the viscountess lost? In her desperate attempt to control her son, to bring him to heel and accept a bride of her own choosing, she had lost his trust. Perhaps forever.

The poor woman was almost to be pitied. Did she really think her stratagem would hold? That they would make no attempt to contact each other? That they would be so hurt they would stay apart?

No, that was too ridiculous. Although now that she thought about it, there was still one question that remained unanswered.

"James." Julia seized his hand and arrested him in his chair-kicking path around the room. "James, it doesn't matter. It didn't work, don't you see? She couldn't keep us apart." She stroked his arm, loving the feel of his muscles leaping beneath her touch. "Here I am. Here I am with you."

As he stared at her, trying to calm himself enough to listen, she drew a deep breath of her own. She had to have him answer that one last question.

"I do want to know, though," she asked in a small voice, "why didn't you come for me? After you knew what had been printed about us, why didn't you try to come for me or contact me in any way?"

He sat down, hard, in the chair across from her again. "But I *did*," he said urgently. "I came as soon as I could herd my blasted mother and that damned prosy baronet out of my house," he said, without the slightest touch of filial respect.

"I don't know what business he thought it was of his, but he honestly seemed to think he was being helpful, and he said he was going to speak with you, too. And my mother was even worse. Gad, the woman simply wouldn't leave. She was clinging to my hand and telling me about how lonely she was, and how glad she was to be having coffee with me."

He snorted in disgust. "It was all a pack of damned lies, designed to keep me there with her until you had gotten discouraged and left."

The fact that this was exactly what *had* happened did

not decrease Julia's feeling of sympathy. She had won; she could afford to be generous.

"Likely she did mean what she told you," she murmured, breaking into James's angry reflection. "I think she must be a very lonely woman. Although she probably did time her revelation for that very reason, to keep us away from one another. There's no denying that was her purpose for coming. Well, maybe not precisely her original purpose, but she certainly seized the opportunity when it arose."

James merely looked skeptical at Julia's placating words, then explained further what had happened. He had gone by the Grosvenor Square address as soon as he could, but the knocker was already off the door. Sheepishly, he admitted, "I pounded on it anyway. And . . . and I shouted for you."

"You did?" Julia was delighted by this mental image. "I imagine you entertained the whole square."

"Probably I did draw rather a lot of attention," James granted, "but I didn't even notice. Once I was sure you weren't there, I thought maybe you—or at least your aunt—really had meant what was said in that letter I received."

"That your mother had forged." Julia was unable to refrain from correcting him.

All right, so she wasn't perfect; she might still be feeling a *little* bit angry. This whole situation really did sting, and maybe it was for the best that the viscountess wasn't present right now, for everyone's sake. Julia wasn't entirely willing to promise that she wouldn't have taken a very unladylike swing at the older woman's face.

"Right," James agreed, continuing with his narrative. "I must have just missed you by a few minutes, though I couldn't have known that. Anyway, I decided to come home—here—and shake the dust of London from my feet for a time. I traveled all day yesterday, practically. I was determined I should get here before another day passed."

"And what about me?" Julia pressed. "What were you going to tell me, and when?"

James stood, without a word, and shuffled through the papers atop his secretaire before laying hands on the sealed missive Julia had noticed earlier. He handed it to her, and she turned it over and noticed that it was directed to her.

"I was going to post this today," he explained. "You can read it if you want to."

Was the man crazy? Of *course* she wanted to read it. She was dying to see what he would have said to her to try to make things right.

Julia, my love,

  I don't know what happened in London, or how things went so terribly wrong yesterday. I came to your aunt's house and you had left for Stonemeadows Hall. I felt like the worst sort of fool for letting you go, regardless of what your aunt might want.

  I wish I could have spared you even the smallest amount of worry. I love you still—always—and I would like to be married as soon as possible. If you feel the same, please let me know and I'll come for you at once, special license in hand.

                    Yours ever,
                    James

"Special license in hand," Julia whispered, joy bubbling up in her. He meant it. He wanted her. He always had.

"It *is* in hand, as I said," James replied, an answering grin on his face. "Well, practically. Here it is on my desk. I was determined to keep it until either we were married

or I knew you didn't want to have anything more to do
with me."

There followed a gleeful few minutes, during which
the couple eagerly sorted out the last few lingering uncertainties with kisses, laughs, and hurried explanations.
They decided to be married as soon as possible from
Stonemeadows Hall. James was all for being married the
next day, as soon as they could return to the barony;
there was no one, he insisted, that he wanted to invite.

"I'm soured on London," he said. "Honestly, Julia, I
think you are my truest friend." He looked warmly at her
as he said this, but then a little bleak as he continued, "I
don't know if any of my others were ever even real."

"That's no way to talk," Julia said, even as his compliment caused her to flutter inside. "You should at least
have your family present at your marriage."

She corrected herself conscientiously. "That is, you
should at least have your sister at the wedding. I can't say
I'm eager to see your mother right now. But you must
have your sister there."

She cast her memory back a long way, to a Christmas
fireside, and James's trust that she could help him bear
the weight of his family's honor. "I'll stand at your side,
and we'll offer her and your nieces a respectable home,
just as you always wanted. I intended to invite them all to
the country anyway. And they really should get out of
that terrible house."

James smiled and traced a fingertip over her face.
"You remembered," he wondered.

"I remember everything," Julia replied. "Though
I'm not sure I'll always be able to be as respectable as
you hoped."

He threw back his head and laughed. "You're just as

respectable as I'd want you to be." He touched the tip of her nose. "My dear viscountess."

So it would happen. They were going to get *married.* They would be able to spend their lives together. During the day, and at night . . .

James's thoughts seemed to be roving as well; his expression grew wolfish. "Now that we've got all the details sorted, what shall we do next?"

His hands roamed down her back and cupped her bottom, pressing her against him. Those hands positively stole the thought right out of her.

Julia felt warm, liquid, and eager, savoring his touch, allowing it to raise fires inside her even as her own hands began to explore his body with passionate curiosity.

Then an idea bobbed into her head that she was *sure* James would like, and she would, too.

After all, they were going to be married so soon . . . what would be the harm in anticipating the ceremony, just once more?

"I'll show you what we can do with our time," she said, and with a gentle shove, she laid him out, amazed, on the study's sofa and then turned the lock of the door.

Simone remained lost for two hours before she returned to the study to check on *mademoiselle*. Putting a cautious ear to the door, she quickly whipped her head back at the sounds from within.

"Nom d'un nom," she murmured, a small smile playing on her lips as she scooted away from the door. "All is well. They will certainly be getting married now."

And then she became dutifully lost again for several more hours.

Chapter 34

In Which They All Live Happily Ever After, and Even Have Plum Pudding

The weather, in the days before the wedding between James, Viscount Matheson, and Miss Julia Herington, turned unromantically cool and overcast. Watching the skies, the Stonemeadows tenants reflected with avid superstition among themselves as to whether this was some type of omen for "the young miss's" wedding day.

The bride and groom never even noticed the clouds, however; they were too wrapped up in one another and in the press of final arrangements. The five days that elapsed between Julia's visit to Nicholls and the marriage ceremony seemed to them like an eternity, even though they hardly left one another's presence (except to sleep, of course, since under the supervision of Lord and Lady Oliver, strict propriety as to bedroom matters was observed).

These five days were needed to bring an eager Gloria and her daughters from London and establish them in Stonemeadows Hall's best guest bedrooms. Besides the usual inhabitants of the hall, these were the only guests, since the hurried nature of the wedding made it desirable to keep it as selective as possible.

James's letter of invitation to his sister had included a rather ungracious postscript about how he supposed his mother could come to the wedding as well if she wanted to. Lady Matheson declined the honor of this invitation, finding herself not up to the rigors of the journey.

"Laziness," decided Lady Irving. "Laziness, and vulgarity."

In her stead, however, the dowager sent the couple a most unexpected wedding present.

Julia first opened the package, which Gloria brought from London with no idea as to its contents. When she saw what it was, her mouth fell open in surprise. She poked her finger into it to make sure her eyes weren't deceiving her. Could it really be just what it seemed? Wasn't it more likely that James's mother would send her an artillery shell, disguised with a thin layer of confection and ready to explode in her face when she cut into it?

No, it was a plum pudding, all right. Interesting.

She carried this unusual gift around the house, looking for James, until she finally found him sorting through some correspondence. As she presented it to him, explaining its source, she added, "This should prove how much I love you. I didn't even cut a slice."

James was bemused at first, turning the partially wrapped sweet around in his hands as if he expected it to transform into a croquet ball.

Finally he shrugged and handed it back to Julia. "I suppose this is a peace offering of sorts. Do you remember when you came to dine at Christmas, and there was that—"

"Yes, yes, of course," Julia cut him off, embarrassed to remember her faux pas in pointing out the absence of her favorite dessert on the viscountess's table. "I know what you mean."

Her cheeks turned pink, but she had to ask him. "Do you think she is being kind, or is she trying to remind me that I tend to say the wrong thing? Because I know I do, and maybe she is hinting that I won't serve the title well. But I think I will, or at least I will certainly try my best, because I know how to run a large home, and of course there is your man of business to help with much of the estate management."

James dropped a reassuring kiss on his bride-to-be's lips, stopping their flow of words. "Everything you say is delightful," he replied. "Even when it makes no sense. And I agree that you will make an excellent wife and viscountess. I don't know what my mother meant by sending an unseasonal pudding, but let us assume it was kindly meant. It might be nice to serve it at the wedding breakfast."

Satisfied, Julia rose to leave James alone with his letters again. As she reached the doorway, he added, "Except for that piece you poked your finger into, of course."

So they were married, quietly and cozily, on a gray March morning. In honor of Julia's long-lost father, they had arranged for the humble parish curate to officiate the wedding, a fact which, when drawn to Lady Oliver's attention, caused her to clap her hands in misty-eyed delight.

The bride wore the ivory silk ball gown made for her by Madame Oiseau, the same one she had worn so recently to the ball at Alleyneham House. Lady Irving, looking at her niece before the wedding, told her that it was completely unsuitable.

Julia, feeling not a bit of pre-wedding nervousness,

was unbothered by this statement. "Is it vulgar? Unlady-like?" she asked, not bothering to hide her dimples.

The countess looked at her suspiciously. "I suppose it isn't as bad as all that," she allowed. She took in the details of the gown, and her expression turned knowing. "I dare say you have your reasons for choosing that one, anyway."

Indeed she did; Julia felt warm just from the memory. The last time she was in this gown, she and James had first admitted their love for one another. Now, little more than a week later, they would pledge their love forever. It seemed only right.

Besides, it was the most beautiful gown she owned, and a girl did want to look her best for her wedding.

Louisa attended the bride in a gown of the pale prim-rose shade that suited her rich coloring so well. She had been unfailingly supportive of Julia through what had been one of the strangest and most trying weeks the sisters had ever lived through. When Julia begged her to wear her Helen of Troy costume for the marriage cere-mony, though, she put her foot down.

"I won't do it," she said, though her eyes were twinkling with amusement. "I'd look ridiculous. Besides, it would be very odd for people to be thinking of Twelfth Night, con-sidering how there's been a change of bride since then."

She made this statement without a hint of resentment or constraint, but Julia deemed it best not to press the issue. Mainly because that would then give Louisa cause to demand that Julia wear the terrible fortuneteller costume at her own wedding someday, and she would have to stand up next to her beautiful sister looking like a tomato.

Of all the possible uncomfortable situations at a wedding, that of the former fiancée serving as a brides-maid to the hastily traded bride—who also happened to be her sister—held great potential to be among the most awkward. Because of the small, close-knit nature of the wedding party, however, everyone carried it off without the least bit of self-consciousness.

Julia granted much of the credit for the success to her sister, who, once she broke her engagement, truly did feel that she had no further hold on James, or he on her. Following the ceremony, Louisa congratulated the bride and groom both with heartfelt embraces. To James, she said simply, "You've made the right choice. She truly shall be your better half, as I never could have been."

James smiled gratefully. "I'll accept the slander to myself, but not to you." He cleared his throat, and added in a choked voice, "I'll be very proud to be a part of your family."

"Not just that," Julia chimed in. "She'll be with us quite a bit of the time, I hope. That is"—she looked questioningly at Louisa—"if you still want to catalogue the library?"

Louisa drew in an eager breath, and looked from Julia to James. "Really? I wouldn't be in the way?"

James put his arm around Julia and gave her an affectionate squeeze. To Louisa, he nodded his willingness and replied, "If you can keep your sister off the library ladders, you can have every single Gutenberg Bible you find."

As she had at Lord and Lady Oliver's wedding so many years before, Lady Irving made a trenchant observation. She had told her brother, long ago, to marry "a snip in her first season," someone without a family of her own to complicate his life. Amazingly, he remembered this, and he reminded her of it as they all progressed into the dining room for the wedding breakfast.

"Stuff and nonsense," the countess replied, seating herself next to her brother. "You can't possibly recall what I told you before your remarriage."

"I do; I remember it well," Lord Oliver insisted. "I had just told you I met her at Tattersalls, where she had been looking at the most beautiful dapple gray mare."

Lady Irving cast her gaze up to heaven, believing this animal-related explanation for his uncannily accurate memory only too well.

"Someone without a family of her own," she repeated, musing, as she cast her eyes down the long table.

Where the four young Olivers kicked their chair legs, chattered happily, and threw bread across the table at one another.

Butternut the parrot sat on young Tom's shoulder, stretching his neck and opening his beak for a morsel of food.

Lady Oliver chatted with Gloria, who was letting her younger daughter unpin her hair and create small, messy plaits in it.

Louisa wiped a smut of pudding from Julia's nose, laughing, as Julia cheerfully motioned to a footman to serve her far more food than any bride ought to have an appetite to eat.

And James sat smiling at his new wife, with such love in his eyes that the countess, who had thought herself immune to this sort of sentimental silliness, actually felt tears well up.

To choose someone without a family . . . if he had, none of this would ever have existed.

Lady Irving turned to face her brother again, a repentant expression on her face. She leaned in close to his ear, and spoke to him in a voice pitched for his ears alone.

"Brother, dear, you are only going to hear this from me once in my whole life, so enjoy it."

She paused, sighed heavily, and said, "I am afraid I have to admit, I was full of rubbish."